NEVER RESIST A *Rake*

MIA MARLOWE

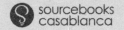

sourcebooks
casablanca

Published by Sourcebooks Casablanca, an imprint of Sourcebooks, Inc.
P.O. Box 4410, Naperville, Illinois 60567-4410
(630) 961-3900
Fax: (630) 961-2168
www.sourcebooks.com

Printed and bound in Canada.
WC 10 9 8 7 6 5 4 3 2 1

One

One of the things which distinguish the young from the old is the youthful ability to go blithely into folly. We who are blessed with a wealth of years are guilty of foolishness from time to time, but we do tend to blunder into it with our eyes wide open.

—Phillippa, the Dowager Marchioness of Somerset

1817, The Green Cockerel
Whitechapel's most notorious boxing crib

JOHN FITZHUGH BARRETT EYED THE PRIZEFIGHTER IN the opposite corner. John's friends rallied around him, crowding on either side, but however supportive they might be, John would be the only one climbing into the roped-off ring.

"The blighter's never been defeated." Pitcairn barely restrained a shudder. He was a foxy-faced little fellow who would never be accused of an overabundance of courage, but John liked him in spite of his nervous nature. Besides, John couldn't be too choosy when it came to friends. The *bon ton* wasn't exactly lining up to take him to heart, even after he'd been suddenly elevated to the title of Lord Hartley.

"Edgar Meek, they say he's called," Pitcairn said.

"Don't fit him much, do it?" Smalley chimed in. His name didn't fit him either. With a protruding belly straining beneath his cutaway waistcoat, he wasn't the least bit small. He always claimed "Smalley" referred to the miserly allowance on which his titled older brother forced him to subsist. He'd been keen to try this illegal boxing crib for weeks and had finally convinced the rest of the Daemon Club to join him. Smalley was Oxford educated, as they all were, but he always affected a country accent when the club went slumming. "If any of the meek are like to inherit the earth, it'll be him. Gor, look at the size of him."

"Perhaps he goes by Meek because Attila the Hun was already taken," Viscount Blackwood said in a bored drawl. Before John learned he was heir to the marquessate of Somerset, Blackwood had enjoyed the highest rank among them. The viscount drained his jigger of whisky and smoothed down his russet mustache with the back of his hand. "What do you say, Hartley? Can you take him?"

John had difficulty thinking of himself by the new name. It seemed odd to answer to "Lord Hartley," one of the marquess's lesser titles. He was still the same person he'd been when he was thought to be nothing more than a great man's by-blow. But it had recently come to light that John's mother's marriage to Lord Somerset had never been properly annulled, making him the unexpected *legitimate* heir.

High ranking or not, John was the best brawler among the members of the Daemon Club by a long chalk. None of the others could hope to challenge the boxing-crib favorite. John reassessed Edgar Meek.

The fighter stripped off his shirt, revealing a broad chest and biceps rippling with muscle. A goodly sized man himself, John stood a bit over six feet. Hard work had left him well-muscled and tough. He'd emerged the victor in his share of fisticuffs during his school years, but Meek topped him by half a head and probably outweighed him by two or three stone.

Common sense told John to walk away, but he'd abandoned such gentle nudges of good judgment of late. The purse for this illegal prize fight was substantial. However, the real money was made with side bets. Since the reigning champion was a crowd favorite, the odds were heavily weighted in the challenger's favor. If John won, it would be a golden chance to put a bit of blunt into his friends' pockets. The Daemon Club wasn't made up of the most dependable of fellows, but through the years, they'd treated him a great deal better than his family had.

Still, Edgar Meek was a monstrous big chap.

"Oh, and did we mention the real plum that goes to the winner?" Blackwood said. "Here they come with her now."

The greasy proprietor of the boxing crib and one of his bulbous-nosed henchmen came out from the back room, dragging a kicking and scratching girl between them. Her chestnut hair was disheveled, hanging down to obscure her face. With dear lace at the bodice and hem, her pale blue gown was of obvious value, but it was also dirtied at the knees and ripped in several places.

"What's this?" John asked with a frown.

"A lost lamb," Blackwood said. "And a sacrificial one at that. She's no game girl, if that's what you're thinking. The fight promoters have the devil's own time convincing anyone to get into the ring with Meek. So when they find a young lady of quality who happens to wander where she shouldn't, they snatch her off the street and offer her up as a prize to the winner to do with as he will." Blackwood licked his lips as he gazed at the struggling girl. "A tasty bit of baggage and probably a virgin to boot. Doesn't it make a man feel alive when a woman wants a bit of subduing?"

John ignored Blackwood's carnal preferences, which always sank to the lowest mark. Instead, he followed the progress of the captive onto a raised block beneath the sagging stairs. The proprietor trussed up the girl, tying her to one of the posts supporting a narrow interior balcony off the rickety upper story. Then he lifted a lantern near her face and pushed back her hair.

"Here you are, gentlemen," he bellowed to be heard over the din as men crowded cheek by jowl in the boxing crib. "Pretty as a daisy, she is, and fresh as one too, if you catch my meaning."

In the yellowish light of the lantern, the girl's eyes were wide with fear, but her mouth was set in a tight line. She obviously wouldn't give her captors the satisfaction of hearing her cry out.

John's gut clenched. He'd seen that girl somewhere. Oh, yes, the British Museum. She and another young lady had been standing before the Rosetta Stone. John had barely spared a glance for the acclaimed artifact, partly because he'd already studied it on a previous visit and partly because he was captivated by the girl's delicate profile. The tip of her nose turned up just slightly, which saved her from being so devastatingly pretty he wouldn't dare approach her.

He'd been the recipient of so many cuts direct since he came to London, he'd lost count. Even though it had proven false, the taint of bastardy still clung to him.

"The same decree is inscribed on the Stone three times," the girl had read from the guidebook to her companion, her properly gloved finger following the words on the page. "In—"

"In hieroglyphic, demotic, and Greek," John had finished for her as he joined the two young women before the display.

Her companion had "hmphed" and pointedly looked away, her sharp, longish nose in the air. But the girl he'd been drawn to peered up at him. Her perfectly oval face was enhanced by a few chestnut curls that had escaped her bonnet at her temples. Her eyes were an unusual shade—the minty gray-green of the sea before a storm. A squall brewed behind them.

"Do you make a habit of interrupting the private conversation of others, sir?" she asked. Her voice was low and musical, instead of the girlish whine he'd come to associate with wellborn misses.

"Only if I wish to make their acquaintance more than I care whether it's good form to interrupt or not." He gave her his best bow. "My only excuse is that you captivate me and if that be a sin, I ask your pardon, my lady."

It wasn't at all the done thing, but she'd smiled at him in any case. The luminous expression erased any deficiency in the tilt of her nose and rendered her as exquisite as a Botticelli angel. If he'd seen her smile first, he'd never have screwed his courage enough to speak to her. But then her companion had grasped her wrist and flounced away, towing her along like a dinghy bobbing in the wake of a frigate under full sail.

John supposed her friend was right. They hadn't been properly introduced, but how was he to manage a proper introduction to anyone when the *ton* shunned him as if he carried the pox?

The girl had seemed an angel in the museum. In the boxing crib, the young lady's face was pale as a ghost, and her hovering friend was nowhere in sight. John warranted she'd be more than grateful for his company now, however improper their meeting might be.

"Well, Hartley, is she worth the risk?" Blackwood asked.

Without a word, John removed his jacket and waistcoat and handed them to Blackwood. Then he reached inside himself for strengthening rage. He found it as quickly as the tip of the tongue finds an aching tooth.

"Lay your money down, gentlemen," John said as he climbed into the ring and strode toward his opponent with fists curled. "The meek will not be blessed today."

❧

Miss Rebecca Kearsey strained against her bonds, but what her captor lacked in hygiene, he apparently made up for in knot-tying skills. She couldn't wiggle free.

Still, part of her heart sang a hopeful little song. She'd been praying for days to stumble across that handsome gentleman she and Lady Winifred Chalcroft had seen at the museum again.

She just never expected to have her prayer answered like this.

Winifred would call her a goose for looking for a bright spot in such a dire situation, but it was better to have found the fellow from the museum than not. Rebecca had stewed for several days after their encounter over who he was and why she'd never seen him at any of the usual assemblies or gatherings. She shouldn't have allowed Freddie to drag her away from the Rosetta Stone that afternoon. It wasn't every day that a gentleman professed to be captivated by the daughter of an impoverished baron. Most of them took one look at her minuscule dowry and looked elsewhere.

Besides, surely this gentleman who knew about the Stone without reading from a guidebook had to be a cut above the usual dandies and bucks who sought her out. If he spent time in museums, surely that spoke to a depth of feeling and a contemplative nature beyond the common.

But if that were the case, she could almost hear Freddie arguing, what was he doing in this boxing crib? And what were his intentions toward her should he win?

Botheration! This was not the best of outcomes, after all.

Of course, it didn't appear as if Rebecca would have to worry about the gentleman's intentions. He was about to be pummeled to death before her eyes.

There seemed to be no proper rules to the fight, no referee to keep any semblance of order. Each of the combatants came out swinging and, though her gentleman was more agile, he was holding the short end of the stick when the fighters came together to exchange blows.

The bald giant connected another punishing jab to the gentleman's ribs. Rebecca's own side ached in sympathy. The one the crowd called Meek was so big, he completely blocked her gentleman from view at times. Meek was tough, too. The first time the man from the museum struck him solidly in the jaw, the fellow had merely spat out a bloody tooth and laughed.

The small candle of hope in her chest began to gutter.

But then Meek took a wild swing which the gentleman managed to duck. The ham-sized fist grazed the top of his dark hair, but evidently it was a glancing blow. The missed punch threw Meek's balance off. Before he could right himself, her gentleman clocked him a good one upside the head, at the spot where the thinner bone of his temple provided less protection for his brain pudding.

The champion staggered, dropped to his knees, and then toppled face forward like a felled oak. He did not rise.

The entire room went silent for the space of three heartbeats. Then it erupted in shouts and thrown fists as the onlookers realized most of them were on the losing side of their wagers.

The gentleman from the museum clambered over the ropes and elbowed his way toward her, knocking heads together when the ones in his path didn't clear out quickly enough to suit him.

A little thrill shivered over Rebecca's skin. During the course of their historical studies, Freddie had told her that in ancient times, women were counted as spoils to the barbarian victors and, according to her research, displays of masculine strength were said to be most invigorating.

Rebecca had no idea what that meant until now. A warm lump of something she'd never felt before flared to life, glowing in her chest.

A trio of well-dressed fellows fell in behind her gentleman, whether to serve as his rear-guard or to follow in his protective wake, Rebecca couldn't be sure.

"What are you doing here?" he demanded of her as he pulled out a pocketknife and sliced through her bonds with a couple of slashes. An evil-smelling fellow stumbled toward them, but her rescuer's fist lashed out. It connected with the fellow's jaw, and the odiferous man fell backward.

"I could ask you the same thing," Rebecca said. Her gentleman—Freddie would scold her for thinking of him like that, but she couldn't help herself—didn't belong here any more than she did. He should be strolling through an astronomy exhibit with her while she basked in an artificial representation of the stars.

"Time is of the essence." One of his companions, a red-haired fellow, scanned the crowd, a nervous tick making his cheek jerk. "Hurry up with the girl, Hartley."

Hartley. The name seemed vaguely familiar. Freddie had been waffling on about a Lord Hartley once, but then Freddie waffled on a great deal about a great many people. Rebecca would go dotty if she tried to recall every *on dit* her friend insisted upon sharing.

The ginger-haired gentleman hefted a small pouch which clinked loudly enough to be heard over the crowd. "I've collected our winnings, but we'd better leave with promptness if we hope to spend it in good health. Come. I know where the back exit is."

The redhead slithered through the crowd along the edge of the room. Hartley put a protective arm around Rebecca and followed, with the smaller fellow and the paunchy one close behind. They squeezed through the rioting swarm and pushed through a filthy excuse for a kitchen. Then the group fled through a door that was half off its hinges. The narrow alley behind the crib smelled better than the kitchen by only the barest of margins.

"This way." The red-haired fellow took to his heels down the dark lane. For a gentleman, he moved very fast indeed.

Hartley half carried Rebecca to keep up as they flew after him. The soles of her kid slippers barely touched the grimy cobbles. Sounds of pursuit echoed behind them.

When they broke into a better-traveled lane, the leader suggested they split up to make it harder for the gang from the boxing crib to follow.

"Smalley and Pitcairn, that way." He pointed toward a corner where a sputtering gas lamp cast a flickering circle of light. It was a measure of his control over them that the pair started off immediately. "Hartley and Miss Prize"—he swept a mocking bow to her—"you're with me."

"No, we need a hackney," Hartley said.

"Good idea. We can all make a hasty exit that way. Any idea where we might find one at this hour and in these environs?"

Hartley lifted his head, and with the sense of direction Rebecca usually associated with country-bred men, he looked opposite of where the other fellow had sent his friends. "Aldgate is west of here. We might find a cab there, but not for you and me, Blackwood. I need to escort this young lady back to wherever she came from."

Blackwood. That was a name Rebecca knew. Viscount Blackwood was anathema in respectable circles. When she'd asked why, she was told she ought to guard the innocence of her ears more carefully; some things didn't bear retelling.

So why was Hartley keeping company with this man?

Lord Blackwood handed Hartley's waistcoat and jacket back to him. "Fancy the chit, do you? Well, that explains a good bit. Very well. If you won't work with me, you're on your own." He trotted away after the other two. Then he stopped with a hand to his temple as if something had just occurred to him, and turned back. He tossed the money pouch to Hartley. "Your winnings, though I've a feeling you value the prize with feet far more."

Blackwood cast her a sly smile and loped after his friends. Hartley shrugged on his waistcoat, tucking the money pouch into the interior pocket. Then he draped his jacket around Rebecca's shoulders.

She hadn't even realized she was shivering. She wasn't cold, exactly. The shakes were probably due to the delayed realization of how very dire her situation had been. Lord Hartley took her by the elbow and hurried her in the opposite direction from his companions.

A heartfelt thank you danced on the tip of her tongue, but he interrupted her thoughts before she could form the right words.

"You shouldn't have come here," he said bluntly.

As saviors went, Hartley was a surly one. He certainly didn't sound captivated by her now. "You don't think I'm here on purpose, do you?"

"Only a ninnyhammer would wander into Whitechapel by accident."

Not captivated at all. Rebecca swallowed back her indignation. "There's no need for name-calling. If you must know, I was abducted near Leadenhall Market."

She'd journeyed across town with her maid because the market was supposed to have the freshest produce from the country. Her mother had been craving Ashmead's Kernel apples. The fruits weren't much to look at, being a drab color, but they were known for pear-like sweetness. Her mother's cough had gotten worse as the autumn weather turned colder. Rebecca hoped the treat would tempt her dwindling appetite.

As she'd wandered among the stalls, she'd become separated from her maid. Then, before she could cry out, those foul men from the Green Cockerel had seized her and borne her to Whitechapel.

"Who's your father, and why does he allow you out without a keeper?" Hartley demanded.

"I do not require a keeper." The man still hadn't bothered to formally introduce himself or inquire after her name. Some of what Freddie had said about Lord

Hartley leaped to the forefront of Rebecca's mind. *Vulgar upstart. Raised in obscurity. Questionable parentage.* "Not that it's any of your concern, but my father is Baron Kearsey and—"

He clamped a hand over her mouth and yanked her into a darkened doorway. A loud gang from the boxing crib crossed an intersection behind them. Once the ruffians passed, Hartley stood motionless for the space of ten heartbeats before he released her.

"Come." He took her hand and pulled her along, not moderating his longer stride to accommodate her narrow column gown one bit.

"Instead of manhandling me," Rebecca said as she skittered to keep up, "you might have simply asked me to be quiet."

"Fine. Be quiet."

Lord Hartley was the most insufferably rude man she'd ever met. Freddie had been right to cut him. The warm glow in her chest faded completely. "Haven't you any notion of how to treat a lady? No. I suppose not. Not after the way you pushed yourself forward at the museum."

"I don't recall hearing you complain of the way I pushed myself forward in the Green Cockerel." He kept looking back for signs of pursuit.

Ahead of them, Rebecca made out the dark outline of a hackney waiting for a fare. The horses' heads were drooped and so was the cabbie's, on his perch above the coach. Lord Hartley put two fingers between his lips and whistled loudly. The cabbie chirruped to his nags, and the hackney moved toward them with a rattle over the uneven cobbles.

Lord Hartley opened the hackney door and practically shoved her in. "Where are you staying?"

"Our town house is in Grosvenor Square." It was a lease her father had prepaid before the start of the Season. Otherwise, her family would have been turned out to pay off the baron's latest gambling debts. But Lord Hartley didn't need to know that.

"The heart of Mayfair." He snorted. "Of course it is. Everyone who's anyone lives there."

He relayed the address to the cabby and climbed in after her, taking the opposite squab. The hackney lurched forward, and they clattered over the cobbles at a surprising pace.

Rebecca laced her fingers on her lap to keep her hands still. She was grateful to have escaped from that horrid Green Cockerel, but if the incident became known, her reputation would not survive the night. *Botheration, it probably won't survive a hackney ride with a strange man either.*

Freddie was right. No matter how handsome he was, no matter that he'd rescued her from what her friend would call "a fate worse than death," there was no doubt about it: this gentleman from the museum was trouble.

Two

Favoring one son over another never bodes well for either of them. Consider Cain and Abel. Let us hope I can undo the damage of Somerset's past before it comes to that desperate pass. Yes, yes, I know I'm the one who did the damage, but that's all the more reason why I should be the one to mend it!

—Phillippa, the Dowager Marchioness of Somerset

THE WHEELS OF THE CAB CLACKED LOUDLY, BUT THE silence inside the conveyance was deafening. Since light from the occasional gas lamp only lit the hackney for fleeting moments, it was too dark to see Lord Hartley properly most of the time. Despite that, Rebecca was uncomfortably aware of his presence. He was a large enough man not to fold neatly into the small space. His knees brushed hers at intervals, sending uncomfortable prickles up her thighs. He was entirely too…too male to be cornered in a cab with.

Finally, Rebecca could stand no more of the silence. If he wasn't going to be civil, at least she would.

"My family will be very grateful to you, Lord Hartley."

"So it seems you know my name without benefit of proper introduction," he said. If a voice could be said to have a flavor, his was a dark, chocolatey sort of sound. It poured over her in luscious waves. "What about you, Miss Kearsey? Yes, I paid attention when you said your father was the baron. Aren't you grateful too?"

"Of course I am." Why was he scolding her like some underpaid tutor? "I...thank you too. It was... kindly done."

"Tell that to my ribs."

Silence descended on them again, like a flock of crows that had been disturbed briefly before settling again to pick at the bones. The image reminded Rebecca of gossips as well, and some of what Freddie had told her about Lord Hartley came back to her.

"Your family is looking for you," she said.

"Is that so?"

"Yes, by all accounts, your brother and sister-in-law—"

"Half brother," he corrected.

Yes, that squared with Freddie's information. "And your grandmother is here in London as well. I understand she is most upset not to have found you at your family's town house."

"Far be it from me to upset the dowager," Hartley said in a tone that suggested he'd prefer to do exactly that. They'd reached a better neighborhood where gas lamps were more frequent, and she could see his face at every corner. She wondered that she'd found him merely handsome before. Now his well-sculpted features were so forbidding, he was like some vengeful minor deity.

She might have even feared him a little if he hadn't just saved her from an awful situation. The silence was back, and she felt as if something inside her might burst if she didn't fill it. "If you aren't staying at the Somerset town house, where have you been?"

"Here and there. It didn't take long to discover I don't belong in Mayfair."

His eyes took on a hard look. He didn't bear much resemblance to the affable gentleman from the museum any longer. In that moment, Rebecca wasn't sure she'd have known him if she passed him on the street.

"I'm like water," he said.

"Running incessantly?"

"No, seeking the lowest place."

"Why do you seek that?"

"Because it's where I belong." He pretended great absorption with the blur of houses on the right as they moved along. "Where I've always belonged."

Now she remembered more of the gossip that dear Freddie had tried to pass on about this Lord Hartley fellow. It seemed he'd been raised in the country as the unwanted child of an anonymous gentleman and his light-o'-love. In deference to his absent father's station, he'd been educated at Eton and later at Oxford. But then, in a sudden explosion of scandal early in the summer, it was learned that the Marquess of Somerset had actually wed this new Lord Hartley's mother.

The entire line of inheritance in one of the greatest houses of England had been disrupted. It was not the sort of transgression the *ton* readily forgave. The new Lord Hartley bore the brunt of Polite Society's collective displeasure.

The hackney slowed as they entered Grosvenor Square. All the town houses were dark, save one on the left side. In that four-story edifice, every window blazed with light. The entire household was awake. Her father had probably sent for a team of Bow Street Runners to hunt for her in the Leadenhall Market district. Rebecca hoped they'd somehow kept the situation from her mother. Strong emotion made her breathing even more labored than usual.

"That must be your home," Lord Hartley said. When she nodded, he rapped on the ceiling of the cab to signal a stop. Then he opened the door and handed her out with instructions for the cabbie to wait for him. They were a few houses down from hers, so he offered her his arm. She expected him to escort her up to the door, but he stopped just outside the wrought iron gate that enclosed the minuscule front garden.

Rebecca rested a hand on the gatepost. "You're coming in too, aren't you?"

Hartley shook his head. "Trust me, they don't want me there."

But I want you danced on her tongue. She bit the words back. Where on earth had those wholly inappropriate sentiments come from?

"I'm certain my father will want to thank you personally."

"Perhaps, but I doubt it will improve your reputation if I intrude at this time. Besides, my friends are still in a dicey neighborhood. I need to discover whether they have found safety or if they require my assistance."

He'd lost that belligerent look somewhere between

the cab and her front door. When she glanced up at him now, she caught a glimpse of the boy he must have been—unacknowledged, inconvenient, and unwanted; always on the fringes of the great, but never allowed into the inner circle. Her chest constricted a bit.

"But why must you return to Whitechapel? What of *your* family?" Rebecca said. "As far as they know, you've been missing for far longer than I was. Won't you please go home to Somerset House?"

He shook his head and pushed open the gate for her. "I'll watch till you are inside."

Rebecca gave up and dipped in a shallow curtsy. "Thank you, Lord Hartley. For everything."

Then she hurried up to her door and slipped inside. She didn't latch it though. Instead, she watched as Lord Hartley strode back to the hackney, his gait swift and determined. Then, with her eye to the slit in the door, she lingered until the cab pulled away and was swallowed up in darkness.

Lord Hartley had saved her this night. She owed him. He might not want her interference. He might resent her sticking her oar in. He might fight her tooth and nail, but somehow Miss Rebecca Kearsey was determined to save him as well.

⁓

"Where did you find him, my lord?"

"Whitechapel."

Concerned voices reached into the blackness and dragged John back up to skim the surface of consciousness. He didn't open his eyes, but he was vaguely aware that he no longer reeked of blood. He seemed to be tucked into a feather bed whose crisp linen sheets smelled faintly of lye soap.

"A dicey place, that Whitechapel, and no mistake." John recognized the speaker as Aloysius Porter, his new valet and the first servant he'd ever had.

"I only wish 'dicey' was the operative word, Mr. Porter. He'd have been much safer if he'd been embroiled in a game of hazard." The second voice belonged to John's nearly perfect half brother, Lord Richard Barrett. They'd met after the scandal first broke. Richard had been deputized by the Marquess of Somerset to travel to Wiltshire and tell John who he really was. John hadn't believed much of what Richard was saying at the time. His half brother seemed to be taking the loss of his preferential place far too calmly. John recognized the same even-tempered tones now.

"My brother engaged in a bare-knuckle brawl in one of those back-alley sparring cribs," Richard was saying. "Apparently, there was a considerable purse wagered."

"And apparently, his lordship lost." Porter sounded appropriately downhearted over the situation, but then John's valet often sounded like that for no reason at all.

"Actually, no." Richard's voice, on the other hand, was laced with a combination of disbelief and grudging admiration. "Lord Hartley won. Miss Kearsey said, and I quote, 'You should have seen the other fellow.'"

Miss Kearsey? What the devil does she have to do with anything?

John didn't open his eyes even now. It seemed the wiser course to allow his valet and half brother to assume he was insensible while they fussed over him and smoothed down the sheets. Besides, he was quite certain he couldn't open the left one in any case.

He was evidently back in the Somerset town house, whether he willed it or no.

"Not wanting to speak out of turn, my lord," Porter began as he always did before he intended to go ahead and speak out of turn, "but this is only the latest in a long string of peccadilloes his lordship has been involved in since coming to London. He's been carousing with a disreputable group of gentlemen who do not deserve the name. I fear they have led him into all manner of mischief."

John's lips twitched. How like Porter to name the activities of the Daemon Club as "mischief." If his friends heard it, they'd feel honor bound to lower their standards to earn a more wicked rating.

"Why is his lordship engaging in such unseemly activities?" Porter asked, his tenor drifting even higher in pitch than usual.

"God knows," Richard said, "and perhaps we should leave it with Him. At any rate, Lord Hartley paid for his sins handsomely this evening. That'll be quite a shiner."

John wondered if it was hard for his half brother to refer to him as Lord Hartley. For all of Richard Barrett's privileged life, that had been *his* title.

"From what I could learn from the link boy on the scene," Richard went on, "after his lordship won the boxing match and escorted Miss Kearsey home in safety, he returned to Whitechapel to look for his friends. He was subsequently set upon by a gang of some dozen ruffians who relieved him of his newly bulging purse and left him bleeding in the street."

In the pause that followed, John imagined his half brother shaking his head in reproof.

"The friends who urged him to wander into that district in the first place evidently fled without him," Richard finished.

And why shouldn't they have? John almost said aloud. The credo of the Daemon Club was "Do as thou wilt." A man was answerable to no one but himself. John made his own choices and stood by them. He couldn't fault his friends for making theirs.

A door opened with a soft snick of the latch, and the swish of feminine skirts was followed by a fresh scent of violets. Lady Richard, no doubt. His brother rarely went anywhere without his new wife, Sophie Barrett, née Goodnight. Richard had even brought her with him when he first came to see John in Wiltshire. She was a fabulous heiress and, even though she had a reputation for meddlesomeness and doing the unexpected, when the fellows of the Daemon Club heard about her ponderous dowry, they all said Richard was deucedly lucky to land her. It was more than enough blunt to make a fellow forget she was common.

But John doubted they'd dare say that in Richard Barrett's hearing.

"Her ladyship sent me to relieve you." The woman who entered the room wasn't Lady Sophie after all. John's fingers curled into frustrated fists under the sheets. The gentle voice belonged to Miss Rebecca Kearsey.

She was the last person John wanted to see him like this, all weak and miserable. In fact, after the danger she'd been subjected to already this night, she shouldn't see him at all. She was from another world. He didn't want her to face any more ugliness from Whitechapel, and judging by how he felt, he was the personification of it. As she drew near his bedside, he heard her sharp intake of breath.

After the beating by that mob, he must look even worse than he imagined.

"The doctor says he likely hasn't suffered any permanent damage," Richard said. "But he hasn't stirred."

"He will. He seems to have a very hard head," Miss Kearsey said without a drop of womanly sympathy. "Please, my lord, take your ease. I'll sit with him till he wakes. I often nurse my mother when she has a bad spell. If he should take a turn for the worse, I'll call you on the moment."

"Here. Let me fetch a chair for you, miss."

John heard the sound of Porter dragging the heavy Tudor-styled monstrosity across the room and depositing it beside his bed. Richard made a halfhearted protest about leaving, but Porter managed to shuffle him out of the room. Silence descended. Blood stomped in John's ears like a retreating giant's footfalls.

"You needn't pretend, you know," she said softly. "I can tell you're awake."

He forced open his one good eye. Now that she wasn't all tied up and terrified, she was as lovely as ever. Her mint-green eyes were filled with concern, but the soft brown brows that arched over them were drawn into a frown.

"How did you know I was awake?"

"I lied," Miss Kearsey said smoothly. "I wasn't sure,

but I thought it was worth a try. Really, it's too bad of you to worry your brother like this."

As if his half brother gave a flying fig about him. After all, John was the only thing that stood between Richard and their father's title and estate. Since the secret first marriage of the marquess had come to light last summer, Richard's expectations had plummeted. John's standing in society, on the other hand, had soared, from being the living proof of his mother's light heels, to the dizzying heights of the scion of the House of Somerset.

"I can't believe you lied," John said woodenly. "That's not at all the done thing. Where did a debutante from Mayfair pick up a trick like that?"

"You may as well learn right now that I don't always do the done thing," she said with a sniff. "For instance, if you thought I wouldn't cajole and bully my father into accompanying me here to tell your family where they could find you, then you have no idea what sort of debutante I am."

"To be honest, I have no experience with debutantes."

"That's obvious. In fact, you've little experience with Polite Society, by all accounts," she said. "But this life you're living…whatever it is you're doing here in London, it's hurting your family. After the kindness you showed me, I must believe that's not like you either."

"Then you have no idea what sort of man I am." If she knew the half of what he'd been up to, she'd flee from his presence and never look back. Since the *ton* was determined to shun him, he'd done his best to give them reason.

John decided to fit in with the *beau monde*'s seedy underbelly. He'd gone to school with Pitcairn, Smalley, and Blackwood, but he'd never had the funds to join his old classmates in the activities of the Daemon Club before. Now they were pleased to take him, and the line of credit due the heir to the Somerset marquessate, under their leathery wings and initiate him royally. They'd introduced him to the sporting life—to bear baiting and cock fights. He learned to drink, and drink hard. John hadn't consumed as much alcohol in his entire life as he had in the last few months.

And the women! He'd come to London a virgin. Now he considered his education in matters sensual thorough, if a trifle jaded.

"This life is like me now," John said. "Haven't you heard? I'm Lord Hartley, a heartbeat from being a peer of the realm. Short of being caught red-handed doing murder, I can do whatever I damn well please."

Miss Kearsey's lips tightened into a thin line, and she glared at him. He'd only spoken the truth. A titled lord could do no wrong.

But he'd sworn in her presence. A bit of shame washed over him, remnants from his stern upbringing in Wiltshire. She deserved to have him keep a civil tongue in his head.

Then it occurred to him that Miss Kearsey wasn't wearing the soiled and torn blue gown any longer. A fine shawl draped over her shoulders. Her off-white muslin column dress was embellished with delicate embroidery at the bodice that curled around her breasts enticingly. Even her hair had been dressed and was tied up with a satin bandeau.

"You're looking much better than you did earlier this evening."

"Careful, Lord Hartley," she said with a roll of her eyes. "That sort of compliment will turn a girl's head."

"I didn't mean—"

"I know what you meant. I'm teasing you. Unfortunately, you're looking much *worse* than you did earlier this evening, my lord." She rose gracefully and went to the pitcher and ewer on the washstand. She wet a cloth and returned to press it over his swollen eye. Even though her touch was gentle, pain shot through his eye socket to his brain.

"Ow!" He took the damp cloth from her and held it over the eye himself. "If you insist on torturing me, do you think you could do it without 'my lord-ing' me left and right? My name is John. John Fitzhugh."

"John Fitzhugh," she repeated. Miss Kearsey's face lit with that beguiling smile again. "If we're being familiar, you must call me Rebecca." Then her smile faded. "But that's not strictly correct. You're John Fitzhugh *Barrett*. You see, while we were waiting to learn whether your brother Richard could find you in Whitechapel, I got a chance to get to know your sister-in-law and grandmother. They told me all about you."

John didn't know what to say. Unfortunately, Rebecca did.

"You're shaming your family," she accused.

"That assumes the Barretts are capable of shame." What with a secret marriage, a scheming dowager marchioness who kept John's true parentage a mystery, and a marquess who even now reportedly had more holes in his memory than a moth-eaten cloak, the Somerset legacy was not something to boast about. "Besides, you're wrong. I have no family."

"Nonsense. You're a Barrett, rightwise born. You're the marquess's heir, for pity's sake. You have four half siblings and a lovely stepmother who are ready to welcome you home to Somerfield Park with open arms."

John snorted.

"You haven't given them a chance," Rebecca said.

"After the chance they gave me, what can they expect?"

John had been six years old when his mother died, penniless and alone. After a few days in the foundling home, someone came to collect him and bring him to a farm in Wiltshire, where he was fostered by Sir Humphrey Coopersmith and his wife. John was reared by the genteel yet threadbare couple. They were distantly kind to him, but he was always conscious of being someone else's son—someone who didn't want to admit John was his son.

The very next week after John was placed with the Coopersmiths, Lord Somerset had wed Lady Helen and built his real family with her.

"I don't owe the Barretts anything," John said.

"Yes, you do. They might have abandoned you forever, but they didn't. The dowager could have taken the secret of your birth to her grave, but she didn't." Rebecca leaned toward him, and he caught a whiff of her violet scent again. "Don't you see? You have a chance to make everything right and you're frittering it away in pursuit of...well, in whatever it is you've been in pursuit of."

Anger boiled in him, worse than when he was beating the stuffing out of Edgar Meek in Whitechapel. She was trying to make this his fault, and it wasn't.

"Don't beat around the bush. An unusual debutante like you knows full well what I've been pursuing—drinking, gambling, and wenching. That's what lords do, don't you know?"

Her cheeks flushed with color, but she stood her ground. "Then it's too bad you became a lord. I rather suspect you were a much nicer person before you learned who you were."

She rose and made to go, but he caught her by the wrist. Her pulse point jumped under his grip, fluttering like a hummingbird's wing.

His chest ached. She was right. No matter what he did now, he'd never get back the innocence of that boy from Wiltshire.

"You're right. I did used to be…" John couldn't claim to have been nicer. As long as he could remember, he'd had a bitter taste under his tongue and a driving need to prove himself. But he hadn't always been such a bounder. "Well, I was different from the way I am now. Don't go, Rebecca." He swallowed hard. "Please. Even if you hate me, stay. No one tells me the truth anymore."

She fixed him with a pointed look, her chin determined, her eyes overly bright. Then she nodded and sat back down, giving her hand a slight tug. He released her with reluctance.

"I could never hate you," she said. "Not after the way you came to my rescue this night. I'll stay. But I want you to promise you'll do something for me, John."

Something inside him relaxed. It was as if every bit of his body had been holding its breath till she said his name. She caressed it a bit, let it linger on that beguiling little tongue of hers.

"Anything you want, I'll do it." He was feeling magnanimous and more than a little fuzzy-headed after the beating he'd taken, but he realized it was true. He would do anything for her.

"It sounds to me as if you're not sure of your place in the world."

He nodded slowly. She'd cut to the heart of his problem in no time at all. He didn't belong anywhere.

"Then I want you to do something that will help you figure out where you belong. Go home to Somerfield Park," she said. "London isn't for you."

He wished he'd kept his mouth shut. Maybe he could talk her into changing her request.

"There's nothing for me in Somerset either. My half brother Richard is running the estate. He keeps things humming, I'm told. I'd be as useful as..." He stopped himself before he said "tits on a boar," deciding even an unusual debutante like Rebecca wouldn't appreciate this poetical, if somewhat coarse, observation. "Well, not useful at all."

"You were decidedly useful to me this evening, but that's beside the point," she said. "And there *is* something for you at Somerfield Park. There's your father. It's almost time for his annual hunt. From what your grandmother told me, his lordship is still not himself after taking a tumble off the roof. He needs you."

Each year, the marquess hosted a grand hunt at Somerfield Park, inviting influential lords from all over the realm to shoot mallards and teal. His lordship's guests went deer stalking and generally attempted to kill anything furred or feathered that roamed the thick woods near the coastline. John remembered hearing about it during his days at Oxford. Blackwood's father had even been invited once.

John was a crack shot himself. Sir Humphrey had taught him, but they didn't hunt to put a trophy on the wall. Lady Coopersmith always needed meat for the stewpot.

However, according to Blackwood's father, more went on during the Somerset hunt than the quest for antlers for the hall. Deals were made about initiatives in the House of Lords. With a little diligence, John could study all the titled gentlemen who'd be there, their fields of influence, their interests and political leanings.

And thanks to his friends in the Daemon Club, who loved to tell tales, he'd learn more than a few of their weaknesses as well. That might be very helpful.

Perhaps John could be of some use after all.

Even though he hated himself for it, the need to have the marquess recognize him, not just as the legitimate heir but as his son, burned in his gut.

"All right," he said slowly. "I'll go to Somerfield Park, but only on two conditions."

Her lips lifted in a hopeful smile. "What are they?"

"You have to come too."

"I can't. My family hasn't been invited."

"I just invited you—and your father and mother and anyone else you care to bring." He took her hand again and was surprised when she didn't pull it away. "In a big house like Somerfield Park, there'll be room for everyone. Blast it all. I doubt even the maids know how many bedrooms there are."

"Language." She cocked a reproving brow at him. "Again."

"I'm sorry. For both times." He wasn't, but it seemed expedient to act as if he were. When her lips twitched in a smile, he decided he just might have a future in politics. Lying had become much easier of late.

"In that case, I forgive you." Rebecca flicked out her tongue and drew it across her lower lip. John wanted to take that little bottom lip between his and suckle it.

"I suspect it will be hard for Lord Hart—" John caught himself before he called Richard Barrett by the title that he now possessed. "For my half brother to be under the same roof with me."

"Nonsense. You're under the same roof right now. As soon as your brother found you, he brought you back to the Barrett family town house. He could have put you up in Mivart's, you know." The posh hotel was located in the heart of Mayfair and was a favorite of the *ton* during the Season. "Doesn't the fact that Lord Richard has been looking for you everywhere for the last two weeks mean anything to you?"

But John had been in London for much longer than two weeks. The day after he discovered his true identity, he'd shaken off the Wiltshire dirt and legged it to Town, dragging the long-suffering Mr. Porter with him. His newfound family hadn't sought him out before now. Whatever the reason they wanted him at Somerfield Park, he'd bet his best shoes—and now he finally had more than one pair!—it had little to do with Lord Somerset's annual hunt.

"The fact that Richard came looking for me doesn't mean as much to me as the fact that you want me to go to Somerfield Park," he said. "I won't go unless you agree to come."

"All right, I accept," she finally said, tugging her hand from his grasp. "My mother doesn't travel well, but one way or another, I'll convince my parents."

John laced his fingers behind his head and gave a self-satisfied sigh. "You know, that's one good thing about becoming the marquess's heir. People say yes to me a lot more than they used to."

She swatted his shoulder as if he were still a cheeky hanger-on. "Don't get used to it from me."

He caught up her hand again. "I'd better. Remember, there are two conditions."

"I've already agreed to go to the country for you. What more could you want?"

"Kiss me."

Her eyes went wide. "That's not the sort of thing a gentleman asks of a lady."

"I'm not asking. I'm offering. It's your choice. If you want me in Somerfield Park, you know what you have to do. Kiss me. Right now."

Anyone who thought Miss Rebecca Kearsey was a pattern sort of debutante had never seen her angry. John recognized the signs. Her sweet mouth went all pinched and her chin quivered.

But however she might feel about it, she leaned forward, grabbed him by both ears, and kissed him right on the mouth.

Three

While one cannot disregard the importance of bloodlines, great men are made, not born. Most often, however, it takes a woman to find and shape that bit of greatness.

—Phillippa, the Dowager Marchioness of Somerset

JOHN FITZHUGH BARRETT WAS NOT GOING TO MAKE a fool of Baron Kearsey's daughter. No, sir. From all accounts, the new Lord Hartley had been running with a fast crowd and had no doubt kissed dozens of women.

Fancy women. Loose women. Women whose kisses would turn a man's knees to water.

Rebecca would show him. A virtuous girl was just as good as a bad girl. Better. She'd kiss him, all right. She'd kiss the man into next week.

She prided herself on reasoned thought and knew she was being illogical, but before she could untangle all the invalid syllogisms running through her head, she pressed her mouth against his with such force, their eye teeth knocked together. No matter. He wasn't going to think her a missish little thing who kissed like an awkward first cousin. She was going to put some passion into it.

As much as she knew about passion, at any rate.

He covered her hands with his and she realized he was trying to encourage her to soften her grip on his ears. So she uncurled her fingers and slid her hands down to palm his cheeks.

He groaned into her mouth.

I'm getting good at this.

Then when he groaned again, she decided it was probably not a good thing. There was a definite edge of pain in the sound. Her fingertips were pressing too hard on the skin around his swollen eye.

Botheration! There were so many things to think about all at once. She eased up. Her lips softened and she slanted her mouth over his.

This time the groan was different—pleased and needy all at once. A little feral.

The thrill of danger danced on her spine. Imagining kissing a man was safe. Holy, almost. She could envision a perfectly acceptable setting for the kiss—a garden in full bloom, an elegant parlor after a well-spoken proposal, before an altar and a church full of witnesses. Heaven knew she'd dreamed of a kiss often enough.

Kissing a man for real as he reclined in his bed was wicked beyond imagining.

Her imagined kisses were always chaste, too. This one was decidedly not. Something inside her went all warm and liquid.

John cupped the back of her head with gentleness as he teased her lips to part by tracing the seam of them with the tip of his tongue. She gave up, and he invaded her. His breath swirled into her, filling her, drawing her back into him.

His tongue, oh Lud, his tongue...

Rebecca had never suspected a kiss could be so... so...*involving*. It wasn't just their mouths meeting. Every fiber in her body strained toward him.

She had to stop right now or she'd never be able to. She pulled back and, to her surprise, he let her go. She almost expected him to drag her down onto the feather tick with him.

A wicked part of her was disappointed when he didn't.

Then her instinct for self-preservation won out. She and her friend Freddie had practically been weaned on cautionary tales about young ladies who lost their virtue. Granted, this was just a kiss, but in all the warnings, a kiss was how "it" started.

Whatever "it" was. Somehow, without knowing all the particulars, she was expected to be careful not to engage in the wicked activity that ended in ruin.

"Rebecca, I—" John began.

"Miss Kearsey," she corrected, her voice coming out as fluttery as her insides felt. She straightened to sit as tall as she could in the uncomfortable Tudor chair, wishing she felt as upright as her posture. Her insides were still soft and pliant. "Please, my lord. I know we agreed on informal address earlier, but I think I should be Miss Kearsey to you. No more, no less."

"Oh, you're more, Rebecca." His eyes were dark brown to begin with, but now the pupils expanded to make them nearly black. "Much more."

She rose to go quickly, lest he stop her again. She'd accomplished her goal of convincing him to leave London, and now she had to make good her escape. "I'll send Mr. Porter to attend you since you're awake."

Without waiting for a reply, she fled the room. As soon as the door latched behind her, she leaned against it, knees sagging.

She and Freddie had made it their business to study the art of flirting, as they studied everything that interested them. Freddie, for example, was an expert on the language of the fan. Unfortunately, she was unable to use her facility often, since she rarely met another who was so well versed in the silent mode of communication. Still, Freddie faithfully reported to Rebecca every time she was able to use her fan to send a message. The two girls had always shared everything. Freddie would expect a full report on this meeting with Lord Hartley and would be filled with horrified fascination to learn that Rebecca had kissed a man.

But that kiss was something Rebecca would never share with anyone. Not even Freddie.

༺❦༻

It was nearly three in the morning when Rebecca sent for Mr. Porter to sit with his lordship. Then she was shown to a guest room and was assured that her father had been similarly accommodated owing to the lateness of the hour. A message had been dispatched to Grosvenor Square, so her mother wouldn't expect them back until tomorrow.

The room Rebecca had been given was lovely, decorated in the French style with a fresco of cherubs cavorting in splendid nakedness across the azure ceiling. It was a restful chamber, but Rebecca tossed and turned until the longcase clock in the foyer chimed half past four.

When she came down to breakfast at ten the next morning, Lady Richard and the dowager marchioness had already begun their meal.

"Well?" Lady Somerset asked as if she expected Rebecca to read her mind.

Fortunately in this instance, she could. "He has agreed."

"My, but that's wonderful, Rebecca." Lady Richard turned from the side table laden with buttered eggs, sausage, and kippers. She'd already insisted on informal address between them, inviting Rebecca to call her Sophie, but it was difficult for Rebecca to use someone's Christian name after so short an acquaintance. "So Lord Hartley will be returning to Somerfield Park with us. I told you she'd manage it."

This last remark was directed toward the dowager marchioness, who was seated at the head of the long table. Lady Somerset cast Lady Richard a thin smile between bites of her dry toast.

"How lovely a thing it must be to be right all the time, my dear," the old lady said. "Of course, one suspects you might find it taxing after a while. What's life without a few surprises?"

Rebecca studied the chafing dishes, silently debating the merits of lamb's kidneys in a spice sauce or cold veal pie. She settled on the pie and took her seat, avoiding eye contact with either of the women.

Last night, before Rebecca had been sent in to try to convince Lord Hartley to return to Somerset's countryseat, a spirited discussion had broken out between Lady Richard and the elder Lady Somerset. Neither of the strong-willed women minded saying whatever popped into their heads, devil take the hindmost, while they debated how best to get Lord Hartley to come to heel with their plans. While they didn't seem to mind the volleys between them, Rebecca felt like a deer cowering between two determined stalkers.

Even invading an unconscious man's bedchamber had seemed preferable to remaining within range of that verbal barrage.

Lady Richard, however, didn't seem a bit distressed by the marchioness's little barbs. She was looking fresh and comfortable in a deceptively simple morning gown of pale pink muslin. Her dark hair was gathered up by a matching beaded bandeau.

"I'm so ready to go back to Barrett House. London becomes just another noisy city after a while," Lady Richard said, her startlingly blue eyes bright. "Besides, autumn is such a vital season for plants. I need time to put the garden to bed before winter."

"I hope you don't feel I'm putting myself forward, but Lord Hartley only agreed to return to the country if my family and I came for his lordship's hunt," Rebecca said. She'd never tell anyone about John's second condition, even though she could still taste him on her lips.

The dowager looked as if she'd just swallowed a bit of bad kipper, clearly not enamored of the idea that a mere baron and his family should visit Somerfield Park. But Lady Richard leaped into the fray.

"Why, there's nothing easier. You've been so very

helpful; of course you must come," Lady Richard said. "In fact, Lord Hartley and I seem to be thinking along the same lines. I've already spoken to your father about a visit to Somerset, and he agreed to allow you to travel with us when we leave for the country tomorrow. He and your mother will come later."

"Thank you, my lady."

"Sophie, please. Call me Sophie. At least when we are in private, if it makes you uncomfortable otherwise."

"Thank you...Sophie. Your Barrett House garden sounds lovely, but I hope you don't have your heart set on living there again." Rebecca remembered John saying something about having his half brother with him under the same roof. "It seems his lordship expects you and Lord Richard to take up residence at Somerfield Park as well."

The dowager erupted in a fit of coughing and settled her teacup back in its saucer with a loud clink. "I say, he certainly makes free with ordering others around."

Lady Richard rolled her eyes. "As if you never arranged the affairs of others to suit yourself."

Rebecca trembled a bit, wondering how Sophie dared speak to the dowager so. The old lady had the reputation of being a veritable dragon. After all, she was a marchioness, the highest-ranking individual Rebecca had ever shared a breakfast with in her life.

"To my mind, this bit of imperiousness is proof positive that John is your rightful grandson," Sophie said before popping a bite of bun that dripped with marmalade into her mouth.

"As if there were any doubt!" Lady Somerset said with vehemence. "No matter what he may have inherited from his mother's side, he's a Barrett to his bones."

Rebecca dared a glance at the dowager. She'd heard the whole story several times now. John's mother had been a pretty opera dancer who married young Hugh Barrett, who was now Lord Somerset, without his parents' knowledge or permission. Once they learned of the misalliance, they offered her a large sum of money to do with as she pleased if only she'd work with the Somerset solicitor to convince the court that fraud had been involved in the union and swear never to contact Hugh again.

"She was young enough and flighty enough to want the money instead of trying to squeeze herself into the role of lady of a large country estate where no one wanted her," Lady Somerset said. "How were we to know that in the short space of a week she'd conceived a child?"

"I have to admire her though," Sophie said. "A bargain was a bargain and she lived up to her end of it. She never contacted Somerset again. Right up until she died."

"Yes, well, by the time we knew there was a little boy, my son was engaged to marry Lady Helen." The daughter of a respectable earl, Lady Helen was someone of whom old Lady Somerset did approve. The sudden news of a previous marriage, and especially one which had resulted in a male child, would surely have upset the wedding. A foster family in sleepy Wiltshire and a more-than-adequate education seemed a fair solution for one considered to be born on the wrong side of the blanket.

"Of course, we made the mistake of trusting a

gaggle of lawyers and didn't realize that the issue had never been satisfactorily resolved, which meant John Fitzhugh is Somerset's legitimate heir. As soon as we learned of this oversight, we made him aware of his status." The dowager sipped her tea. "If that discommoded you and your plans to become part of the aristocracy, my dear Sophie, I'm terribly sorry."

"Nonsense," Sophie said. "My father was the one who wanted me to be the next mistress of Somerfield Park. I fell in love with Richard despite his title, not because of it. I'm ever so much happier not to be a marchioness in training."

"Not half as glad as I that I don't have to train you." The dowager gave a delicate shudder. "That, my dear, would have been a task of herculean proportions."

Rebecca suspected Lady Richard and Lady Somerset were, if not friends, at least allies most of the time. However, the way they sniped at each other reminded her of a pair of biddies in the barnyard. She rose before one of them could draw first blood.

"If I'm to go with you to the country, I'd best return home to pack, my lady...I mean, Sophie."

"A word before you go, Miss Kearsey," said the dowager, who would never dream of addressing anyone outside of her family informally—or allowing them to do so to her. "It has occurred to me that you may be of further assistance to his lordship as he settles into his new station."

"How so?"

"Help him feel comfortable in social situations when you can. I remember how young ladies are. Gossip is your mother tongue. Smooth the way for him by spreading good things about the new Lord Hartley to your friends."

"Of course I will," Rebecca said and dropped a shallow curtsy. It would be easy to say good things about John.

"You will find me appreciative." The dowager lifted a meaningful eyebrow.

Rebecca hadn't felt comfortable trying to convince John to return to Somerfield Park. Before she had gone into John's chamber last night, she'd made a bargain with the dowager. If Rebecca succeeded in talking Lord Hartley into going along with the family's plans for him, Lady Somerset would advance Rebecca's father enough money to cover half of his current indebtedness. That arched brow was the old lady's way of telling Rebecca she might well earn enough to retire the rest of her father's IOUs.

"Thank you, my lady. I'll do my best."

The dowager nodded approvingly, and the girl skittered out of the breakfast room. "Well, she should prove useful."

Sophie sighed. Rebecca Kearsey was more than half smitten with Lord Hartley. That was plain for anyone with eyes to see. Sophie only hoped the dowager was too caught up in her own Machiavellian plans to mark the paleness of Rebecca's face or the way her brows drew together wistfully whenever she spoke of the new Lord Hartley.

"I admit you were right to suggest I task that girl with bringing Hartley to heel. As a mere baron's daughter, she undoubtedly knows what it's like to linger on the fringes. Like calls to like, they do say.

She speaks his language." The dowager allowed the ubiquitous footman to refill her teacup and then dismissed him with an imperious wave of her bejeweled fingers. She waited for the door to close, so she could speak privately. "However, now we must teach my grandson to speak a new language."

"If you wish to have any influence at all with John, perhaps you should simply treat him as a grandson instead of someone to be managed," Sophie suggested. The Barretts were a staunchly loyal family, but they weren't given to displays of affection. She suspected the new Lord Hartley would do more for a kind word or a spontaneous hug from the dowager than he'd ever do because she tried to maneuver him into a position to her liking.

"I would like nothing more than to coddle the lad," the dowager proclaimed, she who'd never coddled anyone in her life. "But time is running on apace and he's in need of so very much instruction."

"Why? John grew up with gentry in Wiltshire. He was well educated and constantly surrounded by the wellborn while he was at school. Surely he's managed to pick up on how you speak, how you carry yourselves, how you think."

"What a terribly naive observation." The dowager sent her a withering glance. "It's times like this that remind me I only put up with you because you amuse me, Sophie."

"I'm glad to have gratified you." She stuck out her tongue.

"Don't try to rile me with your impertinence when we have important work to do." The dowager took a leisurely sip of tea. "Yes, what you say is true. Hartley does know how we live, but there's a difference. Consider the distinction between being a native-born speaker and one who learns a language later in life. One may develop the vocabulary, but rarely the fluency."

"Back to language again. And pray, what language is it that John needs to learn?"

"The language of a man going a-courting," the dowager said with a smile. "Nothing will put a man right so much as the right woman."

"Not that I disagree, but surely you can't mean he must marry now."

Young girls had their come-out in their late teens, and if they didn't "take" in a couple of Seasons, they'd retire to life "on the shelf." Gentlemen had a much easier time of things. They simply decided for themselves when it was time to enter the marriage market. They could look around as long as they liked without becoming the least stale. Sophie thought John would benefit from waiting.

"I don't think you should rush matters. John is not yet adjusted to his new station," Sophie said.

"And he'll never rise to being Lord Hartley if he's allowed to run rampant with the riffraff of London."

"I don't see how you can keep him from doing whatever he pleases. He's a man fully grown and, what's more, the future marquess," Sophie said. "I hardly need remind you that in this family, we tend to do any foolish thing we like."

"Richard could leash him," Lady Somerset said. "He still holds the power of the purse. If Hartley won't behave himself, Richard will have to cut him off."

"Careful. There's nothing to stop John from going to court and relieving Richard of his duties as the estate's agent. I think you and I agree that it's in Somerset's best interests for my husband to continue managing the estate for the time being."

The dowager huffed out a disgusted breath, but conceded the point. She enjoyed her comforts in the sumptuous dower house known as Somerset Steading. Richard's stewardship ensured those comforts would continue unabated.

"Well, perhaps there's not much we need do, actually, except point Hartley in the right direction," Lady Somerset mused. "I've set the stage. We'll simply let nature take its course."

"What do you mean you've set the stage?" Sophie asked suspiciously.

"My son has sent his invitations to the hunt and I've sent mine. Nearly every lord about to descend upon Somerfield Park also has a daughter or a niece of marriageable age."

Sophie's eyes flared. "You didn't."

"Oh, but I did."

"But won't the fact that John's upbringing was… unconventional put them off?"

"Clearly, my dear, you underestimate the value of becoming a marchioness one day. But then, you always did."

"Silly me," Sophie said. "I was always more interested in the man who came with the title. Good thing, since his title went away."

"You showed good sense in that, I'll grant you. Richard is a fine man, no matter that he no longer succeeds his father. And he was fortunate to have chosen a young woman who doesn't care about such things." From the dowager, that was high praise indeed. "But back to the problem at hand. You needn't think I came right out and broadcast the news that Hartley was wife shopping. I simply wrote to the wives of the lords usually invited to the hunt. I explained that when their gentlemen weren't gallivanting about the estate trying to kill things, they might enjoy some genteel activities— card parties and dances, lawn bowling and archery. To that end, they might bring their marriageable daughters to Somerfield Park for the duration of the hunt."

The dowager tittered at the double entendre of "hunt," since poor John would definitely be in the crosshairs of all those hopeful misses.

"Perhaps we might organize some musical evenings," Sophie suggested, getting into the spirit of the plan.

"Only if we can find a few debutantes who aren't tone deaf, which—trust me, my dear—is a very tall order indeed." The dowager leaned forward for emphasis.

"Still, this whole plan seems terribly contrived."

"Well, of course, it is. If we women didn't contrive to arrange marriages, how many do you think would actually come to pass?" Lady Somerset asked without pausing for an answer. "Besides, everyone I invited wrote back to accept. And not a one of the young ladies who'll be in attendance is less than the daughter of an earl. An important consideration, given Lord Hartley's humble beginnings."

"Well, then perhaps John won't be in for a terrible time at the hands of the *ton* after all."

"I should say not when it is seen that his whole

family is behind him. If only he'd come directly to Somerfield Park in the first place, instead of haring off to London on his own—well, there's no putting the milk back in the jug." The old lady sighed. "I simply want to see the succession settled for another generation before I shuffle off this mortal coil."

"What sentimental rot." Sophie chuckled. "You'll outlive us all and dance on our graves."

"Oh, I wouldn't dance, my dear. Cutting a reel at my age causes far too much to jiggle that shouldn't."

They laughed together at that. Sophie rose and came down to the dowager's end of the table. She gave Richard's grandmother her arm so they could take a turn through the pint-sized garden behind the Mayfair town house.

"You know," Sophie said, "I've noticed that you are the only one besides me who calls my Richard by his Christian name."

"I call all my grandchildren by their given names, even my grandchildren by marriage, my dear Sophie," she added with a sly smile. "Why wouldn't I?"

"You don't call John by his name," she pointed out. "He's only Hartley to you."

"Much has been made about what an adjustment this has been for the young man. However, he is not the only one who finds difficulty in accepting these changes." The dowager's lips pinched together. "You know what they say about old dogs."

"Oh dear. If I repeat that to anyone, they'd never believe you referred to yourself in such a manner."

"But I do sometimes feel as low as a dog about my involvement in the whole affair," the dowager admitted with a quiver of her chin. She was the one, after all, who had surrendered young John to the nurture and training of Sir Humphrey and his wife, instead of taking him into the Somerfield Park nursery. She had known John was her son's issue. She just didn't know he was her *legitimate* grandson.

Sophie patted her arm. "You may indeed feel as low as a dog, but I think folk would be more surprised to hear you call yourself 'old.'"

The dowager gave a choking cough of a laugh. "Quite. A momentary lapse, I assure you. I trust your discretion, my dear, not to reveal that I sometimes think myself a veritable Methuselah."

"I am a vault. Your secret is safe with me."

So it was guilt that kept the old lady from reaching out to John. Perhaps that was something Sophie could help mend. Somehow, she needed to reconcile this grandmother with her grandson, so they could both put the past behind them. But even as she thought about it, Sophie shook her head.

"Is something troubling you?" the dowager said.

"No, I'm just bemused over how alike you and I are. We both think we can rearrange the lives of those around us and expect the recipients of our meddling to be grateful."

"And well they should be!" the old lady said.

Lady Somerset wouldn't think so if she knew she'd just been added to Sophie's list of people to manage.

What the dowager doesn't know won't hurt me.

As they strolled out into the brittle autumn garden behind the Barretts' Mayfair town house, Sophie added another name to her list.

Miss Rebecca Kearsey.

Watching John be hunted like the biggest trophy buck of the season might be amusing for Sophie and satisfying for his grandmother, but it would be a special circle of hell for any girl who harbored a *tendresse* for him. And since Rebecca was only the daughter of a baron, and a rather minor one at that, Lady Somerset wouldn't consider her highly placed enough for him to return the favor.

Four

The trick to any hunt, I'm told, is to make sure the quarry is unaware it is about to be snared.

—Phillippa, the Dowager Marchioness of Somerset

"SHOULD YOU BE UP AND ABOUT, MY LORD?" PORTER cringed a bit at the sight of Lord Hartley's left eye. The swelling had gone down since that morning, thanks to the housekeeper's knowledge of the use of leeches. But now in late afternoon, the skin around the offended orb had darkened to a ripe plum color with yellowish undertones. Just looking at it made Porter's own eyes ache.

"I'm fine, Mr. Porter," Lord Hartley said as he sat down to allow Porter to help him into his polished Hessians. "Honestly, you fret like an old woman."

It was Porter's job to fret. He was practically paid by the worry, and the position of Lord Hartley's valet was a goldmine of opportunity to earn that particular coin.

Not that Porter wasn't grateful for the rise in standing he'd enjoyed when John Fitzhugh Barrett had come into his own. A servant's place among the downstairs folk was dependent upon the status of the noble person they served. But honestly, being valet to the heir of Somerset was a daunting situation all the same.

There had been much palavering below stairs about who would take the post for the newly discovered heir. Mr. Hightower, who made all the personnel decisions from his fusty office as butler of Somerfield Park, deemed it too difficult for any of the existing servants to step in as the new lord's valet—not when they'd served Lord Richard and thought of him as the next marquess for so many years. It was bound to lead to confusion.

But neither did Mr. Hightower want to bring a total stranger into this new position. The Family needed someone of proven loyalty for this delicate task. For decades, Porter had been the butler at Barrett House, the cottage set aside for the estate's pensioners when there was need. He was counted as one of the Somerfield Park below stairs folk, yet he was somewhat set apart. Porter had been rendered nearly speechless with gratitude when Mr. Hightower gave him the nod for the post as the next marquess's valet. It was a gift from heaven to be handed a position that could see him through the rest of his working life.

Porter was proud to accompany Lord Richard to Wiltshire to fetch his half brother and welcome him into the bosom of his family. But when the new Lord Hartley learned of his elevation, he didn't return with Lord Richard to Somerfield Park. He abandoned country life altogether for London, forcing Porter to toddle along behind him. The job seemed much less of a gift then.

"Can't say I'm sorry to be going home," Porter said as he neatly folded one of Lord Hartley's new shirts.

The one his lordship had been wearing when Lord Richard dragged him home last night was probably a lost cause, stained as it was with blood and a number of other substances Porter couldn't identify. However, like any good valet, he was obligated to try and salvage it.

"I'm used to country hours, you see, your lordship." When Porter rose at dawn, as was his habit, Lord Hartley often hadn't even come home yet. So-called "morning calls" didn't occur till afternoon, and a gentleman might have supper as late as midnight when he was in Town. It was madness. "Things seem so topsy-turvy here in London."

"Do they? I expect I'll feel even more turned about at Somerfield Park than I do here," Lord Hartley said softly. "Everyone there knows I was once considered a bastard. Here in London, I'm simply a mad gentleman with a bit of blunt to pass around."

"I hadn't thought of it that way, my lord. But back home, even if things do seem odd to you, you'll be among friends. You'll see."

"I wonder." Lord Hartley shrugged on a violent pink waistcoat before Porter could skitter across the room to finesse it from him or, failing that, to help him put it on.

Porter had tried to dissuade him from ordering the outlandish thing at the tailor's shop, but some of his lordship's friends had assured him it was "all the crack." Those Daemon Club gentlemen—and Porter used the word very loosely—were likely having fun at Lord Hartley's expense behind his back.

The new lord started to pull on his tailcoat.

"A moment, my lord, and I'll set you to rights." Porter scurried over in time to smooth down the collar of the jacket and make sure the shoulders lay straight.

"Do you think you could address me just once without 'my lording' me?"

"Yes, my…I'll try."

"Never mind, Porter. It's not your fault."

Perpetual guilt was deeply ingrained in Porter's soul. If things didn't go well, it was almost always deemed the servant's fault.

"Tell me, Mr. Porter. Is there someone special at Somerfield Park that makes you want to return so?"

A vision of Mrs. Culpepper, the pleasingly plump cook at Somerfield Park, wandered across his mind along with a parade of several platters of her delicious food.

"Happens there is, at that," Porter said.

"Well, that explains your eagerness to hie yourself back to the hinterlands."

Porter might harbor tender feelings for Mrs. Culpepper, but he'd never gathered the courage needed to act upon them. The most he'd managed were a few brief conversations with her, none of them of any consequence.

But once he was finally living in the fourth-floor servants' wing of Somerfield Park, he'd be sitting down to her savory meals three times a day. After the needs of the Family had been met, he'd pass quiet evenings in the below stairs common room with the other servants. Surely with all those opportunities, he'd find the gumption to ask her to walk out with him some night.

It'd be a fine, soft evening with a whiff of the sea on the breeze. Overhead, the stars would shimmer like an upset box of diamond cuff links on a square of dark superfine.

"Never thought I'd be stepping out with the valet of a future marquess," Mrs. Culpepper might say.

And once again, he'd be grateful that there wasn't now nor had there ever been a Mr. Culpepper. The *Mrs.* before her name was only a term of respect due her position as cook in the great house.

"Never thought I'd be squiring 'round a kitchen witch, either."

"A witch, ye say?" When she was miffed, her cheeks always pinked up like a girl's. He loved to see her that way, though it was more likely to be Toby, the popular footman, who teased her into a fit of blushing than Porter.

"A witch in the best sense, if you follow my meaning," he'd hasten to explain. "I only mean you make magic with your mixing bowls and wooden spoons."

"Well," she'd say, somewhat mollified, "so long as that's the way ye feel. Otherwise, I'll have to find another use for one of those spoons…on your backside."

"Not until I've done something wicked enough to warrant it, I hope," he'd venture with a slight waggle of his brows. He'd summon his courage and reach for her hand. Then—

"I say, Porter, if you're done woolgathering, do you think you might find my pocket watch?"

Lord Hartley's voice yanked him out of his

pleasant, vaguely naughty musings, and he leaped to be of service.

"Yes, my...yes, indeed. Here it is." Porter arranged the chain to drape properly from the fob to his employer's pocket, where the dear gold watch resided. "What about you, your lordship? Aren't you the least curious about Somerfield Park and the folk whom you'll meet there?"

"Yes, but I'm not thinking of the family, if that's what you mean." Frowning, his lordship tugged at the abominable pink waistcoat as he surveyed himself in the long looking glass. "There's at least one person I'll be glad to see. Miss Kearsey will be there. I've seen to that."

That was a mercy. Porter liked Miss Kearsey very much indeed. Perhaps his lordship was getting better about judging the quality of character in others. Heaven knew his friends in the Daemon Club weren't the right sort at all.

Lord Hartley fiddled with the knot in his cravat that Porter had worked so hard to fashion. Fortunately, he abandoned it before he did too much damage, and pulled on his fine kid gloves. Porter eyed his lordship from the tips of his spit-shined Hessians to his tousled head of hair. Barring the hurt-your-eyes pink waist-coat and the shiner, Lord Hartley was as well turned out as the prince regent himself. Then Porter's gaze wandered back to his employer's face, and he nearly staggered back a step at the abject misery he saw there.

"But as it happens, I probably shouldn't be eager to see her. For her own good." Lord Hartley didn't wait for Porter to hand him his topper. He whisked the hat off the end of the bed himself and popped it on his head. "The best way to save Miss Kearsey from having to spend too much time with me is to fill up the house with other people, people who won't feel uncomfortable around a lately made lord, so it falls to me to invite my own guests to the country."

Porter shuddered to think who Lord Hartley might be considering inflicting on Somerfield Park. "Not wanting to speak out of turn, but—"

"But you fully intend to in any case, don't you?"

Porter wrung his hands and nodded. "I do, beggin' your pardon. Even in a great house like Somerfield Park, there are only so many guest rooms. Oughtn't you discuss the matter with Lord Richard or perhaps your lady grandmother? She's in residence here, part of the party what came looking for you, my—" He caught himself before he said "my lord," but only just. "Sorry, my lord. I can't help when a term of respect passes my lips. I fear it's force of habit."

"Don't fret. I've been called worse and probably deserved it more. But no, I won't be asking my brother's permission to invite my friends to what is, after all, *my* estate." Lord Hartley tilted his topper into a rakish slant. "And I have no grandmother."

He strode from the room without a backward glance.

❧

Lady Chloe Endicott leaned back on the settee and let Lord Blackstone tease a ripe strawberry along her lower lip before he popped it into her mouth.

"Mmm." She licked her lip to make sure she didn't miss a single drop of sweetness. What was life if one didn't savor every pleasure to the fullest? "Where on earth did you get strawberries at this time of year?"

"Believe it or not, I won an orangery in a game of poque at White's last week. The gardener who came with it forces a number of delectable things to grow year-round." The viscount leaned down to nibble at her earlobe. "Though none of them are as delectable as you."

She pushed him away playfully. "Stop it, you rogue, or I'll have to make you my next husband."

Blackwood pulled back the next berry he'd begun to offer, a startled look on his aristocratic features. "Oh, that's an honor I shall be forced to decline, my dear Lady Chloe. Becoming your husband is not conducive to a man's health."

"Never say you believe everything you hear about me."

"Well, let's see."

He put the berry back in its box and began fiddling with one of the long, golden locks that draped alongside her neck and ended in a curl just below her bosom. Chloe's French maid had advised her to leave a few strands dangling, in order to encourage this very behavior. When it came to matters sensual, the French were rarely wrong.

"Stop me if I say something that is untrue." Blackwood began her litany of misfortune. "The first time you wed, the church where the ceremony was held burned to the ground within a week of your nuptials."

"But I was nowhere near the church when—"

"True or false?"

Chloe huffed out a disgruntled breath. "True."

"That unfortunate event was seen as a harbinger of things to come. At least that's what the tongue-waggers claimed when your bridegroom failed to survive the honeymoon in Venice."

"Lucius fell off a gondola." Chloe crossed her arms under her breasts knowing full well the gesture only accentuated her charms. "You can hardly blame me if the man couldn't swim."

True to form, Blackwood's gaze dipped to her décolletage. Men were so very easy to predict.

But Blackwood pressed gamely on, refusing to be distracted. "Your husband wasn't helped to fall off the gondola, was he?"

"Of course not," she said in a properly scandalized tone. "Well, not unless one believes a bottle of amaretto could be guilty of such a crime. Poor Lucius did imbibe an overabundance of the liquor. I had no idea when I married him how fond he was of drink."

"And the gondolier couldn't be bothered to fish him out of the canal?"

"Despite what you hear about how romantic Venice is, the water is terribly dirty. The gondolier couldn't see a thing in that murk." She shrugged and then smiled. "Dear Giovanni. He was such a comfort."

"I'll just bet he was. Especially since your dearly departed Lucius left you a bequest large enough to make you a considerable heiress." Blackwood smiled unpleasantly, as if he knew more than he was saying and could somehow prove it. "Then there was your second husband."

"Viscount Cavendish," she supplied helpfully.

"If memory serves, he lasted a scant six months before you were forced to don widow's weeds again. True?"

"True," she admitted. "But you must realize, Cavendish was rather elderly to begin with."

"Forty years your senior, by all accounts." This time Lord Blackwood's gaze held grudging admiration. "You simply wore him out."

She giggled and returned his wicked smile. "That's true. But believe me, he died a happy man."

"I'm sure, but he didn't succumb amid the delights of your bed until after he'd redrafted his will, making you the sole heiress of his liquid assets," Blackwood said. "I hear it left the son from his first marriage with a venerable title, a crumbling estate, and no funds with which to run it."

"Cavendish was never good at thinking things through."

"But you are, you delightful little hussy, you."

She wished he'd call her worse. A bit of the vulgar tongue was just what she needed sometimes. Cavendish used to say she was his "dirty doxy," and it made her feel deliciously wicked. "Oh, Blackwood, you say the sweetest things."

"Which brings us to husband number three." Blackwood used the end of her long curl to tease along the edge of her bodice. "Your third husband was a lawyer, I believe," Blackwood said.

"He was. Mr. Benedict Longbotham, Esquire."

"And the only one of your husbands to be without a title."

"True, but what did I care that he was in trade? Since I'm the daughter of an earl, I'll always be Lady

Chloe no matter who I marry, and besides, Bothy was simply swimming in lard." She examined the sparkling ruby set about with diamond baguettes that adorned her right pinky. She'd almost forgotten that the ring was a gift from her late lamented third husband. "Most of the money was actually his, too."

Blackwood dropped her long curl, propped his arm on the back of the settee, and leaned his fist against his temple. "I've forgotten. Whatever became of your solicitor?"

"Oh, it's too distasteful," Chloe said with a shudder before she dove into the gory details in any case. "An unhappy client waylaid him as he came out of Boodle's one evening and shoved him into the path of a coach and six. It was a beastly way for Mr. Longbotham to meet his end."

"Quite." Lord Blackwood wasn't able to stifle a chuckle. "But you didn't mourn him long before you married husband number four."

"Can you blame me? Would you want to be known as a *Longbotham* for any longer than you could help?" She sighed. "And besides, when I met Sir Aubrey Endicott, it was love at first sight."

"He was younger than you."

She glared at him. "Only by ten years, but oh, what a difference those ten years made. I must admit, Blackwood, there is much to be said for younger gentlemen." She closed her eyes, the better to savor the delicious memory. "They're so…vigorous."

"He was barely out of the schoolroom." Blackwood laid a hand on her knee and squeezed gently. "Besides,

I assure you there's much to be said for a man of experience as well."

"Dear Blackwood." She caressed his cheek, and then pointedly removed his hand from her leg. "I wouldn't doubt it for worlds, but you've already said you don't wish to marry me."

"With your track record for husbands, can you blame me? Even young Sir Aubrey met his Maker in an untimely fashion." He tapped his temple. "Let me see if I remember what unhappy accident caught up with him."

She narrowed her eyes. "He fell out a fourth-story window."

"From the chamber of one of your maids, I believe," he said with a decidedly nasty sneer.

"Which just goes to show, there is such a thing as being too…vigorous."

Drat Blackwood for making her revisit Aubrey's unfortunate peccadilloes. He really had been a delight when he wasn't shagging the help.

Evidently his heart was not as strong as his other attributes. It was a good thing that window had been large enough for Chloe to shove him through. She'd have had the devil's own time wrangling his body to the head of the stairs to make it look as if that fall had done him in.

Sometimes she thought she ought to have left him in the maid's chamber and let the authorities see him in all his naked shamefulness. He deserved it if he couldn't be more circumspect about whose bed he was caught in. But in the end, Chloe decided it was better that she dressed him and let folk think he'd taken a flying leap out the window on his own.

"Now I'm all alone and out of mourning again. I'm told that black becomes me, but honestly, it is tedious after a while. And jet jewelry is so very uninspired." Chloe walked her fingers down Blackwood's chest. "Are you sure you don't want to tie the knot with me?"

"I'd like to tie something with you." He leaned forward and nuzzled her neck.

He leaned in to try for a kiss again, but she pressed against his chest to keep him at bay. "No doubt we'd both find it delightful, but I make it a firm rule not to tumble into bed with anyone I haven't promised to stick with till death do us part."

"Till death do us part," he repeated. "Aye, there's the rub. I understand a woman's desire to be wed, but never say you don't indulge in *affaires de coeur* on the side."

"I respect you far too much to play coy. Yes, of course, I enjoy the company of men. But my life is complicated. It's all a matter of timing, you see. When one is freshly bereaved, one must have comfort, mustn't one?" She blinked languidly at him. During the early days of each of her bereavements, she often had more than one lover at her beck and call. "But once I am actively seeking a husband, as I am now, it is not practical to take a lover. Gentlemen tend to resent that sort of thing in a prospective bride."

"Your logic is unassailable."

"So I go into a period of nun-like abstinence when I'm on the husband hunt." She sighed.

He shook his head. "The life cycle of the man-eating she-spider is endlessly fascinating."

"You beast!" She swatted him on the chest.

"I take it back, but you must admit you are unlike most women," he said, hands raised in surrender.

"Only in that I am more honest about my needs and wants than most."

"Point taken," he conceded. "Help me understand, my dear. Once you marry, I take it you are faithful to your husband."

She slanted him a sly glance. "As faithful as he is to me."

"So, no."

"Not so far. You see, I've yet to find a man who can love with singleness of heart—not even Lucius, my first husband. Do you know I caught him in the linen closet with a chambermaid while we were on our honeymoon?"

"The dog."

"He was, but his behavior wasn't all that remarkable from what I hear of other marriages. It's naive to expect fidelity," Chloe said. "Of course, if a gentleman is discreet, there's no real harm done. If a husband of mine keeps a ladybird in a discreet nest somewhere, who am I to complain? He has his life. I have mine. I simply engage my own lover and everyone's happy."

"Especially your lover, I expect."

"Use your imagination." She leaned forward so he could get a good look down her décolletage. Lord Blackwood understood her. They'd be good together. "What do you think?"

His mouth went slack below his neat mustache, and he dragged his eyes back up to meet her gaze with difficulty.

"I think it's in my best interests to see you wed posthaste." Blackwood leaned toward her, tilting his head in preparation for a kiss. She was of a mind to let him have it this time.

However, before their lips met, someone cleared their throat in the open doorway to the parlor with a loud "ahem."

Chloe straight-armed Lord Blackwood and turned to find Wilkenson, her butler, standing under the lintel, his back stooped, his face frozen in its perpetual hangdog expression. Whether happy or sad, his eyes were always droopy and his jowls sagging.

He'd be a wizard at the poque table. Fair hand or foul, it would never show. "What is it, Wilkenson?"

"A Lord Hartley to see you, my lady." Wilkenson advanced toward her bearing a single card on a silver salver. "Shall I show him up?"

Five

"Will you swim into my net?" said the angler to the trout.
"You'll love its charms so very much, you never will
*   want out.*
But if by chance you do, you see, don't cry that life's unfair.
I'll take you home and fry you up and then you'll cease
*   to care."*

If this is the sort of thing they read to children these days, I
wash my hands of the next generation altogether!

—Phillippa, the Dowager Marchioness of Somerset

"HARTLEY, HOW GOOD OF YOU TO VISIT ME." CHLOE
rose and extended her hand to the handsome young
lord. And how nice that she was at home, *en dishabille*
and not wearing gloves. Men loved to touch a bit of
skin in private that was forbidden to them in public.
Besides, if done correctly, the tip of a man's tongue
placed at the juncture of the index and middle finger
could create a remarkable sense of stimulation in
another place on a woman's body. "I don't believe

you've ever called on—goodness me! What's happened to your eye?"

"Oh, that. It's nothing. I'm sorry if the sight of it distresses you, but please don't be concerned." Hartley removed his topper and took her hand, bending to brush his lips across her knuckles with correctness. Clearly the newly elevated lord had picked up a few high-toned manners along the way—*more's the pity*. "The bruise looks much worse than it feels."

Chloe returned to the settee and draped herself artfully across it. In a little while, she'd tuck her neatly shod feet up beside her on the seat, taking care to make sure she displayed more ankle than she ought. But she'd do it in such a way as to make it seem inadvertent. Chloe did so enjoy teasing gentlemen with what she wasn't prepared to give them.

Yet.

She waved Hartley to the striped chintz Sheridan chair across from her.

"Never say you engaged in a boxing match and I didn't get to watch," she said with a pout.

Lord Hartley's face brightened like a little boy who'd just been invited to display the toad in his pocket for her inspection. "As a matter of fact, I did, but it was no place for a lady. Besides, I fear it was all quite illegal."

"So much the better." Chloe gave a shiver of delight that wasn't entirely feigned. "Do sit down and tell me all about it."

Blackwood had already described the match to her in some detail. She loved watching half-dressed young fellows go at each other hammer-and-tongs and was quite put out at Blackwood for taking Hartley to the boxing crib without her. She had a full suit of men's clothing she kept for just such occasions, when women weren't allowed. She often joined the Daemon Club on their jaunts about Town that didn't involve ladies of light virtue.

Even if she didn't go incognita, since Chloe was a widow many times over, her movements weren't as restricted as most ladies. If the evening involved cards or dice, she could often venture out and she wouldn't be the only woman present. Chloe wasn't received by the fashionable set in any case, and thus she had very little reputation to protect.

Hartley settled in to give a blow-by-blow account of the match that was worthy of a boxing coach.

"But I didn't get this in the ring," he said pointing to his shiner. "That came later, after I left the crib."

The thought of his being set upon by ruffians sent a thrill rippling through her. She wondered how she'd have fared if she'd been with the Daemon Club when that pack of human wolves gathered around. Perhaps if she'd pulled out the little pistol she always carried in her reticule, Lord Hartley would be able to see out of both of his soulful, dark eyes now. The floor-to-ceiling draperies that were pulled shut over her Palladian windows moved slightly. Blackwood was hiding there.

"I didn't come here to talk boxing with you, Lady Chloe."

"You have me on pins. Why did you come?"

"To invite you to Somerfield Park."

Chloe blinked at him in surprise. He was too good,

this country mouse her city friends had brought to her notice. No one ever invited her anywhere respectable, and the seat of the Somerset marquessate was the pinnacle of respectability. "Me? Go to the country with you? Why?"

"Lord Somerset is hosting his annual hunt, and the house will be filled with his friends," Hartley said. "I'd like to see a few of mine there as well. That's why I'm asking you to come for the next fortnight. Please say you will."

Chloe had heard of Lord Somerset's annual hunts. Each fall, the cream of English aristocracy repaired to the marquess's vast estate. By all accounts, they had a simply marvelous time procuring dead heads with antlers to hang on the walls of their own country manors.

"I am not received by Polite Society," Chloe reminded him.

"Neither am I. That's why my...my *family*..." He seemed to stumble over the word. "At any rate, they seem to feel a turnabout is in order. If I'm in a position to *receive* Polite Society rather than be received, it will change matters. As I understand it, being at Somerfield Park will give some of the *ton* a chance to reconsider me and my unusual circumstances."

He leaned forward, balancing his elbows on his knees. "Perhaps if they have the chance to spend time with you there in the country, they'll reconsider you too."

Chloe hadn't been welcome in a proper parlor since she returned from Italy in widow's weeds. Since her very first bereavement, she hardly knew what it was like to meet a respectable woman on the street. Most of them crossed over to the other side rather than be forced to acknowledge her. She'd suffered more than her share of cuts direct before she decided to thumb her nose at the *ton* and stop seeking their approval.

"I don't know," Chloe said with a sigh. "I don't want to hurt your chances, Hartley."

Where on earth had that come from? She hadn't had an altruistic thought in years. Clearly Lord Hartley was a bad influence on her.

"Let me worry about that. If the *ton* chooses to cut me over my choice of friends, so be it. When I first came to London, you were one of the few who didn't make me feel as if I had a bit of dung on my shoe and then tracked it into the parlor. Can you blame me for wanting to be sure of a few friendly faces in Somerfield Park? I hope one will be yours." He ran the brim of his topper through his thick, capable-looking fingers. At least, she'd like to learn what they might be capable of. "If you're concerned that you won't know anyone, don't be. I intend to invite Blackwood, Smalley, and Pitcairn as well."

"Now I know you're trying to bungle your chances."

Hartley laughed. "Those fellows aren't so bad. At least they're lively and will keep the party from becoming stodgy."

"That's God's truth." The Daemon Club was an entertaining lot…if they didn't burn the manor house down in the meantime.

"Then you'll come?" Hartley said.

"I will." Someone had to watch out for this lost lamb. Chloe hadn't realized before this how very gullible he was. She rose to her feet and he did too. Then a new thought crossed her mind, and with it, her estimation of his intelligence and cleverness ticked up. "Oh! Now I understand. You wish to tweak Somerset's nose. Inviting the Daemon Club and me will not bring your family any ease, will it?"

A smile tugged at the corners of his mouth. "How well you know me, my lady. I confess, the fact that having Blackwood, Pitcairn, and Smalley at Somerfield Park will discomfit the dowager marchioness out of all knowing *does* add to my enthusiasm for having them there. But that does not apply to you."

"Does it not? Surely your family will be horrified to have a merry widow in residence. In some quarters, I am considered beyond the pale."

"Not by me," Hartley assured her. "You ought not to be condemned for having had bad luck. And if I can help your luck change, I will be gratified. I understand Lord Somerset invites the most important lords for his annual hunt, and you've made no secret of the fact that you are open to taking another husband. No doubt you'll embark on a hunt of your own."

"Why, Hartley, you've a positively devious streak I never suspected."

"I've always heard it's the quiet ones people ought to worry about," he said with a grin. "As for inviting the rest of the Daemon Club, no matter what the Barrett family may have to say on the matter, they are my friends. If a man doesn't stick by his friends, he's not much of a man."

"But if I may? A word of advice as you prepare to mingle with the fashionable set. It doesn't do to greet the world with too open a heart."

A shadow passed over his face. "Don't worry on

that score. My heart is safely tucked away where no one can touch it."

"I just mean, don't be too trusting. Even…" How could she tell this fresh-faced young man that the ones he thought of as his friends would sooner laugh at him than with him? "Be careful, will you?"

"I can take care of myself, my lady," he said, bowing over her proffered hand as he prepared to take his leave. "Don't let the shiner fool you. Several of the other fellows looked much worse."

After Hartley left, Blackwood came out from his hiding place. "Seems as if I should be going too. I wouldn't want to miss my invitation to Somerfield Park. What a bag of moonshine. This is going to be a golden opportunity to make a proper bumble-broth of everyone involved."

"Hartley believes you're his friend. Have you no conscience at all?"

"None, and neither do you." He ignored her offered hand and leaned in to buss his lips on her cheek instead. "Otherwise, you wouldn't be considering young Lord Hartley for husband number five."

"Who said I—"

"No one had to. I could tell from the way your voice went all soft and squishy-sounding while you spoke with him." He pitched his baritone into a breathy falsetto. "'It doesn't do to greet the world with too open a heart.'" Then he laughed. "What rubbish. But good luck to the pair of you. The sooner you wed that bumpkin, the sooner you can take me as your lover."

She whacked his shoulder. This time it was not at all playful.

"Good day, my lady. See you in the country."

Blackwood strode from her parlor, leaving a cloud of his strong cologne hovering in his wake like a bergamot-and-musk-scented ghost.

Chloe sank back onto her settee. "John Fitzhugh Barrett," she mused.

She hadn't been considering him as husband material before, but now she mulled over the possibility. He was on the youngish side, perhaps five years or so her junior.

That would bode well in the boudoir. And Hartley struck her as the sort who could be trained to give her what she needed.

She'd heard the Somerset estate had been on shaky financial ground, but from all accounts, the younger Barrett son, Lord Richard, seemed to be taking those matters firmly in hand.

Besides, money was not her immediate concern. Her collective late husbands had left her comfortably well off. She'd simply have to have her solicitor draft a contract that allowed her to retain control of her own funds even after she married.

But the real strawberry in the situation was that someday, Lord Hartley would become Lord Somerset. Chloe would be a marchioness. She'd take precedence over all but a duchess.

No matter how sordid her marital history might be, the ladies of the *ton* who shunned her now would be toadying up to gain her favor then. Countesses would curtsy deeply to her. Baronesses would plead with her to come to their teas.

She'd be able to destroy any of them with a single withering glance.

Her decision made, she rang for Wilkenson. Despite his hunched posture, her butler appeared with surprising speed.

"How may I serve you, my lady?"

"Send Suzette up to my chamber to pack. Apparently, we are going to the country."

"For how long, my lady?"

She'd heard much of the splendors of Somerfield Park and now happily imagined herself as its mistress. "Let's leave that open-ended, shall we?"

Six

While I'm all in favor of planning—no one can live a well-ordered existence without it—sometimes, it is the things we don't plan that make life worth living.

—Phillippa, the Dowager Marchioness of Somerset

HALF A DOZEN GOWNS WERE SPREAD OUT ACROSS Rebecca's bed. Her off-white gown with the clever embroidery on the bodice was the best. The blue one that had been utterly ruined at that horrid boxing crib would have been next, but it was now fit only to wear while gardening. Rebecca's wardrobe went downhill from there.

"Can you turn this pale green muslin one more time, Crosby?" Rebecca asked the lady's maid she shared with her mother.

Agnes Crosby adjusted her spectacles and eyed the worn gown carefully. "I might just do. Think there's enough fabric left at the hem and the sleeves to tuck the frayed bits once more. But this is the limit. It'll be too short for modesty another turn after this."

Crosby took the green muslin and left to do the sewing while Rebecca continued packing for her fortnight in the country. With each folded gown, each rolled up stocking, Rebecca's insides did a little jig.

She loved to look at the stars from her terrace and imagine what sort of worlds might be swirling around each point of light. She was about to enter a world as seemingly unreachable as those distant orbs. Rebecca was acutely aware of her position on one of the lowest rungs of the aristocracy. It would be different if her father had the chinks, but his gambling left the family teetering on the edge of ruin. Though she was a baron's daughter and technically considered an "honorable," the rarified air of a marquessate would normally be too thin, too high for the likes of her.

However, even if she didn't really belong there, she'd still been invited to join the house party—not only by John, but by his family as well. She ought to think of him as Lord Hartley. It would be safer all around, but how quickly he'd been transformed in Rebecca's mind from her nameless gentleman from the museum to simply John.

Everything was happening at such a breakneck pace, she forced herself to plop down on the foot of the bed and take a deep breath. Rebecca had lived through a perilous adventure in Whitechapel. She'd kissed a man in his bedchamber and now she was going to Somerfield Park to rub elbows with the crème de la crème.

She didn't know which of those things was the most dangerously exciting.

"Rebecca!" Freddie's voice echoed down the hallway, the clack of her sensible half boots on the hardwood preceding her to Rebecca's room. Her friend paused at the door and braced her arms on the frame as if she were being confined by the space and would push it back by sheer dint of will. "What's this I hear about you going to Somerfield Park?"

Rebecca skittered to her friend and caught up both her hands. Then she danced her about the small chamber. "You heard correctly. I leave in the morning with Lord Hartley's family."

"Not to be a dash of cold water," Freddie said as she stopped their circuit of the room, "but why?"

Rebecca halted mid-step. "Why what?"

"Why have you been invited?"

"What do you mean?"

"Oh, my dear. Among the upper strata of society, nothing is ever done without reason. What reason do the Barretts have for inviting you to this event? The word is that Lord Hartley is looking for his bride among the guests coming to his house party." Freddie sat on the foot of the bed and patted the spot beside her. "You know I love you like a sister, Rebecca, but let's be honest. You're hopelessly outmatched, and I would be dreadfully upset if you've been invited solely to become a target for mean-spirited barbs. You see, I have it on good authority that all the other young ladies planning to attend the house party are daughters of earls at the least."

Rebecca perched beside her. "So I assume you've been invited, Lady Winifred."

Freddie stuck out her tongue and waved away

Rebecca's use of her title. "There's no cause to be formal, not between you and me. You know I care nothing for that."

Rebecca would have said that was true, but now Freddie seemed to have erected a small wall between them with her pointed questions. They'd been friends since Rebecca first climbed over the rock wall that separated her father's small holding from the Chalcroft country estate. The girls had gone birding together all that summer and had been inseparable ever after. They were both of a scholarly bent, so their shared interests were legion. Freddie, who could have been at the heart of a social whirl by virtue of her father's rank, was content to avoid balls and routs alongside Rebecca, in favor of lectures and art exhibits.

Until now.

"You didn't answer my question. Have you been invited to Somerfield Park too?" Rebecca asked.

"Yes, I've known for weeks that my father was on Lord Somerset's guest list." To Rebecca's surprise, Freddie actually preened a bit, patting the thin blond curls that graced her temple. "Mother and I hadn't thought to attend, but then we received a personal invitation from the dowager marchioness."

So had Rebecca, but she wasn't as annoyingly puffed up about it. "Does this mean you wish to be in the running for Lord Hartley's bride?"

Freddie shrugged. "Let us be honest. We must marry sometime. Men can lead productive, full lives without benefit of matrimony, but as much as I wish it were otherwise, a woman needs the security of a good match."

"That sounds like your mother talking."

"It does and I've decided she's right. For once. Besides, think of all the good I could do as the Marchioness of Somerset." Freddie was keen on making improvements, especially as they applied to other people's lives.

"I was under the impression that you didn't think much of Lord Hartley," Rebecca said as she folded a handkerchief and set it aside to be packed later.

"Whatever gave you that idea?"

"Perhaps the way you dragged me away from him at the British Museum."

Freddie's face paled to the color of a fish's belly. "That was him? Oh dear. Oh no. Do you think he'll remember me?"

"How should I know?"

"Well, you do seem to have...some special connection to the family since you've been invited to the Somerfield Park." Freddie frowned in obvious puzzlement. "I know all your associations. Why is it that I've never known you to be on such friendly terms with the Barretts?"

Rebecca normally would have told Freddie about her brush with disaster in Whitechapel and the way John Fitzhugh Barrett came to her rescue. Once, she might have even shared what it was like to kiss Lord Hartley. Now, something inside her warned her to hold her secrets close.

"How should I know why I've been invited? I only know I have, and I've never been invited anywhere to speak of." Rebecca took her favorite bonnet from the wardrobe and examined it for flaws. Fortunately, it was still in good repair. "With all the high-ranking ladies about to descend upon Somerfield Park, it rather takes all the pressure off me. I'm obviously not under consideration as a match for Lord Hartley so I intend to enjoy myself thoroughly."

Freddie gave her an assessing gaze as if weighing her words for veracity. What was happening to them? Rebecca would have said their friendship would stand up to anything, firm as a tower. Apparently it was teetering a bit over Lord Hartley.

"Frankly, I don't understand your interest in the gentleman," Rebecca went on. She knew why *she* was interested in John Fitzhugh Barrett. He was bold and brash, but also a bit damaged. Rebecca ached for the boy inside the man. "I thought you said the *ton* wouldn't accept the new Lord Hartley."

"Normally, they wouldn't, especially after his behavior since his elevation has been just shy of beyond the pale. But that was before the dowager stepped into the situation. Now that she has, it's a signal to society that the succession is secure and the new Lord Hartley is being groomed for his station. He's definitely the heir to Somerset and—"

"And a marchioness's coronet is no small matter," Rebecca finished for her.

"Exactly. Someone has to wear it. It might as well be me," Freddie said. "Let's have a look at what you're packing. We can't have you looking like last season's rose."

Freddie usually pooh-poohed fashion. Her own wardrobe was a paean to functionality, not frivolity, but that didn't mean she didn't have good taste. She pawed through Rebecca's gowns, approving some and shaking her head in dismay over others.

"What do you have that's suitable for a ball?" Freddie asked.

"This gathering is supposed to be a hunting party at its heart. What makes you think there will be a ball?"

"It's a hunting party, all right, but not all the game has hooves and antlers." Freddie cocked her head to one side and sighed as if putting up with Rebecca's obtuseness was a trial to her soul. "If the future marquess truly means to choose a bride, there will definitely be a ball. The dowager will see to it. Now, what do you have?"

Rebecca pulled a tired peach silk from her wardrobe.

"Oh no. No, no, no," Freddie said, making clucking noises with her tongue against her teeth. "This might do for Almack's or a country assembly, so long as you were sure you'd never see any of the attendees again, but not for Somerfield Park."

"I can't afford a new gown, and there isn't time in any case."

Freddie dug into her reticule and came up with a tape measure. "Let me take your measurements. I have a sweet little pink gown that I'll never wear. It's far too pale for me. Mother says it washes me out something fierce, and I have to agree."

"You and your mother seem to be marching in lockstep all of a sudden."

"No, she still has antiquated notions about so many things, but when it comes to fashion, I defer to her expertise," Freddie said. "I'll have my modiste alter my pink gown and bring it for you when I come to the country in a few days."

"That's so kind of you." Rebecca took back

everything she was thinking about how Lord Hartley was coming between them. She gave her friend a hug and then held her arms up while Freddie wrapped the tape around her at the bosom and hips. Rebecca's friend muttered to herself about how fashion made fools of them all, but what else could one do? After she finished, Freddie scribbled down Rebecca's measurements on a scrap of paper she'd squirreled away in her reticule and then stuffed it and the tape measure back into her beaded bag.

"What will you be wearing to the ball?" Rebecca asked.

"Mother and I ordered new wardrobes for the occasion as soon as Father received his invitation. My ball gown is robin's egg blue with a white lace overlay. The new French styles really aren't as hideous as I'd previously thought," Freddie said.

Rebecca's brows arched. Freddie, who never kept anything from her, had kept this secret. Truly, bringing a man into the mix changed things.

"Seriously, Freddie, do you really want to try to catch Lord Hartley's eye?"

Her friend looked affronted. "You think I can't."

"No, it's not that. I just wonder what you'll find in common with him, that's all."

"I'm not certain that signifies in the least," Freddie said. "My father and mother have virtually nothing in common, and they've been successfully married for twenty-five years."

Successfully, but not necessarily happily.

Even though Rebecca's father had a terrible gambling habit, he and her mother clearly adored each other. There were times when Rebecca was embarrassed to be in the same room with them because they still sent smoldering looks to each other. Her mother's illness had only intensified their passion, because her days seemed numbered. Even though no one spoke it aloud, the whole family knew Lady Kearsey was in the early stages of consumption.

Sometimes, Rebecca wondered if that was why her father gambled. Perhaps he hoped to win enough to be able to afford to take his wife to a spa where she might regain her health.

"However, in the interests of uncovering every bit of intelligence that might aid the cause," Freddie said, "what sort of things do you think Lord Hartley likes in a woman?"

Rebecca knew Lord Hartley liked kissing her. He liked having his own way. But she had no idea what sort of young lady John might choose for his wife.

"I shouldn't worry about that if I were you, Freddie. The best thing you can do is be yourself," she said. "If his lordship is going to find you attractive, shouldn't it be the real you? Otherwise, you'll have to pretend to be someone else for a very long time."

"You've gotten very wise very quickly." Freddie sighed. "But what if sometimes I wish I *were* someone else?"

"Never say that. You are quite the most amazing scholar I know. You're an intrepid birder, a fount of information about historical events and cultures, and no one knows more about the poems of George Chapman than you do."

"No one *should* know as much about George Chapman as I do," Freddie said morosely.

She was right. The sonnets of that Renaissance poet were the epitome of obscurity.

"Never mind, Freddie. Just decide to join me in having fun on this lark. We don't need to figure out what Lord Hartley wants. We should be more interested in what *we* want."

"Rebecca, you will never be accused of being a pattern sort of girl."

"Good. I can't imagine anything more repugnant. Now help me finish packing!"

Seven

A BRIGHT SHAFT OF SUNLIGHT SHOT THROUGH THE freshly opened window and stabbed John in his good eye.

"Begging your pardon, my lord," the nervous footman standing beside John's bed said. "Mr. Porter left with the baggage some time ago. I didn't wish to wake you, but it's only…well, everyone else is waiting on you."

"What ungodly hour is it?"

"Half past ten."

John had spent his last night in London carousing with the Daemon Club. It was the best way he knew to try to put that kiss of Rebecca Kearsey's out of his mind. He really hadn't expected she'd do it. He'd only intended to tease her.

Instead, she'd teased him.

Her kiss wasn't practiced or even particularly sensual, at least not at first. But it was honest. And honesty was in short supply in John's life.

It made everything else seem false by comparison, and he couldn't bear that. So he got roaring drunk. He'd only returned to the town house when the sun began to lighten the eastern sky. He didn't remember collapsing crosswise on his counterpane without undressing, but he must have done. He was still wearing his boots. He pulled a pillow over his head and uttered an obscenity into it.

"Surely Mr. Porter informed you of the Family's plans," the troublesome voice came again. "You're to return to the country today, my lord."

Now he remembered. Porter had said someone else would be on hand to help him dress this morning because the Somerfield Park servants would leave very early to transport the baggage and prepare rooms at the estate. That way, the Family could rise at a leisurely hour, have their breakfast, and be on their way in the marquessate's opulent coach in the style and decorum due them.

"If you please, my lord, the rest of the Family has already bathed, dressed, and breakfasted. They are awaiting only the pleasure of your company to begin their journey."

"The pleasure of my company is highly in doubt at present," John grumbled into the pillow. "Not even I enjoy my company."

"Perhaps your lordship will feel better after a bath and—"

"You don't give up easily, do you?" John sat up and waved off the offer, though he had seldom needed a bath more. The Daemon Club had wandered into a filthy opium den last night, but John hadn't tried the mind-numbing drug. If he wanted oblivion—and when didn't he?—Scottish whisky was his choice. Still, the slightly acrid, slightly sweet smell of opiates and their additives clung to his hair and clothing.

"Then a shave and a change of attire at least, my lord. Mr. Porter left a traveling ensemble for—"

"No, if they're so all-fired ready to go, far be it from me to thwart the *Family*." He spat the word out as if it were a bite of herring that had turned. "If they don't like the way I'm dressed, they'll simply have to learn to live with disappointment."

God knew he had to.

John threw his legs over the side of the bed and rose to his feet. Then, with the harried footman at his heels urging him to wait, to change his clothes, to at least let his servant run a comb through his lordship's hair, John clomped down the back stairs to the town house's kitchen. There he wolfed down a couple of day-old buns without even a plate held beneath them.

The help was scandalized.

"Lord Hartley's eating in the servants' hall." The news buzzed through the town house faster than a case of chicken pox through a nursery. Quality folk didn't eat in the kitchen. It just wasn't *done*.

"Surely, his lordship's wits are as addled as his father's," someone whispered.

"I'm not anything like my father," he bellowed, which stunned the servants around him into silence.

"And I'm damned sure not deaf. I'll thank you not to talk about me as if I'm not right in front of you. And in any case, Lord Somerset's wits are fine. He just can't remember everything." His head pounded like a smith's hammer, so he lowered his voice. "Where's my coffee?"

The cook scurried to put a hot mug into his hand, and he took a big swig, burning his tongue. He couldn't do anything right.

John looked around the kitchen, his vision bleary even though he could open both eyes completely now. "I'm sorry," he said.

"No need for that. 'Twas my fault. I should have sent a tray up with Gibbons there," Cook said with a nod to the quaking footman who'd been tasked with waking him. "I've packed a luncheon hamper. It's in the coach. Is there anything else you'll be wanting before you leave, my lord?"

"My garrick?"

"Here you are, my lord." Gibbons stepped forward with John's greatcoat and his topper and riding gloves. John let himself be dressed like a tailor's dummy. When Gibbons stepped back and looked him over, he gave John a grim smile that said he'd done the best he could with what he had to work with. "Have a pleasant journey."

They'd all be much happier once he was gone, so John decided to spread a little cheer. Ignoring their pleas that he should leave by the front door, he stomped into the alley at the rear of the house where the coach waited. To John's surprise, it was empty. Two outriders were mounted behind the conveyance.

John recognized his half brother Richard's favorite horse. He'd brought the beast to Wiltshire with him. The white mare beside the gelding had beautiful conformation. It probably belonged to Richard's wife.

Well, of course they'd bring their horses to Town. They wouldn't have wasted all their time looking for him. Every day the Upper Crust rode sedately along Rotten Row to see and be seen. Lord Richard and his new wife were probably both top-notch equestrians and had no doubt cut a wide swath through the glittering horse set.

Behind the outriders, a prime bit of horseflesh danced before a sporty little gig being driven by a groom. Apparently, like John, this conveyance was also being transported to Somerfield Park.

John didn't wait for the coachman to open the door for him. He did it himself and, after rapping on the ceiling to signal the coach to move forward, he slumped into the tufted cushions and closed his eyes. He didn't know where the other Barretts were and didn't care. Perhaps they'd hired another coach and gone on without him. In an empty conveyance, at least he'd be able to sleep his way to Somerfield Park.

He had barely drifted off before the equipage stopped again. Glancing out the window, he saw that they'd merely gone around the block and stopped in front of the Barretts' posh Mayfair address. Richard and his wife came out of the red door, headed his way. His half brother was nattily dressed in buff trousers, an understated beige silk waistcoat, and a black jacket topped by a garrick with a built-in cape draping his shoulders. Lady Sophie wore a matching pelisse and gown traveling ensemble in head-to-toe emerald green.

If John cared at all about his appearance, he might be a trifle embarrassed to greet them in such a rumpled state.

Swathed in a serviceable brown hooded cloak, Rebecca appeared, framed by the open doorway for a moment. She flashed a quick smile in his direction and then, eyes chastely downcast, made her way down the steps after Richard and Sophie. At least his family had kept up their end of the bargain and arranged for her to travel with them. Good thing. If she weren't at Somerfield Park, John wouldn't vouch that he'd stay there either.

Rebecca stopped shy of the gate. Then the dowager came out of the town house, leaning on her silver-headed cane and the butler's arm.

"That tears it," John muttered. He might have been able to bear the trip in an enclosed coach with Richard and his lady. He might even have been able to stand being in such close proximity to Rebecca, though it would have been gut-wrenching.

To be next to her and not able to touch her. To smell her sweet fragrance and not be able to imagine what it would be like to gobble her up. To—

He cut off those unproductive thoughts as old Lady Somerset drew nearer to the equipage. He was *not* going to make pleasant conversation with the woman who'd consigned him to the lot of an unwanted bastard.

He scrambled from the coach and held the door for Richard and Sophie to embark.

"Good of you to join us, old chap," his half brother

said genially as he helped his wife into the equipage. "We'd almost given up on you."

"Don't scold, Richard. Your brother is here now, so no harm done," Lady Richard said, then fastened her bright, blue-eyed gaze on John. "I'm looking forward to getting to know you better. And the first thing you need to know about me is that I'm not a terribly formal person. Please call me Sophie, and may I call you John?"

"Of course, my lady…I mean, Sophie." He was as bad as Porter when it came to those ingrained verbal tics of subservience. He wished now that he'd let Gibbons draw a bath for him and fit him out with fresh clothes.

Richard climbed into the coach after his wife.

"Ah, Hartley! There you are, my boy," came the dowager's commanding voice from behind him. John turned toward her and put on his best "nobody face." He'd first learned to shelter behind it at school. It was the face that hid the fact that he had opinions and hopes and dreams that were just as important as those of his titled classmates. He extended his hand to help the lady into the conveyance. Sir Humphrey and his wife had drummed politeness into him until it became nothing more than a reflex.

"How lovely to have you all to ourselves for a bit," Lady Somerset said, patting the squab beside her once she got herself settled. Her smile seemed almost hopeful.

John wiped off his "nobody face" and let her see what he was really thinking. He'd sooner sit beside a python than Lady Somerset.

"There's only room for four in the coach," John said. "Where is Miss Kearsey going to ride?"

"In Richard's gig, with Simpkins, of course," Lady Somerset said.

"Simpkins can stay in London. I'm going to drive," he said with a curt glance at Richard. He supposed he ought to ask his brother if he could drive his gig, but he'd watched Lord Blackwood demand—and get!—the shoes from off the feet of a doorman at a high-toned brothel when Blackwood had forgotten which lady of the evening's room he'd left his own in.

A man with a title didn't go hat in hand to anyone. He simply demanded and the world delivered. John learned that lesson quickly.

Slamming the coach door and stopping his ears to the dowager's sputtering protests, he ordered the driver off the gig's seat and offered Rebecca his arm. He helped her up onto the narrow seat and then went around to join her from the other side.

"My congratulations," she said softly as the outriders fell back, so that they formed a rearguard for both the gig and the coach. "If being surly and unpleasant is your aim, you succeeded beyond all expectation."

Eight

Those who style themselves "free thinkers" are wrong. They haven't an original thought in their heads. They merely take the contrarian view, complaining that Society places too many demands upon them. What utter nonsense. If there were no demands made, those who eschew conformity would have nothing against which to rebel. Wouldn't they be in a pretty pickle then?

—Phillippa, the Dowager Marchioness of Somerset

JOHN HAD WANTED TO SEE REBECCA, BUT NOW HE WAS acutely aware that he should have agreed to a bath and a shave. "On the contrary, it was surly and unpleasant of them to bar you from the coach."

"As you pointed out, there's only room for four." Rebecca's hood fell back. In daylight, he noticed her brown hair was streaked with strands of auburn that glinted in the sun. "But no one barred me from anything. I offered to ride in the gig. It's a lovely day for it, and frankly, I loathe being enclosed."

She had a point. In the open gig, they'd see much more of the countryside than the occupants of the stuffy coach would. "Truthfully, I wanted to travel in the gig mainly so you could spend some time with your family. I gather you need it."

Time with his family was the last thing John wanted.

"If you're quite ready, we'd better move on," Rebecca said. "The coach is already turning the corner, and I don't know about you, but I don't know the way to your home from here."

"I can get us to Somerfield Park," John grumbled as he flicked the reins over the gelding's back. Once he'd learned he was the marquess's heir, he'd studied a map to find out where the countryseat was located. Finding the most direct route to the great house was no problem.

Finding the way *home* was another proposition altogether. He had no idea where that might be.

London was deep into its midmorning bustle. The milk carts and night soil wagons had made their rounds earlier in the wee hours. Now the delivery carts were stopping by shops to drop off eggs and mutton from the countryside or more exotic goods from distant outposts of the English empire fresh off the ships.

A little later, the fashionable set would rouse for the day, and the streets would be full of dashing curricles, each flashier than the last. They weren't terribly practical as conveyances went, but they made a strong statement about the taste and the depth of pockets of their drivers.

Well-dressed ladies and dandies would bustle along, on their way to make calls at the homes of their friends. The length of those visits was strictly regulated and the etiquette for initiating or returning one was more labyrinthine than the most tortuous maze. The activities of Polite Society seemed as predetermined as a set piece at the ballet.

Of course, John hadn't ever danced any of those steps.

"I understand you've known of your new station since last June," Rebecca said, interrupting his thoughts. "Why did you come to London instead of joining your family in the country?"

"I'd lived in the country all my life. Bolting to the Village seemed like the thing to do." John hadn't been sure quite what to do when he first came to the city. He was only sure he didn't wish to present himself dutifully at Somerfield Park—not after having been shuffled off and ignored by Somerset all his life. "I thought all good little debutantes burned for their Season here. Never say you don't prefer Town life to rusticating in the hinterlands."

"Town and country living each have their charms. But a glittering Season is not the goal of every debutante," she said with surprising candor. "My dowry is not awe-inspiring, so I don't have fellows lining up. Besides, I'm a bit of a bluestocking, which puts some gentlemen off."

"Ah, yes, your penchant for museums," John said, grateful she'd turned the conversation away from him. "So you haven't been snapped up in the marriage market?"

"I'm afraid I've spent too much time in lecture halls and not enough at routs. What about you? I haven't seen you in any of the usual places. Do you even know anyone here in Town?"

He shook his head. "No one you'd know."

That was where the fellows of the Daemon Club had come in. He'd bumped into Lord Blackwood on his second day in London. He and Porter were coming out of the tailor's shop where John had ordered a bespoke wardrobe in keeping with his new station. John hadn't seen the viscount since they'd left Oxford. Blackwood had stood him to a pint at a nearby pub and then encouraged him to try White's, the exclusive club.

"Never fear. You're a member," Blackwood had assured him. "The heir to Somerset is placed on the list from the hour of his birth."

"Come with me, then," John had said.

"Can't. I was expelled from White's last year, and believe me when I tell you, my expulsion was richly deserved. Bunch of pompous toads," Blackwood had said as he knocked back the last of his ale. "But one should try everything at least once. Go on, Hartley."

So John had presented himself at the coffeehouse. After a bit of an altercation with the doorman, he was admitted on the strength of the butler's order. Evidently, word of the scandal in the succession at Somerfield Park had preceded him at White's. Most of the denizens of that exclusive haunt seemed fully aware of the tale of the unknown heir who'd suddenly become Lord Hartley.

He was shown to a table in a dim corner and served a pot of scalding coffee and a plate of biscuits. His server handed him a freshly ironed newspaper. John kept looking over his shoulder to see if anyone was hanging about surreptitiously to discover if he was able to read it. He was tempted to hold the paper upside down to see what they'd do.

But he didn't. He read his paper from first page to last, drank his coffee to the dregs, and left.

No one, other than the server, said a single word to him.

Now, after running with the Daemon Club for a few months, John had a few choice ideas about how to best scandalize the patrons of White's. If he were going to be ostracized by Society in any case, he might as well give them reason.

"I say, you do excel at daydreaming, my lord," Rebecca said. "I'd offer a penny for your thoughts, but I suspect they're worth more than that."

"Oh. I don't mean to be poor company." John had become accustomed to solitude. He needed to remember to hold up his end of the conversation.

"Poor company or not, your family is relieved simply to have your presence. There were some who believed you wouldn't come back to the house last night and they'd have to go looking for you again," Rebecca said.

"In truth, I almost didn't come back." If he'd tried the opium like Smalley had, he'd probably still be in that squalid den. There were some young lordlings sprawled about who looked as if they'd been wearing the same clothing for weeks.

"There was only one who adamantly believed that you'd keep your word to return to Somerfield Park," she continued.

"You?"

She shook her head. "I only gave you one chance

in three. I'm not naive. There are enticements aplenty in London that might give you reason to stay."

She was his only reason to go, but he couldn't say that. He didn't think she'd appreciate it.

"All right," he said. "You've piqued my curiosity. Who among the Barretts is my champion?"

"Your grandmother. The dowager was convinced you were enough of a Barrett to feel the call of familial duty."

"God knows no Barrett would feel the call of familial affection." His mother might have been common and flighty and sometimes even neglectful, but there were other times when she'd showered John with love. He remembered those bright, early days, shining as if through a prism, all glorious and multihued.

"The call of familial duty," he repeated. "The dowager must think Lord Somerset's hunt is pretty important."

"It is. The fact that the hunt can still take place after his lordship's accident is nothing short of providential. But for the hunt to go on while the estate is thick into timber production will set the *ton* on its ear. The visiting lords might start to thinking about what could be done with their own floundering estates. At least that's what Lord Richard says." She glanced at him and then away, her cheeks pinking in the autumn sun. "It's not just the hunt. That's his lordship's bailiwick in any case. Your grandmother thinks you've muffed your chances here in London and need a fresh start."

He frowned at her.

"Can you say she's wrong?" she asked.

He shook his head. No one, other than the

members of the Daemon Club and Lady Chloe, had even acknowledged his existence.

"Lady Somerset says it was a mistake to allow you to hare off to London on your own."

"*Allow* me?" He snorted. "No one *allows* me to go anywhere. I go where I please."

"Said the man who is on a journey he was bribed into making," Rebecca said tartly. "In any case, your grandmother is convinced she can undo the damage and reintroduce you to Society."

"Has the dowager ever had a single doubt that she could accomplish anything?"

"I haven't known her long, but I'd say probably not," Rebecca said with a laugh.

Lady Somerset certainly had no doubts about shuffling him off to Wiltshire when he was inconveniently orphaned.

"She didn't know at the time," Rebecca said.

"Didn't know what?"

"That you were the heir," she said as if he'd spoken aloud. "If her ladyship had realized that, I'm sure your childhood would have been much different."

It bothered him that Rebecca seemed privy to his secret thoughts. Obviously, his "nobody face" didn't work with her. "Excuses don't make much difference to a six-year-old."

She turned to glare at him. "Are you still six years old?"

"What?"

"You're not the only one whose young life was not what it should have been, you know." She lifted her pointed little chin and looked away.

"Rebecca, I—"

"Miss Kearsey, if you please," she said primly. "I deserve it."

"So you do. My apologies."

She nodded her acceptance. "The point is, you're no longer a boy. It's time to put aside whatever's past and look to your future."

It would be a future determined for him unless he asserted himself, but she didn't want to hear his side of things. Bouncing along side by side in the gig wasn't conducive to having an argument, so they rode in silence.

The houses on either side of the street became much less grand and finally became fewer and farther between. At the first stone fence row marking off one field from the next, John's heart lifted, and he inhaled deeply.

He'd forgotten how sweet a lungful of country air could be.

A small whirlwind of fallen leaves, a rust-and-scarlet dervish, twirled across the road in front of them, and the gelding shied at the unexpected sight.

"Easy now," he said sternly. "Don't be such a ninny."

"I beg your pardon!"

"I was talking to the horse, not you." He gave a quick tug on the reins and the gelding settled. "That's better, you wicked beast."

"Don't call him names. He can't help it. He was just startled." She twisted her gloved fingers together in her lap. "You'll hurt his feelings."

"Horses don't have feelings. And they don't understand much of what we say to them. It's the tone they respond to." John had just kept the gelding from bolting, and Rebecca was more concerned about hurting its feelings than she was grateful to him. He began to wonder if he could do anything to suit her. "Horses are strong creatures, but they're cowards at heart. They get silly when they don't know what's coming."

"Can't say I blame them. People are like that too."

"But most of us are smart enough not to worry about what we can't control. Besides, it would be a wise one who'd know what's coming."

"Count me wise, then," Rebecca said with a crooked little smile. "It doesn't take much to see around some bends. Would you like me to play gypsy and predict your future?"

"Can you?"

"Easy as breathing." She drew a deep lungful. "Smell that air. Isn't that much better than London?"

Again he wondered if she read minds. How did she know he'd already decided to be grateful not to be in the city just based on the fact that he could finally breathe deeply again? They were far from the rotting smell of the Thames and the stench of too many bodies packed too closely together, not all of them terribly clean. Now he wondered how he'd borne it for four whole months.

If she knew how he felt about that, maybe Rebecca really could tell his future. She didn't look like a gypsy. Her hair wasn't dark enough, and her eyes were decidedly green, not the snapping black associated with those wandering folk. "Do you claim to be part Roma then?"

She shrugged. "If you go back far enough in any-one's lineage, who knows?"

"So how do you manage your fortune-telling,

Madame Kearsey? Do you use a crystal ball? Or tea leaves?" He put a fingertip of his glove between his teeth and tugged it off. Then he held out his hand to her. "Maybe you read palms."

She ignored his hand, though he wished she'd take it, even if she was still wearing gloves. The miles would pass far more quickly if he could touch her.

"I don't need anything like that. Your future is easy to predict." She was smiling now, and it made his heart rise up even more than the fresh air had. "Your grandmother will see to it that you're accepted by the people who matter and you're sensible enough not to fret about the ones who don't welcome you."

She thought him sensible. That was something.

Then her smile went a little brittle around the edges. "You're a planner. After you've scouted out your options, you'll propose to a young lady of good family, marry her, and sire the next generation of Barretts." She glanced up at him and then fixed her gaze pointedly on a distant spot on the horizon. "And that's the life I see for the next marquess of Somerset."

John tugged his glove back on and stared at the tuft of mane sprouting between the gelding's ears. He feared Rebecca was completely right. "Do you know what I wish?"

"What?"

"I wish I could turn back the sun."

"My goodness. Becoming a lord has given you delusions of grandeur."

"I didn't say I could," he corrected. "I said I wish I could."

"All right. Why?"

"So I could go back to the time before I found out I'm Lord Somerset's heir."

"Don't you want to be the marquess someday?"

"Not particularly." The future she saw for him was stultifying. He was to wed the right lady whether she cared for him or not, sire the right number of sons, and generally be little more than a glorified placeholder for the next generation. He would cease to exist as a person. He'd be only his station, a thing belonging to Somerset. At least as an unclaimed bastard, he'd owned himself. "No, I'd rather not be the heir."

"Then you are a decidedly different man. Most would give their right arm for your prospects," she said softly. "But unique as you are, even you can't turn back the sun."

They drove through a sleepy little hamlet, behind the Somerset coach. There was a smith's shop, a sundry store, and a small church strung along a single street with a few dozen cottages clustered around the edges. It was so like every other English village he'd seen, John wondered if there was an official pattern on file someplace, to which all town fathers adhered.

Just like the pattern villages, now that he was Lord Somerset's heir, his life was pretty well mapped out for him. Far from being in control, as he'd always thought titled gentlemen were, he'd be living out someone else's expectations for the rest of his life—just as Rebecca foretold. Unless he chose to do something unexpected…

He nudged the gelding into a trot as they rumbled out of the village and back into the countryside again. The road widened for a bit. "How do you feel about a little more speed?"

"It sounds exciting," she said. "But aren't we sup-posed to stay with the carriage?"

"That's one of the nice things about becoming a lord. 'Supposed to' holds no meaning if I say it doesn't." He gave a wordless cry, and the gelding leaped into a canter. The gig flew around the more ponderous coach. Rebecca grasped John's arm and held on for dear life.

If it meant she'd touch him instead of scolding or bringing up inconvenient topics, he ought to have done this much sooner.

Nine

What a wondrous age in which to live! Mr. Stephenson has harnessed the power of steam for his locomotive and Herr Beethoven has harnessed the power of passion for his music. From industry to the arts, we rejoice in a thoroughly modern world. Yet, despite all of mankind's advances, something as simple as the ancient wheel can still wreak havoc with a perfectly ordinary journey.

—Phillippa, the Dowager Marchioness of Somerset

THE GIG STREAKED PAST THE SOMERSET COACH. ITS horse's hooves tossed great clods of dirt behind him as they disappeared from sight over the next rise.

"Good heavens!" the dowager exclaimed. "Where are those two off to in such a terrible hurry?"

"The same place we're bound, albeit at a much slower pace, Gran," Richard said, folding his arms over his chest. He'd much rather have ridden in the open gig than taken the backward-facing squab in the coach. Perhaps after a while, Miss Kearsey would be ready to exchange places and take his seat alongside Sophie. He could switch out at the next opportunity and ride beside his new brother for a while.

Lady Somerset signaled to one of the outriders with an imperious wave of her hand out the coach window. When the horseman drew even with her, she ordered him to ride ahead to escort the gig.

"It's not seemly." His grandmother's lips drew into a censorious line once the outrider disappeared after Hartley and Miss Kearsey. "The pair of them driving away like that. Alone."

"How kind of you to have a care for Rebecca's reputation," Sophie said.

"It's not Miss Kearsey I'm worried about," the dowager explained. "It's John. He mustn't be allowed to be entrapped by someone unsuitable, and that means he mustn't be allowed to be alone with a young lady who may have designs on him. Cannier men than he have been ensnared by an unacceptable debutante's schemes."

Sophie rolled her eyes. "It seemed to me that Rebecca's *scheme* was chiefly not to topple out of the gig."

"Sophie's right. There's no harm done. We'll catch them when we stop for luncheon, I expect. After the way John looked this morning, I'm glad to see that he can bear some speed." Richard sensed that John's refusal to ride in the coach beside their grandmother grated on the old lady something fierce. Lady Somerset might try to mask her hurt behind criticism, but she'd been wounded by John's rebuff.

However, he couldn't blame John. If Richard had been brought up on some rustic farm in Wiltshire instead of in the Barretts' spacious, light-filled nursery, he might feel the same.

The marchioness sniffed into her scented lacy handkerchief. "I don't know how you can defend him, since he's the reason you'll not succeed your father as the next marquess."

"On the contrary, I bless him." Richard took his wife's hand and gave it a squeeze. He wouldn't have been able to marry Sophie if he'd still been in line for the title, so for that alone, he was grateful for John Fitzhugh Barrett. Besides, after a lifetime of having only sisters, Richard felt an obligation to defend his new half brother.

"Yes, well, you can't argue that one who is so ill-equipped for the title is good for Somerset," the dowager said. "Despite these unexpected developments, the rest of us must keep the welfare of the estate uppermost in our minds."

"And I do, Gran." Richard had worked tirelessly to turn around the estate's finances by building a timber mill on the property, which provided not only some much needed revenue, but employment for the residents of the nearby village of Somerset-on-the-Sea. After four short months under Richard's husbandry, the marquessate's ledgers were already in a much healthier condition. "I'm always looking out for Somerset. Just not in the same way you do."

"I should say not. You seem singularly unconcerned about whether Lord Hartley gets on with the right people." Gran stuffed her handkerchief back into her beaded reticule. "For example, to which of your associates have you introduced him?"

"He'll know Seymour soon enough." Lawrence Seymour was Richard's best friend and a perpetual visitor at Somerfield Park. "Once the guests arrive for the hunt, I'll introduce him to more of my friends."

"Friends? He doesn't need friends. It's past time when he might rely upon that. He's already been to Oxford, but while he was there, he evidently didn't make the requisite connections." Richard's grandmother cast a squint-eyed gaze at him. She had a point. An education was only part of why one attended the prestigious university. The more important part was developing the relationships one would depend upon later in life. Of course, Richard's half brother could hardly be blamed for that. John had been thought an unacknowledged bastard at the time. It was no wonder he hadn't been popular with his classmates.

"Hartley needs people who can help him be accepted by Society even at this late date and under these extraordinary circumstances." She rattled off a string of lords whose approval she most wanted John to cultivate. "I'm counting on you to assist him during the next few weeks. To guide and counsel him."

"I don't think he'll appreciate—"

"Of course, we'll help him. That goes without saying, Phillippa," Sophie interrupted in time to save Richard from disputing his grandmother's word. As far as he knew, his wife was the only soul on earth who dared call Gran by her Christian name. "What we must do is make John fashionable."

Richard's gaze cut to Sophie sharply. "Fashionable? I never expected to hear such a suggestion come out of your mouth."

"Not fashionable in the usual sense," Sophie amended. "But we need to present John as a sort of romantic figure to the *ton*, a gentleman who overcame an unhappy accident in his childhood, rather like Romulus and Remus."

"But they were raised by wolves," Richard objected.

"Hear me out." Sophie sat forward on the edge of the squab, warming to her subject. "The twins were the offspring of a demigod, and John is the son of a marquess. That similarity will resonate with Polite Society, since they're agog over all things classical. And remember Romulus and Remus rose above their unorthodox beginnings to do great things, like founding the city of Rome."

"So how does this help John?" Richard asked.

"We simply plant the parallels between him and the mythological twins in a few influential minds. We might even plan a Roman-themed ball once the house party gets underway. John can be presented as a classical hero in the same mold as Romulus and Remus, and we'll let the gossip grapevine do the rest," Sophie said with enthusiasm. "By the time someone like Lady Wappington gets hold of this idea, John will be Alexander and Hercules rolled into one, the next founder of a classical dynasty!"

The marchioness shook her head. "I rather doubt Sir Humphrey and his wife will appreciate their fostering being likened to being reared by wolves." Then she brightened. "But I do see your point: Hartley too must rise above his upbringing."

Richard covered his eyes with his hand. Fortunately, his grandmother had not yet realized this scenario cast her as the dastardly Amulius, the villain who threw the mythological twins into the Tiber to die before they were rescued by the she-wolf.

"However, it sounds as if you've done a bit of planning for John's future already," Sophie said to Lady Somerset. "Perhaps you might tell us about the young ladies you're expecting to descend upon Somerfield Park. We'll want to steer John to the right ones."

"There's not a wrong one in the bunch," Gran declared. "But, of course, some are more right than others."

She launched into a recitation of the bloodlines and accomplishments of various debutantes whom she'd vetted for the upcoming "Hartley Hunt," as Richard thought of it.

Of course, he didn't call it that out loud. Both his grandmother and his wife would probably boot him out of the carriage if he did.

So Richard propped his chin in his hand and closed his eyes while the feminine conversation about how to handle the problem of Hartley continued to chirp around him.

Just keep driving, John, he thought as the rhythmic rocking of the coach lulled him to sleep. *Just keep driving*.

❦

Rebecca clung to John's arm as they careened down the road. She was quite proud of herself. She hadn't entertained thoughts of the gig overturning more than half a dozen times. John leaned forward, crooning urgent endearments to the gelding he'd been calling a ninny and a wicked beast only a few minutes before.

Men were as changeable as the weather.

Then, to her surprise, she discovered that women were too. She actually began to enjoy the wild ride. Her hair came undone, loose locks coiling down her back. Wind tore moisture from her eyes, tears streaming back over her cheekbones to slip into her ears, but she didn't want to stop. She hadn't felt this free since she had been a child.

When she was quite young, her father had lost his first serious amount of money in a game of chance. He was forced to petition the House of Lords for the right to sell off more than half his land. Along with the acreage, Rebecca's fat little pony had also been sold to settle her father's debt of honor.

To make it up to her, her father had climbed the big oak and hung a burlap bag swing from the stoutest limb. In the days that followed, no matter how bad things seemed as creditors came and carted off her mother's treasures as well, when Rebecca straddled that scratchy seat and kicked her legs, she felt as if she could fly. Nothing mattered when the wind whistled past her cheeks and teased out the tears in a way she didn't have to explain to anyone.

She didn't have to explain the water leaking from her eyes now either. Besides, so long as she kept riding beside John, she had nothing to cry about. It didn't matter that John's station was so very much higher than hers. She trusted him even when he drove the gig into the field to avoid a log in the middle of their path. They sped back up as John returned the gig to the road. An outrider from the Somerset coach leaped over the log and caught up with them, pounding behind them, matching their breakneck pace.

Rebecca wished they could ride forever, and it seemed as if they would.

Then, without warning, John pulled up on the reins so hard, the gelding almost sat on his haunches. The outrider flew past them before he could bring his mount to a stop and then trotted back to rejoin them. Both the horses were panting and blowing. John was standing up in the gig, staring down the road ahead.

"What's wrong?" she asked. "Has he thrown a shoe?"

John pointed to the horizon. She hadn't been looking any farther ahead than their next few lunging strides. The sky had lowered menacingly. Grey clouds descended to meet the earth in a darkening blur. They boiled black in places and lightning leapt from one cloud bank to the next. Distant thunder rumbled toward them.

"Oh dear. The day started so fine, too," Rebecca said. She rose and looked behind them. "And I don't see the coach anywhere."

"We've left them some distance behind. But the next village isn't far. Tincross Bottom, if I remember right from studying the map."

"Doesn't sound like much of a place."

"It isn't, but there's supposed to be a coaching inn there. Nothing fancy, but it'll do. Let's make a dash for it and wait for the others there."

"But will they know to stop?"

"I'll make sure of it. You there," John said to the outrider. "Return to the Somerset coach and tell Lord Richard we've sought shelter at the Tincross Bottom coaching inn."

"But my lord, Lady Somerset said I…" The

outrider's objection died away under John's intense glare. "Right away, my lord. Very good."

The rider bolted back the way they'd come as a light mist began to fall.

"Lovely," Rebecca said in a tone that meant anything but. "We're in for a drenching."

"If we ride fast enough, we'll slip right between the raindrops." John put up the gig's collapsible hood. "Not much protection from the elements, but it's better than nothing. Come, Miss Kearsey. Let's see what this gelding's got left."

⌘

Richard woke when his head narrowly missed being whacked on the ceiling. The coach came down hard and then listed sharply to the right.

"What on earth!" his grandmother exclaimed.

"I'll see what's happened." Richard waited for the coach to limp to a stop before climbing out. By the time he alighted, the driver had already scrambled down to inspect the damage and was squatting by the side of the equipage, peering up at its undercarriage.

"Sorry, my lord. We came over that little rise, and I didn't see it before we was upon the blasted thing. There was a log in the road, you see. Must have come off a lumber wagon sometime or other. In any case, we hit it at full speed since we were coming downhill." The coachman shook his head. "The front axle's broke."

"Can you fix it?"

"That I can't. We'll have to nip back to the last village." The driver gestured toward the remaining outrider, signaling him to draw near. "We're closer to Rattlebridge than Tincross Bottom from here, and I know a few folk in Rattlebridge who might be of help. We'll see can we get a carpenter and maybe the smith to come back with us. Might be they can reinforce the wood, and if so, well and good. We'll be on our way with only a few hours' delay."

"And if not?"

"We'll have to find another mode of transport for the ladies and see can we put up in the village while another axle is made. Might be a day or two in that case."

"Very well," Richard said. "Give us your best speed now."

The man tugged at his forelock in respect. He and the outrider unhitched the draft horses from their traces. It wouldn't do for the beasts to spook and try to drag the disabled coach forward. Then the driver and outrider started leading the four horses at a dog-trot back toward the village of Rattlebridge. Richard climbed back into the coach just as the first raindrops began to fall. He explained the situation to Sophie and his grandmother.

"Honestly, how could the driver have allowed this to happen?" Gran said.

"You don't imagine he planned it for the privilege of walking back to the village in the rain, do you?" Richard said, more testily than he ought. "Not everything in this life can be foreseen and managed. It was an accident."

"Still," Gran said with a frustrated shake of her head that set her iron-gray coiffure aquiver, "this is most bothersome."

"Accidents usually are," Sophie said unhelpfully.

"Well, what are Hartley and Miss Kearsey to do?" the dowager demanded.

Richard had to raise his voice to be heard over the determined patter of rain. "I daresay they'll seek shelter."

He hoped the coach didn't start leaking. His grandmother was upset enough while she was high and dry. Becoming damp wouldn't improve her mood one jot.

The dowager cleared her throat loudly. "Well, at least I had the forethought to make certain that Hartley and the young lady"—she glared accusingly at Sophie—"are chaperoned. Now that we have become separated from them, dare I say it might have been disastrous?"

"You worry too much, Phillippa," Sophie said.

"And you never worry enough."

"Try to look on this as an adventure, albeit an inconvenient one," Sophie suggested with a smile. She was always game for adventure, the more inconvenient the better. It was one of the many things Richard loved about her. "If John were to be caught unchaperoned with a young lady, you couldn't choose a better one than Rebecca Kearsey. She has a sensible head on her shoulders. Besides, people in a rainstorm are looking for someplace dry, not a way to scandalize the *ton*."

Lady Somerset was not convinced—especially when she spied the outrider she'd sent to chaperone John and Miss Kearsey loping back toward the damaged coach. The gig was nowhere to be seen. "Oh dear. It's just as I feared. Honestly, Richard, aren't you going to do something?"

"Yes. Yes, I am," he said decisively as he lifted the luncheon hamper from under their feet. "I'm going to hope Cook packed a bottle or two of that Madeira."

Ten

The German poet von Schiller admonishes us that "there is no such thing as chance; and what seem to us merest accident springs from the deepest source of destiny." Sounds persuasive, does it not?

On the other hand, what do the Germans know?

—Phillippa, the Dowager Marchioness of Somerset

"I'M THAT SORRY, MY LORD. IT'S MARKET DAY, YOU see." The innkeeper wrung his hands on an apron that probably used to be white but was now a dingy shade of gray. "Ordinarily, we'd have rooms and to spare, but the inn is near to bursting at the seams now. I've only one room left, and it's a small one at that. O' course, if I'd known you was coming, Lord Hartley, why, naturally, I'd have saved you the best in the house, but as things stand…"

The fellow waved a hand in a helpless gesture before his midsection, probably waiting for John to fill it with a purse fat enough for him to justify evicting some of his other guests. But after a quick check of his pockets, John realized he'd have to arrange lodging on credit, at least until Richard and the others arrived. Since John was soaking wet, it was less obvious that he'd slept in his well-tailored clothing last night. He had no trouble convincing the innkeeper that he was a gentleman, albeit a damp one. And fortunately, he was wearing his signet ring, a heavy sapphire carved intaglio style with the Somerset crest. He could press the ring into wax as a seal for a debt with the weight and prestige of the marquessate behind it.

"This way, my lord, miss." The innkeeper cast a leering look at Rebecca. "I'll show you to the room."

"The lady will be the only one staying in the chamber. In fact, we expect more members of our party to join us shortly." It was important to John that he protect Rebecca's reputation. It wasn't her fault she was caught in this situation. He was the one who'd driven so far ahead of the Somerset coach. "I assume you allow extra guests to bed down in the common room when the inn is full."

"Of course, my lord." He scratched his head, clearly confused. The idea that John intended to bed down like a vagabond in his common room made the innkeeper twist his apron in his work-rough hands. "Who are you expecting to join you?"

"My half brother and his wife, Lord and Lady Richard Barrett." John paused for effect. "And the Dowager Marchioness of Somerset."

"Oh! Lady Somerset is coming here!" the innkeeper said with a decided wobble in his voice. The dowager's reputation obviously preceded her. "When her ladyship arrives, I'll clear out some more rooms.

Indeed I will. Just a bunch of farmers come to the village, mostly. Of no importance at all. Forgive me, my lord, I thought you and this young lady were just…"

Obviously, the man still thought Rebecca was a lightskirt and John merely meant to have a bit of sport with her at a country inn on a rainy day.

"Perhaps you'll wish to see the chamber at least, my lord," their host said. "To be sure it is adequate for your purposes."

John decided it was futile to argue with him. "Very well. Lead on."

He followed the innkeeper and Rebecca up to the first story, where doors led off from the narrow corridor on either side. Her dripping cloak left a wet trail behind her. Their host thrust a key into the last keyhole on the right.

"It's small, as I said, but since it's on the end, there are two windows instead of one," the innkeeper said. "Makes for a nice breeze when the weather's fine. O' course, that don't do us much good on a day like today, do it?"

The rain fell in blinding sheets, blurring the view from the windows into runny shades of grey and green.

"But there's a small fireplace," the innkeeper said. "Just let me stir up that blaze for you, my lord. Have you dried out in no time."

The man knelt before the banked fire and soon had it dancing cheerily with very little smokiness. "Will this do for you, my lord?"

"I suppose it'll have to, since it's raining as if a second Flood is upon us," John said. "But more importantly, will this do for you, Miss Kearsey?"

She made a slow turn in the center of the space, taking in the small bed which, despite the innkeeper's disreputable apron, seemed to be dressed in fresh linens. There was a washstand with a pitcher and ewer on it, as well as a dressing screen leaning against one wall. A single chair hunkered near the fireplace.

"Yes, my lord." Rebecca pushed back the hood of her cloak. "This will do nicely. If your other rooms are as clean as this one, I believe Lady Somerset will be pleased as well."

John was much less sure of that. The dowager was a stickler for detail and liked her comforts, but the innkeeper was ready to take Rebecca's word as gospel.

"Thank you, miss. Thank you kindly, I'm sure." The innkeeper was near to groveling as he handed John the key and backed out the door.

"I should go too," John said. "Shall I have them send up a tray for you?"

"How can you think of food at a time like this?" she asked.

He'd known hunger as a child before he was fostered in Wiltshire. John could think of food pretty much any time. "What should I be thinking of?"

"For one thing, you're soaked to the skin," Rebecca pointed out as she shooed him to the center of the room. She peeled off her dripping cloak, hung it on a peg, and pulled the door closed, shutting out the noise from the common room below. "You need to get out of those wet things and dry properly or you'll catch your death of cold."

"So might you."

She rested her hand on the brass doorknob. "I'll go

down and sit by the fire in the common room while you…"—she colored up becomingly—"peel out of your clothing and dry off here."

John closed the distance between them in two strides and kept her from opening the door with a broad palm pressed against the old oak, trapping her between the door and his body. Her sweet violet scent rushed into him. "I can't let you do that."

His gaze swept over her. Despite her cloak, the rain had drenched her muslin gown as well, rendering it nearly transparent. The cloth molded to the outline of her stays. A bit of red and pink embroidery, wandering French knots, and chain stitches at the neckline of her chemise showed through the sodden fabric. The toes of muddy slippers peeped from beneath her hem.

"You're all wet too," he said. "A gentleman can't precede a lady in need."

"The daughter of a *baron*"—she stressed the word to emphasize the cavernous social distance between them—"can't precede the heir of a marquess."

"There is another solution, if you think about it for a moment," he said, willing her to come to his vaguely naughty conclusion on her own. "Besides, if you don't see to those slippers right away, I expect they'll be ruined. Probably the other bits of your wardrobe I can't see are just as fragile."

"Don't be troubling yourself about what you can't see," she said, her eyes flaring. "You know perfectly well that we can't both dry off here at the same time."

It pleased him that she'd thought of that possibility too, even if she rejected it. "Why not?"

She made a low growling noise in the back of her

throat and brought one of her soggy slippers down hard on his foot. The action would have been more effective if he hadn't been wearing such heavy boots.

"Ow!" she yelped.

He scooped her up and carried her to the one chair in the room. Then he knelt before her and eased off her slipper. Her stockinged foot was wet and cold and she flinched when he ran a hand under her instep.

"You should wear boots when you mean to travel," he said.

"And when I mean to stomp on a man's foot, evidently."

"Perhaps you should give that up," John said as he turned her foot this way and that. He didn't think she'd broken anything, but she'd probably bruised her arch pretty badly. "Petulance doesn't become you."

"And lechery doesn't become you, either."

"If there's lechery in this room, it's in your mind, not mine. I didn't suggest anything improper."

She narrowed her eyes at him. "Didn't you?"

"Here's our solution." He lifted the folded dressing screen from its place by the wall and stood it before the fireplace at right angles to the cheery blaze. "There. The problem is solved with no threat to your sensibilities. We can each stay on our own side of the screen and dry off at the same time."

"But you can see over it." Rebecca was right. The screen came up to her crown, but he topped it quite handily.

"What if I give you my word as a gentleman that I will not peer over it?"

"You haven't been a gentleman very long."

Rebecca slanted a skeptical gaze at him. Then she rubbed her foot and stood, testing it for soundness. She sneezed, a soft, implosive squeak that seemed to take her by surprise since she barely had time to bring a handkerchief to her nose. "I'd rather you give me your word as my friend."

Was that how she thought of him? Just a friend? Disappointment fizzed in his belly. Still, she needed to get out of those wet things, and quickly too, if that little sneeze was any indicator.

"You have my word," he promised.

༺⁂༻

"Very well," Rebecca said, her heart pounding. This was highly improper. Even if Lord Hartley didn't peek at her, she was about to disrobe in the same room with him. It was beyond scandalous. Freddie would have a conniption if she heard about it. Rebecca sneezed again and shivered.

On the other hand, the ague was not something to be trifled with.

Rebecca skittered over to the bed to remove the blanket and faded counterpane. She handed the blanket to John and laid the counterpane on the back of the chair, which he'd thoughtfully moved to her side of the screen.

"Good idea. We'll need something to wrap up in while our things are drying," he said as he draped his blanket over the screen. "One of the things I've learned about the clothing of a gentleman is that they are designed for inconvenience. I hesitate to ask, but these boots are the very devil to remove. I can never manage it without Porter's help." John plopped down on the foot of the bed and lifted one boot. "Do you think you might lend a hand?"

"If I must." Rebecca had done this often enough for her father after he let his valet go because he could no longer afford to keep him. Somehow, the humble request took some of the naughtiness out of the situation. Rebecca took hold of his boot and gave it a yank while John pushed on the heel with his other toe. After a good deal of effort, the Hessian finally slid off. She wrestled the second one free with only a little less tugging and pulling. "There."

"Thank you."

"Now, if you please, my lord…" She waved him to his side of the screen, but he didn't budge.

"John," he corrected. "Call me John. We can't be expected to maintain formal *address* while we're getting into a state of *undress*."

"All the more reason our discourse should remain *quite* formal," she said primly.

Rebecca breathed a sigh of relief when he shrugged and moved to his side of the dressing screen. She needed some distance from him. He was too big. Too deliciously rumpled-looking.

Too standing near her in the same room as a bed.

"I understand removing feminine clothing can be a trial at times too," he said. "Do you require assistance?"

"No," she snapped. He sounded pretty familiar with the undressing of women. "Remember, no peeking over the top."

John chuckled. "No peeking over from your side, either."

"And how, pray tell, would I manage that?"

"You might stand on the chair."

Rebecca snorted. "You have a very high opinion of yourself to imagine I'd do such a thing."

However, she was seriously tempted. She and Freddie had studied any number of Greek statues of men who were bare as an egg except for a frustrating fig leaf or drapery covering the more puzzling aspects of their anatomy. But Rebecca had never seen a flesh and blood man in the altogether. She wondered how Lord Hartley would compare to the classical ideals of his gender.

But it would be beyond mortifying if he were to catch her standing on the chair to peep at him. So instead, Rebecca plopped into it. She reached under her hem and untied her garters, so she could roll down the wet stockings. From her seated position, she couldn't help noticing that there were a few slim gaps in the dressing screen where the frame folded. Against her better judgment, she leaned forward and put her eye to the narrow slit.

Rebecca couldn't see much, just glimpses here and there. His horrific pink waistcoat was lying in a crumpled heap on the yellow plank pine floor. She looked up and a wide expanse of white filled her vision.

His shirt.

Once he drew the shirt over his head, there seemed to be an oatmeal-colored fabric dominating the narrow slit.

His smalls, Rebecca realized. *Oh my stars, I'm staring at a man in his underclothes. I'm going straight to hell.*

But she didn't look away.

He peeled out of the upper portion of the under-garment, letting the long sleeves drape over the dark wool of his trousers. Then she saw a broad swath of flesh tone.

The skin on his back.

It was beautifully smooth and taut over his large-boned frame. She felt like throwing rocks at those Greek statues now. The muscles in John's shoulders and arms were a study in masculine proportion and grace.

Then he must have turned to face the screen because a brown nipple with a dark whorl of hair around it flashed past her limited field of vision.

His chest.

Her own rib cage tightened. She knew she should tear her gaze away, but she couldn't bring herself to. If she were bound for perdition, she might as well deserve it. Then she heard a rustle of cloth and the dark fabric of his trousers slid down to the floor.

Oh Lud, his…

John was a goodly sized man, broad of shoulder and narrow of hip. Rebecca had wondered if he'd be, well, proportional in all his parts.

No fig leaf could have done him justice.

"You're awfully quiet over there," he said.

Rebecca jerked away from the slit in the screen. "I don't think disrobing requires conversation. Don't let your clothing lie on the floor." Even that abominable pink waistcoat deserved not to puddle on the pine planks.

"How did you know that I—"

Oh dear! He was about to realize she'd been peeking. Then a rush of inspiration saved her. "You haven't hung any of your wet things on the screen."

"Neither have you."

"There." She flung one of her stockings toward the top of the screen, expecting it to catch on the top, but it sailed over.

"You don't have to throw things at me. Nice stocking, though." The stocking reappeared, draped neatly over the screen. "A little French lace wouldn't hurt, but—"

"You have a very commonplace mind, my lord."

"Because I like the idea of a woman wearing lace even where a man cannot see? Why do women wear lace in secret places if they don't want us to think about it?"

"Well, I don't wear lace." She peeled off her other stocking and stood to primly hang this one over the screen instead of lobbing it at him.

"No lace at all?"

"None." The teeny bit at the hem of her chemise didn't count. "I'm a practical girl. I don't need lace." Besides, her father's slender purse couldn't afford embellishments of that sort.

"Pity. I'd like to see you in nothing but lace."

Her cheeks heated at that. Part of her would like for him to see her that way too, to see that curious, wanton part of her. She did her best to keep that bit of her nature in check, but it would be wonderful for John to accept it, maybe celebrate it. But then she remembered John had done probably more than his share of "celebrating" while he was in London.

According to Freddie, gentlemen were really dogs who walked upright.

"It sounds to me as if you've seen far too many ladies in nothing but lace," Rebecca said waspishly.

"And it sounds to me as if you know far too much about the lower habits of gentlemen for your own good."

More articles of his clothing began to be spread over the top of the screen. When his socks and garters finally appeared, Rebecca realized he was naked as Adam in glory just inches away from her, albeit separated by the screen. Her mouth went dry.

"You're right," he said softly.

"About what?" She'd never felt more wrong. She'd peeked at him in a way no respectable woman should. Freddie would think her the most shameless hussy.

"I have been with too many women," he admitted.

Her belly spiraled downward. She'd flung out that comment about ladies in lace because it popped into her head and out her mouth before she had thought it through.

And it didn't bear thinking of. She dreaded what he might say next. It was one thing to be aware that John had spent a profligate time in London. It was quite another to hear chapter and verse of his misdeeds.

"I'm not your confessor." And she wasn't about to give him absolution. Not for this.

Eleven

After a certain age, none of us float through life carefree as a bubble. Regret is the price of experience.

—Phillippa, the Dowager Marchioness of Somerset

"When I left Wiltshire, I was feeling pretty empty," John admitted. "Everything I thought I was, everything I'd been, was suddenly gone. So I decided to try to fill up that emptiness."

Rebecca sank back down on the chair. Her knees wouldn't hold her any longer.

"I bought new clothes," he said, "but no matter how fine, a garment doesn't make a man."

"That's a good thing," Rebecca said with a nervous chuckle. "I'd hate to see what sort of fellow you'd have to become to live down to that pink monstrosity of a waistcoat."

"Don't worry. I only wear it to irritate people into looking the other way."

"Then I suspect it serves its purpose." Whatever tailor had convinced him that color was the height of fashion should be shipped off to New South Wales for fraud. "But you know, you can't blame others for leaving you alone if you push them away."

"You're right," John said. "Perhaps I thought I'd beat them to the punch. And speaking of punch, since I'd been told I was a lord, I decided to drink like one. I poured enough liquor down my gullet to drown myself several times. And while I was foxed, I thought I was all the crack, but once I sobered up, the emptiness remained."

In the silence that followed, Rebecca heard only the determined dripping from her hem to the floor. She knew she ought to continue disrobing, so she could get warm and dry, but she couldn't seem to move as she waited for John to go on with his litany of sins.

"I filled my days with sport and idle games. I filled my nights with…"

She waited for him to say it.

"With women." He exhaled noisily. "Women were such a mystery to me when I first arrived in London. The wellborn ones looked right past me, but there were others who…well, who didn't."

"You don't have to tell me." She didn't want to hear. "You owe me no explanations. I have no claim on you."

"That's true. And I suspect you'll hate me if I continue. I don't blame you. As I look back on the last few months, I despise myself. But I want you to understand that even dallying with women didn't work."

She fisted the fabric of her gown and squeezed. "What do you mean?"

The silence from Rebecca's side of the screen was like the London fog creeping up from the Thames to fill in the narrow streets. It smothered him, chilled him, blotted out the sun. He leaned toward the screen, hoping to hear something, anything, from her, but not even the sound of her soft breathing traveled to his part of the room.

"I'm not going to lie to you. Being with a woman is pleasurable, even when it doesn't mean a damn thing."

There was no reaction. The silence grew, fingering its way through the narrow slits in the screen and curling around him like cords binding a condemned man. Rebecca didn't scold him for swearing this time. That depressed him. A woman really didn't care a fig about a man if she stopped trying to improve him. Still, he was compelled to press on, in case there was a chance he could make her understand.

"But a thing can feel good at the time and still not fill up the emptiness," he said softly. "In fact, every time it was as if more pieces of me were being sheared away."

John lost part of himself with each mindless coupling. A bit here, a bit there, a chunk from his heart, a fragment off his soul, the man he'd been dissolved and sizzled away in the heat of rutting. He didn't know what was being reassembled from the remnants of his former self, but he didn't much like it.

He didn't think Rebecca would either.

"So now I'm a dry husk," he said. "I've spent myself, like the Prodigal. Riotous living has left me so riddled with holes, I'll never be filled again."

She drew a shuddering breath, the only sign there was still someone else in the room.

"Never is a very long time," she whispered.

It wasn't much, but it gave him the courage to go on.

"The last few months seem like a dream and not a very good one at that," he said. "To be honest, the best thing about being in London was meeting you."

"I don't see how that's possible," she said, louder this time. "The first time I met you, Freddie and I practically snubbed you in the museum. And the second time, you took a beating for me."

"I don't know what it is about you, Rebecca, but you make me remember what my life was like before I became Lord Hartley," he said. "What *I* was like and maybe could be again…"

If I were with you.

There was something clean and honest about her. He hadn't found that in his circle of friends in London. He doubted he'd find it at Somerfield Park either. She made him want to live up to his best self—if he still had a best self…

"Don't give up on me."

"Oh, John."

Her voice quavered, but she called him by his name, not by his title. It was like being reborn. In that instant, he knew who he was because she seemed to know him.

He tucked the blanket around his waist and walked bare-chested around the dressing screen. Rebecca was seated on the straight-backed chair, still fully dressed, still dripping onto the plank floor. She gasped at the sight of him.

"Don't be afraid." He knelt before her and took her hands.

"I'm not afraid, but you promised," she said. "You said you wouldn't peek."

"I didn't peek. I came around. I didn't promise not to do that."

"You…are a…a very bad man." Her hitching breaths made it hard to complete her sentence.

"That, my dear, is not in dispute."

Her sweet face crumpled. "And I shouldn't care a bit about what happens to you."

"No, you shouldn't."

"You should leave right now."

"I agree completely, Rebecca. I'm a very bad man. You shouldn't care about me a bit, and I ought to leave immediately. And yet, I'm not going to because I don't think you can get out of this wet gown without my help."

He stood and raised her to her feet. Then he wrapped his arms around her and held her close. To his great relief, she didn't fight him. She melted against him, her whole body shaking.

Damn, I've turned into a selfish lout. Only an absolute cad would be grateful for a shivering woman in his arms. John wished he could kick his own arse up between his shoulder blades, but he couldn't wish that he wasn't holding her. He had ceased being surprised by the depths to which he could sink.

"Come," he whispered. "Let's get you out of those wet things."

He turned her in his arms. She obeyed when he told her to stand still, but couldn't seem to stop her slight tremble. He made short work of the row of buttons marching down her spine and peeled off her gown. Then he tackled her stays, removing the light corset-like garment until she was standing in only her chemise and pantalets.

She turned around and faced him, her eyes enormous, her lower lip quivering. The chemise was wet enough that all his questions about her figure were answered, and in a very affirmative way. Her waist, always a mystery in the current Empire styles, was supple and slender. Her breasts were high, their rounded shape about the size of carnation blossoms. Her nipples showed all rosy through the damp fabric, small points that had come to attention for him.

Her eyes held a question. What was he going to do to her?

John didn't claim to know everything about women, but he knew enough to realize he could seduce Rebecca now if he wished. She was in a weakened state. Vulnerable. A few minutes of kissing and caressing and he'd have her naked in that string bed, ready for anything.

But that would be like gambling with a stacked deck. He might win a quick pot or two, but when his cheating was discovered, he'd lose it all.

Rebecca was going to be a long game if he had any chance with her at all.

John picked up the counterpane that was folded over the back of the chair and held it up between them. Then he shut his eyes.

"All right," he said. "You do the rest."

He fought against the urge to peek as he heard the rustle of fabric. His imagination ran riot as he heard her pull her chemise over her head and untie the drawstring at her waist that held up her pantalets. "Ready?"

"Mmmhmm."

Eyes still closed, he wrapped the counterpane around her. It was torture to feel her hills and valleys under the fabric and know she was in nothing but her glorious skin. John was determined that, for once, he'd behave as if he were still a decent gentleman.

He scooped Rebecca up and carried her to the bed and then laid her down on it with all the tenderness he felt for her. He didn't know why she should bring on this unexpected warmth in his chest, but she did. He was glad to feel it.

He didn't know he could still feel something so fine and good.

Her shoulders were bare. Her thin clavicle was a fragile line beneath smooth skin, inviting him to trace its path with his lips. The slight indentation at the base of her throat throbbed with her pulse, making him ache to kiss it. He didn't dare look her in the eye or he'd lose his resolve not to seduce her.

So John turned away. He strode purposefully back to the dressing screen and draped all her items of clothing over it. After that, he crossed back to his side of the room and got dressed.

His clothes were still slightly damp, but if he were going to continue behaving as if he were a decent gentleman, he needed to leave the room with some urgency. She didn't say anything from her counterpane cocoon, but he heard occasional hitching breaths.

Once he shrugged on his tailcoat, he walked over to the bed and looked down at her. Her mouth was kissably slack, her eyes wide. She was achingly beautiful, but too fine for him to touch.

"Please believe me when I tell you I'm sorry I burdened you with my sins," he said.

"We all have things in our pasts of which we are not proud."

"I doubt it in your case," he said. "But I thought you weren't my confessor. That almost sounds like absolution."

A small smile lifted one corner of her mouth.

A tenuous bridge between them was all he could hope to build, but he'd take it. John leaned down, bracing himself on his palms on either side of her, lest he lower himself to her completely. He wanted more than anything to kiss her deeply, to make love to her sweet mouth.

But he didn't deserve to kiss Rebecca like that. Instead, he brushed his lips on her cheek.

Softly. Reverently. Then he straightened and walked out the door.

They were the hardest ten steps he'd ever taken.

Twelve

*They say that travel is broadening, that one is enriched by
new sights and sounds, by the experience of life in a different
venue. But they only say that to distract one from the general
inconvenience of it all.*

—Phillippa, the Dowager Marchioness of Somerset

PORTER PACED THE LENGTH OF THE BELOW STAIRS
common room in Somerfield Park. It was a pleasant
enough space, dominated by the long pine table at
which the servants gathered for communal meals.
There was a cozy fireplace to warm the room, and Lord
Somerset didn't stint on firewood as some employers were known to do, letting their servants shift for
themselves to find wood to burn or be forced to bundle
up even inside when the weather turned foul. In the
evenings, ample tallow candles released a faintly beefy
scent into the air along with light enough to read or do
some mending or play a hand of cards. Now that Porter
was finally settled into the great house as Lord Hartley's
valet, he thought he'd be happy all the day.

Instead, he was wracked with worry.

"Something must have happened to them," he muttered.

"Still fretting, Mr. Porter?" Mrs. Culpepper bustled in with a tray laden with a steaming pot of tea, a sugar bowl, and a pitcher of milk.

The servants wouldn't be given their supper till the Family was done with theirs, so this late afternoon fortification was essential for keeping everyone sharp as the workday slid into the evening. Mrs. Culpepper's new helper, Theresa Dovecote, followed the cook with a basket of fresh buns and a pot of clotted cream. The girl so closely resembled her sister Eliza, Porter had to look twice to make sure which of them it was. Of course, Theresa wore her blouses ever so much tighter than Eliza did. The little horn buttons that marched down the center of her bosom were taxed mightily by remaining fastened.

Porter feared that looking twice at Theresa might get him into trouble some day.

"If I'm fretting, it's with good reason," Porter said as he plopped into one of the chairs around the table. Worried or not, he wasn't about to miss an opportunity to sample some of Mrs. Culpepper's baked goods. Her cooking was one of the best things about his position as Lord Hartley's valet.

And if something horrible happened to Lord Hartley, he'd lose his livelihood and access to her cooking, almost before the appointment had begun. It was nearly enough to kill his appetite.

"His lordship ought to have arrived home last night," Porter said as he held up his teacup for her to fill. "Thank you kindly, Mrs. C."

"But ye don't know for certain when Lord Hartley left London, so how can ye know when he should arrive?" Mrs. Culpepper plopped a brown lump of sugar into his tea without him having to ask for it.

She remembers how I take my tea, he told himself and did a little self-congratulatory jig in his mind. Of course, he usually liked two lumps, but he could get used to just one.

"Ye ought not to borrow trouble," Mrs. Culpepper went on, moving down the long table to serve Sarah, Drucilla, Toby, and the others who'd gathered for a bite and a respite.

Porter noticed that she gave each of the others a single sugar lump too. So she didn't remember how he took his tea…or how he could learn to take his tea. *Oh, bother and confound it!* He was in a state of constant befuddlement when Mrs. Culpepper was around. This business of fancying a woman was making a muddle of his usually orderly mind.

"Ye don't know if they decided to stop along the way—oh, I know ye can make the trip to Town in a day, but it's a long, hard day by all accounts, and then only if the weather's fine." Mrs. Culpepper rounded the end of the long table and started back up the other side. "And old Lady Somerset isn't the traveler she used to be. She might not want to pound out the miles as vigorously as a young man might. Likely that's why Lord Hartley and the rest are taking their time."

Privately, Porter thought that the dowager could put them all under the table at whatever she decided to attempt. But Mrs. C's words did comfort him a bit.

"You're right," he said. "Women don't travel as well as men."

"Hold a moment, now. I expect I could travel just as well as any man," Theresa said as she deposited a fragrant bun on the plate before Porter and slapped a dollop of clotted cream beside it. "I'd make the trip on my knees if only I could see London, so I would. Tell us, Mr. Porter, was it wonderful?"

London was loud and dirty and Porter was nearly beside himself each time Lord Hartley left the town house because he never knew when his lordship would deign to return. He might be gone for hours or days. There was no way to tell.

Being a servant with no one to serve meant time had hung heavy on Porter's hands. Of course, his lordship's activities while in London were hard on his wardrobe, and that kept Porter stitching and cleaning. But one could only polish a pair of shoes or brush a jacket so often while waiting for freshly dirtied items to appear.

London wasn't a bit wonderful. It was one big knot in Porter's stomach. That's what it was. But when he saw the wistfulness on Theresa's face, he couldn't disabuse her of her dreams.

"Of course, I spent most of my time at the Family's home in Mayfair, you understand," Porter said. While the Barrett family town house was properly elegant, it didn't hold a candle to Somerfield Park in his estimation. "But I did manage to walk down to attend services at Westminster Abbey one Sunday."

He spent his time in the gothic cathedral praying that the new Lord Hartley would come to his senses and go home—or at least start keeping country hours.

"Westminster Abbey? Ain't that the place where all them dead people are buried inside the walls and under the floors?" Theresa asked, her eyes wide.

"Well, if they're buried there, I'd hope to shout that they're dead," Toby the footman said with a laugh. "It'd be silly if they tucked live ones into the walls."

Theresa stuck out her tongue at Toby and whisked the bun she'd just given him off his plate. He snatched it back from her and held it out of her reach until Mrs. Culpepper threatened to box both their ears and withhold their suppers later if they didn't mind their manners now. The maid and the footman murmured contrite apologies to the cook, but exchanged dagger glares at each other behind her back.

"Actually, Theresa is right, Toby," Porter said. "The Abbey is the final resting place for many of our kings and queens."

"I'm all for the royals like any good English girl, you know I am," Theresa said, "but gorblimey, Mr. Porter, didn't you go nowhere where there was live people? No plays? No trips to Vauxhall? I hear that's ever so lovely."

"What do you know about it?" Toby challenged.

"More than you, pudding-head," she returned tartly. "They say there's tightrope walkers and balloon rides. And once the sun goes down, the whole park is lit by gas lamps, so it's bright as day."

"All but the Druid Walk," Toby said. "That's the part of the park what isn't lit at all, and for my money, folk are more like to spend the better part of their evening there than watching some bloke wobble on a tightrope."

Theresa arched a brow at Toby. "What is there to do in the dark?"

"Walk out with me some evening and I'll show you."

Theresa laughed and one of the buttons on her blouse lost its battle with remaining fastened. A bit of lace at the bodice of the girl's unmentionables peeped through the slit. Porter glued his gaze to the bun on his plate.

"That's enough, now," Mrs. Culpepper said crossly, "or I'll toss a tub of wash water on the pair of ye. Toby, if ye say another word, I—"

"What's this?" Mr. Hightower's gruff tones interrupted as the butler entered the room and made his stately way to the head of the long table. All the others assembled leaped to their feet and stood at attention as if Hightower were still a sergeant in the military and they were his raw recruits. "Has Toby been causing trouble again?"

Mrs. Culpepper moderated her tone. "No trouble, Mr. Hightower."

"There had better not be," he warned, "or Master Toby shall celebrate the beginning of the hunting season by hunting for a new position."

A somber pall fell over the entire assemblage. As far as Porter was concerned, to lose a position as sought after as one at Somerfield Park was a tragedy of biblical proportions. No one wanted to see anyone sacked, not even one who pushed himself forward as often as that irritating Toby.

"The arrival of the new Lord Hartley marks a sea change in the life of the estate," Mr. Hightower said. "It is incumbent on all of us to do our utmost to help the Family through this difficult period."

David Abbot, Lord Richard's valet, clattered down the back stairs and into the common room. "There's a coach coming up the drive."

"Right. Well, that's likely our travelers, home from the city. Sharp's the word, everyone," Hightower said as he led the way to form a receiving line at the front door. "We must put our best foot forward."

"Don't you mean feet, sir? Best feet forward," Toby said, his mischievous face a mask of seriousness. "If we're all doing it, shouldn't it be feet, not foot?"

Not many could get a rise out of Mr. Hightower when he was set on leading his troops into behaving with the utmost decorum, but now he stomped up the steps, muttering imprecations under his breath.

"Mr. Porter, sir, a word, if you please." Theresa caught him by the elbow before he could follow Hightower. As a kitchen maid, she wouldn't be allowed to join the liveried footmen and uniformed chambermaids to greet their new lord. But as said lord's valet, Porter had better make an appearance with the rest of them, and on the quick too. Still, her hazel eyes were so importunate, he didn't have the heart to pull away from her.

"No one ever tells me much down here in the kitchen," she said in a furious whisper. "You'd think as I was a mushroom and could live on only darkness and dung, the way they treat me."

"If you're unhappy, you should take up the matter with Mrs. Culpepper," he said.

"Oh, I'm not unhappy," Theresa said quickly. "If you say I am, I'll dispute it with my dying breath. No, it's not that. I only want to know a thing or two, that's all."

If he yanked himself away from her now, he'd still have to take the stairs two at a time to catch up to Mr. Hightower. Porter sighed. "What do you want to know?"

"Well, as I hear tell it, Lord Richard didn't spend much time here when he was Lord Hartley, what with his time at university and traveling abroad and suchlike. It don't seem as if having the heir about is all that important, but Lord Richard and his lady traveled all the way to London to find him. Even old Lady Somerset went to fetch him back here." A lock of her mouse-brown hair had escaped her mobcap and she twirled it on one of her fingers. "Why is the Family so set on making sure the new Lord Hartley comes home, in any case?"

Porter didn't care why the Family wanted Lord Hartley home. He was just grateful that his lordship was. "Well, I suppose they want to get to know him."

"Balderdash," Drucilla, the head chambermaid said with a sniff as she breezed past them and started up the stairs. "They want to get on the new lord's good side while they can."

"Why would they need to do that? They're all lords and ladies up there, ain't they?" Theresa followed Porter and Drucilla up a few steps. "They don't need to be on anyone's good side. Their side *is* the good side."

"Shows what you know, ninny." Drucilla stopped and turned around to sneer down at her. "The new Lord Hartley is the son of his lordship's *first* wife. And the rest of them are the current marchioness's children."

Theresa scratched her head. "I don't see as that makes a difference. They're all still lords and ladies, ain't they?"

Drucilla snorted. "Once the old marquess dies, and may he be spared for many a year yet, the new marquess is under no obligation to provide for the family of the old one. It happens all the time with second marriages. The children from the second wife are turned out with naught but a handful of fingers."

Theresa's eyes widened. "But her ladyship didn't know she was his lordship's second wife when she married him, did she?"

"No, that she didn't," Porter said. "Now we'd best get on with our jobs or Mr. Hightower will turn us out with naught but a handful of fingers too."

Thirteen

The best time to mend one's fences is before the livestock has escaped. Unfortunately, such events rarely occur in that order.

—Phillippa, the Dowager Marchioness of Somerset

JOHN RODE ALONGSIDE LORD RICHARD ON THE narrow seat of the gig, trailing the Somerset coach. After the debacle on the road, Lady Somerset wasn't about to allow them to become separated again. Repairs to the coach had been made with record speed, and the others had straggled in to join John and Rebecca at the inn at Tincross Bottom shortly after midnight. After a late-morning country breakfast—and according to the dowager, a wholly inadequate one at that—the party set out for Somerfield Park. Once they reached the estate, they stopped long enough to deposit old Lady Somerset at Somerset Steading, the dower house.

Richard, Sophie, and Rebecca had helped the old lady into her house. John had remained in the gig the entire time. He hadn't regretted his decision until

Rebecca had shot him a reproving glance as she climbed back into the coach with the wife of his half brother.

He knew he was being churlish, but he didn't care. These people had no claim on him. Not really.

"Gran seemed happy to be home," Richard said, obviously trying to fill the silence that yawned between them.

"And well she should be. Somerset Steading is a veritable palace." At least it seemed so compared to the humble Wiltshire cottage in which John had grown up. He'd rarely seen such a fine home as the dower house, with its gray-slate roof and intricate brickwork. Of course, that was before he caught his first glimpse of Somerfield Park.

At the end of the tree-lined lane ahead of them, the imposing manor of Somerfield Park rose in four glorious stories of Georgian majesty. It was stately, elegant, and most astonishing of all, the place John might live in for the rest of his life.

His chest constricted. No matter how impressive, bricks and mortar did not make a home.

"Your grandmother seemed relieved to be back in the country," John said, "which is not quite the same thing as being happy."

"She's not a good traveler under the best of conditions." Richard chuckled. "You must admit that coaching inn at Tincross Bottom is not up to the dowager's usual standards."

Neither was John, evidently.

"But she was impressed that you were able to command rooms for us all, and on market day too," Richard said.

After John had left Rebecca in that tiny chamber the day before, he'd used his pent-up frustration to behave in the worst of lordly fashion, demanding that the innkeeper turn out his current guests in favor of the party from Somerset, which had yet to straggle in. He'd rank his performance as only slightly more imperious than when Blackwood demanded that poor doorman's shoes, but his lordly fury got results.

However, if the dowager felt he deserved any praise for making sure she didn't have to share a room with Miss Kearsey once Lady Somerset's coach had limped into the village, he hadn't heard it from her.

"You might be a bit easier on Gran, you know," Richard said. "She's already well past her allotted threescore and ten."

John's lips tightened into a thin line. "She disavowed me once. I'm just returning the favor."

"Gran didn't mean it badly. You must allow that she didn't know all the facts at the time."

Oh, well, that makes it all right. Was that what his half brother wanted from him? Easy for him to say. He grew up here in the bosom of his family. Sheltered. Privileged. Sure of his place in the world. It was easy to be magnanimous when you had everything.

Of course, Richard didn't have it all now.

Why wasn't he angry about that?

"This must be difficult for you, the change in your inheritance, I mean." John would have added that he was sorry for it, except it wasn't his fault.

"On the contrary, learning that I am not our father's heir could not have come at a better time. It meant I could marry Sophie. Believe me, I am more than happy to step aside for you, old chap."

John gave Richard a sharp, assessing gaze but could detect no guile. "Keep that up and I may decide to like you."

"Good. I'm partial to the idea of having a brother myself. We'll have to join forces if we hope to prevail against the Barrett women. And speaking of women, Miss Kearsey seems to be quite a fine one."

"She is."

"Since you invited her here, am I right in assuming you harbor a *tendresse* for the lady?"

"Assume what you like," John said. Then he regretted his surliness. Richard had been trying very hard to befriend him. It had been so long since someone had, it was hard not to respond with his reflexive brand of standoffishness. Better to be the first to withdraw, he reasoned, than to be set aside by others. "In truth, I shouldn't have invited her."

"Why?"

"Because…" How could John explain to the man whose title he just usurped that he felt unworthy?

"If you fear Miss Kearsey will be scared off by the Barrett family, I confess you've got reason."

"What's wrong with the family?"

"I wouldn't say there's anything *wrong* with us Barretts. Not exactly. I'd rather class us as 'unconventional.' In order to keep the estate afloat, I'm hip-deep in trade. That's enough to set tongues wagging. After his accident last spring, Father is becoming dottier by the day. Dr. Partridge predicted a full recovery, but Father seems determined to run to foolishness just to spite him."

Richard gave a weak chuckle, but John could see his father's illness worried him.

"My sisters are a force to be reckoned with, both separately and en masse. Ella is constantly harping on the fact that she hasn't had her Season yet and is certain I'm conspiring to make a spinster of her. Petra, who's only a year younger than Ella, is more interested in books than boys and doesn't care who knows it." Richard sighed. "Then there's Ariel. The only governess she wasn't able to run off was the one who threatened to blackmail Father over his first marriage. Since that plot was uncovered, our youngest sister has sent three successive governesses fleeing for the hills."

John laughed and found himself suddenly looking forward to meeting Richard's family. If the Barretts weren't the perfect, ever-correct members of the *ton* he'd envisioned, he might, just might, have a better chance of fitting in with them.

"I don't think Miss Kearsey is the type to be put off by a little eccentricity," John said. If she were, she wouldn't have accepted his invitation. "I notice you haven't mentioned your mother."

"That's because she's the only one of us who's at all normal. A rock, that's what she is." Richard lifted his hat and waved toward the great house. "Look. There they are, spilling out of the front door to welcome us."

Welcome you, you mean. No matter how unconventional the Barretts were, none of them could be truly happy to see John here. He'd been the stray on the edge of the group, never quite allowed into the inner circle. Now the whole Somerfield Park pack clamored to greet him.

The servants flanked the left side of the great double doors. They were lined up with near military precision in two straight queues.

On the right side of the door, he saw only women—well-dressed women in gauzy gowns that fluttered in the slight breeze, like eiderdown on a swan's neck.

His father was not there to meet him.

As the coach rolled to a stop, John was quick to climb down and beat the footman, who was on his way to open the coach's door. John wanted to hand Rebecca down himself. He knew he ought to stay away from her, but he couldn't resist this chance to touch her, even if it was only her gloved hand.

"Thank you, John," Sophie said as she climbed down first.

Rebecca followed. She murmured her thanks and gently tugged her fingertips from him when he didn't release them quickly enough. But she still rewarded him with a smile.

It was like a full plate of nourishing fare, that smile. A warm fire on a cold night. Shelter for his unworthy soul. Lord, he could live on just one of those smiles a day.

For the rest of his life.

He batted away that thought. He didn't deserve someone like Rebecca Kearsey, and he knew it.

Still, he couldn't help admiring her as she moved toward the receiving line. She knew how to carry herself, curtsying prettily before Lady Somerset the younger and then nodding to each of Richard's sisters in turn.

John, on the other hand, felt all knees and elbows as he walked behind her.

The current Lady Somerset was not at all what John had envisioned. He'd expected her to have that imperious, dragon-like quality so common in wellborn matrons. Instead, she was a woman in the final bloom of beauty, her face unlined but for a few wrinkles at the corners of her brown eyes. There were more smile lines around her mouth than frown lines between her even brows.

"Whatever face a person has at twenty, God gave 'em," his foster mother, Lady Coopersmith, used to say. "The face they wear at fifty, they earned for themselves."

If that was so, Lady Somerset had lived a good life, for her face was still quite lovely. She surprised John by offering him a deep, graceful curtsy.

"Lord Hartley," she said, "I know you've traveled a long way and must be tired, but I wonder if I might offer you tea and refreshment in my parlor before you repair to your chamber to rest?"

The request astonished him into stammering, "Yes, of course," when he really ought to have insisted on having Porter draw him a bath and dress him in fresh clothing. He was seriously regretting traveling in the outfit he'd slept in the last night he was in London.

But he followed the swish of Lady Somerset's skirts up a broad, polished staircase to a frilly parlor on the first floor.

"Please be seated and make yourself comfortable," Lady Somerset the younger said.

John perched on the edge of a pink-striped settee. The parlor made him nervous. The furniture seemed too delicate to support him, the space too crowded with knickknacks and oddities for him to move comfortably without knocking some valuable something over.

"How many lumps do you take in your tea, Lord Hartley?"

"None. There was little sugar in Wiltshire. Never developed a taste for it." He accepted the delicate china cup and saucer and took a sip. The tea was an aromatic blend with a hint of orange. "Where is Lord Somerset?"

The lady's brows drew together in distress. "You must understand. His lordship waited all day yesterday for you. He even went up to the roof to watch for your approach, though I chided him so much for it that he finally came down. Even after all this time, it still sends cold chills through me to think of him on that roof."

That still didn't explain why he wasn't there to greet his firstborn.

"His lordship and his valet are in the woods now, scouting out good spots for hunting blinds and such." She added a dollop of milk to her cup and took a refined sip. "He'll be home in time for supper."

But not in time to welcome John.

"I gather Richard has told you about his accident," she continued.

John nodded. "The marquess took a catastrophic fall from the parapet last spring and was only saved from death by a well-placed lilac bush."

"He's much better than we have a right to expect, but he is still not quite himself. In fact, he has deteriorated since his initial injury. His memory is…flawed."

"So you're saying he won't know who I am."

"No, no, he understands that you've been found…"

Found? John was never lost. He was misplaced.

"…and that you are coming here," she continued. "But since he never knew of your existence, he naturally wouldn't have any memories of your earlier life."

"I suppose that makes us even, because I have no recollection of him either."

She didn't seem to catch the irony in his tone.

"Lord Hartley, what I'm trying to prepare you for is that he has no memory of your mother."

For a moment, his mother's face flashed across his mind. She was lovely and young and foolish and sad all at once. It made John's gut burn that she only lived in his hazy recollections from when he was six years old. He didn't remember her favorite song or what color she liked or if she wished her life had been different. Surely someone ought to know who Sadie Mae was.

"But I want to tell you something about Lord Somerset," she went on, as if John's silence were perfectly normal. He blessed her for not requiring him to hold up his side of this unusual conversation. "My husband is a very proud man, an honorable man, and a man of deep feeling. He must have cared deeply for your mother, even if he cannot remember her now."

"My lady, I've no wish to contradict you, but how can you know something his lordship can't even remember?"

One of Lady Somerset's brows quirked up. "I

know this because he defied his parents for her. By the time I came to know him, his father was already gone, so I cannot speak to the previous marquess's temperament, but believe me, one does not cross the dowager with impunity. Your mother must have been quite special."

It did his heart good to hear someone say something positive about his mother. Too often the Coopersmiths had cast her in the role of Whore of Babylon and weren't shy of speaking their opinion before John while he was growing up. Passing strange that it should be his father's second wife who praised his first one.

"Yet he let her go," John said, meeting her gaze.

"No doubt he was convinced that it was for the good of the estate, or some such noble reason. However, I have it on good authority that your mother was amenable to the separation. In fact, she insisted upon it." Lady Somerset looked around the room as if it were some gilded cage. "The demands of being a marchioness were perhaps more than she expected. She wasn't prepared for everything that came with being married to your father. I fear our mode of life seemed…too staid and regimented for her."

The little John remembered of his early years were a blur of activity and merriment, alternating with squalor and neglect.

"But this is what I most wished to tell you about your father: He loved your mother. He loves me. But most of all, he loves his children." She set her teacup back into the saucer with a soft click of bone china meeting its mate. "And that, my dear Lord Hartley, will include you in time. I only ask that you give him that bit of it, so he can get to know you."

His lordship could have had all the time in the world with John if the marquess had fought a little harder to keep John's mother. However, looking at the composed, generous woman before him, he couldn't fault Lord Somerset's choice in his second wife. She was more magnanimous than John had a right to expect.

"I'm sorry for the pain this situation has caused you," he said, meaning it.

"It is not your doing. And it is not my husband's either."

John couldn't agree with that.

"I think we should chalk it up to bad luck all around and begin afresh. It is my dearest hope that you are willing to give us a try."

John mumbled something appropriately noncommittal and excused himself.

Bide your time and toss them all out once the old marquess shuffles off, Blackwood had advised him. John wondered if this little introductory tea was Lady Somerset's first sally in the campaign to see who would still be standing once the title passed from her husband to him.

Part of him didn't want to suspect this gracious lady, who'd had kind words for his mother, of such subterfuge. Another part of him, the small boy who'd grown up as an unacknowledged bastard, decided to walk wary.

Fourteen

In the spring, a young man's fancy turns more naturally to hearts and flowers. In the bleakness of early November, it takes a special young lady indeed to bring out a gentleman's softer side.

—Phillippa, the Dowager Marchioness of Somerset

THE CHAMBER JOHN HAD BEEN ALLOCATED IN Somerfield Park was bigger than the entire cottage in which he'd grown up. Porter had his bath waiting and a fresh suit of clothing laid out. He chattered on while John bathed, and kept up a steady diatribe as he helped him dress. Mr. Porter even hummed while he tied John's cravat. Clearly someone was happy to be there.

John still wasn't. It felt as if his life was happening to someone else, as if he were a Drury Lane player acting the part of heir. He simply wasn't *himself* anymore, and he didn't like it one bit.

"Would you like someone to show you over the house, my lord? I'll warrant the place is a bit over-whelming at first."

John had been surrounded by quite enough opulence

while he made his way through the grand foyer, and up the even grander stairs to this chamber. He hadn't dared think for longer than a blink that it would someday all be his. "No, I think I'll take a walk around the grounds."

A dry winter garden wouldn't be as commanding as the rest of Somerfield Park. The very brick and mortar seemed to demand to know who he was and why such a common pretender would dare try to fit into the proud line of Somersets. The house itself was whispering, "What are *you* doing here?"

John stood immobile while Porter draped his garrick over his shoulders. It still seemed odd to have someone dress him as if he were a helpless child, but this was the way things were done among the Upper Crust—one more oddity of life to which he would have to become accustomed. He wondered if he'd be allowed to blow his own nose if he caught a cold.

"Dinner is served at eight. The dressing gong will sound at seven, my lord," Porter told him as John headed toward the door.

"I'm to change clothing again?"

Porter shot him a puzzled look.

John could have kicked himself. He'd visited Blackwood's home once. He knew everyone who was anyone in a great house dressed for dinner.

"Everyone" had just never included him before.

He stomped out of the chamber before he embarrassed himself before his valet again.

❧

Rebecca needed to stretch her legs after the coach trip from Tincross Bottom with old Lady Somerset and Sophie. Not that she didn't think the world of those ladies, but being in an enclosed space with two such forceful personalities made her feel as if she were in the middle of a battledore and shuttlecock match. And she was the shuttlecock!

They had launched into ways she might help Lord Hartley, to smooth his way with the higher-ranking young ladies who would be descending on Somerfield Park in a day or so.

"He'll not have had much experience with polite discourse. Not after growing up in Wiltshire," the dowager had said with a delicate shudder, as if she hadn't been instrumental in situating John there in the first place. "He'll want training in the proper way to woo a lady of quality."

Rebecca could attest to that. First, he'd spoken to her in the museum without benefit of introduction. Then, even though he had saved her from a terrible situation in that boxing crib in Whitechapel, he'd been surly and taciturn to her in the coach as he took her home. In their next encounter, he'd all but extorted a kiss from her. And at the coaching inn in Tincross Bottom, he contrived for her to remove all her clothing in his presence.

To say that John Fitzhugh Barrett didn't know how to properly woo a lady was an understatement of gargantuan proportions.

"Of course," Sophie had added, "it would be best if John were unaware he was being tutored. Men tend to resent female instruction about anything."

Freddie would have looked at this as a challenge. Perhaps she'd have even seen it as a scientific inquiry into whether human behavior might be drastically altered in a limited amount of time. Freddie would have drafted a plan, designed specific scenarios to elicit the desired response, and then presented her findings in a beautifully footnoted paper.

Freddie enjoyed anthropology far more than Rebecca did. More often than not, the study of her fellow humans depressed her. Rebecca loved the stars. She couldn't change them. No one would expect her to. All she need do was lie back on her terrace and watch them parade across the sky.

Rebecca wasn't sure if she could do anything to change John Fitzhugh Barrett. Or if she really wanted to. There was something appealing about a man who was so dreadfully honest, even when it was improper.

She walked along the pea-gravel path that led through Somerfield Park's extensive gardens. In high summer, it would be a riot of blooms, but now dead vines rattled over a trellised stone bench. She strode toward it, seeking shelter from the occasional breeze.

As she drew near, she saw that the bench was not empty. John was seated there, leaning forward, elbows on his knees and head in his hands.

"Hello, John."

He rose to his feet and stood to one side to make room for her on the bench. "I trust you're not wandering the gardens because your accommodations are lacking."

So far so good—John was polite and solicitous. Even the dowager would have found his behavior impeccable.

"Not at all. My room is splendid." She was a baron's daughter and by rights ought to be accustomed to fine things, but her father had pockets to let. The paintings in their ancestral home had been sold to pay his debts of honor. Her mother's jewelry was paste replicas of her original pieces. After her threadbare chamber at home, her guest room at Somerfield Park was like the difference between a starless night and a meteor shower. "You're wandering about too. Isn't your chamber to your liking?"

"Not really. It's too fine, I suppose. Too big."

That wouldn't please Lady Somerset. Nothing was too big or too fine for the future marquess. "You ought to take it as your due. You are the heir, after all."

"I know something I'd like to take as my due." He sat beside her and swept her form with his dark-eyed gaze.

This was not at all what the dowager had in mind when she suggested Rebecca school John on how to woo a lady. Still, her insides capered about.

"Taking is not at all the done thing." She forced herself to frown at him even though a naughty part of her wanted to encourage him to take whatever he wished. "Wouldn't it be better if whatever it is you want was offered freely?"

"I take your point, but you're far too intelligent to be so obtuse. You know perfectly well I'm talking about another kiss." He stretched out his long legs. "And you're right. As I recall, I did enjoy it immensely when you kissed me of your own accord."

"Of my—" Rebecca blinked hard. "Of all the cheek. You practically blackmailed me into that kiss."

"Is that how you remember it?" His mouth spread in a slow grin and the feel of his lips on hers came back to her unbidden, all warm and sure and beckoning her to follow him to darker depths of wickedness.

"I remember kissing you was the only way I could get you to agree to come home."

"And that's the only reason you kissed me?"

"No."

"So you wanted to kiss me?"

"I really don't want to talk about this with you."

"Very well. What would you like to talk about? How about why Lady Sophie and the dowager insisted that you travel here with us instead of coming later with your family?"

"I don't understand. Do you wish me to leave?"

"No, just wondering why you're staying, that's all."

Despite Sophie's advice to the contrary, she decided honesty was the best policy. "When we first met, you committed a social faux pas by speaking to me before we were properly introduced. Your family is hoping I'll teach you a more appropriate expression of social discourse with the fair sex."

"And you agreed?"

"I did. You see, I want to help you." She couldn't very well tell him the dowager had privately offered to settle some of her father's most pressing debts if she succeeded. "Will you let me?"

"I think you know by now that I'll let you do whatever you like with me." One of his brows lifted, and a vision of him with that blanket wrapped around his waist flitted across her mind. For a blink, she imagined unhooking the blanket and exploring him in all his splendid nakedness. Yes, indeed, there were certainly things she'd like to do with him, but none that she should. She shook off those naughty imaginings.

"If you'll allow me to help you, then let me start by

pointing out that you mustn't speak in double entendres to a respectable lady." Of course, a respectable lady might not even have caught his suggestion.

"I didn't mean any disrespect."

He reached over and wound one of the locks of her hair that had escaped her bonnet around his finger. If she weren't careful, he'd be doing the same thing with her heart. She gently unwound the hair and scooted farther from him.

"All right, Rebecca. What subjects of conversation are permissible with a lady of quality? And please don't tell me the weather."

"The weather is always safe, but there are any number of other things. For example, you might discuss books."

"I doubt I've read many a lady would approve."

"Music, then."

"I've a tin ear."

"The theatre?"

"I didn't attend any plays while I was in London. My set tended more toward gaming and cock fights," he said.

"What about the opera?"

"God save me from women who sound like a cat being gutted. How can they call it singing?"

She frowned at him. "You really do have a tin ear. If none of your interests are suitable to discuss, you could ask about the lady's."

"Now we're making progress," he said, his urbane drawl making him sound more like his friend Blackwood than himself. "Tell me. What are unorthodox debutantes like yourself fascinated by other than the Rosetta Stone and trying to manipulate a rake like me?"

"You are not a rake." At least she didn't think he was. It was true that John had sown his wild oats in London, but she didn't think that behavior was typical for him. Even this haughty "milord" facade he presented to her now didn't seem believable. She was still looking for another glimpse of that boy from Wiltshire she'd caught once or twice. The man who fought for her in that boxing crib. The gentleman who left her untouched in that coaching inn when they both knew he might well have had his way with her. He was the sort who could command any woman's heart. "You ought to think more highly of yourself."

"And you ought to listen more carefully," he said. "You're not answering my question."

John took her hand in his. There was a little opening at her wrist where the glove fastened with a tiny button. He undid it and ran the pad of his thumb in slow circles over that patch of bare skin. Pleasure radiated from the spot. It was as if she were a still pond and he'd just dropped a pebble into her center. Concentric rings of sensation surged and ebbed.

"Please tell me your fancy isn't wrapped up entirely in feminine gewgaws and folderols, or worse, demands for women's suffrage."

"As a matter of fact, my friend Freddie and I are both proponents for the women's vote." Rebecca had dozens of cogent arguments in favor of it, but at the moment, all she could focus on were the exquisite tingles John's strokes sent up her arm.

"I'm not opposed to women voting," he said. "I

just don't know why they need to be as shrill as opera singers about it."

She bristled at that and almost pulled her hand away from his beguiling touch. "Maybe because we aren't sure anyone is listening if we aren't 'shrill.'"

"You have my undivided attention, I assure you." When John's intense gaze swept over her, every bit of her tingled with awareness. "Isn't there anything else you find fascinating?"

You, Rebecca almost blurted out. How could she be so irritated by him one moment and drawn to him as inexorably as a lily to the sun the next? Then, to cover her unladylike response, she admitted, "I'm a bit of an amateur astronomer."

She tugged her hand away and did up the button on her glove quickly, before his soft touches removed all possibility of rational thought from her head.

He smiled at her, seemingly unaware of the effect he was having on her. "Stargazing, eh? That sounds like a suitable feminine diversion. Moonlight is supposed to be romantic."

She'd sighed over the moon as much as the next girl, but she'd also taught herself to recognize the constellations and tracked the progress of a number of planets across the heavens.

"Not all women are romantics. My astronomical studies are quite scholarly," she said. "If you wish to impress a lady with your conversational skills, you shouldn't denigrate her interests."

"Sorry. Do most ladies engage in scholarly pursuits?"

"No, they don't," Rebecca admitted. And even if they did, like Freddie, they often tossed their other interests aside in favor of a woman's supposed only goal in life—to marry the right man.

"Then you are as exceptional as I thought. Dazzle me with your knowledge of the stars."

"Just so you know, being confrontational like this is not the best way to advance a conversation with a lady," she said. "But as a matter of fact, I can dazzle you, or rather the stars themselves can. The annual Leonid meteor shower is due shortly."

"Is it? No doubt it will be easier to see here in the country than in London. What do you say we meet on the roof at midnight and count the falling stars?"

"That doesn't sound very safe. Your father fell from that roof, remember."

"We, however, will not. So long as we stay far from the parapet, you will be in no danger. I give you my word."

She might not be in danger of falling off the roof, but she'd be in peril all the same. "I don't think it's a very good idea."

"I'll collect you at your room at a quarter to midnight, and we'll go up to see your falling stars," he said as if he hadn't heard her objection.

"You will do nothing of the sort because you don't know which room I'm staying in." She crossed her arms over her chest.

"Do you seriously think a future marquess can't find out where each of his guests is staying?"

"That settles it. I'll ask to be moved to a different chamber."

"Which is still in my power to discover."

"There are plenty of big chairs and sofas in the

parlors and receiving rooms in the public areas of this house. I can just slip into one of them to sleep. You could look all night and never find me."

He leaned back and shot her a reassessing look. "You'd go to all that trouble just to avoid stargazing with me?"

"No, I'd do it to avoid a scandal," she said. "Can you imagine how tongues would wag if we were caught creeping about the house together in the dark?"

"Which will not happen so long as we're quiet about it."

A delicious tingle sparked down her spine. It could work. They might have a lovely, totally innocent adventure together under the stars. But the more practical part of her nature argued there was nothing innocent in John's suggestion. "Why do you want to take such a risk?"

"Tomorrow, the *beau monde* arrives. Tonight, I simply want to be with you."

A warm glow spread through her chest, but her heart still urged her to caution. "Why do you want to be with me?"

"Because I want to know you, Rebecca." He stroked her cheek with his fingertips. "I can see from your face that this meteor shower will mean something to you. I want to be a part of that."

"Oh." Something inside her melted like chocolate in a steamer. He wanted to *know* her—and not necessarily in the biblical sense. Well, maybe that too, but he certainly gave every appearance of being interested in her for more than rakish purposes. "I thought you were only interested in a tryst on the roof."

"There you have me," John admitted. "I can't deny I'd like another chance to kiss you."

The dowager's promise to settle her father's debts if Rebecca managed to teach John to approach a young lady correctly thudded back into her. She had to proceed with caution. "You've given me every reason to say no. That's not at all a proper request."

"Maybe not, but it's an honest one. Was kissing me that terrible?"

She glanced at him from under her lashes. "No."

It was wondrous. Stirring. Life-changing.

"Good." They sat in silence for a moment, and then he turned to her. John reached over and slid his fingertips under her chin, tipping her face toward him. "For me, that kiss was almost an absolution. If someone like you can kiss me, there may be hope for me yet."

She chuckled. "So I'm supposed to save you by sneaking out of my chamber and engaging in a clandestine meeting on the roof? It sounds as if you're urging me to sin more than I'll be trying to sway you to better behavior."

"And I thought you only wanted to watch the stars." He grinned at her. "You almost sound hopeful."

She swatted his shoulder. "You, sir, are no gentleman."

His smile faded. "You'd do well to remember it."

Then he gathered her close, and before she could protest, he brought her near enough for her to feel his breath feathering over her lips.

Fifteen

Of course I remember the first young man I kissed. He was Leander Higginbotham, the twelve-year-old brother of my best friend. As I recall, it involved a great deal of sighing and altogether too much exchange of saliva. Can't think why I found it intriguing at the time, but my belly fizzed like seltzer water all the same.

—Phillippa, the Dowager Marchioness of Somerset

JOHN HAD EXPECTED REBECCA TO PUT UP A FUSS, BUT instead, she melted into his arms with the rightness of a homecoming. Her eyelids fluttered closed. She wanted him to kiss her.

He wanted to do much more.

Rebecca Kearsey had no idea of the darkness swirling in him.

But as much as he wanted to kiss her, he knew he shouldn't. Not if he wanted her to trust him. So he dropped a quick kiss on the tip of her turned-up nose, and rose.

She blinked at him, clearly surprised.

"Expect me when you hear the longcase clock in the foyer chime a quarter to midnight." Then, before she could tempt him to snatch her up and kiss her thoroughly, he turned and headed back into the great house.

His insides were a tangle of jumbled-up emotions he couldn't identify. Lust, certainly, but there was also tenderness and longing that had as much to do with Rebecca's restful spirit as her luscious body. He wanted her, and he wanted to protect her from himself in equal measures.

He'd been wrong when he thought the garden would be less intimidating than the big house. Any garden which had Rebecca Kearsey in it was devastating.

❧

Rebecca paced her sumptuous room, walking back and forth through the increasingly narrow swath of moonlight that shafted through her window. The moon would sink into the western horizon by midnight, leaving the sky inky black. Perfect for stargazing and exploring the heavens.

Perfect for other sorts of exploration as well.

But the fact that circumstances had given John not one but two opportunities to kiss her and he hadn't done so made her belly swirl with disappointment.

After that first kiss, maybe he didn't really like her in that way at all. She wasn't accomplished in matters sensual. Her inexperience probably amused him more than anything. Maybe John was simply toying with her, entertaining himself until the more important debutantes arrived and he was forced to make a choice from among them.

After her chat with Freddie, she was under no illusions

about what would happen to John during the Somerset house party. All the daughters of the *ton* on their way to Somerfield Park would launch themselves at his head. Even if Lord Hartley was rough around the edges, he was still the highest-ranking bachelor available on the marriage market this year, and now that his family had taken him in hand, he would be irresistibly attractive.

A fox on hunting day had more chance of escape than he.

If Rebecca weren't so irritated about the fact that he hadn't kissed her again when he could have, she might actually have felt sorry for him.

The longcase clock chimed half past eleven.

Rebecca sank into the Sheraton chair by her fireplace and pulled her shawl tighter around her shoulders. Perhaps John wouldn't even come for her. She wondered if he was laughing to himself, imagining her sitting up, waiting for him.

Freddie would say it served her right. Rebecca was getting above herself, imagining that the heir to a marquess, even one as unorthodox as this new Lord Hartley, might find her worth his time.

Still, there was something of the deserted bastard child about him. He presented a hard face to the world, but that facade had slipped in her presence more than once. She didn't think he'd reveal that part of himself willingly to just anyone.

That made him more hers than any of the other debutantes on their way.

She hugged that to herself as the last of the moonlight slanted into nothingness.

Then she heard a soft scratching at her door. She

hurried to open it and found John with a candle in a small glass holder.

He smiled as he took in the fact that she was ready and waiting for him. Then he put a finger to his lips to signal for quiet, and offered his hand.

She slipped her fingers into his and let him lead her into the corridor. Her fingertips were icy with nervousness, but his hand was warm. Silent as wraiths, they passed along the walkway that looked down into the foyer and then slipped up the grand staircase. Once they reached the fourth floor, Rebecca lost track of all the twists and turns they made in the much narrower hallways. John had evidently been doing some exploring since they'd parted company in the garden and led her on without a pause. Rebecca was so turned about she'd be hard-pressed to find her way back to her chamber without his help.

Finally, they reached a door at the end of a long corridor. Behind it, there was an even narrower set of stairs that led up to a hatch-like opening on Somerfield Park's flat roof.

Once John handed Rebecca up the last step, he closed the hatch behind them and straightened.

"Thank you for coming, Rebecca," he said, his voice a dark summons that set her stomach aflutter. "I wasn't sure you would."

"Your invitation had me at a disadvantage," she whispered. "It's hard for me to resist the stars." There was no need to let the man know she felt an even stronger tug toward him.

"No need to keep quiet now," he said. "No one will hear us up here."

"But we might hear something if we listen hard enough."

He cocked his head. "What?"

"The music of the spheres." Rebecca lifted her arms to the Milky Way spilling across the heavens, a frothy band of white against the eternal dark. When she was a child, she imagined the cloud of stars flowed in an unending stream from a giant's upturned milk pail. The image still made her smile.

"Music of the spheres? That's hokum, surely."

"Pythagoras didn't think so. Neither did Sir Isaac Newton," she told him. "There is a demonstrable relationship between sound and mass and movement."

John stood silent for a moment. Wind sighed through the garden below. An owl hooted in the distant woods. No grand symphony dropped to them from the sky.

"I don't hear anything out of the ordinary," he said.

"I'm not surprised. I'm convinced it's not something we can hear with our ears," Rebecca said. "But I believe if I listen hard enough, someday I'll hear the music of the spheres with my heart."

"Then I'll have to trust you to describe it to me, since my heart is probably not able to perceive anything so sublime. But there's nothing wrong with my eyes, and I expect to see some fireworks in the sky. Come."

He led her to a place roughly in the center of the roof, near the octagonal skylights that looked down into Somerfield Park's foyer four floors below. If the foyer's crystal chandelier had been lit, this would have been a wonderful vantage point to spy on the nocturnal comings and goings in the great house.

Next to the skylights, John had made what looked like a camp bed. There were a couple of straw ticks topped with a feather one, so that it reached Rebecca's mid-calf. He'd layered several blankets on the ticks. He blew out the candle and set the holder down on the roof beside the mattresses.

"What's this?"

"It's chilly here on the roof, so I figured we'd need blankets," he said. "And is there a better position for stargazing than flat on your back?"

She'd often taken a quilt from her bed and lain out on her terrace to watch the stars wheel overhead. "No, I suppose not."

He lifted one corner of the blankets.

"John, did you even think for a moment about how improper this is?"

"You mean did it occur to me that this is a thinly veiled attempt to get you into my bed? Of course. But you can't deny it's also a sensible way to stay warm and look at the night sky. Two birds. One stone." He caught up her hand and brought it to his mouth for a soft kiss. "All teasing aside, I promise you that nothing will pass between us you don't wish as much as I. Not a thing."

A brisk breeze ruffled over them. It was early November, after all. Her heavy shawl, which had seemed so warm and snug in her bedchamber, was wholly inadequate now.

As long as we both stay fully clothed, there's not much likelihood that I'll accidentally succumb to performing the mysterious "it."

"Very well. I hold you to that promise," Rebecca said as she sat down on the low, impromptu bed.

"Let me help you take your slippers off." He knelt at
her feet to remove them before she could object. "Your
feet will be warmer without them under the covers."

So much for staying fully clothed.

Then he tucked the blankets around her and went
around to slide into his side of the bed. With the layers
of mattress beneath her, the soft blankets over her, and
a man beside her who seemed to be throwing off as
much heat as a crackling fire, Rebecca was as toasty
as if she were in her own bedchamber with a heated
brick at her feet.

"I don't see any falling stars," John said, lacing his
fingers under his head. It left an inviting space where
she might snuggle close and lay her head on his shoulder. Rebecca forced her gaze back to the heavens.
"Are you sure about this meteor shower?"

"It actually lasts for several nights. Be patient. We
should see some." She rolled onto her side to face him.
"I have it on good authority that you were educated
at Eton and Oxford. Did you not learn a thing about
astronomy there?"

"If I did, it's escaped my memory." He shifted
to face her and half sat up, propping himself on his
elbow. "I spent most of my time avoiding fights at
Eton. An Oxford education is still heavy on rhetoric
and Latin. Any study of astronomy was tucked neatly
into mathematics. But I do know the names of a
couple of stars here and there."

"Do you? Then it's your turn to dazzle me. Which
stars do you know?"

John rolled onto his back and scanned the sky from
north to south. He was closer to her now, his shoulder

touching hers, his muscular arm flush against hers. Instead of resting in two little pockets in the feather tick, John and Rebecca seemed to be sliding together into one.

"Well, I can usually pick out Arcturus." He frowned at the heavens. "It's a reddish star that's sort of off by itself. It's brighter than most in the southern sky, but I don't see it now."

"That's because it's the wrong time of year. You can see it best in our hemisphere in the spring." Rebecca fought off the urge to snuggle even closer to him. The sagging bed seemed to be arranging for that of its own accord. "But Arcturus is not really off by itself. It's part of the constellation Boötes. That's a roughly kite-shaped grouping of stars."

"There's a description worthy of a bluestocking— just the bare facts. I'd have thought someone who expects to hear the stars' music someday would have a bit of whimsy to share about them."

"There are as many myths about them as there are stars in the sky. But instead of accepting someone else's story, I always think the ones we tell ourselves about the stars are more interesting." John's scent, a heady mix of leather and bergamot, wafted by her nose, and she breathed him in. Who knew a man could smell so good? Rebecca forced herself to roll onto her back and focus on the heavens. After all, that was why they were there. "So what about you? Did you tell yourself a story about Arcturus?"

His shoulders lifted in a shrug. "I don't know that I gave it a story, particularly. It just always stood out to me. Solitary. Pulsing a bit. It seemed a little angry to me. Does that sound strange? That a star could be angry?"

Solitary and angry. "No one can say whose story about the stars is the right one. Of course, stars can't really be angry, but a boy looking up at one might be."

He turned to face her.

"You thought you were alone when you were a boy, looking up at that red star," she said softly.

"I didn't just think it. I was."

"You're not alone now." Rebecca reached to cup his cheek. A light bristle of stubble from a day's growth of his beard tickled her palm. "You have…" *Me* almost slipped out. No, she couldn't say that. She amended it to "You have a family here."

He narrowed his eyes at her. "Did I miss something tonight? My esteemed father couldn't be bothered to make it down to the dining room. Doesn't seem like much of a family to me."

Rebecca had bled a little for John when Lady Somerset announced that her husband was indisposed after roaming in the woods all afternoon and couldn't join them for supper. The marquess still hadn't come face-to-face with his eldest son. She felt John's pain over the slight—a dull, keening ache that would not be stilled—as if it were her own.

She and John were lying together under the stars. This was no place for evasiveness. The very setting cried out for honesty, no matter that it wasn't practical, that it could never work. She grasped her courage in both hands.

"You're not alone, John, because you have me."

His breath hissed in over his teeth. "Do you mean that?"

She wanted to say "I do," but it smacked too much of a commitment he likely wasn't ready to make. So she nodded instead.

He raised up and leaned over her, gathered her into his arms, and gave her the kiss she'd been longing for.

Rebecca knew then she'd never need to see another meteor shower as long as she lived. The stars were falling inside her, fiery bursts plummeting to earth, consuming themselves in a heated rush.

And if they burned themselves up in their headlong fall, they didn't care one whit.

Sixteen

When young people find someone whose oddities seem to match with theirs, when their souls' wrinkles fit together with the rightness of fine joinery, they click like magnets and call it true love. It may well be only a case of not enough wrinkle cream. I recommend a thorough dousing with Olympian Dew.

—Phillippa, the Dowager Marchioness of Somerset

JOHN COULDN'T GET ENOUGH OF HER. NO MATTER HOW long he kissed this girl, it wouldn't be enough. He needed Rebecca like he needed his next breath.

He drew the air from her lungs and replaced it with his own. He was inside her in a way, he a part of her and she a part of him. Their mouths might be the point of contact, but the connection went far deeper.

Lord, she was sweet. She suckled his tongue and shyly offered her own. He'd take it. He'd take all of her. He was someone else when he was with Rebecca, someone he didn't mind being so very badly. He kissed down the satiny column of her neck. Her hitched breaths went straight to his groin.

He'd never been this hard in his life.

John kissed his way under the blankets until he met the turned edge of her bodice. Frustration made him groan. Muslin shouldn't separate them. Buttons? Surely she had some buttons somewhere.

"John?" Her voice sounded distant but tight, as though she were thinking his name at him with clenched teeth.

Not yet. Don't stop this yet. He unhooked her top three buttons with his teeth and nuzzled between her breasts, drunk on her scent—a faint whiff of violets—desperate to draw out this loving exploration, desperate to sink into her sweetness and find release.

Please let it go on.

His lips met a narrow strip of lace on her chemise and he raised up, surprised. "I thought you didn't wear lace."

"Only a little," she admitted.

"Then I'll always think of you in only a little lace." He dove back under the blanket and untied the satin bow holding the chemise drawstring neckline. The next obstacle was her stays. He bumped his jaw on the wooden busk that ran down her breastbone and separated her sweet mounds.

Hooks this time. Buttons, ribbons, and hooks. Why couldn't women settle on one method of fastening their wardrobes? Didn't they realize when a man was in these dire straits, he was easily confused?

He started to work the hooks and was surprised when Rebecca's hands beat him to them.

"Angel woman," he whispered, raising to meet her gaze.

"Hardly. I've never been more wicked." She kissed him, a desperate sort of kiss, a kiss that pleaded for more and less at the same time. Rebecca was clearly torn.

She was a quintessential good girl. Obedient to her parents. Faithful to her friends. Needing the shield of her purity because she had little else of value in the world.

He didn't have any business meddling with her.

"If there is wickedness done this night, let it be on my head," he said and then kissed the sweet hollow at the base of her throat. "I want to love you, Rebecca. I want to give to you, not take. You have nothing to fear from me."

He bared one of her breasts and the nipple hardened, whether from his touch or the chill, he couldn't be sure. He thrummed it with the pad of his thumb, and she made a needy little noise in the back of her throat. He lowered his head and took her nipple between his lips.

She moaned. She moved in slow undulations. She made him feel like a minor deity.

"My mother always tells me too much knowledge is a bad thing, but there's no safety in ignorance," Rebecca gasped as she arched herself into his mouth. "What if I...I don't know anything about this?"

"But I do." He devoured her for a moment, then pulled back when her little moans made his balls tighten in response to her need. "You were a virgin when you set foot on this roof. I swear by...by the stars that you'll still be one when you leave."

"Oh, John." She pushed back the shock of his hair that had fallen forward over his forehead. "The way I'm feeling now, I never want to leave."

"Just keep feeling that." He struggled to hold her gaze and lost the battle. His eyes wandered down to the swell of her breasts. He hoped the hunger on his face didn't scare her. Her nipples drew tight under his gaze.

Her palms smoothed over his head and around his neck. He covered one of her hands with his, their fingers twining. Then he cupped her cheek, tracing her bottom lip with his thumb.

"Trust me, Rebecca." He bent and claimed her mouth.

She answered his kiss with more assurance this time. He covered her lips with his for a moment; then he slanted his mouth across hers, tasting her, teasing her lips open. He tongued her while his hand tormented her breasts.

She arched her back, pressing herself into his hand. Then his mouth was at her breasts, suckling her. He nipped her lightly, and she cried out in aching joy.

"What are you doing to me?" she whispered. "I've never…is it supposed to…throb like this?"

"I can make it better. Will you let me?"

"Yes, please, oh yes," she chanted.

John needed no further prompting. Rebecca closed her eyes as he slid his hand down her body, smoothing over her flat abdomen. He brushed by her crotch and bunched up her gown.

"Spread your legs."

It was a measure of her trust in him that she did. He found the top of her pantalets and plunged his hand in to cup her sex, holding her while she trembled.

"It will be all right. I promise." He kissed her temple, her closed eyes, and then her lips. Her tremble stilled. While his tongue made love to her mouth, his fingers slid along her cleft. She was already wet and slick. His fingertip circled her most sensitive spot, which had risen, all swollen, to be teased and petted.

He moved slowly, not in a heated rush, so he could draw out her torment. While he stroked her, he kissed his way down her throat, pausing to suck at the point of her pulse. She was so sweet, he could savor the thin skin of her neck for hours, but he moved on, past her thin clavicle to the soft mounds of her breasts. He drew circles on them with his lips. He feathered his warm breath across them. By the time he finally took her tight little bud in his mouth again, she was writhing beneath him.

He sucked. He set his teeth around her taut nipples and bit down just enough to make her whimper. Her fingers twined in his hair, kneading his scalp.

"What should I...what do you want...me to do?" Rebecca asked raggedly.

He came up for air, surfacing like a pearl diver, dragging in a sweet lungful of her arousal. His hand between her legs continued to drive her forward.

"I don't want you to do anything," John said as he eased down and nuzzled her navel through the layers of her gown and undergarments. He imagined for a moment how glorious it would be to have her under him without a stitch, skin on skin. He shoved away that wish for another time. If there was a merciful God in the heavens, there would be another time. "For now, I just want you to be. Lie still and let me."

She raised her arms above her head in a gesture of surrender, one forearm draped across her eyes. It was her artless way of shielding herself from him. Later, he didn't intend to let her hide, but this time, it might be easier for her to let go if she thought she could keep her response from immediate view. With a smile, he laid his head between her breasts.

Her heart pounded beneath his ear. His fingers left her sensitive spot to stroke the tender skin of her inner thigh, to brush by the curling hairs and her hidden folds. She made a noise of frustration, and he returned to the glistening entrance to her deepest secrets and her tender nub, erect and quivering.

He intended to serve her and serve her well—to reveal her to herself in ways she'd not yet discovered.

It was time. He dove farther under the covers.

❧

Rebecca clenched her teeth and fisted the blankets. She wanted to touch John, to thread her fingers through his hair, but feared if she lost control and grasped his ears, as she had the first time she kissed him, she might twist them off.

She was trying to lie still as he'd asked, but he was making it so difficult. She wanted to move. The short curling hairs between her legs swayed in the hot breeze of his breath. His fingers had driven her to aching fury, and now she supposed he thought this was a respite.

Then another sensation tickled along her thigh. His tongue. Warm. Wet. Just a little rough. He teased the crease of skin at the apex of her leg.

What on earth? She couldn't imagine what might happen next.

He took one of her throbbing folds between his lips. If she'd had a hundred guesses, she wouldn't have guessed that. But the sensations he awakened guaranteed she wouldn't be able to think clearly enough to guess in any case.

Then the tip of his tongue slid into her cleft, slippery and slickery, moving in slow, deliberate strokes. He circled that spot from which torment and pleasure seemed to flow in equal measure.

Her breath caught. She forced herself to inhale.

He moved his body between her legs. Both his hands cupped her bum, and he lifted her to his mouth. She didn't resist.

It was as if her body didn't belong to her any longer. It was totally his.

His lips closed over that special spot, and he suckled her, ever so gently.

Ache. Throb. Want.

Rebecca felt hollow as a gourd. Longing stretched her out on its rack.

His tongue probed into her, a soft, wet invasion.

Could this be what "it" is?

No. John promised. She would still be a virgin when the night was done. But if "it" was more pleasurable than this, she wondered how women withheld themselves from it at all.

She was wound tight as a ball of yarn. Then John pressed his teeth against her spot and suddenly Rebecca unraveled.

Deep inside her, an uncoiling overtook her. Her body bucked in tandem with the contractions over which she had no control.

"Stop. Oh, stop," she pleaded.

John showed her no mercy, driving her to a higher

peak. She was dizzy and disoriented, but her insides continued to pump. Joy flooded her veins. Her limbs were not her own. She felt lighter, as if she might rise from the warm blankets and float up to the stars.

When it finally subsided, she lifted the blankets and looked down along her body to where his dark head lay between her legs. Was she imagining it? No, the little bit of her exposed skin actually glowed a little. Then the radiance faded and her heart rate began to subside.

But the flush of pleasure remained. She drew in deep breaths, reveling in the brisk November night and John's sharp, masculine tang.

John moved up to lie beside her, slipping an arm under her to pillow her head. He draped the other over her, splaying his fingers possessively over her belly.

"Did the stars fall?" he asked.

"What stars? Oh, I don't know." She'd forgotten all about the Leonid meteor shower. "That was... extraordinary." She turned her head to look at him. "You know a great deal about women."

"I'd rather know a great deal about you."

"I think you already do." A flash of light caught the tail of her eye, and she looked back up at the heavens. "Oh, look. It's starting."

John snuggled her close, and together they watched the Leonids streak across the sky. For a moment, Rebecca thought she almost heard them singing.

Seventeen

One's family is like fire—exceedingly important, but one never knows if they're going to warm one's hands with a cheery blaze or burn the house down around one's ears.

—Phillippa, the Dowager Marchioness of Somerset

HER HEAD NESTLED ON JOHN'S WARM SHOULDER, Rebecca watched the meteor shower with mixed emotions. On the one hand, she was so limp and suffused with pleasure that it was difficult to fret about anything. Still, she kept expecting him to say something. Didn't a gentleman follow such ardent lovemaking with a declaration of some sort?

Freddie would say so. Of course, the sun would rise in the west before Rebecca told Freddie about this night's deeds.

Instead of waxing poetic about his undying adoration for her, John gave the stars the same undivided attention he'd lavished on her a few moments ago.

"I suppose I ought to feel shy in front of you

after what you did to me," she finally said to fill up the silence.

"For you, not to you," he corrected. "Oh, look! That's a good one."

A long tail of light bisected the dark sky.

"Aren't we…supposed to do something else now?" she asked.

He looked at her then and hugged her close. "In a perfect world, yes. What we've done together is just the beginning, but I promised you'd retain your purity, so be grateful there's a light show this spectacular to distract me from carrying on."

This raised more questions than answers. Rebecca suspected she ought to be affronted that anything could turn his attention from her, but all she could feel was bone-deep contentment. She was satisfied to let the world spin beneath her and the stars to fall above without the need to do a blessed thing.

She was untouchable by the world's troubles. Everything would be all right. John was an honorable man at heart. She was certain of it.

In the times between meteors, they kissed and whispered small endearments to each other. Rebecca told him things, things she'd never admit to another soul about her disappointment over what her father's gambling had done to the family. She voiced her fears for her mother's health, something she'd resisted for months, as if not speaking of it would somehow make Lady Kearsey's cough better and cause her blood-spattered handkerchiefs to disappear. Rebecca felt so very hopeless about it sometimes.

Freddie would tell her not to feel that way, as if one

could change how one felt as easily as one changed bonnets. John listened without reproof and without trying to minimize her concerns. It was a relief just to let the words flow without needing to check them because the topics weren't the "done thing." Then when the eastern sky began to lighten from ebony to pale slate, John kissed her once more and rose from their warm bower.

"We need to get you tucked into your own bed or dawn will catch us here."

"We don't want that. We don't want it quite a lot," she said. It wouldn't matter a jot that she was still a virgin if anyone stumbled upon them in their rooftop nest. Rebecca scrambled from the blankets quickly. She turned her back to him, retied the ribbon that held her chemise closed, and rehooked the top of her stays. Somehow in all their entanglements, she'd managed to stay fully clothed, the scheme she and Freddie had hit upon to avoid "ruin." But only just.

A determined lover didn't let little things like muslin and lace get in his way.

A lover. I have a lover. It was the last thing she'd expected when she first met John in the British Museum.

John put his hands on her shoulders and gently turned her around. He fastened the buttons on the bodice of her gown. "It's rather past time for modesty between you and me."

"Allow me a little, if you please."

"Only a little," he agreed. "You have a few secrets from me, and I'll let you keep them, but you're mine now, you know."

"What do you mean?" Was this the prelude to that declaration she hoped for?

"No matter what the future holds for us, Rebecca, I was the first to show you what pleasure you're capable of. You will remember me. And that pleases me more than I can say." He pressed a kiss to her forehead. "It makes me part of you forever."

"What about you?" Was the experience that was so earth-shattering for her so blasé for him it would leave no lasting mark? "Am I not part of you as well?"

"No. I told you I intended to give to you, not take, and I'm a man of my word." He fished her shawl from the tangle of bedclothes and draped it around her shoulders. "Besides, I could not wish for you to surrender the least sliver of your soul to me. You wouldn't find my heart at all comfortable to be on intimate terms with."

"Perhaps you should let me be the judge of that."

John looked away, staring down into the skylight that topped the grand foyer four floors beneath them. A man crossed the space below bearing a single candle. John frowned down at the wandering figure.

"Come." He grasped her elbow. "We need to hurry."

❧

Since there was someone besides them stirring in the great house, John couldn't take Rebecca back to her chamber by the most direct route. They had to stop at every corner and survey the way ahead before he committed them to it. Traveling in silence, they threaded their way through the great house, hand in hand.

When they reached her door, he wished he could say

something to her. Words of love were dancing on his tongue, words he didn't have the right to say to someone as fine as she. Besides, he didn't want to chance being overheard by someone in a nearby room. Instead, he kissed her cheek and hurried away, trying to put some distance between them in case there were any other early risers among the occupants of Somerfield Park.

Someone other than that man with the candle.

It had been difficult for John to see the fellow's features from the vantage point of the roof skylight. The man had moved slowly, stopping to examine objets d'art placed on side tables and running his fingertips over the polished horizontal surfaces as if he were trying to acquaint himself with the place by touch. He was dressed in a dark banyan whose silken folds flowed around his form like water as he moved. It was of obvious quality.

Clearly the man roaming the halls was not a servant.

John hastened to the grand staircase and headed down, breathing a sigh of relief. Rebecca was safe. It didn't matter if he were discovered out of his chamber. He was bloody Lord Hartley, after all. If he wanted to dance naked through every parlor in the house, no one would dare say a word against it.

So who else could wander Somerfield Park by night without purpose and without anyone saying them nay?

John slipped through room after room, looking for the man with the candle. He heard some muttering ahead and followed the sound to a long, high-ceilinged gallery. Row upon row of portraits stared down at him from the canvases, some of them dark with age, some in brighter hues of more recent times.

The man with the candle had stopped before one of them, lifting his light to squint up at the painting. He seemed to be in an earnest whispered conversation with the likeness of a double-chinned fellow whose aristocratic head was topped by a full-bottom powdered wig.

"It's not fair," the man murmured. "You can't expect me to give her up. I can't and I won't."

John drew closer, and when he was about ten paces away, the polished hardwood beneath his foot creaked. The man jerked his gaze to him, wild-eyed.

Now that he was closer, John saw that the man's hair was the same dark honey color as Lord Richard's, but his temples were shot with silver. Still, the resemblance in coloring was striking and that wasn't where the similarity ended. With his fine, straight nose and expressive brown eyes, the man's face might be Richard's, though his square jaw was weighted by another twenty-five or thirty years. John had rarely seen such an obvious stamp of paternity. The man was undoubtedly Richard's father.

And *his* father, he realized.

"Who's there?" Holding the candle before him, Lord Somerset's eyes were so wide, one would have thought he was seeing a ghost. Then he gave himself a small shake. John suspected the older man had been sleepwalking and had only now awakened.

"What are you doing with her eyes?" Lord Somerset demanded.

"Who's eyes?" John asked in surprise.

"Sadie M— No. Mustn't speak of her." The marquess put down his candle on a small side table and wrung his hands. "That's done with. No good thinking on it. What can't be mended shouldn't be kept. Toss it out and think on it nevermore."

John had intended to confront his father, to demand an explanation for his semi-benevolent neglect over the years. Silent rage had been John's companion since his first day at Eton, when one of the boys in a higher form had named him a "penniless bastard" and proceeded to pummel him for something over which he had no control.

Now he wondered if the man he blamed for his troubles could even be made aware of them.

"Are you unwell?" John asked.

"Me? No, I'm fit as a fiddle. I'll live to be a hundred, Dr. Partridge says." His lordship thumped his chest at this bit of bravado. "I simply fell off the roof, they tell me. It happened because… Confound it! I used to remember how it happened. At least I think I remember that I knew once, but now it's… Well, things sort of retreat from one sometimes, don't they?" Lord Somerset paced in a neat little circle. "I mean, first you think you have a thought in your net and then it slips away. Just like a trout, that little thought shakes off the hook and splashes back into the stream."

He stopped pacing and stared up at John, who topped him by a couple of inches.

"You remind me of someone," the marquess said.

"I believe, sir, you were acquainted with my mother." The irony in John's tone was completely lost on Lord Somerset.

"That must be it. Yes. Lovely woman, your mother. Never forget a face. Forgot plenty of other things though." He chuckled self-deprecatingly. Then he pointed an accusatory finger at the portrait of the man in the powdered wig. "He never forgot. Never forgave, either. Not a damned thing."

John came over and stood next to the marquess. "Who is he?"

"Oh, I thought everyone knew. That's my father, Lord Somerset." The current Lord Somerset's voice took on a curiously childish quality. "You won't tell him I was out of bed, will you? He gets frightfully upset if anyone tampers with the schedule. Must do things right. Everything in its place. Everyone in his place. Promise you won't tell."

The smoldering resentment John felt toward his sire began to fizzle out. It was impossible to remain angry with someone whose mind was so disheveled.

"No," John promised solemnly, "I won't tell him."

"Good." The marquess's face split into a smile of unabashed pleasure. "If I don't get any demerits this week, I can ride my pony to Somerset-on-the-Sea on Saturday."

"Perhaps we should see you back to your bed, sir, just to be on the safe side."

"Oh, yes, quite right. Wouldn't do to be caught out of line, would it?" Lord Somerset took a few steps, then stopped and narrowed his eyes at John. "You must be the new footman. What's your name?"

"I'm…John."

"No, the new footman's name is Toby. I remember that distinctly. Hightower claims this new chap's quite a goer. But John…there was something about a John." The marquess thumped the side of his head as if the sudden blow might shake loose a stray memory. "Oh, now I remember. My son's name is John."

"John Fitzhugh Barrett," John supplied as he took up the candle and shepherded the marquess out of the gallery, toward the grand staircase.

"Oh, know him, do you? Haven't met him myself. Can't think why not." Shaking his head, the marquess allowed himself to be led along. "That's a dickens of a thing, not to know one's own son."

"Quite a dickens of a thing." John slowed his pace to match his father's halting steps. Lord Somerset sounded regretful over their relationship now. Why had he not taken action when it might have made a difference?

"Takes his middle name from me, you know. Fitzhugh. My Christian name is Hugh, though no one but Helen and *Maman* ever call me that." He chuckled to himself. "And then only when they're upset with me."

John couldn't be upset with the shattered remains of the man climbing the staircase beside him, but he was frustrated that his pent-up bitterness no longer had a focus. Who could he blame for his childhood if not his father?

No, wait. There was always the dowager. She had been up to her bony shoulders in the scheme to hide John away in Wiltshire. And no doubt now she had her own reasons for bringing him back.

The marquess stopped at the head of the staircase and looked up and down the long dark corridor. "Say, I don't suppose you know which chamber is mine, do you?"

Yesterday afternoon after he left Rebecca in the

garden, John had thoroughly explored the house and learned where everything and everyone was. He had to know, if he was going to spirit her up to the rooftop in secrecy and safety.

"Yes, my lord, I know where your room is."

"Well, that's capital, Toby. Hightower was right. You are a goer!"

John had been elevated from unclaimed bastard to footman in his father's eyes. It wasn't much of a step up. And there likely wouldn't be any more. He doubted Lord Somerset could be made to understand who he was.

His chest constricted. He'd never hear his father claim him as his son.

But he still might glean some information from Lord Somerset. The man knew more than he was aware of and might be coaxed into answers if John could keep him talking.

"You say your son's name is John. Will we be seeing him here at Somerfield Park?"

"Oh, yes, he's on his way, but he's late. Waited for him on the roof till Helen made me come down. Can't think why she was so upset at me being up there."

"You fell off the roof once," John reminded him.

"Oh, quite right. That must be it. Well, can't say as I blame her then, but my son has to come home, you see."

"Why?" John kicked himself for a fool, but something in him hoped to hear his father say that he longed to meet him, that he wanted to ask his forgiveness, that he was sorry for the wasted years, and could they start afresh?

"On account of the hunt," the marquess said as he shuffled along.

John's belly spiraled downward in disappointment. He should have known better. "Oh, you need his help when you entertain the visiting lords."

"Oh, no. We've already set up the blinds and have beaters lined up ready for the shooting. It'll be grand. Always is."

John wondered if everyone in Somerfield Park was dotty. They surely had to be if Lord Somerset was going to be allowed to handle a loaded weapon.

"Then if your son isn't helping you with the annual hunting party, what hunt are you talking about?"

His lordship put a finger to his mouth and made a shushing sound. "*Maman* says we're not to speak of it until it's time."

John's curiosity burned. "That's all right," he assured the marquess. "You can tell me."

"Why, so I can. If one can't trust one's footman, who can one trust? The hunt my son must come home for is the Hartley Hunt."

"The Hartley Hunt?"

"Yes, of course. He's Lord Hartley now, and it's high time he did his duty."

"What duty?"

"Why, to wed and breed a gaggle of sons to ensure the continuation of the line, of course. So *Maman* has invited all the right sorts of young ladies, not a one of them less than an earl's daughter, mind you. One of them will bag him before the season turns." Lord Somerset stopped mid-stride and sighed. "Mark my words. When a woman sets her cap for a man, it's all up with him."

He'd suspected as much, but John swallowed back his indignation at this confirmation that he'd been summoned to Somerfield Park simply to serve as breeding stock. Something in his father's tone suggested he'd recalled a vivid memory, and while it was fresh in Lord Somerset's mind, John wanted to hear about it. "Is that what happened to you? A woman set her cap for you?"

"Yes. She beguiled me," Lord Somerset said.

John was right. The way the older man smiled at the memory convinced him it was clearer than most of what scampered about his father's confused brain.

"I knew I shouldn't," his lordship continued, "but I couldn't take my eyes off her."

"Lady Somerset is a striking woman." During the tea they had shared, his father's wife had impressed John as being equally lovely on the inside.

"Yes, she is, but no, I don't mean Helen. I learned to love her later, after our parents arranged everything. In fact, I loved her so well, we had to rush the wedding a bit." Lord Somerset chuckled. "Shh. Don't tell."

Then his face took on a wistful expression, and John suspected his father was in another time and place entirely.

"When I first saw my Sadie on the stage, her eyes lit with fire, her voice… Lord, the woman had a voice that would tempt angels."

Lord Somerset was speaking of John's mother. So the old man did remember her. John remembered the sound of her voice as well. She used to sing to him sometimes, low and comforting.

"I knew I shouldn't, but I couldn't help myself. I

had to have her. Father was furious. If he could have disowned me, he would have." The marquess hung his head. "Then, as it turned out, she didn't want me either. Father was even more furious."

"What did you do?" John wanted desperately to know how things fell out between his parents. Why his mother had decided not to remain with a marquess was a mystery beyond his ability to unravel.

"I think…I think I need my valet," Lord Somerset said, abruptly changing the subject. "I say, Toby, nip off and find Mr. Cope, will you?"

"Why do you need your valet, my lord?"

"Well, if I'm going to bed, I need my pajamas, don't I?"

"You're already wearing your banyan."

The marquess looked down at himself and laughed. "So I am. You are a sharp one, Toby. Hightower said so. Don't know what Somerfield Park would do without him. That butler is always right."

The marquess went into his bedchamber, leaving John in the dark corridor. Then he walked the short distance down the same hall to the room he'd been allotted.

It was a fine chamber, as befitted the heir to Somerset, firmly central in the Family wing of this floor. To all appearances, he was being welcomed by the Barretts with open arms.

Except now his father had let slip the reason he'd been sought out in London and dragged back to the country. They didn't want him. Not really. His grandmother intended to use him solely to further the Barrett lineage. No doubt once John begat an heir of his own on an approved earl's daughter, his usefulness to the Family would be over. They could relegate him, as the unorthodox heir, to the background and lavish their attention on the next marquess in the making, biding their time until that nameless one could take his rightful place.

And it seemed his future wife's pedigree was important enough that the dowager had decreed she must be at least the daughter of an earl.

Rebecca's father was a threadbare baron.

He shoved that thought away. Even if she met the dowager's requirements, John wouldn't saddle her with his mess. She was too fine, too innocent, too open a person to be burdened with a shut-off fellow like him.

As his hand closed over the doorknob to his chamber, an idea to thwart the dowager's plans for him, and have a bit of fun while he was at it, popped into his head.

"So she wants to see me with an earl's daughter, does she?" he murmured. "As luck would have it, I have one in mind."

Eighteen

When I had my coming out, nothing could separate me from my bosom friends, with one notable exception. If a match with an eligible party was in the offing, all bonds of sisterhood were strained to the breaking point.

—Phillippa, the Dowager Marchioness of Somerset

"THANK HEAVEN SOMERFIELD PARK ISN'T TOO TERRIBLY distant from London. Else I couldn't bear all the sheep." Lady Winifred Chalcroft removed the charming little capote from her blond head and settled on the foot of Rebecca's bed. With un-Freddie-like attention to her wardrobe, she smoothed out her column gown's sheer overlay to ensure it didn't wrinkle. "There were simply endless flocks of them on the way here. Honestly, how can anyone enjoy rusticating in the country when there are museums and plays and lectures to be had in the city?"

Remembered pleasure from her time on the roof with John rushed back into Rebecca. She bit her lower lip, trying to avoid a blush. "Country life has its charms."

"No doubt, if one is content to be a cabbage. I, for

one, prefer to improve my mind. Gallivanting along the hedgerows, trying to avoid animal droppings, is not my idea of time well spent."

"I believe there is an extensive library here."

"Well, that's a mercy." Freddie narrowed her eyes at Rebecca. "You look terribly wan, and there are dark smudges under your eyes. Are you unwell?"

Rebecca pressed her palms to her cheeks. With all the young ladies descending upon Somerfield Park, she had to be in her best looks. "No, I'm fine. I just didn't get much sleep last night."

"Oh?"

"I was on the roof for a meteor shower."

"That's right. The Leonids. Well, where are your notes? Did you time the event? How many meteorites did you observe per hour?"

Nothing could have been farther from her thoughts at the time the stars began to fall. "I'm afraid I only observed the phenomenon."

"What? A cow could merely watch the Leonids shower, Rebecca. Where's your sense of scientific inquiry?" Freddie shook her head. "Well, never mind. The meteorites should return tonight, and I'll make a detailed record. The roof should be a good vantage point, eh? Perhaps this won't be a wholly wasted fortnight after all."

"Does that mean you've given up winning Lord Hartley?" Rebecca wandered to the window and looked down on yet another coach pulling up the long drive. Once it stopped, the butler and footman leaped to open the carriage door for the visiting dignitaries and handed them out with aplomb.

"Oh no," Freddie said, waving a hand airily. "Father is adamant that I give becoming Lady Hartley my best, and you know when I set my mind to something, I rarely fail."

Rebecca smiled at Freddie's roundabout way of patting her own back. Then she spared a moment to pity John. All day, carriages like the one below had been arriving at the house's great double front doors. Some of the finest families in the kingdom spilled from those elegant equipages. If all the young ladies who alighted from those carriages were of the same mind as Freddie, Lord Hartley would have to step lively to evade capture by one of them.

But surely after last night, the fact that these well-born ladies were after him wouldn't be enough to turn his head. She and John had formed a bond in shared pleasure. Rebecca was a part of him now, no matter what he had to say on the subject.

A soft rap came at the door.

"That'll be Olive with your gown," Freddie said, then raised her voice. "Come."

"My gown?" Rebecca said as Freddie's maid bustled in bearing a smallish valise and a largish hatbox.

"Yes, you silly goose, have you forgotten already? I had that pale pink one of mine resized for you." Freddie turned to her maid. "Step lively, Olive. It'll be wrinkled enough without your shilly-shallying."

Since Rebecca had never seen Olive move at less than a flustered trot, she didn't think the maid could be accused of shillying a single shally.

"I'm sure it will be fine," Rebecca said. Beggars couldn't be choosers, in any case.

Olive shot her a shy smile and quickly unpacked the gown, spreading it on the bed and smoothing her palms over the pink silk. It was an ethereal watery color and reminded Rebecca of the eastern sky as night retreated, before the heat of the sun warmed the heavens to a rosier hue.

The color would have washed Freddie out completely, since she was pale to begin with, but it would be perfect for Rebecca, with her chestnut hair and cool-green eyes.

"Oh my," she whispered in awe. "This gown is far better than fine. It might have been made for me."

"Well, don't stand there gaping like a codfish, Rebecca." The smile in Freddie's voice mitigated her harsh words. She was clearly pleased by Rebecca's reaction. "Try it on."

Olive's deft hands helped her out of her thrice-turned green day gown and into the pink silk. Freddie's measurements proved true. The bodice was snug, the décolletage daring but not vulgar. The empire waist rose to the exactly right place. The skirt portion flowed over Rebecca's hips like water and spilled onto the polished floor.

"Oh, that train is *le dernier cri*," Freddie exclaimed, clapping her hands over the foot and a half of silk and lace that trailed Rebecca. The maid shot her a questioning look. "It's something of a pun, Olive. *Le dernier cri* literally means 'the last word.' Won't Rebecca's derriere give everyone reason to watch her walk away with a train accentuating her charms like that?"

"It does make me feel like a princess," Rebecca said happily, as she turned this way and that before the long looking glass in the corner. She couldn't wait to see John's expression when he saw her in it.

Freddie choked on a laugh. "Not quite a princess, my dear. Let's not succumb to delusions of grandeur, but you'll do. Indeed, you will." She nodded approvingly. "Have you any jewels?"

Long ago, her father had pawned every piece of jewelry Rebecca had inherited from her grandmother on her mother's side. It was supposed to form part of her dowry, but nothing was safe from the requirements of a debt of honor.

"I didn't think to bring anything but ribbons to the country," she lied. She'd always rather Freddie think her above such fripperies than unable to have them.

"Well, a ribbon at your neck might be fine for day wear, but it won't do for that gown," Freddie said. "Olive, fetch my freshwater pearls. They're simple but elegant. They should do nicely. Now slip on your gloves. You have some white satin, don't you? Good. Oh, wait till you see the cunning little headdress I had my milliner work up for you."

"You didn't have to do that." She'd never be able to repay her friend's generosity.

"Pish! I wanted to."

Freddie dove into the hatbox and came up with a fetching confection of lace and seed pearls. An ostrich feather curled around the headpiece, and once Freddie positioned it correctly, the plume nodded above Rebecca's head.

The two girls gazed into the mirror together. Rebecca couldn't say which of them looked more pleased by the results of her transformation. Freddie might be brash and abrupt sometimes, but she had a tender heart and a generous spirit.

"You're so good to me," Rebecca said, giving her an impulsive hug.

Freddie waved her away. "Piffle. What are friends for?"

A prickle of guilt niggled at Rebecca. Last night, she'd been all tangled up with the man her friend had set her cap for. She hadn't felt disloyal to Freddie at the time. After all, Freddie hardly knew John, and it wasn't as if her heart was engaged. But now, she and Freddie—and every other woman of marriageable age visiting the great house—would be in direct competition for his favor.

She ought to step aside for Freddie. After all, Rebecca wasn't really up to scratch. She ought to put her efforts into helping her friend's cause. John trusted her. She could do a great deal to improve Freddie's chances.

Her chest ached at the thought. When she and John were together, the difference in their stations didn't matter a jot. She knew things about him, personal things like his astounding confession about how he really felt about having been with too many women. She knew about his boyhood hurts. She didn't think he'd ever tell anyone else about that. She longed to ease the bitterness he felt toward his family. It was eating him up, and she hurt right along with him.

Which of the other wellborn daughters coming to Somerfield Park were interested in John for himself instead of the marchioness's coronet he could offer them?

When Rebecca looked up at the night sky this evening, she wondered if she could find a world where things like rank and wealth didn't matter. Where was the place where love trumped all?

"Oh! I brought the slippers to match too." Freddie began pawing through the valise and hatbox looking for them. "Lovely little beaded things. Your feet may be a tad bigger than mine, but even so, I should think you'll do well with them. It's not as if your dance card will be completely full in any case. Not with all the higher-ranking debutantes available."

Freddie's words made tears press against the backs of Rebecca's eyes. Her friend didn't mean to be cruel, she reminded herself. Freddie was simply devoted to the truth, however unpalatable it might be. In a ballroom filled with earls' daughters, Rebecca would naturally be a wallflower.

But I'll be an extremely well-turned-out wallflower, she told herself.

While Freddie continued to mutter about the whereabouts of those slippers, Rebecca wandered to the window and looked down at yet another coach arriving. A strikingly beautiful woman stepped down from a smart equipage.

Freddie's fashionably blond tresses were so fair as to be almost white. This lady's long curls glinted golden in the sunlight as they escaped her flattering scoop-shaped capote. Her gown and matching pelisse were an eye-catching poppy red, a hue few wellborn misses would dare. However, instead of overpowering this woman, the flamboyant shade only accentuated her natural beauty. From her dainty satin half boot to the *coquelicot* ribbon on her bonnet that matched her outrageously bright gown, she was dressed in the first stare of fashion, despite the loud color.

But her bold fashion sense wasn't what made Rebecca's heart sink to her pelvic floor.

It was the fact that the footman didn't help her alight from the carriage. Neither did Somerfield Park's butler.

John Fitzhugh Barrett stepped lively to hand her down himself.

❧

Lord Somerset wasn't available to greet his guests for the hunt. Lady Somerset had stepped in to welcome the visiting lords and ladies with her typical unruffled dignity. However, by midafternoon it was clear she was flagging, so John had asked that he be allowed to take her place.

"Thank you, Lord Hartley. What a thoughtful and brilliant idea," she said. "I confess to being all in, and there are a number of things I must tend to before our first dinner this evening. I wonder if Richard might join you to make introductions."

His half brother was called away from poring over the estate's ledgers to greet the *bon ton* as they alighted from their equipages. To his credit, Richard introduced John as "my brother, Lord Hartley" and not as "the upstart usurper who stole my birthright." John doubted *he'd* have been half so gracious if their places were reversed.

It was a measure of the prestige of Somerset that the lords to whom he was presented did not shun him as the denizens of White's had when he was on his own in London. Instead of being cut by the ladies, John lost count of the number of giggling debutantes who made dipping curtsies to him or flirted with him from behind their fans on their way into Somerfield Park.

Clearly, the "Hartley Hunt" was in full force.

After all the lumbering coaches, John was surprised to see a single fellow come whipping down the tree-lined lane driving an open gig meant for speed instead of comfortable travel. Richard's face split in a smile as he stepped forward to greet the gentleman, whose sandy hair was disheveled and whose waistcoat was spattered with mud from flying over the country roads.

"In a hurry to meet the Grim Reaper, are you, Seymour?" Richard said.

"Not at all. This gig is devilishly fast, but perfectly safe."

"It's not the gig I'm worried about," Richard said. "It's your driving."

"I'm careful enough." Seymour grinned. "I'm trying to save myself for your sister Petra. She's offered to end me more than once. I'd hate to deprive her of the pleasure."

Then the fellow turned to John. "And you must be the man who rescued my friend from a lifetime of boredom in the House of Lords. Lawrence Seymour, your servant, sir," he said to John as he tossed the reins of his high-stepping filly to a waiting hostler. "Didn't that sound nice? I'm actually philosophically opposed to being treated as a servant on any level."

John shook Seymour's hand and decided he liked Richard's friend.

"I'll see Seymour to his room," Richard said. "It'll

be my last chance to remind him that meddling with any of our sisters will require us to nail him to a stump and set the stump on fire."

John laughed as they headed into the house. "Our sisters," Richard had said. "Us." John wished it were true. All his life, he'd wished for a father and a family. He'd never been part of an "us." With Lord Somerset's growing dementia, the chance to be recognized as a son was slipping away. Was it possible that John might have a half brother and sisters who were truly willing to make him part of their circle?

He pushed the wish aside as childish. Rebecca was right. He wasn't six years old anymore.

Another coach broke free of the tree-lined drive. John recognized the Endicott crest embossed on the side. Family was a dicey proposition. He could choose his friends, and they were all finally here. He pushed past Mr. Hightower and the footman to open the coach once it rolled to a stop.

"Hartley, you've grown even more handsome since I saw you last. Do you suppose there's something to wholesome country air? Gives me hope for poor Smalley and Pitcairn." Lady Chloe Endicott's red cherry of a mouth stretched into a broad smile. John brought her hand to his lips for a correct kiss. "How glad I am to see you."

"Not half as glad as I am to see you, my lady," he said. "How was your journey?"

"Crowded."

Blackwood climbed down from the carriage behind her, followed swiftly by Pitcairn and Smalley. Lady Chloe's saucy French maid scrambled down from her perch beside the driver and, in heavily accented English, stridently instructed the Somerfield Park footman on the proper unloading of her mistress's trunks and accoutrements.

"Crowded, but lively," Lady Chloe amended. "You know how I loathe being alone. The gentlemen's conversation made the miles pass by more quickly."

"We'd have done more than bump our gums," Smalley said, his affected country accent finally finding an appropriate venue, "but Lady Chloe don't allow no cards in the coach."

"Just as well," Blackwood said with a yawn. "I'd have cleaned out you and Pitcairn before we reached Tincross Bottom, and then you'd have nothing else to lose the whole time we're here."

"Nonsense," Lady Chloe said. "All three of you would have been left with nothing but your drawers if we'd gambled away the time and you know it, Blackwood. I can always tell when you're bluffing."

"Why is that, I wonder?"

"Because, my dear Lord Blackwood, it's the only time your gaze is not glued to my décolletage." She laughed. It wasn't the merry tinkle of a green girl, but the full-throated laughter of a woman who was sure of her own femininity and enjoyed flaunting it everywhere she went.

Mr. Hightower, who'd been trying to appear as if he weren't hanging on every word, coughed to cover his shock as his bushy brows shot skyward. The staid butler would only be the first to be scandalized by his friends, John suspected. He was beginning to look forward to this house party very much indeed.

"Mr. Hightower, please see Viscount Blackwood and Messrs. Smalley and Pitcairn to their rooms."

"And the lady, my lord?"

"I'll escort Lady Chloe to her chamber after we have a spot of tea in the parlor. She and I have a few things to discuss. See to it, Mr. Hightower."

"Very good, my lord. Toby." Hightower snapped his fingers at the footman. "Step lively and see to his lordship's tea. This way, gentlemen, if you'll be pleased to follow me."

Whatever his private thoughts about the new arrivals, Hightower was quick to do John's bidding. Sometimes, it was very good to be Lord Hartley.

His friends followed the butler, cracking jokes and warning John not to let Lady Chloe pull out a deck of cards in the parlor unless he wanted to end up in his drawers. Chloe took his arm and smiled up at him warmly.

"They're right, you know. If we cut a deck, I'd see you in your unmentionables," she assured him.

"That's why I won't play cards with you."

"Oh, Hartley, you don't know what you're missing. I'd make certain it was great fun for you, even if you lose."

"Not if, *when* I lose," he admitted. "You are a masterful poque player."

Lady Chloe was also gracious when it suited her, and she deftly turned the conversation to a more socially acceptable topic. She chatted quite properly about the beauties of the Somerset countryside as they strolled at a leisurely pace up to the first-floor parlor, where tea was waiting for them. Lady Chloe nodded to the maid who brought the hurriedly assembled tray.

"I'll pour out myself. You may go," Chloe told the girl. She took her seat on the striped settee as if she were mistress of the place and began arranging the teapot, cups, and saucers to suit her. Her upbringing as the daughter of an earl showed in every graceful movement.

"Thank you, Sarah." John was making it his business to learn the servants' names as quickly as he could. The girl rewarded him with a toothsome smile, bobbed a deep curtsy, and then left, pulling the door closed behind her.

"I freely confess it, Hartley. You have me on pins," Lady Chloe said as she poured the tea into egg-shell thin cups. "What is this mysterious tête-à-tête about?"

"Well, I hope—"

"One lump or two?"

Why did women always try to foist sugar on him? "None. I'm a simple man."

"That I seriously doubt. The quiet ones are always the most complicated. And the most worth unraveling." She handed him a steaming cup and prepared her own with a generous dollop of milk and one lump of sugar. "Tell me, Hartley. What's afoot here?"

His plan had seemed a good one when the idea first came to him. Now he wondered if her role in the game he intended to play would offend her. Still, she was his friend. If she wouldn't help him, who would?

John shared his scheme, and, along with it, his hopes and a piece of his twisted soul. She listened without interruption. When he finished, she leaned back on the settee, teacup halfway to her artfully rouged lips. Chloe peered at him through half-closed eyes, considering him like a tabby studying a mouse hole.

He had no idea what was racing around in her pretty little head. No wonder she was a terror at a poque table.

Lady Chloe smiled at him, her teeth stark white against her red lips. It struck him as a feral smile. Then the smile moved up to crinkle the corners of her eyes, and the predatory impression vanished. His heart-stopping, sleepless night on the roof with Rebecca was making his imagination run rampant.

"Well, what do you think? I can't do this without you, my lady," he asked. "Will you help me?"

"Why not?" She ran the tip of her tongue over her lower lip. "It'll be fun."

Nineteen

I have always subscribed to the adage "One must begin as one means to continue." Fortunately, my grandson Hartley has been given a rare opportunity to begin a second time.

—Phillippa, the Dowager Marchioness of Somerset

JOHN CAME DOWN THE GRAND STAIRCASE WITH A SPRING in his step. For the first time since he had learned he was Lord Hartley, he finally felt in control of his destiny. He had a plan. He wasn't waiting for things to happen to him anymore. He was acting instead of reacting.

He intended to make a memorable impression on the Upper Crust tonight. Mr. Porter had moved heaven and earth to make sure he looked every inch the marquess's heir. The valet nearly had a case of the vapors when John called for his striking pink waistcoat. Porter seemed beyond grateful when John relented and allowed himself to be dressed in elegant, Brummell–esque simplicity.

John caught his reflection in the tail of his eye as he passed the tall, decorative mirror on one of the grand staircase's landings.

Porter was right.

He couldn't look more aristocratic if he'd been born with the proverbial silver spoon in his mouth. So much the better for his plan.

He only wished he'd been able to speak to Rebecca about it first. Perhaps if he arrived in the drawing room early enough, he'd be able to pull her aside for a few moments. When he reached the foot of the staircase, he quickened his pace.

"Hartley, a word in your ear before we go through to our guests." From the shadows in the corner of the foyer, the dowager's voice stopped him in his tracks. They had yet to speak more than a few words to each other, and John was content to keep it that way. However, good manners required him to stop and acknowledge her with a shallow bow. He wouldn't think of her as his grandmother, but he couldn't deny she had been a marchioness.

"My lady."

"I had wished to speak with you earlier, but you have been avoiding me."

"You're mistaken." Avoiding her would require him to be aware of her. Since she had blithely dismissed him for most of his life, he was merely returning the favor.

"Be that as it may…" Leaning heavily on her ivory-headed cane, Lady Somerset the elder stepped from where she'd obviously been lying in wait for him. "My, you're quite…presentable, aren't you?"

"You needn't sound so surprised."

"I'm not. It is to be quite expected." Pulling out her lorgnette and holding it to one eye, she circled him slowly, making a thorough inspection. "After all, you are a Barrett."

"How gracious of you to finally come to that conclusion," he said, his tone biting.

"You might give me a bit of credit." She dropped the lorgnette, letting it dangle on its silver chain, and whipped out her fan, fluttering it furiously before herself. "When one is not in full possession of the facts of a matter, it is easy to make a lapse in judgment."

"A lapse in judgment," John repeated woodenly. "Is that how you explain relegating your own flesh and blood to obscurity?"

"I did not know—"

"That I was legitimate. Yes, I'll give you that. However, you didn't doubt I was your son's progeny. Otherwise, you wouldn't have provided for the Coopersmiths to foster me. I'd have been cast out on the streets to fend for myself."

The dowager's lips tightened into a thin line, like the mark of a spade on an old potato. "How heartless you must think me."

"Madam, I try very hard not to think of you at all."

When he would have moved on, she lifted a hand to stay him. "My husband had died a scant month before Hugh was expected to wed Lady Helen. That match was his final wish. Once I was made aware of you, there were so many decisions clamoring at me and no time to make them. Would you have had me upend my husband's last act as marquess and overturn my son's happiness for a child we all believed was…"

A bastard was left hanging unsaid. John let it echo in the silence.

"Nevertheless," the dowager plowed on, "I wish to express…that is to say, regret is not a very fruitful emotion, but I'd be lying if I said I didn't have any."

John blinked in surprise. It was almost an apology.

"However, the past is the past and has little bearing on our present. You must realize now that everything which has been done was for your benefit."

"I fail to see how growing up as an unacknowledged bastard redounded to my benefit."

"You are very bitter. I understand that."

"How gratifying to be understood."

He took a step in the direction of the drawing room, but the dowager put a bejeweled hand on his forearm to stop him.

"You haven't let me finish."

"Trust me, madam, as far as I'm concerned, you are finished." He shook her off and started to walk away.

"John Fitzhugh Barrett!"

He stopped and rounded on her. "I don't believe I've given you leave to address me by my Christian name."

"I don't believe I asked your leave, you impertinent pup." She glared up at him. "I call all my grandchildren by their given names. Why should you be any different? Now come back here this instant and give me your arm. We'll go through together. You may be the handsomest devil in Somerfield Park this evening, and the most eligible bachelor in Christendom, but even you will benefit from having a veritable institution at your side. And trust me, I am that."

John hesitated, wrestling with himself. Part of him wanted to remain aloof and untouchable.

Don't let anyone close and you won't give them a chance to turn on you.

Another part wanted to offer his arm to this woman who considered herself his grandmother enough to scold him and call him by name.

The six-year-old who still lived inside him won.

"That's better," the dowager said as she slipped her bony knuckles around his elbow. "I knew you were quick-minded."

"This is when good form would oblige me to say I come from good stock."

"Oh, my dear boy, one is never obliged to acknowledge the obvious." She chuckled at her own wit. "Now, this evening, all you have to do is smile and make polite conversation. Think no more upon your past and no one else will either."

That would be easier said than done.

They paused at the drawing room door, and she placed a slightly trembling hand on his chest. "The weight of the entire family is behind you, John. This night, you can do no wrong."

Want to bet? he thought, still stubbornly set on implementing his plan. *This changes nothing.*

The door before them swung open as if by magic.

"Sit here, Mother, and I'll see if the footman will fetch you something to drink." Rebecca helped Lady Kearsey into a chair beside the cheery drawing room fire. The room was so full of glittering people engaged in less-than-glittering small talk, Rebecca was fortunate to find an empty place for her mother to sit. Her parents had arrived that afternoon, along with all the other guests, but Rebecca hadn't seen them until now.

"Oh, no, dear," her mother said breathlessly. The blue vein at her temple showed clearly through alabaster skin. "Don't make a fuss. I'll be fine until we go through to dinner."

"I'm sure you'll start to feel better here in the country, my dear," Rebecca's father said solicitously. "The fresh air alone is better than a tonic."

"Undoubtedly, you're right," Lady Kearsey said with typical agreeableness. She'd have said the same thing if Lord Kearsey had announced that standing on her head would have a beneficial effect. Sometimes Rebecca wondered if her mother had made a bargain with God that He'd allow her to remain on earth so long as she was amenable to all and a burden to none.

Rebecca's father leaned down and whispered for their ears alone. "And our pockets might benefit from this country excursion as well. I overheard Lord Blackwood talking about a poque game later."

"Oh, Father." Rebecca didn't feel the need to whisper. She loved her father, but the lure of a deck of cards was as much a sickness as her mother's consumption. "Please don't."

Lord Kearsey narrowed his eyes at her. "Daughter, because I'm so pleased you provided us with an entry into this little gathering, I'm going to pretend I didn't hear the censure in your tone. It is not becoming for a daughter to reprimand her father."

It's not becoming for a father to need one leaped to the tip of her tongue, but she bit it back. She didn't know what he'd have to gamble with, in any case. She didn't have any more jewelry for him to pawn.

Rebecca was wearing only an ecru-colored ribbon at her throat to compliment the off-white muslin that was her best remaining gown. She'd thought the embroidered bodice exceptionally fine until she saw some of the other ensembles parading around the Somerfield Park drawing room. She'd never seen so much silk and satin in one place, so many furbelows and flounces. It was as if fashion plates had come to life and were on parade.

She heartily wished she still had the blue gown that had been ruined in that boxing crib in Whitechapel. Try as she might, it was beyond redemption and had to be cut up to be pieced into a quilt her mother was working.

"Rebecca, dearest, go on," her mother said, mistaking her intent gaze at the other visitors for a desire to engage them in conversation. "Please don't trouble yourself with us tonight. Your friend Lady Winifred seems to be trying to catch your eye."

Freddie was practicing her fan language. She touched her ivory and silk accessory along the edge repeatedly, while shooting pointed looks in their direction. As nearly as Rebecca could recall, that gesture meant either "You are cruel," or "I'm married. Go away," or "I want to talk to you."

When the plain sense makes sense, seek no other sense. "I'm guessing she wants to talk to me."

"Have a lovely evening, and we'll chat later. Perhaps tomorrow afternoon…" Her mother's voice drifted into a breathy whisper.

Rebecca gave her a peck on the cheek and started across the room to Freddie. At least as long as her mother was up and about, her father was bound to behave himself. It was only once Lady Kearsey was out of sight that he'd be tempted to ruin by a deck of cards. Perhaps she could mention something to John about keeping him occupied once the gentlemen separated from the ladies.

"You look lovely tonight," she told Freddie.

"I should. Father spent the earth on my wardrobe for this house party." Freddie's gown was white with a small print pattern overlaid in the color of a robin's egg on lovely watered silk. A full two inches of matching ribbon and lace from her petticoat showed at the hem. "When this is all over, I'm thinking of donating every stitch of new clothing to the Society for the Improvement of Morals among the Lower Classes. They are doing such important work with the prostitutes in Whitechapel. Correct clothing leads to correct morals, you know."

Rebecca tried to imagine one of the slatternly wretches she'd seen during her brief foray into that district in one of Freddie's castoffs. Chances were the unfortunate recipient of Freddie's largess would simply sell the dress on the second-hand clothing market. The proceeds would probably feed her for a month.

"Yes, indeed, one can tell a good deal about a person from their wardrobe," Freddie went on. "For instance, do you know who that woman is over there? The one who's draped herself so artfully over the chaise longue?"

It was the woman John had handed down from

the carriage earlier today. Now, instead of the gaudy red dress, she was wearing a shocking shade of yellow called *jonquil*. No flower ever bared so much cleavage.

"No, I don't know her." *But John evidently does.*

"She's Lady Chloe Endicott, the one who styles herself the Merry Widow."

"Goodness, that's cold."

"But unfailingly accurate," Freddie said. "The woman has buried no less than four husbands, all of them under suspicious circumstances, and rumor has it that she's looking for number five!"

"She's no debutante." Rebecca noted that every other young lady in the room was flanked by doting parents. "She doesn't seem to fit in with the rest of the party. I wonder why she's here."

"Rumor has it Lord Hartley invited her himself. I greatly fear his lordship is living down to my expectations if he keeps company with her sort."

"Perhaps he feels sorry for her," Rebecca said, grasping at an innocent reason John might have for consorting with the lady. "After all, she is a widow."

Freddie cast her a pitying look, as if she were a not-quite-bright child. "We may hope Lord Hartley notices that Lady Chloe is decidedly long in the tooth."

All the other young women in the room were close to Rebecca and Freddie's age of twenty. Some even younger. While Lady Chloe was still a strikingly handsome woman, she'd never see thirty again.

"That doesn't seem to be a deterrent to the gentlemen." In addition to the three fellows Rebecca recognized as John's companions from the boxing crib fiasco, there were several other men hovering around Lady Chloe. She was holding court, obviously relating a funny tale, for they all threw back their heads and laughed.

"Not to mention that association with Lady Chloe is not conducive to a man's longevity," Freddie continued uncharitably.

"If you know these things about her, surely Joh— Lord Hartley knows them too."

"Yes, but what a man knows with his head doesn't always sway what he knows with his other less contemplative parts." Freddie cast her a suggestive look.

"Freddie, that's positively wicked." The solid feel of John pressed against her hip as he initiated her in delight rushed back into her. Rebecca knew firsthand about those "less than contemplative parts." Where had Freddie come by such knowledge? "I'm surprised at you."

"Nevertheless," Freddie said with a sniff, "it's true."

"Well, I'm not one to believe every bit of gossip I hear. Someone may spread unpleasant lies about me sometime, and I wouldn't want others to believe it without giving me a chance to convince them otherwise," Rebecca said. "Let's go meet her."

"Oh, no, we mustn't. Scandal taints everyone within its reach, and that woman fairly reeks of it."

If John invited the lady to Somerfield Park, Rebecca wanted to know why. "If you won't go with me, I'll go by myself," she said and started across the room.

Twenty

If one catches me smiling when there's nothing amusing afoot, it's because I'm contemplating doing something I really ought not. However, if I'm chuckling under my breath, it means I've already done it.

—Lady Chloe Endicott

Rebecca wasn't sure how to approach Lady Chloe. They hadn't been properly introduced, and she didn't know any of the respectable gentlemen surrounding the lady who might be relied upon to do the honors. Lord Blackwood and his toadies didn't count. It occurred to Rebecca that she was about to commit the same social faux pas that John had when he spoke to her in the museum without benefit of introduction.

Rebecca hoped Lady Chloe would be kinder to her than she and Freddie had been to John. The lady's smile was encouraging.

Rebecca dipped in a shallow curtsy. "How do you do?"

"According to the gossips, I do entirely too well

and far too often." The lady rose to her feet and dropped a correct curtsy in return. "I'm Lady Chloe Endicott, but then you probably know that."

Rebecca repeated her curtsy, still not sure what to say. All the guidebooks for correct behavior she and Freddie patterned their lives after had neglected to give instruction on how to make the acquaintance of a self-admitted merry widow.

"You're very brave, whoever you are," Lady Chloe said. "None of the other women here would spit on me if I were on fire."

"Only because spitting is not the done thing," popped into Rebecca's head and out her mouth before she could censor herself. Had her night on the roof with John removed all her inhibitions?

The lady laughed. Whatever else she was, Lady Chloe didn't take herself too seriously, and she harbored no illusions about her welcome in this company. Rebecca admired her pluck.

"My lady," Lord Blackwood said, his voice as smooth as oil, "may I present Miss Rebecca Kearsey?"

"Oh, so you're Miss Kearsey, she of the boxing crib fame. It must have been wildly exciting to have two men exchange blows over you. I confess it sounds quite…exhilarating." Lady Chloe took Rebecca's arm and started a slow walk around the room with her, seemingly oblivious to the way heads turned to follow their progress.

"Perhaps it would have been, had I not been tied up at the time," Rebecca said in a whisper. From the corner of her eye, she saw Freddie's jaw drop in horrified fascination. Even if her conversation with Lady

Chloe couldn't be overheard, this little promenade firmly equated Rebecca with the infamous Merry Widow in the minds of the other guests.

"Really? I'd have thought being tied up would add something to the experience," she said with a throaty laugh. "Despite your naiveté, I do believe you and I shall get on swimmingly, Miss Kearsey. Lord Hartley has told me so much about you."

"How very surprising." Rebecca's cheeks heated as she wondered what John might have told this wholly unorthodox woman—or even why he was connected with her in the first place. "He neglected to mention you."

"Oh, my dear, you should consider that a good sign. Clearly, he had other things on his mind when he was with you if he failed to drop my name." Her very red mouth tilted in a crooked smile. "But a word of advice. Never believe a man will tell you about other women in his circle of acquaintance. My husbands never did, God rest them. At least, one may hope they're at rest now. I certainly gave them little enough of that while they were alive. But back to your dealings with gentlemen. May I advise lowered expectations where they are concerned? It reduces disappointment, you know."

Rebecca had been prepared to like Lady Chloe for John's sake, since she must be a friend of his. But the lady's words sounded more like a warning than friendly advice.

"And yet expectation seems to be the watchword for this house party," Rebecca said. "What is yours, if I may ask?"

She cast a smile of promise to the group of gentlemen she'd recently abandoned to walk with Rebecca. "Why, the same as every other unattached woman here—to find a husband, of course."

The door to the drawing room opened slowly and Lord Hartley entered with the dowager marchioness on his arm. Framed in the doorway, the two of them were dazzling. A net of gems was set in the dowager's iron-gray coiffure. More winked at her wattled throat and wrists. John needed no jewels to draw every eye in the room. His dark good looks were devastating enough when he'd been in nothing but his shirtsleeves in that boxing crib. In full dress, he made Rebecca's mouth go dry.

"The Most Honorable Phillippa, the Dowager Marchioness of Somerset," Mr. Hightower intoned from his place beside the open door. "And the Right Honorable Earl of Hartley."

Rebecca and her family had been announced in a similar way, but the room hadn't gone still while the butler called out their names and honors, such as they were. Now, she'd have wagered she would have been able to hear a mouse hiccup behind the wall, if any dared invade so grand a place as Somerfield Park.

John didn't catch her eye or even look for her particularly. He and his grandmother moved toward the first group of guests nearest the door. Conversations resumed around the room, the low drone of an agitated hive.

"The man of the hour," Lady Chloe said under her breath. "Perhaps you'd do well to return to your family and friends, Miss Kearsey, to wait upon his lordship to acknowledge you. If you've any goodwill built up with the dowager, it will dissipate quickly once she sees you with me."

"Perhaps you give people too little credit. You might be surprised at who will befriend you."

"With my reputation?"

"For good or ill, reputations aren't always warranted. A wise person makes their own judgment. But you're not giving them an opportunity if you push them away at the outset," Rebecca said. "Lord Hartley has the same habit. He rejects others before they have the chance to reject him."

"Astute as well as pretty. It's clear you haven't rejected him. No wonder he likes you." The lady cast a sidelong glance at Rebecca that made her feel she was being hoisted into a cosmic scale of some sort. Chloe's arched brow said Rebecca hadn't been found wanting. "I hope we'll have the opportunity to become better acquainted."

"Depend upon on it." Rebecca dropped a quick curtsy and left Lady Chloe to rejoin her parents by the fire before John and his grandmother worked their way around the room to them.

No wonder he likes you.

Lady Chloe's words echoed in her mind. Rebecca still wasn't sure if the outcast lady was going to be a friend or a foe, but she was grateful for her words.

He likes me.

After their torrent of kisses, after the world-shifting things John had done with her on the roof, after watching the stars fall together, Rebecca hoped for more than mere liking. But with a man like John, who didn't give his trust easily, who walked warily around anything so ephemeral as a feeling, liking was at least a start.

"I don't see Lord and Lady Somerset here," Lady Kearsey said when Rebecca perched on the arm of her mother's chair.

"Because his lordship is unwell, I believe they are already seated in the dining room," Lord Kearsey said. "Perhaps we ought to have asked for the same consideration for you, my love. I know how it tires you to walk, and it's a long promenade to the dining room from here."

"I don't wish to be singled out for special treatment," her mother said. "I'll be fine."

Lady Kearsey would be red-faced and blown with effort after walking to the dining room, but she wouldn't complain. Ignoring her symptoms was her way of coping with her disease. Rebecca wondered if her father's suggestion that they be seated ahead of the rest of the party was motivated by concern for his wife's condition or if the opportunity to have private speech with the marquess and his marchioness before the other guests arrived in the dining room was the bigger draw.

"Here they come, Rebecca," her father whispered when the dowager and John finally headed their way. "Turn on the charm, girl."

All things being equal, compared to the other wellborn ladies in the room who had the family connections and fat dowries to dangle before Lord Hartley, Rebecca had no chance of charming the new earl. But all things were not equal.

John liked her.

If last night was any indication, he liked her very much.

⤫

John had behaved himself as he squired the dowager around the room. They still weren't on the best of terms, but the ice had been broken between them. Whatever her culpability in the pain of his child-hood, he wasn't likely to get more of an apology than she'd already condescended to give. As much distance as she'd given him as a boy, she seemed to be trying to make up for lost time by actively trying to shape his adulthood.

She'd find him far less malleable now.

However, the dowager wouldn't be able to fault his performance at the moment. He greeted each of his guests with the gravity of his station. He even let Lady Somerset have her head as she adroitly maneuvered him away from the group surrounding Lady Chloe that included his Daemon Club friends.

Rebecca and her family were waiting patiently for John and the dowager to acknowledge them. She glanced his way, and their gazes met for the briefest flicker. A sharp pang bit into his chest. It was enough to make him believe in the stories of Cupid and his darts. She was mesmerizing. He had to restrain himself from dashing across the room and catching her up in his arms.

He'd met many lovely ladies already this evening. Several were witty. Plenty of them dripped with precious jewels, hinting at even more generous dowries. One was downright frightening in her intensity; he'd recognized that one as Rebecca's friend from the museum.

But none made his chest glow the way Rebecca did.

She bent her head to speak to her mother, who was looking very wan despite judicious use of paint. He wondered if there was a way for him to use his new-found wealth and position to arrange for Lady Kearsey to take a cure on the Continent someplace. Surely there was a sanatorium whose treatments would put the roses back into Rebecca's mother's cheeks. He'd speak to Richard about it in the morning.

What point was there in being the heir to a marquess if he couldn't do a little good?

Especially since he was planning to do a great deal of bad in the near future and would need some positives to balance out the scales.

He ached to snatch Rebecca away and shield her, but there simply wasn't time. He wasn't going to be able to say more than a few words to her in front of her parents and his grandmother, and none of those words could give her warning of what was to come.

She was wearing long gloves with her pale muslin gown. He wished she weren't. He wished when he took her hand so very correctly before God and everybody that he could at least brush his lips on her bare knuckles instead of on silk. Maybe he'd even turn her hand over and press a lover's kiss into her open palm.

John cut off the current debutante before him, who had stuttered through their exchange of pleasantries, by offering the hope that she'd enjoy herself at Somerfield Park. Then he started toward Rebecca with the dowager in tow. The longcase clock chimes interrupted their progress.

"It's eight o'clock," Lady Somerset the elder said. "We must cease these greetings and lead our guests through to the dining room."

"We haven't met everyone yet."

"I know, but there's simply no time. I've seen to it that you've met the important ones, so the rest will keep until after dinner," the dowager said in hushed tones. "We must stick to the schedule. Your father cannot bear to be in company any longer than the time we've allotted."

After the disjointed midnight conversation with his confused father, John was surprised they were going to trot out the marquess at all.

"Very well," he said. "But perhaps there's time for me to give attention to one more guest without extending the evening for his lordship. Lord Richard, will you do the honors and escort Lady Somerset to the dining room?"

"Delighted." His half brother stepped up, offering their grandmother his arm. The hand-off was done so smoothly and so publicly, the dowager couldn't object. "Seymour, I assume I may trust you to see my lady to the same place?"

"Also delighted," Lawrence Seymour said, "but I can't promise I won't try to convince Sophie to run away with me between here and the first course."

Sophie laughed. "Trust me, Lawrence, you'd be bringing me back before we reached Somerset-on-the-Sea. I've a wickedly sharp tongue and wouldn't hesitate to use it, but I trust you to walk a few hallways with me. Now, John, since your arm is unadorned, who will you take to dinner?"

This was the defining moment of the evening. His choice would signal the front-runner in the dreaded Hartley Hunt and he knew it. Was counting on it. He surveyed the room and read hope in every pair of feminine eyes. The naked trust on Rebecca's sweet face made his gut burn. This would be tantamount to a declaration.

He set his face like flint and turned away from her, looking for another. There she was, up to her pretty little chin in aspiring swains.

"Lady Chloe," John said as he crossed the drawing room to her side. The other bachelors around her stepped back to make room for him as if he were the dominant bull in the herd. "Will you do me the honor of accompanying me to supper?"

Chloe sidled up to him and draped herself from his proffered arm. "Why, Lord Hartley, I thought you'd never ask."

Twenty-one

The wellborn gentleman's propensity for gambling never ceases to amaze, especially since most wagers are guaranteed ways of exchanging something for nothing. Ladies also have the urge to indulge in games of chance, but they satisfy this need by giving their trust to men...with similar results.

—Phillippa, the Dowager Marchioness of Somerset

REBECCA SLIPPED INTO HER CHAMBER AND LEANED against the closed door. The snick of the latch released her pent-up frustration, utter bewilderment, and simmering rage. She covered her mouth to muffle the keening that threatened to escape. Her knees sagged. She was surprised they still held her up.

So this is what hell is like—or at least purgatory. Painfully aware of what's happening but totally unable to change a thing.

Her cheeks ached from the false smile she'd plastered on her face all evening. She'd hidden behind it as if it were a medieval visor, a place of relative safety from which to view the world around her—a world that had been stood on its ear from the moment John offered his arm to Lady Chloe.

Rebecca had been so monumentally stupid. From the first time John demanded—and received!—a kiss from her, he'd played upon her ignorance. He'd amused himself by toying with her on the roof. John had wakened her sensuality and revealed her vulnerability. Only by the slimmest of margins had she escaped total ruin.

She lit the candle on her dressing table. It would be another half hour or so before the maid she shared with her mother came to help her out of her gown. In the meantime, she sat, toed off her slippers, and peeled off her stockings. She balled them in her fists and then threw them as hard as she could. They fluttered to the floor only a few feet away.

She couldn't identify what she was feeling. She was all hot inside. And miserable. And blaming herself as much as John for her predicament.

The lovely ball gown Freddie had brought for her was still spread across her bed. She had allowed herself the fantasy that, in that gown, she'd so capture John's heart that he'd defy his family and take her for his marchioness despite her lowly status.

"I'm such a fool." Her whisper floated up to the cherub-covered ceiling and swirled around the cornices.

There was little point to the gown now, not if John was as obsessed as he seemed to be with Lady Chloe. Tomorrow, she'd beg her parents to take her back to London. They were out of their depth here. All of them. Her father was likely to make a buffoon of himself with the other gentlemen. Her mother never did as well physically outside of her own home. And Rebecca had left a piece of her innocence, given a sliver of her heart to a man who didn't treasure it on Somerfield Park's flat roof. She narrowly resisted the urge to fly down the grand staircase, out the big double doors, and down the long lane.

She'd never look back.

She promised herself she would not weep. John didn't deserve her tears. She would not—

For some reason, her cheeks were wet.

A soft rap sounded on her door. The maid must have finished with Lady Kearsey much more quickly than Rebecca expected.

"Come," she said, swiping at her face. She didn't want the maid reporting back to her mother that her cheeks were unaccountably damp.

But it wasn't the maid. Instead, Freddie poked her head around the door. "Oh, good. You're still dressed."

Her friend bustled into the room. "Well, don't just sit there. Put your shoes and stockings back on. We haven't much time."

"Time for what?"

"The Leonids, you little goose. They should still be here tonight and the next if we're lucky. I've commandeered a footman who will lead us to the roof and back down again after a few hours."

Rebecca had forgotten all about the falling stars. They were less than nothing to her. Unreal. In fact, everything around her, from the flickering light of her candle to her discarded stockings and slippers, seemed as false as stage props on Drury Lane, as if they were pale symbols of things and not the things themselves.

But Freddie was true. She was comfortingly real—and a friend who could be counted upon to be nosy if Rebecca behaved the least out of character.

She decided to take refuge in a lady's eternal excuse when she didn't wish to do something. "I'm afraid I have a terrible headache."

It was almost true. There was a soft pounding behind her left eye.

"Really? Why?" Freddie asked, plopping down on the foot of the bed. "I mean, I could see why I might have developed one, what with the way that horrid Lady Chloe monopolized Lord Hartley all evening, but why you?"

"I suspect several feminine hearts were disappointed this night, but you're right. I have no reason to be upset over Lord Hartley's choice of dinner companion." It was true, and no amount of flutters in her chest would change it. She had no claim on John. She wished he had none on her. "I don't know why, but my head is pounding."

"Oh, you poor dear. I have some laudanum in my room. Shall I fetch it?"

"No." Rebecca never enjoyed the sensation of floating outside her own body that opiates delivered. Besides, she'd heard some people came to need that brand of oblivion, and she didn't wish to be one of them. "I only need sleep."

"Of course." Her friend rose to remove the pink gown from the bed, and hung it in the wardrobe. Freddie hummed to herself as she worked, as if she hadn't been dealt a setback in her own quest to capture the elusive Lord Hartley.

"You had every right to expect you'd be able to get to know his lordship this evening," Rebecca said. "Why aren't you upset about…about the way things went?"

"Because this evening is of no import." Freddie waved her hand as if she could wave away any obstacle she encountered just as easily. "This is a marathon, not a sprint. Lady Chloe is merely a diversion, a way for his lordship to assert his independence from his family's wishes."

"Do you really think so?"

"Of course. Did you see the look on the dowager's face?" She loosed an un-Freddie-like giggle. Clearly Rebecca's friend was trying on a new persona in her attempt at a future marchioness's crown—a flightier, more insipid version of herself. Rebecca wasn't sure she liked it. If her friend had to be someone other than herself to capture a husband, would it be worth the transformation if Freddie lost what made her unique? "Old Lady Somerset was nearly apoplectic."

"That's true." Perhaps John was motivated by something other than Lady Chloe's superb figure and very red mouth.

"Where is that abigail of yours?" Freddie demanded. "Never mind. Stand up, dear, and let me help you."

Freddie made short work of removing her gown and dressing her in her night rail. Rebecca found herself being tucked in before she knew it.

"You don't need to do this, you know." Once again, Rebecca suffered a pinch of guilt over the way she felt about John. Not that it would make a smidge of difference to the outcome of the Hartley Hunt.

Clearly she was of no import to John, and her feelings one way or another for him wouldn't change a thing. But Rebecca still felt guilty because she'd never kept anything a secret from her best friend before. "You're so good to me, Freddie."

"Pish. It's not just you. I'm good to everyone."

In her own brusque way, she was. "Good night," Rebecca said as she sank deeper into the feather tick. "Oh, do me a favor, will you?"

"Another one?" Despite her words, Freddie paused by the door. "What, dear?"

"Don't monitor the Leonids tonight. We'll do it together tomorrow. They'll still be there." It would also give Rebecca a chance to make sure that damning little love bower on the roof was made to disappear. Freddie was sure to unravel the reason for those blankets and mattresses.

"All right. I hope you feel better." Freddie slipped out of the room.

Rebecca stared up at the painted cherubs on her ceiling and wondered why God had sent her such a good friend as Lady Winifred Chalcroft.

And such a bad lover as John Fitzhugh Barrett.

Lover. I have a lover—had a lover.

She must put it in the past tense, even in her own thoughts. She'd never forget that night under the stars, but she also couldn't allow herself to be silly enough to repeat it.

Of course, John showed no sign of wanting to. He had been too busy laughing and flirting with Lady Chloe all evening.

Her chest constricted as if a heavy weight had been

placed upon it. If he ever did want her again, she'd at least have the pleasure of rejecting him. She promised herself that with fervor. A girl had to have some measure of self-respect.

It was several minutes before she realized she was clenching her fists so tightly, her fingernails left deep marks on the heels of her palms. How foolish to be so self-destructive when John had proven destructive enough. A tear leaked out and slid into her hairline, leaving a salty streak.

There was another rap on the door. It was her long-suffering maid. Rebecca thanked her, but assured her she needed nothing and sent her on her way. Then Rebecca climbed back into bed to stare up at the cherubic ceiling again.

Sleep fled from her as surely as the little naked godlings seemed to flit between the cornices over her head.

She tossed and turned. Her mind might reject the notion of John Fitzhugh Barrett. Her body had other ideas completely.

She kept replaying her time on the roof, all tangled up with John. Remembered sensations made her feel achy and swollen in her intimate parts. She put a hand to her own breasts in an effort to still the determined throb. It made matters worse.

She flopped onto her belly and covered her head with a pillow. It didn't help.

Finally, as she skimmed that twilight place between sleep and awareness, Rebecca was jerked back to full wakefulness by a soft scratching on her door.

Freddie must have decided to come back and check on her since she pleaded that headache.

"I so don't deserve her." Rebecca dragged herself out of bed and went to open the door.

But it wasn't Freddie. John was standing in the hallway.

Rebecca was thankful for her aching palms and the little crescent moon indentations left by her own nails. They'd help her remember her resolve.

❧

Four lovely ladies grinned up at Lord Kearsey. After hours of pitiful fare, this was the best hand of cards he'd held all night. It made the stale fug of cigar smoke and alcohol that swirled around the gaming room bearable again.

What were the odds that anyone still at the poque table could beat his queens?

By thunder, he deserved a bit of good luck for a change. After Lord Hartley all but snubbed his dear Rebecca, he'd been of half a mind to gather his little family and return to London. His lordship had invited her especially to Somerfield Park. Had practically demanded her presence. And then the cad had ignored Rebecca completely, spending the first evening of the house party with that infamous Lady Chloe at his side.

Kearsey would have stormed out after that insult if Lord Blackwood hadn't promised him a poque game once the ladies retired for the evening. It would have been a shame to travel all the way to Somerset for nothing. There were some fat purses represented in this party. At the very least, Kearsey counted on being able to recoup his traveling expenses at the gaming table.

Instead, his pile of chips dwindled steadily as the right cards fled from him with each hand.

But not this time. His four queens were a gift from heaven. Kearsey raised the bid with the last of his chips.

"Too rich for my blood," Lord Arbuthnot said as he stood, scooping up more chips than he left in the poque pools. "I pray you'll excuse me until another time, gentlemen."

Both Kearsey and Blackwood stood to bid the earl good night, and then settled again to fight out this final hand. There had been six players at the start of the evening, but one by one, they'd bowed out after having their pockets lightened considerably. Most of their chips were stacked before Viscount Blackwood. The rest were in the poque pools, waiting for this hand to be decided.

"I could buy this round, you know." Blackwood drummed his fingers on the tabletop as the longcase clock in the hall chimed three.

"Where's the sport in that?" Kearsey said. He'd sunk all his available blunt into his chips. What would his dear wife say if he told her he'd lost the money that was supposed to support them for the next half year? It didn't bear thinking on. If he could draw Blackwood into committing more of his wealth on this hand, Kearsey might yet come out on top. "What do you say to raising the stakes?"

Blackwood knocked back his jigger of whisky and took a pull on his cheroot. "What did you have in mind?" Smoke curled out along with his words, as if he were part dragon.

"I shall give you my vowels." Kearsey took a piece of

paper and the stub of a pencil from his pocket and wrote down an IOU for an amount that would have made his dear wife faint dead away. But she worried more than she ought. It wasn't really gambling if one had the cards. He couldn't let this one get away. With barely a tremor in his hand, he shoved the paper across the slick tabletop toward Blackwood. "What do you say?"

Blackwood lifted the paper and gave it heavy-lidded scrutiny for about ten heartbeats. "I don't know, Kearsey. It runs against my nature to see a man bleed himself."

"Let me worry about that," Kearsey said testily. He was already hemorrhaging badly. Winning this pot would stop the flow. "Do you believe in your hand or not?"

"May as well. Since it's just we two, let's make it interesting." Blackwood shrugged and pushed all his chips into the center of the table. "I haven't done anything especially foolish lately. I suppose I'm due. Show your cards, sir."

Kearsey's heart lifted. This pot would set him up for the next two years if he listened to his wife and abided by her frugal suggestions. It would certainly provide him more than enough with which to play for the duration of this house party. With more luck like this hand full of ladies, Kearsey would secure his family's fortunes for the foreseeable future. He'd be able to pay off their creditors and provide a well-deserved dowry for his Rebecca. He'd find the doctor who could cure his dear wife's persistent cough.

He'd feel like a man again for the first time since he was forced to pawn her jewelry.

Kearsey flipped over the queens with unconcealed glee. "Beat that."

Blackwood loosed a low whistle. "That's a good hand, Kearsey. I understand why you risked so much for it." He began to turn over his cards, revealing one ace after another until four of them lay side by side. "Unfortunately, it's not quite good enough."

Kearsey's stomach failed him and he rushed to the chamber pot set up behind a screen in a corner so the players wouldn't have to leave the table for long. He heaved into the befouled porcelain until he was a dry husk.

Finally, he wiped his mouth on his sleeve and emerged from behind the screen.

"You have ruined me," he said woodenly.

"Nonsense," Blackwood said with disgusting cheerfulness as he scooped up all the chips. Before the men began playing, they had deposited a like amount of money into a strongbox which was then secreted away in Lord Somerset's safe. At the end of the house party, the players would present their wooden markers to redeem their winnings. Now Kearsey would have no claim to any of the cash in the safe at all. "You ruined yourself. I simply happened to be in your path in your rush to do so. Now about your vowels—"

"I cannot satisfy this debt," Kearsey said. "Not right away. I shall have to petition the House of Lords to sell off a portion of the estate."

In truth, it would take the lion's share of his land to satisfy a debt of this size. He would never recover. After centuries of Kearsey men husbanding the Sussex estate and defending it from harm, he'd be the one to fail utterly. The air in the room suddenly seemed as gelatinous as aspic. He had difficulty pushing it in and out of his lungs. His vision started to tunnel.

Damn those queens. They had tempted him as surely as Odysseus was tempted by the sirens. Unfortunately, Kearsey had had no one to bind him to the mast.

"I'm not an unreasonable man, Kearsey," Blackwood said. "There's no need to petition the Lords right away. I'm sure we can come to a…mutually beneficial agreement."

"That's demmed decent of you." The air thinned a bit, and Kearsey was able push back the gathering dark from the edges of his mind. Perhaps everything would come around right after all.

But then he met Lord Blackwood's steely gaze.

"You, sir, have a very comely daughter."

Twenty-two

Every time one loves another person, one takes a risk. The result is either a lifelong bond or a cautionary tale. Both have their uses.

—Phillippa, the Dowager Marchioness of Somerset

REBECCA TRIED TO CLOSE HER DOOR, BUT JOHN stopped it with a splay-fingered hand. He pushed into her chamber and locked the door behind himself.

"Get out," Rebecca said through clenched teeth. Her insides quivered like a plate of gelatin.

"Not yet," he said.

"Then for pity's sake, at least lower your voice. Or do you wish to disgrace me by being found here?"

"You know better than that." He matched her whisper. "But I'm not leaving until we've had a chance to talk."

"That's not necessary." She backed away from him until her spine bumped into the wall next to the banked fireplace. "I understand you perfectly."

"No, you don't."

He closed the distance between them and rested

his palms on the wall on either side of her. A whiff of his scent—leather and spicy bergamot and all things male—made it hard for her to remember that she was furious with him. Her insides stopped shaking and went pliable as a reed by the river.

She couldn't continue meeting his intense gaze, so hers slipped down his face. His mouth was wide, his lips full, slightly parted, and firm. Just looking at them made her remember the feel of those lips on her and the way he'd trailed them over her intimate places. His shirt was undone, revealing a deep V of skin. Her palms began to itch; she longed to tug his shirt from his trousers and run her hands over his ribs.

Her gaze flicked downward.

His trousers. Botheration! Had she actually looked at that hard male bulge? Her cheeks burned, and she could only hope he wouldn't notice the accompanying blush in the dimness of her chamber.

She reminded herself that he'd spent the entire evening pretending she didn't exist. The rage she'd suppressed earlier rose up and threatened to boil over.

"Your station has gone to your head if you think you can force your way in here without my consent," she hissed.

"Scream if you like, and I'll go away. It's the only thing that will convince me you don't want me here." He leaned closer, his chest near enough that her breasts brushed against it. Her traitorous nipples started to ache again.

"We both know how that would end." She ducked under his arm to get away from him. "Ruin for me and a round of celebratory drinks with your friends for you."

He followed close behind as she tried to put some distance between them. "Then don't scream. Listen."

She covered her ears with her hands. "No, I won't."

"Yes, you will." John grasped her wrists and pulled her hands away from her ears. "I need you to know what's happening."

"Anyone with eyes can see that, my lord. You think you're in a bakery shop and that you can help yourself to a scone here and a butter biscuit there and no one can say you nay." She yanked her hands away from him and fisted them at her waist. "Well, this is one little biscuit that isn't going to stay on your plate."

"A biscuit, eh?" A smile lifted the corners of his mouth as he grappled with her till she was back against the wall, her arms pinned above her head. "I like that. You're sweet as one, and I should know."

He was reminding her that he'd tasted her all over. Warmth gathered between her legs, as if her intimate parts were blushing. She yanked one wrist free, balled her fist, and pummeled his chest.

"How dare you speak about—"

He stopped her by claiming her mouth with a kiss. It wasn't at all gentle. Her lips would likely bruise.

It felt wonderful. Primitive.

It called to a deep place inside her, and she responded.

No one ever told her a woman might feel such need. Such fierce hunger.

Such total lack of self-respect.

She wedged both hands between them and shoved against his chest with all her might. After a moment's struggle, he released her.

"No," she said with vehemence. "You are not going to use me."

"Use you? Nothing could be farther from my mind."

She laughed mirthlessly. "You are gravely mistaken if you think I care to follow your Lady Chloe."

"You don't understand. She's not my lady."

"So she rejected you. Good for her. Contrary to her reputation, it shows her to be a lady of taste and refinement. But now you think to come to your poor second. I will not be—"

"You are second to no one, Rebecca. Not to me." He pulled her close again, but she held her body tense, refusing the urge to melt into his heat. "Lady Chloe is my friend, nothing more."

Rebecca relaxed by the smallest of degrees. She rested her palm on his chest, marginally comforted by the way his heart beat steadily but slowly. Surely, if he were lying, it would have been pounding like a coach and six. "That's not how it appeared."

"I know. That was by design. The truth is, Chloe is making it possible for you and me to be together."

"Now I know you think me a fool."

"Never that." He reached up and ran his thumb along the curve of her cheek. Shimmers of pleasure trailed his touch. "I could never deserve you, Rebecca." The words came out haltingly. "But I mean to have you in any case. And if I'm going to saddle you with someone like me, the least I can do is make the process easier for you."

"John Fitzhugh Barrett!" All the tender feelings he'd just stoked in her were suddenly smothered by indignation. "Of all the stupid, ill-considered… How

in heaven is it easier for me to see you dancing attendance on another woman?"

"You've heard the talk. The family expects me
to marry well. Not necessarily for money, though
they wouldn't reject a fat dowry, but for power and
connections. It's no accident that the young ladies here
are all the daughters of earls at the least."

She looked away. "Except for me."

"Except for you, my little biscuit." He slipped his
fingertips under her chin and tipped her face back so she
had to meet his gaze. "Not that it matters one jot to me.
I was a nameless bastard only a few months ago. I'm the
last person to be a respecter of title and prestige."

"But your family does."

"Exactly, and if my true feelings for you were
known, they would be deucedly hard on you and
would try to separate us."

His true feelings? John had feelings for her. He hadn't
named them yet, but simply admitting he had them
was important. Hope surged in her chest.

"Remember what they did to my mother when
she wasn't considered up to the mark," he said. "If
they think I'm serious about Lady Chloe, whom they
wouldn't accept even though she possesses the rank
they crave, they'll be so relieved when I present you to
them as my real choice, they'll accept you with open
arms. And they'll be grateful for you."

All that stood out in her mind from his explanation
was that she was his real choice. Hope rushed through
her entire body like a bracing tonic. "Are you afraid
the dowager will try to buy me off?"

"I know she would. But what I'm really afraid of is

that you'd take it." When she stiffened in his arms, he was quick to amend his words. "Not that you're the mercenary type. I don't mean that, but I know your father has debts and your mother's illness frets you."

"My family is in need of funds, I'll not deny it. But you don't know me at all if you think I can be bought or sold." Freddie would remind her that a lady waits for the gentleman to make the first declaration, but if she tried to contain the words, she feared she'd burst. "I love you, John. And that means with my heart and my soul and my body. My family's purse doesn't enter into it at all."

His face was a study in wonderment and joy. She wrapped her arms around his shoulders and pulled his head down, so she could kiss him on the mouth. Hard.

"And I love you only for you. Do you think I'd care two figs if you weren't Lord Hartley?" she asked when she finally pulled back from him.

"Well, I didn't think plain John Fitzhugh had much chance when I first approached you in the museum."

"Plain John Fitzhugh had every chance. At least, he would have if Freddie hadn't been there to drag me away."

"So you do love me for me," he said, as if it were a miracle on par with the loaves and the fishes. "And I love you for your sweet self. For your heart as much as your beauty. For the way your hair shimmers like chestnut rain. And the way your eyes dance when you're planning some devilment." He cocked his head at her with a sidelong glance. "As they are now. What are you about, Rebecca?"

"This," she said as she tugged at his shirt, pulling it

from the waist of his trousers. *He loves me*, her heart sang. She was determined to show him her love. She slid her hands under the hem and ran her fingertips up his ribs and across his chest, just as she'd imagined doing. Standing on tiptoe, she nuzzled his neck and along the firm ridge of his jawline. Then she dropped a row of feathery kisses down the V of his open-neck shirt. His skin was warm and tasted lightly of salt.

Utterly delicious.

"And this." Rebecca undid the one button over his breastbone that was still fastened on his shirt. She nipped and licked at his newly exposed skin. His breath sucked in harshly over his teeth. She hadn't troubled to braid her hair before bed, and his fingers tangled in her hair, smoothing the long locks down her back.

"And this too." She tugged at the heavy pewter buttons at his waist. Sneaking a glance up at him from under her lashes, she knew from his dazed expression he was hers to do with as she pleased. She pulled his shirt over his head and ran her palms over his chest, grazing the hard nubs of his nipples.

With the buttons on his trousers undone, the drop front of the garment lived up to its name.

"You're not wearing any smalls," she said, her breath hissing over her teeth this time.

"Porter says they spoil the line of dress trousers."

"Remind me to thank your Mr. Porter." Rebecca teased her fingertips along the line of hair that ran from his navel and spread as it disappeared into the trousers.

She knew she was dancing close to ruin, but she'd avoid doing "it" so long as she remained clothed. Freddie had been adamant on that point.

However, that didn't mean John had to remain so.

She slid her hand down the front of his trousers and grazed him with maddening, short caresses. His hard rod was hot in her hand, almost feverish. And below it his bollocks, soft at first, but then drawing up tight under her touch.

What a wonderful thing a man is, granite strength and softness, side by side.

His breathing became short and ragged as she tormented him. A heaviness, a dull ache built in her as well, a response to his need.

"Rebecca." The warning in his voice turned his tone husky and deep. "You're playing with fire."

"Then let me burn."

He took her mouth, ravaging and demanding. She met his longing with her own. His hands slid over her shoulders and down her arms to entwine fingers with her. Then his hands went wandering. A light brush down her spine, a gentle squeeze at the curve of her waist, relentless strokes on the undersides of her breasts. She cursed the thin linen of her night rail, aching for him to touch her bare skin.

"Oh, John. All this scheming." She sagged against him, a low drumbeat throbbing in between her legs. "Are we never to have a little peace together?"

"We will, darling," he murmured into her hair. "After we convince the family that my choice is the best choice."

She pulled back and grinned up at him. "You're assuming that I'll accept you without actually being asked."

"Won't you?"

"Yes, but a girl does like to hear the words." *Say them, John. Please.*

"I'll ask them as soon as our plan has worked its magic," he said. "I promise."

She tamped down a smidgeon of frustration. It was hard to stay disappointed when such a fine man was pressed up against her. "I'll hold you to that."

"As long as you hold me," he said with a wicked smile. "And now, we'll have a bit of what I want to hold."

He knelt and slid his hands under the hem of her night rail. Then he rose slowly, gliding his fingertips up her shins, past her knees, and over her thighs. By the time he cupped her with his hot palm, she was trembling with need.

"Let me love you, Rebecca."

Once, when she was bathing off Brighton, she'd been swept into a dangerous undertow. Fortunately, a nearby boater had fished her out before she could be carried farther out into the Channel. She had the presence of mind to recognize a similar danger now.

"But if we do this"—by which she meant "it"—"I will be ruined."

"No, you'll be mine," John said. "And then, when I officially ask you to be my countess now and my marchioness later, you'll have no choice but to accept."

"How incredibly devious, my lord. No wonder you warned me against playing with fire." She smiled up at him, but then her expression turned serious. "How can you think I wouldn't accept you? But you draw me close with one hand and push me away with the other. Why is that?"

"I have to be sure you want me."

As a boy, he'd never felt wanted. It left a mark.

"I will always want you," she assured him.

He moved his hand then, sweetly invading her secret place which was already hot and moist and ready to receive him. Delight radiated through her entire body.

His fingers found her sensitive spot, and her insides began to coil. He buried his nose in the curve of her neck. "Shall I stop?"

"Please God, no," she said as his lips brushed her temple, her closed eyelids, the hollow of her throat. All the while, his wicked fingers played a lover's game on her sensitive flesh. She moaned when he stopped and started to withdraw, and then moaned louder when he resumed his gentle assault. She seemed to have grown a second heart. The new one pounded between her legs.

He bent his head and suckled her nipple through the thin linen of her chemise. She begged him to stop. She urged him to go on. This must be what madness was. Soft, meaningless sounds escaped her lips, and she was powerless to control them.

He straightened and covered her mouth with his own then, to still her. When his tongue matched his finger's stroke, a sun burst forth inside her, sending warmth and light to every corner of her body. Deep bliss radiated in concentric spasms. Intense joy. More than she could hope.

Rebecca let her head fall back. Was it her imagination or were the stars falling again? Her breath caught with the glow of tiny aftershocks. He gave her sensitive spot one last stroke and pulled his hand away.

"Oh, don't leave me," she whimpered.

"You couldn't drive me away." He picked her up and carried her to the waiting bed. He laid her out with such tenderness, she wept. He stroked her cheek. "What's this?"

"I'm so happy, I can't hold it all."

He frowned for a heartbeat. "But I want to give you more."

"Oh, yes, please. If the happiness leaks out, so be it." She lifted her arms to him as he lowered himself to settle on her. She welcomed the weight of his body, the hardness, the raw maleness of him. Only a moment ago, all had been light and peace, but now emptiness yawned inside her again. The ache that had seemed fully assuaged roared back to life, and she helped him position himself between her legs with greedy hands.

John grasped her bum. She tilted her hips to guide him to her hot wetness, and he entered her in one smooth stroke.

She gasped at the sudden rending, but then the pain dissolved with the joy of stretching to receive all of him. In one blinding moment, she knew she'd committed the infamous "it."

"But how did this happen? We're dressed. I'm still wearing my night rail," she whispered in disbelief. She thought she would have had a bit more warning. "Your trousers are still bunched at your knees."

"Sorry, Biscuit." He kissed the tip of her nose. "I was in a hurry. I'll take my time now."

And without any further ado, Rebecca bid her virginity farewell. She wrapped her legs around his waist as he thrust into her again and again. Slowly, deeply, the man surged inside her. Rebecca moved in tandem with him, rising to meet each thrust.

John raised himself up to look down at her as he moved. She didn't shrink from his intense scrutiny. She read the love on his face and knew he accepted all of her. All she was—good and bad—he was welcome to know, to handle. She'd let him push her to the limits of her flesh and to the farthest edge her spirit could reach.

A muscle twitched in his cheek, and she chanted his name softly. A deep groan tore loose from his throat, and she felt his seed course into her, hot and deep. She strained against him, reveling in his pulsing release.

When it was over, he gathered her close, unwilling to separate from her yet.

"I love you," he whispered. "I'll love you till my last breath."

"And I you." She pressed a hand to his dear cheek. The stubble of his beard prickled her palm. Together, they'd sweep away the pain of his past and build a future worth having. Only the present was a source of worry. "I wish we didn't have to steal these moments."

"It won't be long," he promised. Then he frowned, seeming to change his mind. "No, blast it all, it's not fair to you to wait. I see now it was pigheaded of me to believe I can outscheme the Barrett family. I don't care what they think. We'll announce our engagement tomorrow and devil take the consequences."

John slipped from her body, and the separation left her strangely bereft. Then he eased off her to stretch out beside her and smoothed down her night rail to cover her.

She silently blessed his thoughtfulness. Somehow, he'd known that now that they'd done "it," she was feeling a little shy.

"No, John. We shouldn't make any announcements yet." Rebecca considered helping him tug up his trousers, but he didn't seem a bit shy, letting his big body rest against hers. She liked the feel of him there too much to offer to cover him. "Your plan to make me more acceptable by comparison is a good one. Lady Chloe is…well, if not beyond the pale at least halfway over the fence. And you said she knows of and agrees with your plan?"

"She thought it would be fun, actually. She's happy to help."

Rebecca quickly reevaluated the beautiful lady. Lady Chloe had a generous, if somewhat devious, spirit. "If your family thinks you're likely to offer for Lady Chloe, perhaps they would decide I was a more conventional choice. It would smooth the way for them to accept us."

"I don't care about making it easy for them." A little bitterness crept back into his tone. "It's you I'm concerned about. I don't want them giving you a moment's grief."

She kissed him again, gently this time, unhurried by passion. The kiss was almost unbearably sweet.

John was honest, intelligent, and devoted—all she'd ever wished for in a man. She couldn't hold a single drop more happiness if her hope of heaven depended upon it.

From deep in the house, the longcase clock chimed.

"I need to go. I won't have you face scandal on my

account." John rolled out of bed, tugging up his trousers. He didn't move quite quickly enough. Rebecca was treated to a glimpse of his tight bum. The sight made her sigh.

"You're right, but it hurts my heart for you to leave." She climbed out of bed and helped him slip his shirt over his head. "Good night, my lord."

"My lady." John backed away from her, holding her hand, then just her fingertips until he'd exceeded the length of his reach. Then he unlocked the door, slipped out, and closed it softly behind himself.

Rebecca couldn't return to the bed. It would seem too empty without him. Instead, she pushed back the thick damask curtains and peered into the southern sky. A single falling star streaked the blackness.

Now that John was gone, Rebecca realized she'd taken as big a gamble as her father ever had. She'd wagered everything on a man's promise. When he was with her, it hadn't seemed such a leap of faith, but now prickles of unease ruffled over her.

She watched the sky for another quarter hour, but no other meteorites appeared. The solitary one she'd seen seemed cold and lonely.

She shook off the fancy that it was a harbinger of things to come.

Twenty-three

Plenty of game in the thickets, loaded rifles, and shaky-fingered men who shoot only once or twice a year—what could possibly go wrong?

—Phillippa, the Dowager Marchioness of Somerset

"My lord, ought we not stop for a moment? Her ladyship may be fatigued with all this mucking about in the weeds," Porter said hopefully.

"Don't worry about me, Mr. Porter," Lady Chloe Endicott said airily. "I live for adventure, and this hunt is the merest lark. Now, if Lord Hartley offered to take me on safari to darkest Africa, I might become a bit winded, but believe me, I'd jump at the chance."

She'd jump at any chance where his lordship was concerned, Porter thought sourly, but he kept his expression carefully neutral. He was no judge of such things, admittedly, but he couldn't help but wish Lord Hartley were spending the day with that nice Miss Kearsey instead of this bold—dare he say *garish?*—woman.

He trudged after Lord Hartley and Lady Chloe, shifting the weight of the lady's shotgun and its accoutrements from one shoulder to the other.

"But I'm a valet, my lord," he'd told his employer when his lordship first proposed that Porter act as the lady's bearer. "I'm not trained for such things."

"All you have to do is tramp through the woods with us while carrying the lady's weapon," Lord Hartley said in a tone that brooked no refusal. "How much training does that require?"

Evidently more than Porter possessed. He'd never gone hunting in his life. He'd been in service since he was a boy and prided himself on securing employment that allowed him to work inside, thank you very much. He was happiest when keeping as far away from dirt and insects and creeping things that scuttled through the underbrush as he could. Porter was no woodsman and didn't wish to become one.

The forest was so thick in this section, he'd tripped on a root that snaked across the ground and went sprawling once. The shotgun had discharged when it hit the ground, though thankfully no one was hit. His lordship seemed more concerned about the gun than about Porter, and was relieved that it had suffered no damage.

The same could not be said for Porter. He had a bruise on his right shin that hurt like billy-o. His ears were still ringing, and if the weapon accidentally fired again, he couldn't promise he wouldn't need a change of drawers.

After that mishap, Lord Hartley told him it was all right for him to carry the gun empty. If Lady Chloe saw something she simply had to kill, she'd have to take the time to load first.

However, as much noise as the lady made, laughing and talking as they blundered through the undergrowth, Porter suspected any self-respecting prey would have removed itself to the next shire by now.

"I hope we get a big buck with a simply enormous rack of antlers," Lady Chloe said. "I need a trophy for my drawing room."

"I suspect you've trophies aplenty already, but I'd wager they're of the two-legged variety," his lordship said.

Lady Chloe laughed again.

Honestly, Porter thought, *the woman must have a feather trapped in her unmentionables, the way she goes giggling, chuckling, and downright guffawing through life.* He purposely let himself fall a little farther behind the pair, but he was exceptionally keen of hearing and could still make out her words.

"How well you know me, Hartley," the lady said. "I have indeed dined on my share of hearts, but society would frown on me even more than it already does if I tried mounting all those heads!"

It wasn't Porter's place to say the lady was gauche in the extreme. But nothing could keep him from thinking it as loudly as he pleased.

"Hush," his lordship said as he crouched down to the ground. "Fresh scat. There may be game nearby."

The report of a rifle sounded, but no other hunters were visible. It made Porter nervous. He pitied the deer who'd done no one any wrong. He pitied the pheasant and quail whose only crime was having tasty flesh when properly roasted. He pitied himself.

He might not provide a trophy or fill a dinner plate, but was he in any less danger?

Another sharp crack echoed through the trees, and suddenly Porter felt as though he'd sat on a hot nail. Then something warm began to trickle down the back of his leg. Porter reached around and found the seat of his trousers sticky.

He brought his hand up in front of his face. His wet fingers shook. Darkness gathered at the edges of his vision, which began to contract into an ever-narrowing tunnel.

"I say, my lord," he said in a quavering voice before he winked out completely, "is this blood?"

❧

"Hurry, Mister... Well, hurry up, will you?" Not being able to recall his bearer's name made Lord Somerset short-tempered. He was sure the man had been with him for years, carrying his weapon and helping him track game whenever Somerset was of a mind to go hunting. Why couldn't he recall his name? "It's a monstrous big buck, and I'm sure I hit him, but confound it, I can't be certain it was a clean kill. We must find him before he drags himself deeper into the undergrowth."

He handed his weapon back to his bearer and started off in the direction of his prey. It had been a difficult shot. He'd heard the low murmur of conversation and discerned a couple of people in the woods, but a few yards behind them he'd seen the characteristic hesitant ruffle in the distant underbrush that signaled the presence of a grazing animal. It felt good to take the shot.

In fact, he felt more himself while he tramped in

the woods, more in control when hunting his land. It was as if the bracing November air cleared his head and allowed him to think cogent thoughts for the first time in weeks.

Except for not being able to recall that blasted man's name.

Somerset broke into a trot and felt his years slough away as the low-hanging branches flayed his cheeks. It was as if the fall off the roof never happened. He was the same man he'd been last year for the hunt. He was the marquess again, not a pale shadow of himself. He was—

Doomed.

As Lord Somerset broke into a clearing, he found a man and a woman kneeling around a third prone figure which boasted neither horns nor hooves.

"Oh Lord, no."

It hadn't been a deer foraging in the thicket. He'd shot a man. Accidentally, to be sure, but the man was down all the same.

The confidence he'd experienced only a few seconds ago withered like the season's last rose. He shrank into himself. Richard was right to have him declared incompetent. He was unfit to wander without a keeper. He ought to be committed to Bedlam where he could do no harm. He ought—

"Your lordship," the kneeling man shouted to him. "A little assistance, if you please."

That damnable mist was descending on his mind again, sending rational thought scurrying like vermin before a lit candle. But the kneeling man seemed vaguely familiar.

"John?"

The man's face lifted in a smile which faded quickly when he turned back to the fallen fellow.

Oh, that's right. He's John Fitzhugh, a new footman. No, that wasn't it. He was... This tall man with Sadie's eyes...he was... *Oh Lord, he has her eyes.*

"My son," he said. "You're my son."

"Yes, my lord." The man glanced up at him and then down at the still fellow on the ground again. "Yes, I am, and I'm gladder than I can tell you to hear you say so, but right now I need your help. Porter has been shot."

"I know. I did it. I thought he was a deer." Even though this was a horrible turn of events, it felt right to take responsibility for it. That was what a man did, wasn't it? Porter was lying facedown in the bracken. He didn't so much as twitch a muscle. Somerset's heart clenched like a fist. "Is...is he dead?"

"No, only fainted. You shot him in the bum. I doubt it's mortal, but he'll need a pillow to sit on for a while. Here, my lady, can you carry the weapons?" John handed his rifle to the woman who was gamely holding a lacy handkerchief to the valet's backside to stanch the bleeding. "Come help me, sir. We need to carry him back to the house and call a doctor."

"Dr. Partridge." Somerset was surprised at how quickly that name sprang to his lips. Perhaps the mist in his mind was clearing again. "A good man, that. Partridge will see Mr. Porter right as rain."

Somerset knelt and helped his son lift the valet from the forest floor. His son, his lost son, his heir. Where did he lose such a fine young man? How could he have allowed such a terrible thing to occur? How did he happen to find him again? He shoved those questions aside for the moment and concentrated on the job at hand. With him on one side of Mr. Porter and his son John on the other, they started carrying the valet through the woods. The lady who'd been accompanying Lord Hartley followed after them, helpfully bearing the weapons and refraining admirably from female histrionics.

Somerset's bearer came puffing up to them then. "Here, your lordship. Let me take your place."

"No, it's my responsibility, Dawson." His servant's name suddenly came nimbly to Somerset's tongue. Even though he'd shot a faithful retainer like Porter, his heart lightened. His mind was his own, for the moment at least. "I'll carry Mr. Porter home. My son John will help me."

❧

"There you are, Mr. Porter," Dr. Partridge said as he tied off the last stitch on Porter's throbbing bum. The sweet, tarry smell of carbolic soap used to scrub the wound still lingered in the air and burned his insulted flesh.

Porter gripped the iron rail at the foot of his bed to keep from crying out. He'd already disgraced himself by fainting away like a little girl at the sight of his own blood. The last thing he wanted to do was squeal like one.

"The bullet went through the…ahem…gluteus maximus and out again without doing any lasting damage. A fairly shallow wound track for a gun shot," Dr. Partridge said. "You'll be sore for a while, but all things considered, you're a very lucky man, Mr. Porter."

Porter didn't feel very lucky. He felt very humiliated.

"I'd like to see this left to the open air to heal, but I don't suppose that's practical," the doctor said.

"No, indeed," Porter said through clenched teeth. Bad enough to have been shot in the backside; he wasn't about to lie there with his nether crack smiling at the ceiling, his buttocks bare as a matched pair of river stones. Not even if, as Lord Hartley's valet, he did rate his own room in the servants' wing, and it was unlikely anyone would barge in and see him.

"Well, then, this bandage will have to do for now. I'll be back tomorrow to see how you're getting on." Dr. Partridge repacked his supplies into his medical bag and covered Porter with a sheet up to the waist.

Porter was still in his shirtsleeves, so he was more or less decently covered. He breathed a relieved sigh.

"I expect you'll be uncomfortable tonight, but I don't recommend doses of laudanum for this sort of thing," the doctor said. "Too easy to lean on that particular crutch."

"No, I wouldn't have it, in any case. Thank ye kindly." He wouldn't say no to a dose of Mr. Hightower's private stash of spirits. He thought a tot of rum was likely not to be forthcoming though. The butler was very parsimonious with liquor for the below stairs staff.

"Doctor," Porter said, stopping him as he reached the door. "Does...does everyone know where I was shot?"

Dr. Partridge's lips pursed in an amused moue. "I wish I could say no, but Toby relieved Lord Somerset when he and Lord Hartley were bearing you up the stairs. He learned about the location of your…wound and…" A chuckle escaped his lips. "You mustn't blame the young fellow. It's just too good to keep."

The doctor slipped out the door and Porter quietly banged his forehead against the iron footboard. He'd be a laughingstock for weeks…months…possibly years. How would he ever face the rest of the below stairs folk?

Most especially, how would he face Mrs. Culpepper?

Then, as if he'd conjured her, she opened his door with her helper, Theresa, at her side, bearing a supper tray.

"Oh, good. Ye're awake, Mr. Porter."

He'd give anything to be able to faint again right now. He'd felt decently covered a moment ago, but he was wearing only his shirt. Without his jacket, he'd be considered as good as naked so far as society was concerned if he were standing upright. Crivens! Beneath the sheets, he *was* naked from the waist down, barring his stockings. What on earth was the woman thinking to come to his room like this?

"Theresa, set that tray down and then hie yourself back to the common room." The cook moved the only chair in the room from its place in the corner to his bedside. "Mr. Hightower will be wanting tea for the others, and ye'll have to see to it. Make me proud, girl."

"Yes, Mrs. C. I hope you're feeling better, Mr. Porter," the girl said between suppressed giggles.

"Never ye mind about how the man feels. How should he feel after being shot in his nethers?" Mrs. Culpepper drew herself up to her full yet unimpressive height as she continued to scold the girl. "Just ye keep *your* mind on your work and your hands busy. If I hear ye've been mooning around in the gallery again when ye think no one sees, I'll send ye packing, and that's a promise. Now scoot."

Theresa scurried out of the room as if her skirt were on fire.

"Well then, how can I make ye more comfortable?" Mrs. C asked.

By pretending I'm not lying here with naught on my backside but a bit of gauze and a thin sheet of linen. But of course, he couldn't say that. "Perhaps a pillow from the head of the bed?"

"Of course." In her brusque way, Mrs. Culpepper made a strange angel of mercy, but Porter did feel marginally better when she plumped the pillow and positioned it so he could lay his forehead on feathers instead of banging it on iron.

"Now, I know ye likely wish to sleep, but if ye can hold up your head for only a bit, I'll help ye with a bite or two." She plopped into the chair and took up the soup bowl and spoon.

"Do ye think that's wise? I mean, ought ye to be in my room as long as that will take? Alone, I mean."

"I'm not alone, silly." She gave his shoulder a playful swat. "I'm with ye."

"But your reputation…"

"Honestly, Mr. Porter, if ye feel up to threatening my reputation after taking a gunshot wound to the bum, I'll swear that Dr. Partridge is some sort of miracle worker." She tilted her head at him. "Ye don't feel up to that, do ye?"

He sighed and plopped his head down on his pillow. "The spirit is willing but the flesh is weak."

Mrs. Culpepper loosed a chortling laugh. "Well,

we shall have to see about building up the flesh then. Come now. Lift your head and have some of my chicken soup. It'll have ye fit to chase me 'round the bedpost in no time."

"Mrs. C!" Porter's conventional soul was deeply scandalized.

"Well, did ye not say the spirit was willing?" Her eyes sparkled like a green girl's.

"Yes, I did. I do. It is. I mean, I'd...well, what I want is..."

She held a spoonful of the soup a few inches from his mouth. "Yes?"

"Will ye walk out with me sometime?" He took the offered spoonful so he wouldn't be expected to say more.

"That I will," Mrs. C said. "But let's get ye feeling up to it first. Have a bit more of my soup. That'll put ye to rights."

The soup was savory and rich, with much more chicken in it than usually appeared in the common-table fare. After a few spoonfuls, she laid the spoon and bowl aside.

"Actually, Mr. Porter, I was hoping ye'd ask for summat more than for me to walk out with ye some night."

"Oh? I can't imagine what more I could wish for. After all, I couldn't expect...that is, I mean... Well, I know I'm not a handsome man."

A smile lifted her cheeks. "Handsome is as handsome does, my old mam used to say. Reckon ye're handsome enough by those lights."

"Well, then, I guess...that is to say, I've heard

tell…" Frustrated with his own hemming and hawing, Porter came to the point. "They do say that when one has suffered an injury, a kiss makes it all better."

Mrs. Culpepper broke into peals of laughter. "Surely, Mr. P, ye can't expect me to kiss ye *there*!"

"No, no indeed." He blushed so furiously and so hotly he was sure even his bum had a rose glow. "I meant…" He put a finger to his lips, unable to say the words.

"Well, if that's the way of it, of course I'll kiss ye and make ye better."

Mrs. Culpepper knelt beside his bed and took his face between her work-roughened palms. Then she brought her lips to his.

All of a sudden, he didn't feel gawky and awkward and like a man about to slide into the twilight years of his adult life. Porter felt strong. Capable. Handsome.

In a wholly unconventional sort of way, of course.

Then Mrs. C pulled back and sat on the chair again as she launched into a one-sided conversation about the dainties and trifles she'd been called upon to make for the upcoming ball a few days hence, all the while spooning her nourishing soup into his mouth. She didn't mention the kiss. Talking about what had just passed between them would only detract from the magic of it.

At least, it had been magical for him.

Porter sighed. The woman was a goddess in an apron, and she'd kissed him.

He was beginning to feel lucky after all. Very lucky indeed.

Twenty-four

The cautionary tale of Faust aside, sometimes a deal with the devil is the only deal one can make.

—Phillippa, the Dowager Marchioness of Somerset

IT HAD BEEN A WEEK SINCE JOHN TOLD REBECCA OF HIS plan to court Lady Chloe openly so as to confound his family's designs for him. He'd done so with devastating conviction. Lady Chloe still accompanied him when he went on his daily hunt, even after the unfortunate accident with his valet. She sat beside him at supper each evening, and if there were any games to be played after the meal, she was always hovering nearby.

To interested observers, and they were legion in the great house, it seemed the merry widow held Lord Hartley under her spell and he was well on the way to becoming her husband number five. Freddie and the rest of the hopeful debutantes were understandably distressed.

If John hadn't continued to slip short love notes into Rebecca's pocket or under her chamber door

at least once a day, she'd have been tempted to
believe the night he'd declared his love for her was
only a dream.

However, his scheme seemed to be working. The
dowager marchioness was beside herself over this turn
of events.

"My dear, I thought you understood that you
were to assist my grandson in the proper way to woo
a lady," she said to Rebecca over her after-supper
sherry. On this particular evening, the gentlemen and
ladies had not split up along lines of gender, and the
whole party congregated in Somerfield Park's massive
drawing room. The dowager eyed her grandson across
the room with a pointed look.

Rebecca did not follow suit. She didn't need to
look at John to know that Lady Chloe was there with
him, hanging on his every word.

"He seems to be doing quite well with wooing and
needs no instruction from me."

The entire house party was spread out in a glittering
array, the *beau monde* in miniature with all its foibles,
pettiness, and grandeur. Tables had been set up for
numerous card games. Even Lord Somerset was evidently feeling up to taking part in the lively game of
charades in one corner. He and his lovely wife were in
the center of a boisterous circle of players. Since he'd
accidentally shot John's valet, his lordship had become
much more gregarious. It was odd in the extreme, but
Rebecca had reached the point where nothing about
the Barrett family surprised her.

John was in the opposite corner, playing loo with
a group of five others, and try as she might, Rebecca

couldn't keep her gaze from straying there. One of the other players was the ubiquitous Lady Chloe. She leaned toward him to whisper into his ear. Whatever she'd said must have been amusing because he laughed loudly enough to be heard across the room. Rebecca's insides did a slow burn.

"Perhaps I did not make myself clear," the dowager said. "Gentlemen need guidance, and gentlemen who are courting need it most of all. It is not Hartley's method of wooing which troubles me, but the object of said wooing."

"On that score I cannot help," Rebecca said. "Your grandson seems to have made his choice."

The dowager leaned toward her. "Then we shall have to unmake it for him."

"How?"

The dowager frowned. "If I knew, I wouldn't be asking you for help, would I?"

"Have you spoken to him about Lady Chloe?"

"I daresay anything I said on the subject would be tantamount to tossing more kindling on an already roaring fire. If I try to dissuade him from this misalliance, he's more apt to flee toward it." She drummed her bejeweled fingers on the arm of her overstuffed chair. "He's as stubborn as his father on that score."

"Have you spoken to the lady, then?"

The dowager made an undignified noise that sounded suspiciously like a snort, though she would have denied with her final breath that one of her exalted rank was capable of such a vulgar response. "Lady Chloe is not like John's mother."

"You mean she cannot be bought."

"It's not only that, though heaven knows the fact that Lady Chloe is independently wealthy does make it difficult to tempt her with more. The money was a secondary consideration for John's mother." The dowager's eyes took on a slightly hazy glaze as she reached for the distant memory of the last time she'd interfered in a match involving one of her progeny. "It's true that she was dazzled by the prospect of her own funds and the freedom to use them as she wished, but she was also motivated by her feelings for my son. She realized she'd damage him by staying with him. They were from two different worlds. She could never have hoped to span the chasm between them. She would have diminished him forever."

That wasn't only the dowager's opinion, Rebecca realized. There was nothing the *bon ton* hated so much as a disruption in the natural order of things. An opera dancer as a marchioness would have offended their collective souls so deeply that they would have been merciless over the uneven match.

Would they feel the same about the daughter of a debt-riddled baron? No, Rebecca assured herself. If the Barrett family accepted the match, gossips would say Lord Hartley had married beneath him and that Rebecca had done exceedingly well for herself. That should be the end of it.

"Lady Chloe, however, is not motivated by her feelings for my grandson," Lady Somerset went on as if there hadn't been a lull in the conversation. "She is without doubt the most self-centered person I've ever encountered, and I've met the prince regent on numerous occasions, so that's saying something. Lady

Chloe's own wishes are her sole guide. She rules by fiat and expects the rest of the world to fall willy-nilly in line with her plans."

Well, if that wasn't a case of the pot coming face to face with the kettle, Rebecca didn't know what was. However, she didn't think Lady Somerset would appreciate having her similarities to Lady Chloe pointed out to her.

"So you see, we must make Hartley see reason, and you're just the one to help him do it," Lady Somerset said. "He must make a different choice."

"Whom did you have in mind?"

The dowager surveyed the room. If she said even Rebecca would be preferable to Lady Chloe, John's plan would have succeeded and the farce could end. Instead, Lady Somerset's gaze fell upon Rebecca's friend.

"Lady Winifred would be ideal. Such a bright young lady and, more importantly, so well-connected. Or the Earl of Montfort's daughter. Her name escapes me at the moment, but she's biddable as a lamb. She'd be an excellent choice." A biddable wife for Lord Hartley meant Lady Somerset could continue to rule Somerfield Park by means subtle and overt even after her son's tenure as marquess was over. "In truth, any unattached young lady in this room would be an acceptable improvement over that…that woman."

It wasn't a ringing endorsement of Rebecca, but at least she might consider herself lumped in with the "acceptables." It was a start.

The dowager shot a smoldering glare across the room that by rights should have reduced Lady Chloe, as well as anyone within ten feet of her, to smoking cinders.

"Go talk to him, Rebecca."

"What? Now?"

"Yes, at once, before you lose your train of thought."

She was quite capable of keeping a train of thought where John was concerned, thank you very much. But extricating him from an active card game was a daunting prospect. "What would I say to him?"

"I don't know. You're his friend. Ask for his help. You'll think of something." The dowager waved her away and then fluttered her fan toward her own face. "Now go, girl."

Rebecca stood and started across the long space. Several couples were congregating around the table where tea was laid. Card games abounded, but since they were in mixed company, no actual wagering was going on. That was reserved for the gentlemen in the smoking room, after the ladies retired for the night. No one paid her any heed as she headed toward John.

She'd decided she would tell him that Mr. Porter had taken a turn for the worse—a touch of fever, perhaps—and would he come see what was to be done for his valet? Most gentlemen wouldn't give two figs for the health of their servants, except as it related to how their inability to serve would impact their wellborn employers, but John would care. He'd leave the loo game immediately. But before she could reach him, her father intercepted her.

"We haven't had much chance to speak lately, Daughter," Lord Kearsey said. "Are you enjoying yourself?"

"Yes, Father. Mother is fine, if that's what you're concerned about," she said, anxious to shake him off so she could continue across the room. "I saw that she was settled after supper, and she said I should come back down to spend time with the rest of the company."

"To be sure, she doesn't wish her infirmity to dampen your pleasure. She's considerate in that way."

Didn't he realize that if Rebecca thought her mother needed her, she couldn't enjoy herself anywhere else but at her side?

"What do you want, Father?"

"To speak to you privily. Come." He led her to a little alcove, where a cushioned window seat would provide a spot to sit and converse without being overheard.

"I know you had hopes of Lord Hartley when you came here, dear," he said, taking her hand between his. "He led you a merry chase, and I'd thrash the young pup if it would do any good."

"There's no need for that." Besides, though she loved her father, Lord Kearsey was a stick of a man. John could break him like a twig. "Lord Hartley didn't deceive me. If I had hopes, it was my own fault."

"I won't believe that for a moment. But let us consider your options honestly. While it's doubtful you could bring down the trophy buck at this little gathering—and I'm first to admit the fault lies with me and your poor dowry, not you, my dear—you may yet be able to capture a lesser beast."

"Father, you've been hunting far too often of late. What girl wants a beast of any sort? Speak your mind plainly."

"Lord Hartley is beyond your reach, but there are other gentlemen here who might well do for you."

"You mean second sons and such." John's friends,

Smalley and Pitcairn, came to mind and flitted right out again. Rebecca would end her days a spinster before she'd wed either of those fellows. Smalley was more interested in his dinner plate than anything, and Pitcairn was such a nervous little fellow, he infected everyone around him with the fidgets just from being in close proximity to him.

"No, dear," Lord Kearsey said. "I think you might raise your sights a bit."

Her sights were already on Lord Hartley, the "trophy buck." And John wanted her. It amused her to hear Lord Kearsey's thoughts on a suitable match for her. Wouldn't he feel foolish once John revealed his true choice! "So, Father, upon whom do you think I should set my cap?"

"Viscount Blackwood."

"Blackwood?" She still remembered being warned off him in the strongest possible terms.

"Unlike Hartley, he doesn't have to wait for his father to die to come into his own. Blackwood is already a peer. His income is not staggering, but neither is it insubstantial."

"I don't like him," she said firmly.

"You don't know him."

"I know *of* him. And that's quite enough."

"You'll have a chance to change your mind now," her father said. "He's headed this way."

"I don't care to—"

He took her by the shoulders, his eyes wild. "Rebecca. You must. Please. I have promised him you'd... Just hear him out, will you?"

She'd only seen desperation like that in Lord

Kearsey's eyes once before—when his gambling debts had forced him to confiscate and sell her jewelry. "Father, what have you done?"

Before he could answer, Blackwood stopped before them and gave a correct bow from the neck. "Miss Kearsey, may I say you're looking particularly fetching this evening."

Rebecca thanked him and dropped the requisite curtsy.

"I was wondering," the viscount said. "Have you seen the portrait gallery here at Somerfield Park?"

She shook her head.

"Then I should be delighted to show it to you. There are some rather fine works on display." He offered her his arm in a way that brooked no refusal. With her father standing by, encouraging her, it would be an insult of the first water to decline.

"Thank you, my lord." A flash of inspiration burst in her mind. "I believe my friend, Lady Winifred, would be interested in the gallery as well. She's much more knowledgeable about art than I and—"

"Tut, tut," her father interrupted. "Blackwood has invited you to view the portraits, not give him an art history lecture. Go along now."

The only way to avoid going with the viscount was to defy her father and make a nasty scene. Neither was in her nature. Rebecca laid a hand on Blackwood's forearm and allowed him to lead her away.

Twenty-five

It is never good to eavesdrop. It diminishes both parties, the spy as well as the one being spied upon. But sometimes, it is the only way to learn anything worth knowing.

—Phillippa, the Dowager Marchioness of Somerset

THERESA OPENED THE SECRET DOOR THAT LED FROM the back staircase into the gallery, but she was careful to open it only a crack. She did it slowly and without making any more noise than a mouse fart. Then she put her eye to the slim opening and checked to see if anyone was in the high-ceilinged room.

She was in luck. No one was wandering the long, narrow space. Theresa slipped through the door, taking care not to let it close completely behind her. She sometimes had a dickens of a time finding the hidden latch from the Family side of the portal.

Like her sister Eliza, Theresa Dovecote loved sneaking into the gallery. She hadn't believed her sister when she first carried tales of the magical space. Now she didn't think Eliza had told her the half of it. The ornately painted ceiling was so lovely, so chock-full of phantasmagorical wonder, it made tears gather at the corners of her eyes. The walls of the room were lined with images of long-dead ladies in gorgeous gowns with glowing gems accenting perilously scooped necklines. Then there were the debonair gentlemen in suits of armor or plumed hats.

It was a faery world on canvas, filled with whimsy. Theresa had made up dozens of stories for herself about the people in the paintings. As often as her duties allowed, Theresa slipped into the gallery, so she could stop being a cook's helper, even if it was only for a few moments, and become one of those fancy ladies in her imagination.

If Mrs. Culpepper hadn't warned her off wandering into the gallery, would she still have felt compelled to visit the place? Probably not at this time of day. She usually tried to sneak into the forbidden upstairs world early in the morning when most of the Quality were still abed. But since the cook had brought it up, it was all she could think of as she washed up after the servants' tea. Mrs. C's threats to her hadn't helped her resist the gallery's tug one jot, and she nipped up to it the moment she was free.

Theresa didn't waste any time, but went promptly to the painting of *Him*. She didn't know his name. It might be on that brass plate at the bottom of the painting, but Theresa had never learned to read or write more than her own name. She had to content herself with the knowledge that her mystery gentleman was one of the Barrett ancestors. He was dressed in a suit of armor that still gleamed despite the patina of age on the canvas. His hair was the same dark honey color of the current Lord Somerset and his son Lord Richard. His eyes were a warm amber peering at her from the past. He seemed to be looking right at Theresa, as if he knew her, as if he could see her secret dreams and approved them.

"Oh, how I wish you weren't dead as a doorknob," she whispered to him. "Indeed, I do."

Toby the footman was fun to flirt with, but this long-departed gentleman called to her with his soulful eyes in a way the very much alive Toby didn't. Would she ever find a living, breathing man fit to take the place of her dream fellow?

Theresa very much doubted it. So she came here as often as she could to wallow in melancholy over her unanswerable love. Sometimes it hurt so badly, it was downright pleasurable.

She knew there was no reason to that, but knowing didn't make it any less so.

Theresa might have stood there for another quarter hour if she hadn't heard the clack of a man's boot on the polished hardwood, headed her way. She scurried back to the secret door, slipped through it, and pulled it nearly closed behind her just as a couple was framed in the broad opening that led from the foyer into the gallery. Most of her life was lived in the dim realm of "Below Stairs." She couldn't resist peeping at these living examples of the rarified beings that inhabited the "Above Stairs" world.

The gentleman was dressed all in black save for his very white shirt front and intricately tied cravat. His trousers were cut close to his muscular thighs, his knee boots were glossy enough to cast reflections of the gilt spindle legs of the side table nearest him. His strong-featured face might be called striking, but it could not be called pleasant. His expression was far too severe for that.

The lady would have had a sweet face if her mouth weren't pinched so tight. Her gown was pale green, and now that Theresa considered it with a critical eye, she'd swear it wasn't silk. While it was a good deal finer than anything Theresa had ever owned or was ever likely to, the green gown looked as if its sleeves and hem had been "turned" a time or two to hide fraying edges.

Theresa knew she ought not to eavesdrop. Mr. Hightower was very specific on that point. Servants were expected to be seen and not heard. Except for her, of course. Theresa might have been content with merely being seen, only she wasn't even allowed to do that. She wasn't supposed to venture above stairs once the Family was up and about. But as for the other below stairs folk, once any of them crossed the threshold into the public areas of the house, they were assumed not to see or hear anything that wasn't directly related to their serving. It was rather as if the butler expected them to go about their duties like draft horses wearing blinders. Nothing could distract them while they used all their energy to pull Somerfield Park into the good opinion of all the respectable guests.

Phoo to that, Theresa thought as she huddled closer to the crack in the door. *I'm here. They're here. I'm going to see how the Upper Crust behaves themselves when they think no one's looking if it strikes me blind.*

❦

"There are some very fine pieces here," Rebecca said as she strolled down the center of the gallery, stopping from time to time to admire one painting after another. "If you'd let me send for my friend Lady Winifred, I'm sure she could tell us who the artists are."

"I don't care a fig for that. The artists don't figure at all. It's the subjects, the Barretts, that you're supposed to be interested in, you know." Blackwood stopped before a canvas showing a gentleman in early-eighteenth-century knee breeches. A cutlass dangled from his belt and a Letter of Marque was curled in his defiant fist. "Pirates, rogues, and thieves, all around, they are."

"Surely not all. The Barretts are a venerable old family that has held Somerset since the time of William—"

"The Conqueror. Yes, so I've heard," he drawled in a bored tone. "And do you not think it would take a string of ruthless lords to be able to hold this not inconsiderable piece of earth since then?"

"I suspect any man can be ruthless when the occasion calls for it," she admitted. "But the present Lord Somerset seems a proper gentleman."

As opposed to her present company. Not that Lord Blackwood had done anything untoward, but there was something in his manner, in the way his gaze drifted downward that made Rebecca feel as if one or more of her buttons had come undone. She didn't dare check, for fear of drawing more attention to her bosom than he was already giving it.

"The present Lord Somerset is a befogged scatter-wit, and that's being charitable. But don't fool yourself. He was undoubtedly a wolf of a man in his prime." Lord Blackwood leaned against the wall, looking more than a little wolfish himself. "Even my friend Lord Hartley has a rod of steel where his spine should be. I don't say that to condemn him, you understand. Pride of place and privilege is all it's cracked up to be. It is a fine thing to be in a position to have one's every want gratified."

"I don't think that's how Lord Hartley would class his situation." In fact, John seemed to feel himself particularly powerless where his family was concerned and hence wasn't as demanding of them as he could be. John would never cut off the current Lord Somerset's entire family once he became the marquess, despite the way they'd treated him as a boy. However, she had no doubt it would be first on Lord Blackwood's list if he were in John's shoes. "He never expected to become Lord Somerset's heir, you know. I don't believe his change in station will change him."

"Don't be too sure about that. He'll come around to it soon. Just because he wasn't raised with certain advantages doesn't mean he won't learn to love them and demand them in a short time."

Rebecca walked farther down the gallery, pretending interest in the myriad canvases but really just trying to put some distance between them. "I thought you were his friend."

Lord Blackwood laughed. "I am. I'm not tarring him with any brush I'm not tainted with myself. You see, I too know what I want, and I know I can have it."

"I collect you have high expectations since you're a peer of the realm."

And according to Freddie, he was a well-heeled peer. "Poor taste and an empty purse don't always go hand in hand," Freddie was fond of saying. "Low habits and a high income, that Lord Blackwood."

"But even you can't have everything you want, my lord. It wouldn't be good for you."

"Please, call me Blackwood." He closed the distance between them, crowding her as she tried to stroll along the length of the room. "It's friendlier that way."

She didn't feel the least friendly toward him. In fact, the way he matched her steps around the long hall made gooseflesh rise. But she thought it best to humor him. "Blackwood, then."

"Good. Come now, Miss Kearsey. Surely you can guess what I want."

She never expected he'd move so quickly. Before she knew what he was about, he had her pressed up against the polished mahogany wall next to a distressing portrait of old Lady Somerset in a most unfortunate hat.

"I want you, of course," he said, his voice the rumbling growl of a predator.

She pressed against his chest, but he didn't budge an inch. "In that case, you are destined for disappointment. I am not to be had for the wanting."

"You are gravely mistaken, my dear." He bent his head to sniff appreciatively at her hair. His nearness made Rebecca feel as though she needed a bath. A scalding hot one, for choice. "You see, Lord Kearsey and I were the last to leave the poque table on the first night of the house party. He thought he had a winning hand with his four queens, but I dissuaded him of the notion with my four aces. As a result, I hold your father's vowels."

Her stomach began to swirl and then sink. Whatever his failings, her father could be counted upon to pay his gambling debts. She just wasn't sure what the Kearseys had left to sell. The family already dined on pewter instead of china, and the staff that served them had been cut to the bone. Still, he'd find a way to satisfy the debt. Her father might be quite run off his legs, but no one could accuse him of failing to pay what he owed.

"My father always makes good on his debts of honor," she said staunchly.

"I'm depending upon that. But I suspect he's never been this far into dun territory before. You see, the only way he can manage to pay this time is to petition the House of Lords to allow him to carve up his land and sell it off piecemeal."

This was devastating news, but Rebecca tried not to let him see how it affected her. The meager rent from the tenants who farmed the land surrounding the Kearsey countryseat was the only dependable source of income for the family. The home place might be ever so shabby since there was never any extra money to do the upkeep the manor house so desperately needed, but it was all they had. When her father had lost at the gaming tables badly before, Rebecca had been so embarrassed at the way their home fell into disrepair, she declined to invite anyone to visit but Freddie, who could be depended upon not to care about their reduced circumstances.

But this was more than merely an embarrassment. She'd never considered that her father might someday lose even what little remained to them. The Kearseys would be ruined this time.

Unless...

So that's why her father was so insistent that she consider Blackwood as husband material. Likely the return of his IOUs was part of a marriage bargain they'd discussed.

She crossed her arms over her chest, a small shield from Blackwood. "I don't know what sort of scheme you and my father have concocted between you, but nothing could be more repugnant to me than a forced match."

"A forced match?" Blackwood threw back his head and laughed. "Oh, bravo, Miss Kearsey. Innocence played with such devastating conviction. Are you certain you've never trod the boards in Drury Lane?"

As if a lady would engage in so common an activity as acting on the stage.

"But I—" *am innocent* almost tumbled out her mouth before she remembered it would be a lie. John had well and thoroughly initiated her into the world of the sensual. Did Blackwood somehow sense that? Like a smallpox scar, did carnal experience leave a mark for all to see? More to the point, why was the man still laughing?

"You think I intend to offer marriage?" he finally managed to wheeze out.

She cocked her head at him, ready to believe him crackbrained, the way he chuckled through his words.

"Do you mean to say your father didn't tell you? No, I can see from the expression on your pretty face that he didn't, the coward." Then the laughter faded and he suddenly grabbed her and pressed her against the wall again, his body flush against hers. "You, my dear, are the down payment on your father's debt. First, you will give yourself to me unreservedly. Do you know what I mean by that?"

She narrowly resisted the urged to scream. If she did, her father would be well and truly ruined. Blackwood would see to it.

"It means I use you in any way I like." He put two fingers to her mouth and brushed the tips across her lower lip. "If I want you to take me in your mouth, you will, my lovely. And you'll smile when you do it."

She jerked her face to the side. It would serve the man right if she retched on him. "Anything you think to put in my mouth will be in extreme danger of being bitten off."

"Spirit. I like that. In small doses. It gives me reason to discipline you." He grasped one of her arms and forced it behind her until she was bent over at the waist. Then he snugged her bum against the hard bulge on the front of his trousers. She gasped in shock and struggled to get away but stopped when he twisted her arm so hard that she saw stars and feared he'd snap her limb like a dry twig.

"Let me go this instant or I'll scream," she spat out.

"No, you won't. By the time anyone came, I'd be on the other side of the room, shaking my head over your attack of the vapors. No one will believe I said such things to you—or did such things to you."

He reached under her hem and ran his hand up her leg to squeeze her buttocks painfully.

She cried out, but then clamped her lips together. He was right. She would be the one who would be publicly censured if she made a fuss that drew a crowd.

"If I want to ride you like a mare in heat, you'll get down on your knees and beg me prettily to do it harder. And if I wish to pass you around to my friends, you'll serve them as you would me. I'll know because I'll be watching. I may even charge admission for others to do so as well. It's not every day of the week a baron's daughter plays the whore, and believe me, that's what you'll be by the time we're done."

Rebecca squeezed her eyes shut but couldn't shut out the ugly images his words slammed into her brain. "And then you'll cancel my father's debt."

"No, that's only the down payment. If I like you, and you'd better pray that I do, I'll set you up as my own little ladybird. Nothing too ostentatious, you understand, but we'll need some privacy for what I have in mind, my dove." He twisted her arm again until she whimpered. "You see, I've lately become enamored of the writings of the Marquis de Sade. He's convinced me that pleasure and pain exist side by side. Of course, I mean to conduct my own inquiry into that philosophy. There are depths of pain I cannot plumb with the game girls of Whitechapel. The bullies who protect them always interfere just when things become interesting."

Rebecca tried to draw breath but found nothing about her was working right. Her vision darkened, but she fought to stay conscious. Who knew what he'd do to her if she passed out?

"You will be my willing participant," he hissed.

"You'll work off your father's debt one stripe, one pinch, one prick at a time. You'll come to love it, need it even, eventually. At least that's what the marquis discovered in his subjects, a deep-seated need for pain. I shall be happy to oblige you in yours."

The darkness began to seep toward the center of her vision. If she didn't get away soon, she'd drop in a heap. "You are beyond vile."

"Oh, my dear. Just you wait. I shall exceed your every expectation."

Desperate, Rebecca raised her knee and kicked backward, landing a solid blow to his shin. It wasn't enough to hurt him as she wished she could, but it surprised him enough so that she was able to wiggle free and skitter across the room.

"My father can't have known what you're planning."

"He can and does. You see, while your father is a fool, he'll sacrifice anything to protect his wife—even his dear daughter. How do you think being destitute will affect Lady Kearsey's already-precarious health?"

"No, no, no," she chanted as she backed away. "John won't let that happen. He'll take care of my mother. I know he will."

"John, is it? You think yourself safe because you're cozy with Lord Hartley? Calling him John doesn't mean a thing. I called him Fitzhugh for years and had no inkling of who he really was. You don't know him any better. But I suppose you think he'll come to your rescue like he did in that boxing crib. John the backwoods bumpkin who's lately fallen into Lady Chloe's clutches? That John?"

"Yes. He won't allow you to hurt me or my family."

"He doesn't have any say in the matter. And I'd advise you against telling him anything about our little agreement."

"We have no agreement."

Blackwood pulled a piece of paper from his waistcoat pocket. "I have your father's IOU, remember. The law, the *ton*, even Lord Kearsey's own twisted sense of honor is on my side. Nothing can stop me from having him prosecuted for this debt. Except you."

Rebecca wanted more than anything to flee, but it was as though her slippers had been nailed to the floor.

"I'll take your silence as consent. Here's how we'll begin. On the night of the ball, you will profess a headache and repair to your chamber by midnight. I will join you shortly thereafter, and we shall…become better acquainted."

In the silence that followed, there was a little squeak, as if someone were suppressing a cry followed by the loud snick of a latch.

"Who's there?" Blackwood demanded.

Rebecca didn't wait to see. Suddenly her feet felt free. She hiked her skirt and fled out of the gallery as fast as she could. Blackwood had to be lying. Her father couldn't have known what the man had planned when he practically shoved her into Blackwood's arms. He simply couldn't.

❧

Oh Lud, now I'm for it. Theresa clattered down the back staircase as if the hounds of hell were on her heels. *I never should have gone up to the gallery tonight.*

And I especially shouldn't have stayed to listen to the Quality Folk...only now I know some of 'em ain't such Quality after all.

It shocked her to her curled toes that a highborn lady might be treated as if she were a common gutter tramp. Her mum was right all along. Women had no say in this world. None at all.

Well, Theresa was going to have a say. She was going to tell...

That was just it. Who could she tell? Mr. Hightower would likely be as shocked as she at the treatment of Miss Kearsey, but Theresa would have to admit to eavesdropping in order to have known about it.

Such a thing was likely to cost her her position.

She couldn't lose that. Her mum depended on the extra blunt Theresa sent her each week.

But she couldn't let that horrid Lord Blackwood get away with his plans, either. And while she mulled over what to do, she'd do what she could as Cook's assistant.

With a little finagling in the kitchen and a little help from the footman Toby, at the very least, she'd see to it that nice Miss Kearsey was avenged. Lord Blackwood would find a spider in the bottom of his breakfast teacup on the morrow.

Twenty-six

Adversity brings allies together. Well, it would, wouldn't it? If there is no common foe, nothing is more likely than squabbles among even the dearest of friends.

—Phillippa, the Dowager Marchioness of Somerset

JOHN PUT ON A GOOD SHOW OF BEING ATTENTIVE TO LADY Chloe while they played loo, but he knew to within a finger-width where Rebecca was at all times while she was in the drawing room. When she left on Blackwood's arm, he watched the minutes tick by on the ormolu clock on the mantel and resented each one that passed.

Blackwood was the only titled gent who'd befriended him when he'd first arrived in London. John owed him a bit for that kindness. Compared to the raucous time they'd spent together in London, the viscount had behaved like a choirboy at Somerfield Park. John knew of Blackwood's darker proclivities, even if he didn't share them. The thought of Rebecca being alone with the viscount, even within the confines of the great house, made him uneasy.

He excused himself from the card game after throwing the last hand and headed through the doorway Rebecca and Blackwood had used. All the rooms on the ground floor of the house seemed to run into each other, one after another. John hurried through parlors and salons, a music room and library, before he turned a corner and Rebecca practically ran into his arms.

She didn't seem to recognize him in the dimness. "No, let me go," she demanded when he snatched her to him.

"Steady on. It's me," John said, hugging her tight. She collapsed into him then. He cupped her head and pressed it to his chest. Her cheeks were damp. Had she been crying? "What's wrong?"

"Oh, John. I...I can't tell you." She trembled like a birch in a breeze.

"Did Blackwood hurt you?" he demanded.

"Well of course he did, or she wouldn't be so beside herself." Lady Chloe's voice came from behind them. She lifted the candle she carried and lit a wall lamp, sending the shadows scurrying away. "Honestly, men are so thickheaded sometimes. By the way, if the two of you are still trying to convince everyone that Hartley prefers me above all, holding each other so tightly I couldn't slip a piece of parchment between you is probably not the best way to go about it."

Rebecca stepped out of the circle of John's arms. "You're right, my lady," she said. "It's a good thing it was you who happened upon us."

"Assuredly," Chloe said. "Come now, Miss Kearsey. What did that cur do?"

Rebecca bit her lower lip. "I can't say."

"Of course you can. If you don't, Hartley and I will be forced to guess what foul thing Blackwood's up to, and I haven't the patience for it. If I wanted to play charades, I'd have joined Lord Somerset's group in the far corner of the drawing room. Lud, what fools they were making of themselves over there, all that capering about. Now, tell me, dearie. And don't leave anything out."

Lady Chloe reached out her hands, and to John's astonishment, Rebecca took them. Chloe truly did possess the ability to charm everyone she met. He had no idea why she didn't unleash that ability on the *ton*.

Perhaps, like him, she preferred to push Polite Society away before they had time to reject her.

"She's right, Rebecca," John said. "You should know by now that no harm will come to you while I breathe."

"It's not my harm I'm worried about." The stricken look on her face put the lie to that. She was truly afraid. "It's my parents I fear for."

"Oh, you poor lamb." Chloe put her arm around Rebecca and led her to a nearby settee. "Tell us everything."

It occurred to John that Chloe had cut him off from Rebecca as effectively as another gentleman cutting in on the dance floor. He narrowed his eyes at the lady, wondering what her game was now.

But he couldn't fault her results. Rebecca's troubles spilled out of her as if the floodgates had been opened. John grimaced at the tale of her father's feckless gambling and ground his teeth together when she told about how Lord Kearsey all but shoved her into Blackwood's arms to settle the debt. Rebecca was certain her father believed the viscount was making an offer of marriage for her, and the threats were simply his way of making sure she couldn't refuse. She couldn't accept that Lord Kearsey knew anything about Blackwood's true intentions, but John wasn't so sanguine.

A gambler would do anything to feed his habit— even make himself believe the unbelievable.

"Well, there's nothing else for it," John said. "I'll call Blackwood out."

"No," both the women exclaimed in unison, then Rebecca went on. "I won't have you dueling over me."

"But he insulted your honor."

"Which will not be made whole by letting Blackwood blow a hole of a different sort in your chest," Chloe said.

"You're assuming he's a better shot than I am," John said.

"It's no assumption. It's a fact." Chloe rolled her eyes expressively. "Lord Blackwood has been involved in no less than three duels to my certain knowledge, and he killed his man in two of them. The third lived, but…well, suffice it to say he will never father children."

Eyes pleading, Rebecca stood and put a hand on his arm. "Please, John. Don't risk yourself on my account."

Didn't she know by now that he'd risk anything for her?

"Besides, a duel would be pointless in any case,"

Chloe said, tapping her fingernails on her very white front teeth as she considered the matter. "The problem isn't merely the insult to Rebecca, though that was horrid and not to be excused. But the fact is, she escaped unharmed."

John put an arm around Rebecca's waist and drew her close. "She won't remain so if Blackwood has his way."

"Then we must make sure he doesn't." Chloe stood and paced, her skirt swishing on the hardwood as she made each pass. "As I see it, the crux of the matter is that IOU. If we can retrieve that, Blackwood has nothing but a handful of fingers. He'd have no way to demand anything of anyone."

"My father would still owe him a debt," Rebecca pointed out.

"But not an enforceable one," Chloe said. "It would be Blackwood's word against Lord Kearsey's. Did anyone else see them enter into the wager?"

Rebecca cocked her head to one side, searching her memory. "No. Blackwood said he and my father were the last two in the poque game."

"Then by whatever means, we must relieve him of those vowels," Chloe said.

"Where would he keep them?" John asked.

"I think I know," Lady Chloe said, pulling out her fan and waving it languidly before her. "But it would be indelicate of me to say where and even more indelicate to say how I know."

John and Rebecca both sent her looks of indignation.

"Oh, very well." Chloe snapped the fan shut. "Blackwood keeps important things tucked into his smalls. Now, none of that. Wipe that smirk off your face, Hartley, or I'll not help you a bit."

"I'm not smirking," John said, trying to school his expression so the smirk he felt inside wouldn't show outside. "I'm sure you have a perfectly innocent reason why you know Blackwood keeps his valuables in his smalls, but the deuce of it is, that certainly makes them hard to steal," John admitted grudgingly.

"But we can't simply steal them. It's dishonest. That would make us as rotten as he. My father must have lost to Lord Blackwood fairly, or he'd never have…" Rebecca stopped herself. It was still too painful for her to admit Lord Kearsey had tossed her at Blackwood as if she were a stack of banknotes.

"Well, that settles it. If you don't want me to shoot the blackguard, and your sense of rightness won't let me lift the vowels from him, I shall have to win Lord Kearsey's IOU back," John said.

"Blackwood will never hazard them," Chloe said.

"He will if he doesn't know he's doing it," John said. "I have a plan."

~

John escorted Rebecca to her chamber. Once she went through her door, he leaned on the doorjamb to keep her from closing it right away. He knew he shouldn't hang about her room, but he couldn't help himself. He wanted more than anything to be invited in, but she'd had enough trouble from men this night. He didn't want to add to her unease.

"I'm sorry to be such a bother," she said.

"You could never be that. I don't want you to

worry about your family or anything else." He cupped her cheek. He couldn't seem to help himself. He'd kept his distance from her over the past few days, and his insides were strained to the breaking point. It was touch her or die.

Just that, he promised himself. *I'll only touch her face.*

"I've been meaning to tell you that I asked Richard's man of business to make inquiries about the right physician for your mother. He found one in Bath who specializes in treating illnesses of the lungs. After Christmas, I'll send her and your father there, so she can take the waters and regain her health."

"Oh, John, do you think it will work? How wonderful if it does." Her eyes glistened with unshed tears. Rebecca stood on tiptoe and kissed his cheek, obviously not caring if anyone popped out of one of the other bedchambers and happened to see them. However, the other guests seemed to be either abed already or still in the drawing room. No one else roamed the dark hallway. "Won't I be going with them?"

"No, you'll be my countess by then, I hope." Her sweet scent wove itself around him, an intoxicating summons. He forced himself not to act on it. She'd been manhandled enough for one night. He needed to prove he respected her, idolized her a little even.

"And yet..." She walked her fingers up his chest. John was certain she had no idea how she was teasing him. "You still haven't officially asked me to marry you."

"I'm getting to it." *Her hair. I'll just stroke her hair.* There was one chestnut lock curling past her shoulder. He ran its silky length through his fingers. "I'm waiting until we can announce your answer right away."

"Then maybe you'd better come in." She gave his arm a tug, pulled him into her room, and quickly shut the door behind him. "If someone were to catch us all tangled up by my door, you'd likely be forced into marrying me, and I wouldn't want that."

"You wouldn't?" His body cheered the whole "tangled up" business with an aching cockstand.

"No." She looped her arms around his neck and peered up at him in the dimness. "What girl wants to be a bride merely to satisfy the sense of propriety of the *ton*?"

"I see your point." She was making him crowd his trousers till the seams strained. He ached to lose himself in her.

"I want to marry for love," she said. "Undeniable. Irrevocable. Love without an ending. Doesn't that sound wonderful?"

It sounded like a tall order. John hadn't known much love in his life. His flighty mother had left him too soon to deliver love without an ending. His foster parents offered a strict, prickly sort of halfhearted affection, dependent upon his deportment and willingness to work without complaint. His family hadn't shown him any love at all.

"That's how I feel about us," she went on as she hugged him close. "What about you?"

"I've told you I love you, but I can't honestly say I know what that means. It's too high for me. Too fine," he admitted. "Sometimes, I don't know what I feel. I collect there's something different about you, Rebecca. I recognized it right off that day in the museum. It's as if…there's something missing in me and you've got it hidden inside you. I need you, you see. That's love, isn't it?"

She stood on tiptoe and kissed him again, this time on the mouth. "Close enough."

She slipped her arms under his jacket to run her hands along his ribs. Then she let them slide down to tease his bum. Much more of this, and he'd be on her in a heated rut. John grasped both her hands and held them tight between them.

"What are you doing?" he demanded.

"Don't you like it?"

"More than my next breath, but, Rebecca...I don't want to press you for anything tonight."

"Don't you see, John? I need you too. Blackwood made me feel so very dirty. The things he said, and...I need you to wash me clean of him. Please."

⁓

"I am without doubt the luckiest almost-bastard in the world," he whispered in awe.

"Yes, you are." She grinned up at him and unfastened the top button on her bodice. Then his hands replaced hers and he undid the rest of the row.

Slowly. Carefully. His fingertips slipped beneath the muslin to brush her newly exposed skin. His breath tickled warmly on her neck as he kissed his way along her neckline. He touched her with deliberation, with tenderness, with a sense of wonder.

She'd cringed with distaste when Blackwood laid a hand on her. With John, she tingled with awareness. By the time he bared her breasts and bent to take a taut nipple in his mouth, she was trembling with need.

Articles of clothing sloughed away and fell to the floor. Whatever barriers might yet have existed between them slipped away too. Skin on skin. Heartbeat on heartbeat. Rebecca felt herself fade into John and he into her. They danced a tipsy sort of waltz to no discernible time signature, backing and advancing, turning and lifting, to make the most of the way their bodies fit together as they moved across the room.

John's breath filled her. His sharp masculine scent overwhelmed her. His mouth was the whole world, his hands the stuff of magic.

When they finally tumbled into the waiting bed, there was no more sense of being two separate people. They were one. One flesh. One heart.

One shared soul between them.

They hadn't said the words that would bind them together forever yet. Their bodies made the vow for them. There was no need for words.

Twenty-seven

In the theatre, the first and second acts plod along like a draft horse, while the final one races like the swiftest courser. As one nears the end of life, the same thing happens, only with days.

—Phillippa, the Dowager Marchioness of Somerset

AFTER THERESA DOVECOTE FINISHED HER WORK FOR the night, she plopped down on the bottom step of the back stairs and held her head in her hands. She couldn't confide in Mr. Hightower what she'd seen. Mrs. Grahame, the housekeeper, would be as aghast as the butler over the way she'd spied on folk in the upstairs world. She definitely couldn't break protocol and speak to anyone from the Family. Yet she wanted so desperately to help that nice Miss Kearsey. If she didn't, it would plague her for the rest of her days.

She never should have eavesdropped. Her mother, who was cursed with an overlong nose, always said it grew that way because she never stuck it into other people's business. Theresa wished she had her mother's long nose instead of her pert, short one.

"That'll teach me," she mumbled.

"What'll teach you?"

She jerked her head up to find Toby grinning down at her. "Never you mind."

"Oh, but I do mind. It's plain you've got some troubles, and I've a nice broad shoulder." He sat down next to her and flicked off a little imaginary dust from the shoulder of his smart blue livery. "There you go. Have a good cry if you like. It would certainly be a novelty. You've a reputation for being a coldhearted wench, you know."

She and Toby flirted with each other madly, but sometimes, it felt as if he was merely teasing her to amuse himself, to fill up his time until someone better came along. As the scullery help, she was far beneath a footman, and he often made her feel it.

"You'd like that, wouldn't you? Then you could brag to your friends that I was weeping and they'd think you're the cause," she said. "The day you make me cry will never dawn, Toby Hollis."

She made a low growling noise in the back of her throat, stood, and legged it to the back door off the common room in long strides. Toby was on her heels.

"Don't take on so, Theresa," he said. "I was only funning. Of course I don't want you to cry, only you just looked so serious. I thought a little joke would cheer you up."

She pushed through the doorway and into the little courtyard behind the servants' part of the house. Sometimes, the grooms came there to smoke their pipes since smoking in the stable would earn them the sack quick as a wink. But there was no one in the windswept courtyard now. Theresa was glad. She was in no mood for company.

Least of all the company of a self-important twit like Toby.

"That's just the trouble. Everything's a joke with you," she said, not slowing her pace until she reached the waist-high stone wall enclosing the space. Then she hefted herself up to sit on it, letting her legs dangle.

"Life *is* a joke until there's a real problem," Toby said. "In all honesty, what's wrong? You know I'll help you, if I can."

There was enough moonlight to make out his handsome face in planes of light and dark. Maybe that was Toby's trouble. He was so devilishly good-looking he'd rarely had to work hard at anything. No wonder life was a joke to him.

Still, the temptation to unburden herself was more than Theresa could bear. The whole story came tumbling out of her with barely a pause for breath. To his credit, Toby didn't laugh, not even when she confessed her infatuation with the fellow in the suit of armor on the gallery wall.

After she finished, Toby was silent for the space of several heartbeats. "Well," she finally said, "what do we do about it?"

"We don't do anything."

She whacked him on the shoulder. "I thought you said you'd help me."

"I did. I will." He rubbed his shoulder and shot her an accusing look. "What I mean is *you* aren't to do anything. I'll take care of it."

She eyed him suspiciously. "How?"

"I'll speak to Lord Hartley about it," Toby said. "He strikes me as a fellow of sense, and since he's not been a lord long, he's not so puffed up with himself that he'll be affronted if a servant takes it upon himself to speak up about something. Especially something this important."

"But I suspect Lord Blackwood is his friend, else he'd not have been invited here," Theresa said. "What makes you think Lord Hartley will do anything?"

"I've noticed the way he watches Miss Kearsey when he thinks no one sees. He'll be ready for some help in dealing with Lord Blackwood, I'm thinking. Ofttimes, a well-placed servant can do things a lord can't."

"Oh, Toby, that's so wonderful of you." Tears pricked at the backs of her eyes, but she'd told him he'd never make her cry, so she couldn't let him see. She threw her arms around his neck and hugged him close. Toby was her new hero. He was even better than that fellow in the armor. He was flesh and blood and warm and—

"Gorblimey, Theresa!" Toby said as he stroked her back. "If I'd thought it would get me a hug, I'd have tried to get you into a pickle long before this."

Disappointment made her belly sink. He had to go and spoil the moment by being himself. The gentleman in the armor would never have said such a foolish thing. She yanked herself out of his arms and gave him another swat on the shoulder. "Just you tell me what his lordship says. We'll have to look sharp now."

"Indeed we will." Toby rubbed his hands together, not at all troubled by her assault on his person. "This is going to be better than a play."

❧

It was nearly noon the next day when Lady Richard made her way down to the breakfast room. Ordinarily, Sophie took a tray in her room, as married ladies frequently did, but there was an odd buzz in the house today, and she felt the need to be up and about, so she could locate its source.

She wouldn't have said she was particularly sensitive about these sorts of things, but somehow the very air in Somerfield Park seemed pregnant with secrets about to pop. She filled her plate at the sideboard with stewed kidneys and buttered eggs, and then seated herself at the long table in a room that was empty save for the handsome young footman named Toby. He leaped to fill her teacup and provide her with an assortment of fresh rolls and potted jams.

"I seem to be the last one up," she said.

"Yes, my lady."

Since it wasn't proper to engage in conversation with the help, Sophie decided to eat in silence. Not that it would bother her in the least to talk to Toby. He probably knew more about what was afoot in the house than she, but if he were caught speaking with her, he'd be the one in trouble for it.

However, she wasn't destined for a quiet meal. She hadn't had time to blow on her tea long enough to cool it before the dowager marchioness appeared at the breakfast room door.

"Hightower said you'd be here."

"And here I am." Sophie wondered how Mr. Hightower managed to know the whereabouts of everyone, whether he'd actually seen them or not. "How are you this fine morning, Phillippa?"

Lady Somerset glowered at her. "I don't see what's fine about it. The weather's turned sharp. My rheumatism is acting up, and Hartley is still chasing about after that horrid widow. I can't see what's to be done about it."

"We can't help the weather. I'm told Mrs. Grahame has an efficacious poultice for the rheumatism if you can bear the smell, but about John and Lady Chloe, I expect you're right. If he's serious about her, we're as powerless to change that as we are to change the weather."

"Dash it all, I probably am right. What are the odds I'd be wrong?"

"Very small," Sophie allowed, "but while you are right in this, you are wrong about something else."

"What? No, wait a moment. If you mean to instruct me over an error in my ways, I'd as soon not have you do it before the help." The old woman settled into the chair the footman thoughtfully pulled out for her. "That'll do, Toby. Leave us, if you please. You can come back later to do the... well, whatever it is you do once Lady Richard has finished eating."

"Yes, my lady. Very good." The young man bowed and left the room with a spring in his step. It seemed to Sophie as if he'd just been excused from a school term and an endless summer was set to begin. She almost envied him. He wasn't stuck in the breakfast room about to take the dowager marchioness to task.

"Now, you were about to explain that I'm wrong about something," Lady Somerset said.

"You're wrong to think it's your place to try to control who John fancies."

The dowager shook a bony finger at her. "And you're wrong if you think the marriage of a future marquess is about anything so prosaic as 'fancying' someone.'"

"That may be true for most, yet settling on the lady he fancies is all a match is about to John."

"How can you know this?"

"I have eyes." From what Sophie had seen, it appeared to her John was merely putting on a grand show of courting Lady Chloe. In truth, his gaze rarely strayed far from a certain baron's daughter. Sophie already suspected Rebecca was sweet on John. Now, she believed the affection was returned, but why he was playing a double game with Lady Chloe was a mystery. However, if the dowager hadn't tumbled to John's duplicity, who was Sophie to unmask him?

"But this Lady Chloe. She's so unsuitable." Lady Somerset looked as if she'd just swallowed a bit of pottage that had been left in the pot far too long. "Surely you agree that the pedigree of the young lady John chooses is vital to improving his acceptance among the *ton*. It's all well and good to say that John will be the marquess of Somerset eventually, but a title is no guarantee, you know. If the lady patronesses of Almack's can refuse the Duke of Wellington, they can refuse anyone."

The dowager always used to refer to John as Lord Hartley. Sophie was glad to hear her calling him by name.

"You specified that he should wed at least the daughter of an earl," Sophie pointed out. "Lady Chloe is that."

"That and so much more." The dowager rolled her eyes. "Honestly, to have buried four husbands at her tender age smacks of either skullduggery or monstrously bad luck. Either way, I don't want her near any grandson of mine. Besides, Lady Chloe is uniformly cut by anyone who's the least respectable."

"I don't think John cares much about that."

"He ought to care. The ones with whom he spends time reflects upon his character. He simply *must* be made to care. If not for his family's sake—and he does have three unwed half sisters to consider, you know—he ought to care for the sake of his future children. Knowing the right people, being received in the right parlors is so frightfully important. I cannot emphasize it strenuously enough."

Though not for lack of trying, Sophie thought as she dabbed her lips with a linen napkin. "It doesn't seem to be important to John, and whether you like it or not, he is a grown man and future peer. He'll do whatever he pleases, devil take the hindmost."

"Oh, my dear, there's no use being vulgar about it." The dowager shook her head and made a tsking noise. "Believe me, if I thought it would help, I'd join you in your gutter tongue."

Sophie suppressed a chuckle. If Lady Somerset thought "devil take the hindmost" was gutter tongue, she'd led a very sheltered life indeed.

"Don't you wonder why the comfort of his family is of so little consequence to him?" Sophie asked.

"Indeed I do. It's most unnatural."

"Not if one was raised by strangers," Sophie countered. "In that case, it's perfectly understandable that

John doesn't consider how his actions might affect the Barretts. After all, his real family never considered how their actions might affect *him*."

"He was fed, clothed, and educated. I saw to that."

"But was he loved?"

The dowager looked pointedly away. "The Barretts are not noted for their demonstrative natures."

"I'm well aware of that. And yet I married into the family in any case. Whether you show it or not, I know you care deeply for your grandchildren."

Lady Somerset banged the tip of her cane in indignation. "Of course I do."

"Then I think now would be the perfect time for you to demonstrate how you feel about John by supporting him in whatever choice he makes with regard to his future wife."

"Even if it's that…" The dowager gave an exquisite shudder. "That woman, Lady Chloe Endicott?"

"Especially if it's Lady Chloe. If you show John you are behind him in even this decision, you'll have proved that you love him."

"Love? Do let's not be maudlin."

Sophie leaned forward. "Don't you love him?"

"Of course I do. What sort of unnatural monster do you take me for?" The dowager made a great show of rearranging her skirts so she could avoid meeting Sophie's direct gaze. "Just because I haven't the need to wallow in my feelings, it does not signify that I do not have them."

"Of course not."

"I simply want the best for him and that is assuredly not Lady Chloe."

"And yet, you cannot make that choice for him. As I see it, the only choice you have before you is whether or not you'll show your grandson you love him by offering him unconditional acceptance."

"But mightn't I—"

"Unconditional," Sophie repeated. "Love is not love if it tries to make us earn it. It's freely given, or it's not worth a groat. Love takes us as we are, warts and all. And isn't that a good thing? Otherwise, none of us would ever taste a bit of that heaven this side of the grave."

The dowager rose and walked slowly to the doorway. She paused at the opening. "Sophie, my dear."

"Yes, Phillippa?"

"It vexes me so when you're right."

Twenty-eight

Sometimes a plan must be enacted violently and without need of further discussion. More talk would undoubtedly lead to more mistakes, and heaven knows we've already seen those in abundance.

—Phillippa, the Dowager Marchioness of Somerset

TOBY HAD TO STEP LIVELY TO CONVINCE MR. Hightower he'd left his post in the breakfast room for a good reason. It helped that the butler nearly idolized old Lady Somerset. If she'd sent Toby away, then away he had to go, provided he'd not given cause for offense that led to his dismissal. Toby had to revisit the whole conversation twice before Hightower was satisfied with the young footman's explanation. Then Toby asked where he might find Lord Hartley.

"His lordship is in the marquess's study, which some might find to be a bit presumptuous given that his father, Lord Somerset, is still with us," Hightower said with a sniff. "Do not relay Lord Hartley's location to anyone else."

Toby thought it would do the current marquess no good to spend time in the study, since his mind was obviously on holiday. The room might as well be put to use by someone who needed it, rather than left to gather dust. But he was careful not to share these sentiments with Mr. Hightower.

"Why do you wish to know Lord Hartley's whereabouts?"

"I've a message for him." Toby failed to mention that the message was from the Cook's helper. It wasn't his fault if Mr. Hightower assumed it was from the esteemed dowager marchioness.

"Very well. Deliver the message and then nip back to the breakfast room. Lady Sophie is not one to linger over her plate if she's not holding court at a full table."

Getting past the butler was one thing. Broaching the subject of the behavior of one of his lordship's guests, a guest who was likely one of Lord Hartley's bosom friends, with the future marquess himself was a much more daunting prospect.

"I'd better get another hug for this. In fact, a kiss would not be beyond reason," Toby muttered as he rapped softly on the study door. At Lord Hartley's order to "Come," Toby marched into the room and, with as much confidence as he could muster, launched into the telling of what Theresa had seen through the crack in the gallery door. Toby was, of course, careful to leave her name out of it. If anyone was going to come to grief over this breach of protocol, he'd make sure it would be him.

But once Toby finished, Lord Hartley didn't scold him for spying on Somerfield Park's guests or question the truthfulness of Toby's account. It was almost as if Lord Hartley had known about the incident already and Toby was merely confirming the facts of the matter.

"I'd thought of asking Mr. Porter to help me deal with this problem, but now that I think on it, he might not be the best choice. Don't misunderstand me. I think the world and all of Porter, but he's the nervous sort," Lord Hartley said, closing the heavy book on the desk before him. "You, however, are not. How good are you with your hands, Toby?"

"Sir?"

"Could you act as a valet?"

Toby straightened to his full height. Was Lord Hartley about to promote him? He never expected to be rewarded like this. "I've not trained as one, but I daresay I could rise to the occasion."

"More to the point, can you pick a pocket?"

"My lord?" Perhaps Lord Hartley didn't intend to reward him after all.

"What I mean is, are you quick enough of hand to lift something from someone's person without their knowledge?"

"I collect what a pickpocket is, sir." A bead of sweat slid down his spine. Toby had lived hand-to-mouth as a lad, and if he hadn't been light-fingered on occasion, his stomach would have been knocking on his backbone regular-like. Somehow, Lord Hartley must have heard about his less-than-stellar past and was using this opportunity to expose him as unfit to work at Somerfield Park. But his lordship's face held no censure, just honest inquisitiveness. Toby decided to risk the truth. "Yes, your lordship. If you need a pocket picked, I'm your man."

"Good. Then here's what I want you to do."

❧

No sooner had Toby left than Lady Somerset the elder appeared in the doorway of the marquess's study. Richard had left last month's ledgers for John to look over. If this steady stream of visitors kept up, he'd never get through the long rows of sums demanding his attention.

John rose as she entered the room. There might not be much love lost between him and his grandmother, but he would still afford her every courtesy. She moved slowly toward the desk, as if her years weighed more this day than usual.

"Please be seated," John said.

"Actually, I prefer to stand." She cleared her throat noisily. "That way I'll get right to the point with no shilly-shallying. We are both people of consequence, you and I, and our time is valuable."

"Very well." John clasped his hands behind his back and, still standing, waited for her to speak.

After the space of ten heartbeats, he was still waiting.

"Perhaps I will sit after all," the dowager said as she settled into the overstuffed chair on the opposite side of the desk from his nail-studded leather one. "Heavens, this room is warm. Might you open a window, please? Just a sliver, mind."

John had been comfortable enough, but the dowager's color was high. He could well believe she was too warm. Or too anxious about something. He cracked the window behind the desk to allow in a stream of cool-ish air.

"Now, how may I be of assistance?" he asked, crossing his arms over his chest and leaning against the windowsill.

"Perhaps...if you could just listen for a bit while I get through this... Yes, that will do. No questions until I'm finished."

"All right." When she still didn't speak, he added, "Of course, one has to begin before one can finish."

Her face contorted into a scowl. "Dash it all, it's difficult to know where to start. The beginning, I suppose, though we have discussed the circumstances surrounding your birth ad nauseam. However, I fear I must revisit it one last time. You must believe that I did not realize you were my legitimate grandson when I arranged for you to be cared for in Wiltshire."

"I do not doubt it." He didn't forgive her for it either. Whether he was legitimate or not shouldn't have made a particle of difference. He'd been an unwanted child who knew to his bones that he was unwanted. The mark left by that knowledge was deep.

"What I want you to realize is the turmoil Somerfield Park was in during that time." She hitched herself forward to perch on the edge of her seat. "My husband had died only a month before Hugh, your father, was to wed Lady Helen. When word came of your mother's death only a week before the wedding, I was left to deal with the consequences of her passing on my own. And remember, I did not know then that my son's first marriage had indeed been a valid one.

With a husband to mourn, a wedding to oversee, and a son who was barely beginning to understand his role as the marquess at the time, I could only see how the knowledge of your existence would complicate matters beyond bearing."

John resisted saying a little complication might have done Somerset a world of good. Besides, she'd told him all this before. Instead, he set his mouth in a hard line, determined not to interrupt her.

"However, I was wrong," Lady Somerset said.

She hadn't told him *that* before. "What did you say?"

"I. Was. Wrong. In error. I made a mistake. No matter my situation, I failed you in the most miserable of ways. Even if I thought you born on the wrong side of the blanket, that circumstance was not your fault."

Her eyes were overbright, but surely Lady Somerset wasn't about to let her emotions course down her withered cheeks. It would be beyond shocking. She dabbed at her eyes with a lacy handkerchief to keep such a monumental thing as a tear from materializing.

"The fault was mine for trying to have the marriage between your mother and my son put aside in the first place," the dowager said. "I shouldn't have meddled."

John sank into the desk chair in shock. He never expected her to acknowledge guilt in such a forthright manner.

"You are my grandson. I should have had you brought here, so you could grow up knowing your father. I greatly fear the way his mind is going. The time when you might have been able to know him now is slipping away." She shook her head. "Perhaps it is my punishment."

"I doubt that," he said. "Besides, I believe the Almighty visits the sins of the fathers on the children, not on their aging parents."

She shot him an imperious glare, all signs of humility gone. "Mock if you like. I'm trying to be serious."

"I am too. Lord Somerset may be slightly out of countenance"—that was being too charitable by half. If the marquess had been an ordinary man, he'd have been shipped off to Bedlam for his follies and frequent non sequiturs. Unless a miraculous cure could be affected, he'd never truly be able to serve as Lord of Somerset again— "but his lordship calls me his son and seems to know who I am from time to time. For that, I'm grateful."

Her pursed lips showed her feathers were still ruffled. "Then you might show your gratitude by refraining from insulting your grandmother. I resent being called aging, you know."

"My apologies."

"That's exactly why I'm here," she said emphatically.

"So that I can apologize to you?"

"No, John. So that I can apologize to you. I did you a grave disservice when you were a child. I ask your forgiveness for that offense, knowing I don't deserve it. I ask humbly and with no expectation that you will be gracious enough to respond. Though I dare not—"

"Enough! If you keep talking, you'll have me painted as a horrible monster who holds a grudge against his defenseless grandmother for a mistake she made years ago." As the words left his lips, it occurred to him that's exactly what he'd been doing. John had been lugging around his resentment all his life. Perhaps that did make him a bit of a monster.

But he didn't have to stay one.

"For whatever hurts you might have done me in the past, I forgive you...Gran." He decided to try out the name he'd heard Richard use for the dowager. It seemed right as it slid over his tongue.

It pleased Lady Somerset out of all knowing. Her wrinkles bunched into a wreath around her smile. "Thank you, my dear boy. Now I have a bit more to say to you on the subject of your choice of wife—"

John held up a hand to signal a halt. "Stop right there. We've made a fair bit of progress, you and I. It feels as if we're starting fresh. Let's not muck it up with an argument right out of the gate."

"If you'll allow me to finish, you'll find there's no argument ensuing. I simply wished to tell you that I shall not repeat the error of my past," the dowager said. "It was wrong of me to separate your father and mother. She was Hugh's choice, and if I'd have accepted the match, you and I should never have had this divide between us."

John shook his head slowly. "That's true, but in that case, you wouldn't have had Richard and his sisters. I doubt you'd wish them away. I don't think much good is served by wondering what might have happened."

"You're right. The past is fixed, and we are powerless to alter it. However, in the here and now, I shall not interfere with your choice of a bride. You have my solemn promise that I'll not attempt to sway you to one young lady or another. Whomever you decide upon..." The dowager swallowed so hard that the folds of skin on her neck undulated. "No matter who the lady is..." She sighed deeply, clearly pained but doggedly determined to go on. "I shall support your selection."

John leaned back in his chair, deciding to put her to the test. "Even if I wish to marry Lady Chloe?"

She erupted in a coughing fit, then finally managed to choke out, "Even if...if that lady is your choice."

"Cheer up, Gran. I have no intention of marrying Lady Chloe."

"Oh, that's a mercy." Her shoulders slumped in obvious relief. Then her gray brows drew together in agitation. "You wicked boy. You gave me such a start. Tell me now, upon what fortunate maiden have you cast your eye?"

"Before I tell you that, answer me this, Gran: Are you game for a bit of fun while you help me settle a score?"

The old lady smiled, a beguiling expression that made her entire face lift and her pale gray eyes sparkle. John caught a glimpse of what a beauty she must have been some sixty years or so ago.

"At my age, a bit of fun for any reason is something to celebrate. Having fun while settling a score is icing on the cake," Lady Somerset said. "What would you have me do?"

Twenty-nine

It is all well and good to have a plan. Essential, in fact. However, one can never provide for all possible contingencies, so once a course of action is put into motion, the best plan in the world at times flies right out the nearest window.

—Phillippa, the Dowager Marchioness of Somerset

FEW THINGS HAD GONE RIGHT FOR LORD BLACKWOOD since he'd arrived at Somerfield Park. When Hartley had gone shooting with the most influential lords, Blackwood had been cordially *not* invited to join them. The debutantes in attendance at the house party had been warned away from him by that meddlesome Lady Winifred Chalcroft, so there'd been no opportunity for him to make any new conquests in that department. Even the Somerfield Park chambermaids skittered shy of him.

To make matters worse, Smalley and Pitcairn seemed to be moving out of his sphere of influence. He'd cornered them one evening with plans to host a Daemon Club party of his own in a few weeks featuring Miss Kearsey as the guest of honor. She owed him, he explained, and he had some inventive ways in mind for her to pay off the debt.

"Of course, I'll have her broken in so well by then," Blackwood had boasted, "she'll even service you two caper-wits."

The pair of them traded a sheepish glance. Then Pitcairn spoke up. "Not Miss Kearsey. She's a fine lady. And kind, too."

"That she is. She didn't make a bit of fun of me when I was at the archery butts and my shafts didn't fly as true as I'd like," Smalley said, making a great show of studying his boot tips, which, given the girth of his waist, was no mean feat. "Lord knows I'm no Nimrod the great hunter, but she was exceedingly gracious about helping me retrieve some arrows that had gone astray, with nary a word of censure. I'll not be a party to bringing her grief."

"You're no great anything but a fool," Blackwood had snarled.

Did they suddenly think that because they were rubbing elbows with the Upper Crust, they'd soon be on every society matron's guest list? The idiots were too stupid to know they'd have no standing at all without him. He'd stormed away, determined to have nothing more to do with them.

Pitcairn and Smalley would be easy to replace. They were almost deadweight, in any case. Never a truly imaginative wicked idea between them. There were surely other like-minded free spirits in London who shared Blackwood's sense of carnal adventurism. He'd think no more about his toadies' unexpected defection to the respectable side of the *ton*.

At least his luck at the gaming table had held. Since his big win on the first night of the house party, he'd stayed even or a little ahead each evening. And Lord Kearsey's IOU was still safely tucked into the drawstring at the waist of his smalls.

The dressing gong sounded two hours earlier than usual this evening. He made his way to his bedchamber to prepare for the ball, followed by a midnight supper, which would signal an end to the house party's festivities.

Then, his festivities with Miss Kearsey were set to begin. He grew hard just thinking about invading her bedchamber later and plucking her maidenhead as easily as picking a daisy. He'd go easy on her tonight. After all, they were in a great house filled to capacity with guests. He wondered if she'd bite her lip to keep from crying out. Would it be hard enough to draw blood?

He hoped to taste a little of that coppery substance and relish the tightly contained despair that brought it to the surface of her lips.

There'd be time enough to hear her sob and scream later, when they had more privacy.

When he opened the door to his bedchamber, he was surprised to see a servant in Somerfield Park livery waiting for him.

"Good evening, my lord," the young man said with a proper bow. "As you brought no man with you, and it's a special evening what with the ball and all, Lord Hartley sent me to act as your valet. I took the liberty of drawing your bath and laying out your ensemble."

Blackwood's cutaway tailcoat and knee britches were spread across the bed. His best shoes had been spit-shined to within an inch of the leather's life, and the silver buckles gleamed.

"Hartley sent you, eh?" Perhaps Blackwood hadn't lost touch with the new lordling after all. Nice to see someone remembered who his friends were. "What's your name?"

"Hollis, sir. Toby Hollis."

"Very well, Hollis, help me out of these boots, and look sharp about it. While I bathe, see what you can do to put the shine back into them. I want to see my reflection in them by tomorrow morning."

Blackwood stripped, letting his clothing fall where it may. Then he sank into the inviting copper hip bath. He leaned back into the suds and commanded Hollis to nip down and bring back a jigger of whisky for him to enjoy while he soaked.

"Of course, sir. Just let me gather up your things first." The valet picked up the items of clothing, folding them carefully and stowing them away. Lastly, he retrieved Blackwood's smalls and gave them a shake. The neatly folded IOU fluttered to the floor.

"Pick that up, you clumsy oaf. Lay it on the foot of the bed where I can see it."

"Yes, sir. I'm ever so sorry, sir. No harm done. There it is." Hollis placed the paper on the bed as instructed. Then he smoothed down the brocade waistcoat that was spread out on the bed for Blackwood to wear that evening. "Lovely workmanship, this."

"I should hope so. The entire ensemble is the creation of one of the finest bespoke tailors in London. Brummell himself used to frequent the shop. Now get me that whisky!"

Hollis skidded out of the chamber as if his trousers were afire. Blackwood took a last look at the IOU on the foot of the bed. It was his ticket to the heaven between Miss Kearsey's legs…and any place else on her delectable body he cared to claim.

She does have the loveliest little pink mouth.

With that delightful thought in mind, he decided to see if he could imagine defiling her mouth hard enough to spend before Hollis returned or the bathwater got cold.

❦

"Oh, you look even better than I'd hoped in that gown." Freddie adjusted the clever little headdress for Rebecca and smiled at her in the dressing table mirror. "There. If only I weren't an earl's daughter, I'd have a real future as a lady's maid."

Rebecca laughed. "Being an earl's daughter *is* a real future."

"I suppose, but it hasn't availed me much this fortnight. Lord Hartley only has eyes for one lady it seems."

"Oh, yes. Lady Chloe." Rebecca cast her gaze downward, lest Freddie see her duplicity. She felt terrible keeping things from her friend, but the fewer people who knew of John's plans, the better.

"It won't answer, you know," Freddie said. "I collect you're up to something. And you and I both know perfectly well that the lady Lord Hartley favors is you."

Her gaze jerked back to Freddie's reflection. "What? How can you say that?"

Freddie rolled her eyes. "Because he's a veritable

mooncalf. He covers it well, to be sure, but no matter how much time he spends in the company of that merry widow, it can't trump the way he looks at you in unguarded moments."

This didn't bode well. John was adamant about keeping their secret until the right time. "Does everyone know?"

"Of course not. How many of the *ton* have my powers of observation and keen reasoning skills? Not many," she answered her own query. "Even the book at White's has Lady Chloe leading the pack of future marchioness hopefuls."

"How on earth can you know what the White's wager book says?"

"Believe me, I have my sources. But that's of no consequence since we know who the real front-runner is." Freddie gave her a quick hug. "I'm so happy for you, my dear, but also curious as to why the need for subterfuge?"

Even though Freddie was dearer to her than any sister could be, she couldn't share the terrible situation in which her father had placed her with Lord Blackwood. Instead, Rebecca settled for telling Freddie about a complication she would understand. "The dowager is set on John marrying no less than an earl's daughter. Lady Chloe meets that standard, but is wholly unacceptable to her ladyship in other regards."

"I should think so."

"No, don't say that. Chloe has proved to be a friend." Rebecca rose and paced the room. "In any case, John thinks his grandmother will be so relieved when he tells her that he won't be offering for Lady

Chloe, she'll be much more accepting when he pro-
poses to me."

"That is probably a good plan. Well, *if* you decide
to accept him, he'll be an extremely lucky gentleman.
Hold a moment." Freddie stooped to spread the short
train of Rebecca's gown so that it swept behind her as
lightly as faery dust. Then she straightened and gave an
approving nod. "Now, is your father coming to escort
you to the ballroom?"

Rebecca shook her head. Her father had scrupu-
lously avoided her since the night he all but shoved
her into Blackwood's arms.

"Mine isn't either. I do believe they're all plotting
to disappear to their wicked little poque game again at
some point in the evening, instead of supporting the
dancing." Freddie linked arms with her. "Let's go down
together then. I hear the string quartet warming up."

Rebecca called her courage and headed toward
the ballroom with her friend. So much more was
riding on this night's work than putting the right foot
forward before the *ton*. Though John had promised
he'd settled everything in one stroke, Polite Society
expected him to marry extremely well, and she still
didn't signify in that case. Her father was still deeply
in debt.

And Blackwood still expected her to pay.

⁂

The first dance called by the dancing master was the
minuet, the most correct and elegant dance with
which to begin any ball. Since not every couple dared
attempt the intricate steps and figures, it was more a

display piece. Once the reels and quadrilles began, the entire assembly would line up to be included, but now only a handful of dancers glided to the center of the floor to take their positions.

Rebecca and Freddie had settled in to watch as the quartet continued to torture their instruments into tune with each other. She nearly toppled out of her chair when John appeared before her and asked most correctly for the honor of this dance.

"I didn't know you could dance the minuet," she stammered as she rose and made the obligatory curtsy.

"There are many things you don't know about me yet." His eyes glinted with promise. "But trust me enough to lead you through a few figures, will you?"

"Yes, my lord, of course. The honor is mine."

As he lead her out, he whispered, "That's better. You know you're always supposed to say yes to the marquess, don't you?"

She turned to make her first pose and pulled a quick face at him. "You're not the marquess yet."

He grinned. "Consider it practice for the future."

"And what about saying yes to the marchioness?" She had to play as if her heart weren't pounding like a coach-and-six, as if nothing was more important than whether she missed a dance step. If she let herself think about Blackwood coming to her at midnight, she'd melt into a terrified puddle in the middle of the floor.

"Oh, a yes to the marchioness is a given. It comes standard with the coronet and jewels."

He brought her in close for the first figure, which allowed them to look adoringly at each other as a matter of course. To her surprise, his lead was sure and correct, if not the most refined. That was fine with her. One of the things she loved most about John was his rough edges.

"Besides," he whispered, "I could never say no to you."

"Then tell me, is everything in train for your plan this evening?"

He hadn't confided the whole plan to her. In fact, he claimed not to have told anyone all of it. If everyone did their part, it would all come together. Nothing would be helped by worrying about the bits for which others were responsible, John had said. She desperately wanted to hear him say yes now, that everything was going to work out exactly as they hoped.

But John didn't answer. Instead, his gaze swept over the room, as if he were looking for someone. She followed the direction of his gaze until he finally settled on a footman moving smoothly around the room offering a tray of canapés to the matrons who were seated along the walls to observe the dancing. The footman never glanced toward John.

"Does that footman have something to do with our plans?" she asked.

John pulled his gaze away and smiled down at her. "If he does, he strikes me as a handy fellow at whatever he's tasked to do. Don't fret. Please, Rebecca. I need you to trust me tonight. Do you?"

They drew together for the stylized kiss required by the dance. Even though it couldn't be the kiss she wished for, John's mouth was firm and warm on hers. It settled the unruly flutters in her stomach and gave her a small measure of peace.

"Yes, John," she whispered. "I'll always trust you."

Thirty

Losing at cards doesn't build character. It reveals character.

—Phillippa, the Dowager Marchioness of Somerset

BLACKWOOD WAS MIGHTILY PUT OUT THAT THERE WAS no waltz on the program. He considered the minuet a throwback to the previous generation and had no interest in moves designed merely to showcase a lady's charms. All the other dances were country reels or formations with other couples, which precluded any private speech with his partner. He'd so looked forward to waltzing with Miss Kearsey, so he could whisper under his breath all the deliciously wicked things he intended to do to her later. Watching her flush and go short of breath as she tried to maintain her composure would have been the high point of his public evening.

But he couldn't get near enough to menace her with more than a few glances, which she refused to meet.

No matter. There'd be time enough to bedevil Rebecca Kearsey later. He'd make sure she couldn't look away then if he had to tie her to the bedpost, which, now that he thought about it, was an idea with real appeal.

He chanced to see Lord Arbuthnot and Lord Kearsey slipping out of the ballroom door between sets. Even without their host, Lord Hartley, who couldn't be spared from the dancing, a card game was clearly in the offing. Kearsey had nothing to buy into the pot with except his cuff links, so Blackwood couldn't figure why the gentleman was even bothering to sit in for a hand. But Arbuthnot had yet to be skinned for more than a quid or two.

Fresh meat.

It would do Blackwood's heart good to make the old curmudgeon bleed freely. Lord knew Arbuthnot had the chinks, right enough. He'd hardly miss the blunt Blackwood intended to win from him. If the cards didn't fall Blackwood's way naturally, he had a special deck in his jacket pocket that would ensure a win. He made his way toward the exit but was stopped shy of it by a feminine hand on his forearm.

"Where do you think you're going in such an all-fired hurry?" Lady Chloe said. "We're already short of eligible gentlemen. Never say you'd leave a ballroom full of debutantes to dance with the graybeards."

"If all the little darlings want to do is dance, yes, I'm content to let the dotards have them." He offered her his arm because it made him feel pleasurably male for Chloe to snug against him. Her breast was soft against his elbow as she sidled up to him. "If the angelic young ladies want some carnal adventures, I'll be happy to oblige them, but what I have in mind cannot be accomplished on a dance floor."

Lady Chloe laughed, the full-throated laugh of a woman who understood and enjoyed pleasure. "I'm guessing it could be accomplished on the dance floor at one of your Daemon Club parties." She slid a hand from his chest to his waist, stopping their progress toward the door. "I've heard clothing was not required for a full sennight at one of them."

He grinned wickedly. "You should come to the next party."

"You know my rules. I must remain chaste...well, relatively chaste," she amended and turned so they could continue walking on, "until I've found my next husband. And after our nuptials, I'll stay true to him until he's demonstrated an inability to remain faithful to me."

Blackwood led her on to the door but didn't pass through it. "People like you and me shouldn't be bound by rules."

"Never fear. I have only one or two, but I do adhere to those few religiously. Not that I think there's one chance in a hundred that I'll ever discover a faithful husband, but it's only sporting to give a gentleman the chance to keep me at his side by remaining by mine. Now, tell me. Where are you off to in such a clandestine fashion?"

He leaned down and whispered in her ear, "There's a poque game in the second-floor parlor."

"Oh, good. I'm ever so tired of playing loo."

"The table has rather high stakes."

"All the better. It'll be more interesting that way. Lead on, Blackwood." She cocked her head fetchingly at him. "Or don't you think the other gentlemen will welcome me at the table?"

The way the neckline of her gown was cut, if Lady
Chloe leaned forward to collect her winnings just so,
there wouldn't be a man at the table who'd begrudge
her the pot.

"No, I'm certain you'll be a most welcome addition," he said and led her away from the foolish crowd
tripping the light fantastic in the ballroom.

∽

Two hours later, Kearsey was still hanging on in the
game, staying fairly even with each hand. Arbuthnot
had dropped a small fortune and was determined to
win it back. Another couple of players had escaped
with their teeth still intact, but little else. They quit
the game, claiming the coming midnight supper was
calling them, leaving only four players around the
lacquered table. The chips had been transferred to a
new owner in a decidedly lopsided fashion all evening.

However, the largest pile of winnings wasn't sitting
in front of Blackwood. It was stacked up before Lady
Chloe so high it almost obscured her magnificent
bosom. And a good many of those chips had belonged
to Blackwood when the game first started.

"This deck is grown cold," he muttered. "Let us
start with a fresh one."

He reached into his jacket pocket, only to find
it empty.

"What an excellent idea," Lady Chloe said, opening her beaded reticule and pulling out a deck of cards
which looked suspiciously similar to Blackwood's
special one.

When had she managed to lift it from him? Oh,

yes. When she snuggled close to him in the ballroom. He remembered that her hand had surreptitiously brushed his form. He'd enjoyed it at the time. Now he narrowed his eyes at her, the conniving minx. She was as nimble-fingered as a Whitechapel lightskirt.

"Would you care to cut, Lord Kearsey?" she asked sweetly, as if she weren't guilty of purloining Blackwood's stacked deck.

Kearsey merely rapped his knuckles on the cards and Chloe began to deal.

Blackwood's mind churned furiously. How could he accuse a lady of cheating with a deck he knew to be tainted because it was his? Instead, he concentrated on the cards being dealt. He knew without a doubt what cards each player held. Yes, there was the third jack to him. It was being played out exactly as it should except that Chloe, as the dealer, would receive the winning hand.

The longcase clock chimed a quarter to midnight. The game was expected to break up for the supper following the ball soon, and Miss Kearsey would be waiting for him in her chamber while the rest of the party ate their après-dancing repast. It was time he made his exit from this game in any case.

"I believe I will call it a night." Blackwood laid his hand facedown and stood.

"Oh, where's the fun in that?" Chloe said. "At least finish this hand. What will you wager?"

"On these cards, nothing."

"Well, I'm willing to hazard everything I have on mine. Come, Blackwood. If you won't bet a chip, at least wager whatever's in your waistcoat pocket."

Since there was nothing in his waistcoat pocket, he

shrugged and sat back down. Arbuthnot and Kearsey made their bets. This pot dwarfed all the others, so no one wanted to be left out.

Chloe turned her cards over.

She had three tens. It was good, but it wasn't the winning hand Blackwood had expected. The foolish girl had mixed up the cards somehow. He revealed his trio of jacks with mounting excitement. Arbuthnot was holding the anticipated pair of aces, which he tossed down with disgust.

Blackwood could scarcely breathe. He was going to take everything—all of Chloe's winnings in a single lucky stroke.

Kearsey continued to stare stupidly at his cards.

"Throw down, sir. We haven't all night," Blackwood said.

Hands trembling, Lord Kearsey laid down four threes in a crooked row. "I...I guess...I win."

"So you do, my lord," Lady Chloe said with no evidence of envy or displeasure. She pushed her pile of chips in his direction. "Now you, Blackwood. Empty your pocket."

"There's nothing in—" But there was something in his pocket after all. He'd meant to turn the satin lining inside out to demonstrate its emptiness, but his fingers brushed against a piece of folded paper. He drew it out, unbelievingly.

"What's this?" Lady Chloe snatched it from him, unfolded it, and ran her gaze over it. "My word, Lord Kearsey. It appears double congratulations are in order. These are your own vowels. You just won back a considerable IOU to Lord Blackwood."

"No, that's not possible," Blackwood said. But it certainly looked like Kearsey's IOU. It was the same spidery script. "It can't be."

With no scruples for propriety, Blackwood unbuttoned one side of his drop-front knee britches to fumble with the slit opening in his smalls.

"It's here. I know it is." He rummaged in his drawers for the slip of paper that had to be there. Hollis had left it on the end of the bed. While the valet helped him dress, Blackwood had tucked the precious IOU into its usual place himself. "It must be here somewhere."

"Now see here, Blackwood," Lord Arbuthnot said. "There's a lady present."

"I pray you, don't fret on my account, Lord Arbuthnot. I'm a widow, remember. The male of the species holds no mystery for me." Lady Chloe laughed and turned her attention to Blackwood. "My dear viscount, you're not the first to feel himself unmanned by a loss at the poque table, but I assure you, the equipment is still there. It may just take a while for it to work properly again."

Blackwood glared at her, but then his fingers brushed a piece of paper tucked into the cinched waist of his smalls. He pulled it out and threw it onto the table.

"There! See for yourself."

Lady Chloe blinked at the folded paper and then said with sugary sweetness, "Considering where it's been, you surely don't expect me to touch that."

"Dash it all! This will prove the IOU in Kearsey's hand is a forgery." Blackwood unfolded his paper and found…a blank page staring up at him. "How the devil…"

A vivid recollection of young Hollis placing a piece of paper on the bed scrolled across his mind. Then the valet had smoothed down the front of Blackwood's brocade waistcoat admiringly, remarking on the fine workmanship. The blasted fellow must have performed his little sleight of hand while Blackwood was soaking in the tub. One square of folded paper looked very like another. In hindsight, it was easy to see how he'd been duped.

"Hartley," Blackwood said through clenched teeth. "It was Hartley. This is all his doing."

"Ridiculous," Lord Arbuthnot said, rising to his feet. "Our host is clearly nowhere near this poque table and cannot be held responsible for your losses. Come." He gave Blackwood a bracing slap on the back. "Take your lumps like a man. And now, my lady"—he offered his arm to Chloe—"may I escort you to supper, where we can commiserate over our losses and lick our wounds?"

"It might be more interesting if we were to lick each other's wounds." One of Chloe's brows arched naughtily and she took his arm. "But perhaps that's a game for another time."

Arbuthnot's face lit up. "No time like the present. Some things don't improve with the waiting, my dear."

He was a widower with grown children and a sizeable estate. Chloe had clearly identified a candidate for husband number five and was preparing to lead him a merry chase until she caught him.

"Come with us to supper, Kearsey," Chloe called

over her shoulder. "Before Lord Blackwood finds something else in his drawers he feels compelled to show us."

Kearsey skittered after them while Blackwood did a slow burn. He'd lost the leverage he held over the baron and couldn't use Miss Kearsey to settle her father's uncollectable debt.

But Miss Kearsey didn't know that.

He buttoned up his breeches and headed for the guest wing of Somerfield Park. She'd be waiting for him.

He decided he wouldn't go easy on her after all. A gag would do nicely to quiet her screams.

Thirty-one

*When one is burdened by as many years as I am, people assume
I must sigh and shake my head over the past when I was young
and foolish. Balderdash! There's no time like the present. Never
say I've lived long enough to be done with foolish things.*

—Phillippa, the Dowager Marchioness of Somerset

IT ALWAYS PAID TO KNOW THE GEOGRAPHY OF A GREAT
house. Blackwood made his way through the dark
corridors, tracing the map of the place he carried in
his head. He'd followed Miss Kearsey back to her
chamber one evening, careful not to be caught lurking
around corners, in preparation for this very moment,
when he'd need to find her.

He might have lost a king's ransom this night, but
by God, no one was going to cheat him of his con-
quest of Miss Kearsey. As far as she knew, her father
was still in thrall to him. She'd do anything for the sake
of her family. Blackwood could even pretend to be
magnanimous and claim this single night would settle
her father's debt.

Yes, that was the ticket. She'd be so pathetically grateful, her participation in her own debauching might not even have to be coerced. He might not have to take. She would give.

Anything.

Blackwood glanced up and down the long hallway to satisfy himself that no one was there to see him. Then he slipped into Rebecca Kearsey's chamber.

She'd left a single candle burning on the dressing table, its flame magnified by the mirror to bring the entire room into a dusky half-light. The lady herself was already abed, but he doubted she was asleep.

What girl would be able to rest knowing she was destined to lose her maidenhead that night?

The covers were pulled up so far that only a lacy nightcap showed above them. She was trying to hide from him. Her modesty was endearing. Quaint, even. An unexpected swell of something that might be called tenderness in another man warmed his chest.

Perhaps he would be gentle with her. At first.

"Wake up, sweeting," he whispered. "I've been dreaming of making extravagant love to you all day."

"Oh, I sincerely doubt that." The figure in the bed threw back the covers and sat up. Blackwood was horrified to discover the dowager marchioness in all her high-collared, buttoned-up muslin and lace glory. "However, your protestation of designs on my person flatters me, sir; indeed it does."

"Lady Somerset!" he said, aghast.

"Lord Blackwood. Now that we've established the players, tell me, why are you in Miss Kearsey's bedchamber?"

"Why are you?" he sputtered.

"To keep you from accomplishing your nefarious intent, of course." Then she raised her voice. "John! You may enter. It appears Lord Blackwood will not be ravishing anyone this evening."

Hartley, flanked by his half brother, Lord Richard, on one side and Miss Kearsey on the other, strode into the room. Lady Wappington, the *ton*'s most malevolent gossip, was also in train, her bug eyes magnified to even greater proportions by peering at him through a lorgnette.

"Blackwood, in making improper advances toward my grandmother, you have shown yourself to be beyond the pale," Hartley said.

"What? I never—"

"Now, now, Blackwood. Truth is truth. You did claim to have dreamt of making extravagant love to me all day long," the marchioness put in unhelpfully.

"Oh, I say!" Lady Wappington made a noise halfway between a snort and an owl hoot. Then she turned and fairly ran down the hall in her hurry to spread word of the debacle.

Once the *ton* got wind of this, Blackwood would be a laughingstock. The tabloids would likely pick it up. He could imagine the cartoons now, depicting him slavering over a wrinkled old crone in a nightcap.

He'd never been respectable, but at least he'd been feared. Now he'd face only derision.

"The IOU in my waistcoat pocket, the switching of my card deck, my loss at the poque table, even this ridiculous farce with your grandmother—this is all your doing," Blackwood accused Lord Hartley.

His former friend executed a flawless bow. "Freely admitted with pride."

Ire boiled inside him. Blackwood stomped over to Hartley, smacked him with his glove.

"I demand satisfaction." That drove the amused smirk off Hartley's face. He seemed to blanch at the thought of meeting Blackwood on a field of honor. And well he might. Blackwood had never lost a duel, killing two men and maiming a third.

"No, John, please. Walk away. It's not worth it." Distress drawing her brows together, Rebecca Kearsey clung to Hartley's forearm, but he gently moved her behind him.

"That very much depends upon what price your beloved sets upon his honor," Blackwood said with a sneer. "If you feel yourself man enough, my lord, shall we say tomorrow at dawn?"

Hartley nodded. "I'll meet you in the Greek folly."

"Very well. Since you have been challenged, you may choose the weapons, though I warn you I am equally skilled at pistols and blades."

"I am forewarned," Hartley said solemnly.

Blackwood pushed between his former friend and the girl he'd intended to ravish. The total collapse of his plans still stung, but the opportunity to kill Hartley for it and suffer no legal repercussions soothed him immeasurably.

⌒

After Blackwood stormed out, John, his brother, and the dowager left the chamber as well. But Rebecca hadn't even had time to ring for a maid to help her out of her ball gown before John slipped back into her room.

"Oh, thank heaven," she murmured as she flew across the space and into his arms. "Tell me you are not going through with this ridiculous duel."

"I jolly well have to." John pressed a kiss on the crown of her head. "Otherwise, I'll be branded a coward and Blackwood will be vindicated in the eyes of the *ton*."

"Since when do you care what they think?"

"Since I fell in love with a certain baron's daughter. Don't you see? I want to make everything right for you, love. I can't do that if I let Blackwood get the best of me."

She ranted after that, though not very loudly, since her reputation wouldn't withstand being caught with yet another man in her bedchamber on the selfsame night. This was precisely what she'd feared when John first promised to take on the problem of her father's debt.

She'd rather give herself to that odious Blackwood a thousand times than have John killed by the man.

She pleaded. She wept, but she couldn't make him see reason. Finally, despair gave way to anger.

"If you won't listen to me, then get out."

"Now, love, is that any way to talk? No, you're right. Maybe it's best if we don't talk at all." He kissed her then, claiming her mouth by right. He crowded her senses with his strength and his scent and the wonder of his lips on hers. For a moment, longing urged her to forget the morrow. No one was promised even their next breath. Now was all anyone had.

Why not take the man she loved to bed and forget the rest of the world?

But her head overruled her aching body.

"No, John." She wedged her hands between them and shoved against his chest. "If you're determined to kill yourself, you'll not take my blessing—or anything else—with you."

He gave her a long look. "I wish you had more faith in me."

It wasn't that. She had plenty of faith in his intentions. She just had more fear of Blackwood's reputation with a blade and a pistol. She couldn't encourage him in this foolishness.

"So. That's it, then." He brushed a soft kiss on her forehead. "Good night, love. Sleep well."

He was gone before she could respond.

Rebecca wouldn't sleep. This was her worst nightmare, and she didn't even have the option of waking from it.

So weeping silently, she paced the length of her room until the sky lightened to pearl gray. She was still wearing the pink ball gown, but now she wrapped a pale oatmeal shawl around her shoulders and headed for the Greek folly.

The grass was stiff with early morning frost. The cunning slippers Freddie had lent her for the ball would never be the same, but it didn't signify in the slightest. Her chest was a leaden weight. She had no more tears. Nothing mattered but seeing John one last time. Even if she couldn't dissuade him from his course, she'd be with him to the end.

When Rebecca reached the tumbled-down

amphitheater, she was stupefied to discover the stone seats were almost filled to capacity by other members of the house party. It was mostly the gentlemen, who loved nothing better than a fight and the opportunity to wager on it. But a few ladies had arrived early enough to claim a good vantage point from which to view the proceedings. Rebecca passed by Lord Arbuthnot and Lady Chloe, who were also both still wearing their formal clothes from last evening.

"Of course, dueling is illegal." Lord Arbuthnot's breath rose in dragonish puffs while he pontificated to Lady Chloe. "But ignoring a slight to one's honor cannot be legislated."

"I fail to see how catching Blackwood at his own game is a slight to his honor," Chloe drawled.

Rebecca scanned the sloping stones toward the stage area and saw Freddie seated beside Lady Wappington. She scrambled down toward them.

"Naturally, I abhor the notion of dueling," Freddie was saying to her companion. "However, as a cultural phenomenon, it is worth further study. It behooves me to witness one if for no other reason than to prepare a treatise against the practice. Oh, Rebecca, there you are. I'd begun to think you wouldn't come."

More people were arriving over the rise and taking their places in the amphitheater's stone seating as the sky continued to lighten. Rebecca's sense of unreality grew by the moment. "Did someone send out invitations?"

"I might have mentioned it to one or two people." Lady Wappington had the grace to look chagrined. "In strictest confidence, you understand."

"Is John here?" Rebecca didn't bother to call him

Lord Hartley for form's sake. She was trembling for reasons that had nothing to do with the chill morning air. None of the silly things society thought was so important mattered one whit. She knew that now. She shouldn't have sent John away. She—

"Yes," Freddie interrupted her thoughts, "the principals are here, though I gather Lord Blackwood had difficulty finding a second. It seems poor Mr. Pitcairn has been pressed into service."

On the right side of the proscenium, Pitcairn was helping Blackwood remove his garrick and jacket. The small fellow's face was so wide-eyed, Rebecca didn't doubt he'd bolt if given half a chance.

Then John and his brother, Richard, strode onto the left side of the stage, and the rest of the world faded away. Freddie's droning voice became a meaningless jumble of sounds. The gathered onlookers were shapeless blobs of wool and superfine. All that existed, all that was real, all that mattered was John Fitzhugh Barrett.

Her legs propelled her toward him somehow, but she wasn't conscious of commanding them. She was powerless to stop herself until she stood before him. He let Richard divest him of his greatcoat and jacket, and then took both of Rebecca's hands.

"You shouldn't have come," he said softly.

"I had no choice."

"Neither do I."

"I know that now," she said. To refuse Blackwood's challenge, he'd have to deny who he was, who he was desperately trying to be—the next marquess of Somerset. "I love you. I'll love you till…till forever comes."

Despite the grimness of the situation, his face broke

into a wide smile. "That's good, love. But don't look so glum. Forever isn't coming today."

Then he strode to meet Blackwood in the center of the Greek folly's stage. Rebecca hugged her shawl around her tighter, but nothing could warm her. She strained to hear the duelists' conversation over the rumble of the assembled witnesses. Then the crowd finally hushed and Blackwood's voice rang clearly in the open space.

"What will it be, Hartley? Swords or pistols?"

"Neither."

"You mean to concede and apologize then?"

"Nothing of the sort. You insulted both my grandmother and the lady I love. We'll duel, all right, but not with conventional weapons," John said. "I choose fists."

"Fists?" Pitcairn piped up. "There's no precedent. It's simply not done."

"There's no law against it, either," Richard put in. "And Hartley, as the challenged party, is allowed to choose his weapons. You may accept his choice or apologize…with significant damage to your honor, of course."

"Or you can accept with significant damage to your teeth," John promised with a wolf's smile.

"You can brawl to the death, of course. Men have killed each other with naught but their bare hands before, but I hope you're a bit more civilized than that," Richard offered, as John's second. "My brother is not a vindictive man. We propose the winner be decided by first blood."

"Sounds like a good idea to me," Pitcairn said. "A bloody nose is better than a beating."

"Shut up, you bird-wit!" An amused titter rose up from the crowd on the amphitheater steps. Blackwood lowered his voice to a low growl. "You'll rue the day you tried to make a fool of me, Hartley."

"Oh, I think you're doing a fine job of that without any help from me." John raised his fists in a pugilist's classic stance. "Defend yourself."

"So be it."

Then with the skill and lightning reflexes that made him a master swordsman, Blackwood lashed out with a jab to John's jaw. It didn't draw blood, but Rebecca felt the jolt as if the blow had connected with her own face. John staggered back a pace.

Blackwood followed it up with a blow that glanced off John's chin and then another to his gut that connected with a dull thud.

As John doubled over, Rebecca's breath hissed out of her in a rush.

"Hit him back," she chanted softly, not wanting to distract John as he and Blackwood circled each other, looking for an opening. The rest of the witnesses weren't so thoughtful. They called out suggestions and derision to both boxers as the seriousness and civility of a field of honor degenerated into a mill.

John swung wide, but Blackwood ducked beneath the blow.

"Never figured me for a pugilist, did you?" the viscount said as he danced around the bigger man.

"Never figured you'd risk your pretty face," John said with a grunt. Then he threw a punch toward Blackwood's jaw, which he deflected with his forearm.

"You should have taken training, Hartley."

"I did. In every schoolyard, every time I was called a bastard. I learned early to defend myself."

"But not how to defeat your opponent. That knockout in the Green Cockerel was a lucky punch. You may have got the girl that night, but I'll have her this time."

John feinted to the right, which drew Blackwood's guard that direction. Then he moved in swiftly with an uppercut to Blackwood's jaw from the left.

Rebecca could hear the crunch of bone from where she stood. Blackwood fell to his knees, spitting blood and an eyetooth onto the stone stage.

"First blood! Hartley wins!" Pitcairn exclaimed, obviously forgetting that it was his principal who was down.

"It may be first blood," Blackwood growled, "but, by God, it won't be the last." He came up with his boot knife in his hand, slashing at John's midsection with a wild swing. The blade sliced through his shirt and left a string of red beads on his exposed midsection.

The crowd that had been jeering and shouting now fell silent as John pulled out his boot knife and the fight took a deadly turn.

Rebecca covered her eyes. She knew it was cowardly, but she couldn't bear to look. However, hearing the grunts and swearing of the fighters, the gasps and cries of the onlookers was almost worse. Then the worst possible thing happened.

She heard a dull thud, the sound of a body hitting the stone floor. And then there was absolute silence.

When Rebecca finally peered through her fingers, she saw Lord Blackwood splayed on his back, with John's knee pressed to his chest and a blade to his throat.

"Now listen to me very carefully, Blackwood, because what you do next will determine whether you live or die," John said between huge gulps of air. Both fighters' chests were heaving with exertion. "If you understand, blink once."

Blackwood complied.

"Good. Now, here's what you're going to do. You're never to have contact with me or mine for the rest of your natural life. In fact, to acquaint you with your newly hermit-like mode of existence, you will remove to your country estate and not stir from it for the next year. If you agree to these terms, you may blink twice."

Blackwood did.

"If after that time you ever threaten, harass, or even look cross-eyed at Miss Kearsey, you and I will revisit this moment with a very different ending. Now, if you are in accord with these conditions, I want to hear one word from you and one word only," John said, his voice low with silky menace. "That word is yes."

"Y-yes."

"Louder. I want Lord Arbuthnot to hear you up in the back row."

"Yes!"

John rose and glared down at him. "Now get out of my sight and off my land before I change my mind about being merciful."

Blackwood scrambled to his feet and ran away as fast as his legs could carry him.

Rebecca flew across the stage to John and embraced

him. When they pulled apart, her pink gown came away flecked with red. "Oh, John, you're hurt."

"It's a small matter. I'll mend." He put his arms around her and pressed her to his chest again.

"But Blackwood won't. You've crushed him right enough," Pitcairn said woodenly. "I'm his cousin, you know. In fact…since he hasn't wed and sired a son… I'm his nearest kin. His heir." A shaky smile quirked his mouth. "If you'd done for him, Hartley…I'd be Lord Blackwood now."

"If I'd known that, Pitcairn, I might not have stayed my hand."

"But I'm glad you did, John, for your sake," Rebecca said. "You don't want Blackwood's blood on your hands. Besides, you proved what you've been telling me. People do tend to say yes to a marquess, but then you're not one quite yet, are you?"

"No, and besides, I've been trying to warn you I'm an unworthy rake."

"Lucky for you, it seems I can never resist a rake."

"I'm counting on it." John dropped to one knee before the crowd of witnesses. "Miss Kearsey, I love you beyond reason. Will you do me the honor of becoming my bride?" he said loud enough for even Lord Arbuthnot to hear before lowering his voice for her alone. "And remember, if you really can't resist a rake, the only answer I'm expecting is yes."

Rebecca dropped to her knees with him. "Your bride, your wife, your love, for as long as we both shall live. Yes, John. Always and only, yes!"

Author's Note

Dear Reader,

Thanks for choosing *Never Resist a Rake*. I'm thrilled you've decided to spend some time with me and the folk who live in Somerfield Park. My goal is to give you reason to smile, and maybe shed a tear or two. I hope you enjoy your visit and return to us often.

Never Resist a Rake is about finding your place in the world, and if you're very lucky, finding that one person to share it with. Both Rebecca and John have miles to go in their journey of the heart, but the end of the sojourn is worth the trip.

I try to make the history in my books as accurate as possible, but I must admit to one little fudge. In my story, John and Rebecca spend a magical night on the manor house's flat roof watching the Leonids meteor shower. However, it's unlikely an amateur astronomer like Rebecca would have been aware of them in 1817. Though the first record of the Leonids was made in 902, people didn't really get excited about the annual meteor storm until 1833, when a whopping 100,000 meteors per hour were recorded. Talk about the sky falling...

I'd love to hear from you anytime. For more about my books, please visit www.miamarlowe.com.

Happy Reading,
Mia

Acknowledgments

If it takes a village to raise a child, it takes at least a small hamlet to bring up a book.

I'm honored to work with my editor, Deb Werksman. She always encourages me to make the story better, to deepen the characters, and to get it right! Then there are the incredible people at Sourcebooks who take my raw manuscript and transform it into the polished work you now hold in your hands. Thank you to Susie Benton for keeping me on task and on time. I'm grateful to talented cover artist Dawn Adams, production editor Rachel Gilmer, copy editor Gretchen Stelter, and publicist Amelia Narigon and her crew.

No author could have a better agent than Natasha Kern. She's insightful, determined, and frees me to play with my imaginary people while she deals with the real ones.

Deep thanks go to my dear husband and family, the loves of my life. Who else would put up with someone who wanders around in another century half the time?

Lastly, I want to thank YOU again, dear reader. There are many things competing for your time and attention. Thank you for investing a few hours of your life in my book. It means the world to me. Truly.

About the Author

Mia Marlowe is a rising star whose *Touch of a Rogue* was named in *Publishers Weekly*'s Top Ten Best Romances for Spring 2012. Mia learned about storytelling while singing professional opera. She knows what it's like to sing a high C in a corset, so she empathizes with the trials of her historical heroines. Mia resides in the Ozarks surrounded by the Mark Twain Forest. For more, visit www.miamarlowe.com.

"SIT UP STRAIGHT," THE DOWAGER COUNTESS OF Dane hissed at her daughter before turning back to their hostess and smiling stiffly as the marchioness prattled on about bonnet styles this season.

Lady Susanna straightened in her uncomfortable chair. She was wilting in the heat that all the ladies had already remarked upon as being unseasonably warm for June. Susanna fluttered her fan and tried to take an interest in the conversation, but she didn't care about hats. She didn't care about garden parties. She didn't care about finding a husband. If her mother ever heard Susanna admit husband hunting was not her favorite pursuit, she would lock Susanna in her room for days.

Susanna did not mind being locked in her room as much as her mother seemed to think. In her room, she could lose herself in her drawing. She could bring out her pencil or watercolors and sketch until her hand cramped. Sketching was infinitely preferable to spending hours embroidering in the drawing room, listening to her mother's lectures on decorum and etiquette.

Susanna did not need to be told how to behave. She had been raised to be a perfectly proper young lady. She was the daughter of an earl. She knew what was expected of her.

One: She must marry well.

Two: She must *at all times* exhibit good *ton*.

Three: She must be accomplished, beautiful, fashionable, and witty.

That third expectation was daunting indeed.

Susanna had spent two decades playing the perfect earl's daughter. She'd had little choice. If she rebelled, even minutely, her mother quickly put her back in her place. At the moment, Susanna wished her place was anywhere but here. She sympathized with her failed sketches, feeling as though it were *she* tossed in the hearth and browning in the fire. She burned slowly, torturously, gasping for her last breath.

Could no one see she was dying inside? Around her, ladies smiled and laughed and sipped tea. Susanna would not survive much longer.

And no one cared.

Ladies of the *ton* were far too concerned with themselves—what were they speaking of now? Haberdashery?—to notice she was smothering under the weight of the heat, the endless cups of tea, the tinny politeness of the ladies' laughs, and the interminable talk of bonnets. If she were to sketch her life, she would draw a single horizontal line extending into forever.

Susanna stifled the rising scream—afraid she might wail aloud for once, rather than shriek silently and endlessly. Before she could second-guess what she planned, she gained her feet. She wobbled, shaking with uncertainty and fear, but she must escape or go quietly mad.

Lady Dane cut her a look pointed as a sharpened blade. "Do sit down, Susanna."

"E-excuse me," Susanna murmured.

"What are you doing?"

Susanna staggered under the weight of the stares from the half-dozen women in their circle. She had not thought it possible to feel any heavier, but the addition of the women's cool gazes on her made her back bow.

"Excuse me. I need to find—"

"Oh, do cease mumbling." Lady Dane sounded remarkably like a dog barking when she issued orders. "You know I hate it when you mumble."

"I'm sorry. I need to—"

"Go ahead, my dear," their hostess said. "One of the footmen will show you the way."

Susanna's burst of freedom was short-lived. She'd no more than moved away from her chair, when her mother rose to join her. Susanna choked back a small sob. There really was no escape.

"Could you not at least wait until we had finished our conversation?" Lady Dane complained, as though Susanna's physical needs were the most inconvenient thing in the world.

"I'm sorry, Mama."

"Why don't you stay, Dorothea?" the marchioness

asked. "Surely Lady Susanna can find her way to the retiring room by herself."

Susanna's gaze locked on her mother's. Inside, she squirmed like one of the insects her brothers used to pin for their collections. Lady Dane would most certainly defy the marchioness. She would never let her disappointing daughter out of her sight.

Susanna had one glimmer of hope. Her brother's scandalous marriage a few weeks ago had noticeably thinned the pile of invitations the Danes received. The family was not shunned, exactly, but they had spent more nights at home than the debutante daughter of an earl should.

Not that she minded.

Her mother patted Susanna on the arm, the stinging pinch delivered under cover of affection.

"Do not dawdle."

Susanna need not be cut free twice. She practically ran for the house.

"She is perfectly safe here." The marchioness's voice carried across the lawn. "I understand why you play the hawk. She must make a good match, and the sooner the better."

The sooner she escaped this garden party, the better. Every group of ladies she passed bestowed snakelike smiles before raising their fans and whispering. Sometimes the whispers weren't even whispered.

"Dane introduced a bill to establish a central police force! What next? *Gendarmes?*"

A few steps more.

"I heard her brother began a soup kitchen."

Almost there.

"St. Giles! Can you imagine?"

Susanna ducked into the cool darkness of the town house and flattened herself against the wall. She closed her eyes, swiping at the stinging tears. *Breathe, breathe.* Free from the whispers-that-were-not-whispers and the stares and, best of all, her mother, she slouched in smug rebellion.

"May I be of assistance, my lady?"

Susanna's spine went rigid, and she opened her eyes. A footman bestowed a bemused smile on her. She imagined it was not every day a lady ran away from the marchioness's garden party and collapsed in relief.

"The ladies' retiring room. Could you direct me?"

"This way, Lady Susanna."

She followed him through well-appointed though cold, impersonal rooms until she reached a small room filled with plants, several chairs, two small hand mirrors on stands, a pitcher of fresh water and basin, and screens for privacy. Susanna stepped inside and closed the door. Finally alone. She straightened her white muslin gown with the blue sash at the high waist. Her hat sported matching ribbons. She might have removed it if it would not have been so much trouble to pin in place again. At the basin, she splashed water into the bowl and dabbed at her face. One look in the mirror showed that her cheeks were flushed and her brown eyes too bright. She had the typical coloring of a strawberry blond, and her pale skin reddened easily.

In the mirror, she spotted something move, and a woman in a large, elaborately plumed hat emerged from behind the screen. Susanna's heart sank.

The Best of Both Rogues

Samantha Grace

COMING SOON FROM SOURCEBOOKS CASABLANCA

April 1817

EVE THORNE HAD NO MORE TEARS TO SHED. HER BODY had become heavy, sinking into her bed as if it might swallow her. The coverlet beneath her cheek was damp and cool. Subdued afternoon light cast her normally cheerful bedchamber in shadow.

Her maid's sympathetic frown and the porcelain plate she held out to Eve made her eyes burn, dispelling the notion she had cried herself dry. The plate was filled with dishes meant for Eve's wedding breakfast, food that would spoil in a day with no guests to enjoy the feast.

"Lord Thorne will be cross if I cannot coax you to eat something, miss," Alice said.

"Has he returned?" Speaking required more effort than Eve thought possible; her voice was raspy and her throat tight.

Alice shook her graying head. "May I speak freely, miss?"

"Please," Eve said on a sigh.

"You don't want your brother to find you this way. The baron is on a tear as it is."

Sebastian was scouring London for Eve's runaway groom now, determined to defend her honor. Finding her in tears would only make matters worse, but how did one hide the shattered pieces of one's heart?

She blinked up at Alice. "I will try."

Her lady's maid answered with an encouraging smile and placed the plate back on its tray. "Very good, miss. Allow me to help you sit up."

Eve leaned forward while Alice fluffed the pillows and watched in a numbing fog as her maid placed the tray across her lap. The sight of red grapes made her vision blur again.

"Oh, bother," she mumbled. Why did everything have to make her think of Ben?

It was hard to believe it had only been last night when they had teased each other.

Ben's smoky blue eyes—the perfect blending of dark blue and gray—had twinkled with mischief as he'd wrapped her in his arms when Mama had allowed them a rare moment alone for Eve to bid him good night. It was to be their last good-bye, for tonight he should have taken her to his home. Her home.

Once we have spoken our vows, I will expect many things from you, Miss Thorne.

Is that so, Mr. Hillary? Let me hear these expectations, so I might decide if I wish to meet them.

She had been teasing. In that moment of blind devotion, she would have done anything he asked. His amused chuckle had washed her in warm tingles.

Do you want the entire list?

She had nodded, expecting him to recite the usual duties involved with managing a household. Instead, he'd made her laugh and planted the most delicious vision in her mind to take with her to bed: Ben lounging on a fainting couch like some hedonistic god, wearing nothing but a loincloth and laurel wreath in his golden brown hair, while Eve fed him grapes.

Eve had felt so cherished and happy when he'd stolen a kiss and whispered in her ear. *I love you, Kitten.*

She swiped at the wetness leaking from the corners of her eyes. What could have happened between nightfall and this morning at the church to change his mind about her? Or had she been too smitten to recognize reservation in his actions?

He had come to St. George's Church, and by all accounts, seemed prepared to marry her. Surely the love she had felt in his touch last night was no lie. Yet her limited imagination didn't allow for any other excuse for what he had done. Ben left her at the church, humiliated her in front of her family and friends.

A soft knock sounded at her door and Alice swept across the room to answer. Eve's mother paused in the threshold. Her dark gaze flickered over Eve as a small frown formed on her lips. "Eve, there is a gentleman here to see you. Mr. Cooper says Mr. Hillary sent him."

Eve's heart leaped. She knew Ben hadn't truly abandoned her. Something of the utmost importance must have occurred to make him leave so suddenly.

More important than your wedding?

She ignored the logic in favor of having Ben back.

"Should I have Milo tell him you are not receiving?" Mama asked.

"No!" Eve nearly knocked over the tray in her haste, but Alice grabbed it before it tipped. Eve mumbled an apology and scrambled from the bed. She stopped at the washstand to clear the evidence of her tears from her cheeks, although she wouldn't be able to hide the redness of her eyes and nose. "Did Mr. Cooper indicate how he knows Ben?"

Mama came up behind her to place her hands on Eve's shoulders. "He only said he made his acquaintance at the docks this afternoon. Mr. Cooper was seeing his cousin off to India on one of Benjamin's ships."

Why would Ben be at the docks on their wedding day? Eve swallowed against the panic welling up at the back of her throat. There must be a reasonable explanation, and it appeared Mr. Cooper was here to deliver it. She couldn't get ahead of herself.

Draping the cloth over the side of the basin, she took a deep breath. "I suppose I should see what the gentleman has to say before drawing conclusions."

The Beautiful One

Emily Greenwood

COMING SOON FROM SOURCEBOOKS CASABLANCA

MISS ANNA BLACK GAVE A SILENT CHEER AS THE carriage she was riding in lurched and came to an abrupt stop at an angle that suggested they'd hit a deep ditch.

Perhaps, she thought hopefully from the edge of her seat, where she'd been tossed, they'd be stuck on the road for hours, which would delay their arrival at the estate of Viscount Grandville. She had reason to be worried about what might happen at Lord Grandville's estate, and she dreaded reaching it.

It was also possible she was being pursued.

Or not.

Perhaps nothing would happen at all. But the whole situation was nerve-wracking enough that she had more than once considered simply running off to live in the woods and survive on berries.

However, several considerations discouraged her from this course:

1. She had exactly three shillings to her name. Though admittedly money would be of no use in the woods, she would at some point need more than berries.

2. She had agreed to escort her traveling companion, Miss Elizabeth Tarryton, to the home of Viscount Grandville, who was the girl's guardian.

3. If Anna abandoned her duty, along with being a wicked person, she wouldn't be able to return to the Rosewood School for Young Ladies of Quality, her employer.

Anna was nothing if not practical, and she was highly skeptical of the success of the life-in-the-woods plan, but the dramatic occurrences in her life of late were starting to lend it appeal.

"Hell!" said the lovely Miss Elizabeth Tarryton from her sprawled position on the opposite coach seat. Her apricot silk bonnet had fallen across her face during the coach-lurching, and she pushed it aside. "What's happened?"

"We're in a ditch, evidently," Anna replied. Their situation was obvious, but Miss Tarryton had not so far proven herself to be particularly sensible for her sixteen years. She was also apparently not averse to cursing.

Surrendering to the inevitable, Anna said, "I'll go see how things look."

She had to push upward to open the door to the tilted coach, and before stepping down, she paused to tug her faded blue bonnet over her black curls, a reflex of concealment that had become second nature in the last month. The rain that had followed them since they left the school that morning had stopped, but the dark sky promised more.

The coachman was already seeing to the horses.

"Had to go off the road to avoid a vast puddle, and now we're in a ditch," he called. "'Tis fortunate that we're but half a mile from his lordship's estate."

So they would soon be at Stillwell, Viscount Grandville's estate. *Damn*, Anna thought, taking a page from Miss Tarryton's book. Would he be a threat to her?

After a month in a state of nearly constant anxiety, of waiting to be exposed, she sometimes felt mutinously that she didn't care anymore. She'd done nothing of which she ought to be ashamed—yet it would never appear that way. And so she felt like a victim, and hated feeling that way, and hated the accursed book that had given two wicked men such power over her.

She gathered up the limp skirts of her faded, old blue frock and jumped off the last step, intending to see how badly they were stuck.

The coachman was seeing to the horses, and as she moved to inspect the back of the carriage, she became aware of hoofbeats and turned to see a rider cantering toward them. A farmer, she thought, taking in his dusty, floppy hat and dull coat and breeches. He drew even.

"You are trespassing," he said from atop his horse, his tone as blunt as his words. The sagging brim of his hat hid the upper part of his face, but from the hard set of his jaw, she could guess it did not bear a warm expression. His shadowed gaze passed over her, not lingering for more time than it might have taken to observe a pile of dirty breakfast dishes.

"We had no intention of doing so, I assure you,"

she began, wondering that the stranger hadn't even offered a greeting. "The road was impassible and our coachman tried to go around, but now we are stuck. Perhaps, though, if you might—"

"You cannot tarry here," he said, ignoring her attempt to ask for help. "A storm is coming. Your coach will be stranded if you don't make haste."

His speech was clipped, but it sounded surprisingly refined. *Ha.* That was surely the only refined thing about him. Aside from his lack of manners and the shabbiness of his clothes, there was an L-shaped rip in his breeches that gave a window onto pale skin and thigh muscles pressed taut, and underneath his coat, his shirt hung loose at the neck. She supposed it was his broad shoulders that made him seem especially imposing atop his dark horse.

A stormy surge of wind blew his hat brim off his face, and she realized that severe though his expression might be, he was very handsome. The lines of his cheekbones and hard jaw ran in perfect complement to each other. His well-formed brows arched in graceful if harsh angles over dark eyes surrounded by crowded black lashes.

But those eyes. They were as devoid of life as one of her father's near-death patients.

Several fat raindrops pelted her bonnet.

"We shall be away momentarily," she said briskly, turning away from him to consider the plight of the coach and assuming he would leave now that he'd delivered his warning.

The rain began to fall faster, soaking through the thin fabric of her worn-out frock. She called out to the coachman, who was doing something with the harness straps. "Better take off the young lady's trunk before you try to advance."

"No. That's a waste of time," said the stranger from atop his horse behind her.

She turned around, deeply annoyed. "Your opinion is not wanted."

The ill-mannered man watched her, a muscle ticking in his stubbled jaw.

A cold rivulet trickled through her bonnet to her scalp and continued down her neck, and his empty gaze seemed to follow the little stream's journey to the collar of her dampening frock. His eyes flicked lower, and she thought they lingered at her breasts.

She crossed her arms in front of her and tipped her chin higher. Not for nothing had she sparred with her older brother all those years in a home that had been more than anything else a man's domain. Her father had been a doctor who had valued reason and scientific process and frowned on softness, and she'd been raised to speak her mind.

50 Ways to Ruin a Rake

Jade Lee

Coming soon from Sourcebooks Casablanca

There are certain things a woman knows. She knows what the weather will be based on how easily her hair settles into the pins. She knows when the cook has quarreled with the butler by the taste of the morning eggs. And she knows when a man will completely upset her day.

And right now, that man was walking up her front drive as easy as if he expected to be welcomed.

Melinda Smithson bolted out of her bedroom where she'd been fighting with her curls—again—and rushed downstairs. "I'm just going for a quick walk!" she said much too brightly to their butler as she made it to the front door. Rowe hadn't even the time to reach for her gloves when she snatched her gardening bonnet off the table and headed outside. She had to get to the odious man before he rounded the rock and came into view from her father's laboratory. If her papa saw him, she would be done for. So she ran as fast as her legs could carry her.

She rounded the bend at the same moment he arrived at the rock. One step more, and she was doomed.

"Oh no, Mr. Anaedsley. Not today. You cannot come here today." She said the words breathlessly, but she punctuated with a severe tug on her bonnet. So hard, in fact, that three pins dug painfully into her scalp.

Mr. Anaedsley had been whistling, but now he drew up short. "You've punched your thumb through your bonnet." He spoke with a charming smile that made her grind her teeth in frustration. Everything about the man was charming, from his reddish-brown hair to the freckles that dotted his cheeks to the rich green of his eyes. An annoyance dressed as a prince of the realm, for all that he had no courtesy title. He was the son and heir of the Duke of Timby, and she hated him with a passion that bordered on insanity.

Unfortunately, he was right. She'd punched her thumb clean through the straw brim of her bonnet.

"Yes, I have," she said as she stepped directly in front of him. He would not pass around the rock. He simply wouldn't. "And that is one more crime I lay at your feet."

"A crime?" he replied. "To poke a hole in that ugly thing? Really, Miss Smithson, I call it more a mercy. The sun should not shine on something that hideous."

It was hideous, which was why it was her gardening bonnet. "The sun is not supposed to shine on my face either, so it is this ugly thing or stay inside."

"Come now, Miss Smithson," he said as he held out his arm to escort her. "I am well aware that you have dozens of fetching bonnets—"

"But this was the one at hand." She ignored his arm and stared intimidatingly at him. Or at least she tried to. But he was a good six inches taller than her. Average for a man, but for her he was quite the perfect height. Not too tall as to dwarf her, but large enough to be handsome in his coat of bottle-green superfine. It brought out his eyes, which were made all the more stunning by the sunlight that shone full on his face.

"Shall we amble up your beautiful drive and fetch you a pretty bonnet?"

"No, Mr. Anaedsley, we shall not. Because you shall not come to the house today. Any other day, you will be very welcome. But not today."

His brows drew together in worry. "Is your father ill? Is there something amiss? Tell me, Miss Smithson. What can I do to help?"

It was the right thing to say. Of course it was because he *always* knew the right thing to say. Her father's health was precarious these days, a cough plaguing him despite all attempts to physic him. She might have ignored his words as simple politeness, but she saw genuine worry in his eyes. She couldn't help but soften toward him.

"Papa is the same as before. It's worst at night—"

"The gypsy tincture didn't help then." He took her arm and gently eased her hand into the crook of his elbow. Her fingers were placed there before she even realized it. "I'll ask a doctor friend I know as soon as I return to London. He may—"

She dug in her feet, tugging backward on his arm. He raised a perfect eyebrow in query, but she flashed him a warm smile. "An excellent idea. You should go there right now. In fact, pray fetch the doctor here."

His eyebrows rose in alarm. "I shall write down

the man's direction and a message. You can send a footman—"

"No, sir. You must go yourself. Right now. It is most urgent."

He flashed her his dimple. Damn him for having such a very attractive dimple. "Now why do I get the feeling that you're trying to rush me away?"

"Because the first thing I said to you was go away!"

He cocked his head, and his expression grew even more delightful. She would swear she saw a twinkle in his eyes. "Miss Smithson, I thought you were a scientist. The first thing you said to me was, 'Oh no, Mr. Anaedsley, not today.'"

"Well, there you have it. Go away. We are not receiving callers."

And then, just to make a liar of her, her uncle's carriage trotted up the path. Four horses—matched chestnuts—stepping smartly as they pulled her uncle's polished, gilded monstrosity. And inside waving cheerily was her cousin Ronnie. Half cousin, actually, and she waved halfheartedly at the wan fop.

"It appears, Miss Smithson, that we have been spotted. I'm afraid politeness requires that I make my bow."

"No, we haven't!" She'd used the distraction to pull them back from the rock. They were, in fact, completely shielded from all windows of the Smithson residence including the laboratory. "Ronnie doesn't count. And he certainly doesn't care if you greet him or not. The most powerful snub only seems to inspire him to greater heights of poetry."

"A poet is he?"

"Yes," she groaned. "A good one too." Which made it all the worse.

"Ah. Your suitor, I assume?"

"Suitor" was too simple a word for her relationship with Ronnie, which involved a lot of private family history. "He's my cousin. Well, half cousin, as my father and uncle had different mothers. But he has convinced himself that we are fated to be wed."

"And as a practical woman of science, you do not believe in fate."

She didn't believe in a lot of things, but at the top of the list was Ronnie's fantasy. He thought fate had cast them as prince and princess in a make-believe future. She thought her cousin's obsession with her silly at best, but more likely a dark and dangerous thing. "I do not wish to wed the man," she said baldly.

"Well, the solution is obvious then, isn't it? I shall join you today as an afternoon caller, and Ronnie will not be able to press his suit upon you."

"That would be lovely," she said sourly, "if you actually did as you say. But we both know what will really happen."

"We do?" he countered, all innocence.

She tossed him her most irritated, ugly, and angry look, but it did absolutely nothing to diminish his smile. "Oh leave off, Mr. Anaedsley, I haven't the time for it today."

Tremaine's True Love

Grace Burrowes

Coming soon from Sourcebooks Casablanca

"THE GREATEST PLAGUE EVER TO BEDEVIL MORTAL MAN, the greatest threat to his peace, the most fiendish source of undeserved humility is *his sister*, and spinster sisters are the worst of a bad lot." In the corridor outside the formal parlor, Nicholas, Earl of Bellefonte, sounded very certain of his point.

"Of course, my lord," somebody replied softly, "but, my lord—"

"I tell you, Hanford," the earl went on, "if it wouldn't imperil certain personal masculine attributes which my countess holds dear, I'd turn Lady Nita right over my—"

"My lord, you have a visitor."

Hanford's pronouncement came off a little desperately but had the effect of silencing his lordship's lament. Quiet words were exchanged beyond the door, giving Tremaine St. Michael time to step away from the parlor's cozy fireplace, where he'd been shamelessly warming a personal attribute of his own formerly frozen to the saddle.

Bellefonte's greeting as he strode into the parlor a moment later was as enthusiastic as his ranting had been.

"Our very own Mr. St. Michael! You are early. This is not fashionable. In fact, were I not the soul of congeniality, I'd call it unsporting in the extreme."

"Bellefonte." Tremaine St. Michael bowed, for Bellefonte was his social superior, also one of few men whose height and brawn exceeded Tremaine's.

"Don't suppose you have any sisters?" Bellefonte asked with a rueful smile. "I have four. They're what my grandmother calls *lively*."

So lively, Bellefonte had apparently bellowed at one of these sisters for the entire ten minutes Tremaine had been left to admire the spotless Turkey carpets in Belle Maison's formal parlor. The sister's responses had been inaudible until an upstairs door had slammed.

"Liveliness is a fine quality in a young lady," Tremaine said, because he was a guest in this house, and sociability was called for if he was to relieve Bellefonte of substantial assets.

His lordship was welcome to keep all four sisters, thank you very much.

"Fat lot you know," Bellefonte retorted, taking a position with his back to the fire. "If every man in the House of Lords had rounded up his *lively* sisters and sent them to France, the Corsican would have been on bended knee, seeking asylum of old George in a week flat. How was your journey?"

Bellefonte had the blond hair and blue eyes of many an English aristocrat. The corners of those eyes crinkled agreeably, and he'd followed up Tremaine's bow with a hearty handshake.

Bellefonte would never be a friend, but he was friendly.

"My journey was uneventful, if cold," Tremaine said. "I apologize for making good time down from Town."

"I apologize for complaining. I am blessed in my family, truly, but Lady Nita, my oldest sister, is particularly strong willed."

Bellefonte's hearty bonhomie faded to a soft smile as feminine laughter rang out in the corridor.

"You were saying?" Tremaine prompted. When would his lordship offer a guest a damned drink?

"Nothing of any moment, St. Michael. My countess and my sister Della have taken note of your arrival. Shall we to the library, where the best libation and coziest hearth await? Beckman gave me to understand you're not the tea-and-crumpets sort."

When and why had his lordship's brother conveyed that sentiment? Another thought intruded on Tremaine's irritation: Bellefonte knew his womenfolk by their laughter. How odd was that?

"I'm the whiskey sort," Tremaine said. "Winter ale wouldn't go amiss either." Not brandy though. Not if Tremaine could avoid it.

His lordship was too well-bred to raise an eyebrow at tastes refined in drovers' inns the length of the realm.

"Whiskey, then. Hanford!"

A little old fellow in formal livery stepped into the library. "My lord?"

Bellefonte directed the butler to send 'round some decent sandwiches to the library, to fetch the countess to her husband's side when the fiend in the nursery had turned loose of her, and to inform the housekeeper that Mr. St. Michael was on the premises earlier than planned.

His lordship set a smart pace down carpeted hallways, past bouquets of white hothouse roses and across gleaming parquet floors, to a high-ceilinged, oak-paneled treasury of books. Belle Maison was a well-maintained example of the last century's enthusiasm for the spacious country seat, and whoever had designed the house had had an eye for light.

The library was blessed with tall windows at regular intervals, and the red velvet draperies were caught back, despite the cold. Winter sunshine bounced cheerily off mirrors, brass, and silver, and here too, the hearth was blazing extravagantly.

The entire impression—genial Lord Bellefonte; his dear, plaguey sisters; roaring fires even in empty rooms; the casual wealth lined up on the library's endless, sunny shelves—left Tremaine feeling out of place.

Tremaine had been in countless aristocratic family seats and more than a few castles and palaces. The out-of-place feeling he experienced at Belle Maison was the fault of the sisters, whom Bellefonte clearly loved and worried over.

Commerce Tremaine comprehended, and even gloried in.

Sisters had no part of commerce, but the lively variety could apparently transform an imposing family seat into a home. Bellefonte's sisters inspired slammed doors, fraternal grumbling, and even laughter, and in this, Belle Maison was a departure from Tremaine's usual experience with titled English families.

"I know you only intended to stay for a few days," Bellefonte said, gesturing to a pair of chairs beneath a tall window, "but my countess declares that will not do. You are to visit for at least two weeks, so the neighbors may come by and inspect you. Don't worry. I'll warn you which ones have marriageable daughters—which is most of them—and my brother George will distract the young ladies."

After the winter journey from Town, the cozy library and plush armchair were exquisitely comfortable. To Tremaine, who had vivid memories of Highland winters, comfortable was never a bad thing.

"A few days might be all the time I can spare, my lord," Tremaine said, seating himself in cushioned luxury. "The press of business waits for no man, and wasted time is often wasted money."

"Protest is futile, no matter how sensible your arguments," Bellefonte countered, folding his length into the second chair. "My countess has spoken, and my sisters will abet her. You are an eligible bachelor and, therefore, a doomed man."